SO-AVI-451

In the display there appeared many green dots, nineteen of them, clustered at some distance from Lusitania, but surrounding it in most directions.

"Is that the Lusitania Fleet?"

"Those were their positions five months ago." He typed again. The green dots all disappeared. "And those are their positions today."

She looked for them. She couldn't find a green dot anywhere. Yet Father clearly expected her to see something. "Are they already at Lusitania?"

"The ships are where you see them," said Father. "Five months ago the fleet disappeared."

"The whole Fleet?"

"Every ship."

"The ansibles?"

"Silent. All within the same three-minute period. One transmission would end, and then the next one—never came."

"Every ship's connection with every planetside ansible everywhere? That's impossible."

. . . Jane watches everything. She can do a million jobs and pay attention to a thousand things at once. She does have a sensory limitation, however; she can't see or know anything that hasn't been entered as data into the great interworld network.

She has almost immediate access to the raw inputs of every starship, every satellite, every traffic control system, and almost every electronically-monitored spy device in the human universe. But it does mean that she almost never witnesses lovers' quarrels, bedtime stories, classroom arguments, supper-table gossip, or bitter tears privately shed. . . .

She does not understand all of human nature, but Ender has taught her this: to stop a human being from doing something, you must find a way to make the person stop wanting to do it.

ORSON SCOTT CARD

XENOCIDE

A TOM DOHERTY ASSOCIATES BOOK
NEW YORK

XENOCIDE

Several chapters of this book appeared first in *Analog* magazine as the novella "Gloriously Bright."

Quotations from Li Qing-jao are from James Cryer, trans., *Plum Blossom: Poems of Li Ch'ing-Chao* (Carolina Wren Press, 1984), by permission of the translator.

Quotations from Han Fei-tzu are from Burton Watson, trans., *Han Fei Tzu: Basic Writings* (Columbia University Press, 1964), by permission of the publisher.

Cover art by John Harris

A Tor Book
Published by Tom Doherty Associates, LLC
175 Fifth Avenue
New York, NY 10010

www.tor.com

Tor® is a registered trademark of Tom Doherty Associates, LLC

ISBN 0-812-50925-0
EAN 978-0-812-50925-0
Library of Congress Catalog Card Number: 90-27108

First edition: August 1991
First mass market printing: August 1992

Printed in the United States of America

20 19 18 17 16

To Clark and Kathy Kidd:
for the freedom, for the haven,
and for frolics all over America.

CONTENTS

ACKNOWLEDGMENTS

A chance meeting with James Cryer in the Second Foundation Bookstore in Chapel Hill, North Carolina, led directly to the story of Li Qing-jao and Han Fei-tzu at the heart of this book. Learning that he was a translator of Chinese poetry, I asked him on the spot if he could give me a few plausible names for some Chinese characters I was developing. My knowledge of Chinese culture was rudimentary at best, and my idea for these characters was for them to play a fairly minor, though meaningful, role in the story of *Xenocide*. But as James Cryer, one of the most vigorous, fascinating, and generous people I have known, told me more and more about Li Qing-jao and Han Fei-tzu—as he showed me their writings and told me more stories about other figures in Chinese history and literature—I began to realize that here was the real foundation of the tale I wanted this book to tell. I owe him much, and regret that I have passed up my best opportunities to repay.

I also give my thanks to many others: To Judith Rapaport, for her book *The Boy Who Couldn't Stop Washing*, which was the source of the information about obsessive-compulsive disorder in this novel. To my agent Barbara Bova, who called this book into existence by selling it in England before I had ever thought of writing it. To my American publisher Tom Doherty, for extraordinary faith and generosity that I hope will all be justified in the end. To Jim Frenkel, the editor who wisely turned down the first outline of this book when I offered it to Dell back in 1978, telling me—correctly—that I wasn't ready yet to write such an ambitious novel. To my British publisher, Anthony Cheetham, who has believed in my work from the start of my career, and has patiently waited for this book far longer than either of us bargained for. To my editor Beth Meacham, for being a friend, adviser, and protector through the preparation of this and many other books. To the many readers who have written to me urging me to return to Ender's story; their encouragement helped a great deal as I struggled through the most difficult writing project of my career so far. To Fred Chappell's graduate writing workshop at the University of North Carolina at Greensboro, for looking over and responding to the first draft of the Qing-jao storyline. To Stan Schmidt at *Analog,* for being willing to publish such an extraordinarily long portion of the novel as the story "Gloriously Bright." To my assistants, Laraine Moon, Erin Absher, and Willard and Peggy Card, who, serving well in such completely different ways, gave me the freedom and help that I needed in order to write at all. To friends like Jeff Alton and Philip Absher, for reading early drafts to help me ensure that this hodgepodge of characters and storylines actually did make sense. And to my children, Geoffrey, Emily, and Charlie, for being patient with me through the crabbiness and neglect that always seem to accompany my bursts of writing, and for letting me borrow from their lives and experiences as I create the characters I love the most.

Above all, I give my thanks to my wife, Kristine, who has suffered through every arduous step in the creation of this book, raising questions, catching errors and contradictions, and—most important—responding so favorably to those aspects of the story that worked well that I found in her the confidence to go on. I have no idea who I would be, as a writer or as a person, without her; I intend never to have occasion to find out.

PRONUNCIATION

A few names may seem strange to English-speaking readers. From Chinese, *Qing-jao* is pronounced "tching jow"; *Jiang-qing* is "jee-eng tching." From Portuguese, *Quim* is pronounced "keeng"; *Novinha* is "no-VEEN-ya"; *Olhado* is "ol-YAH-doe." From Swedish, *Jakt* is "yahkt."

Other names are either easier to pronounce as written, or repeated rarely enough that they shouldn't cause difficulty.

1

A PARTING

<Today one of the brothers asked me: Is it a terrible prison, not to be able to move from the place where you're standing?>

<You answered . . .>

<I told him that I am now more free than he is. The inability to move frees me from the obligation to act.>

<You who speak languages, you are such liars.>

Han Fei-tzu sat in lotus position on the bare wooden floor beside his wife's sickbed. Until a moment ago he might have been sleeping; he wasn't sure. But now he was aware of the slight change in her breathing, a change as subtle as the wind from a butterfly's passing.

Jiang-qing, for her part, must also have detected some change in him, for she had not spoken before and now she did speak. Her voice was very soft. But Han Fei-tzu could hear her clearly, for the house was silent. He had asked his friends and servants for stillness during the dusk of Jiang-qing's life. Time enough for careless noise during the long night that was to come, when there would be no hushed words from her lips.

"Still not dead," she said. She had greeted him with these words each time she woke during the past few days. At first the words had seemed whimsical or ironic to him, but now he knew that she spoke with disappointment. She longed for death now, not because she hadn't loved life, but because death was now unavoidable, and what cannot be shunned must be embraced. That was the Path. Jiang-qing had never taken a step away from the Path in her life.

"Then the gods are kind to me," said Han Fei-tzu.

"To you," she breathed. "What do we contemplate?"

It was her way of asking him to share his private thoughts with her. When others asked his private thoughts, he felt spied upon. But Jiang-qing asked only so that she could also think the same thought; it was part of their having become a single soul.

"We are contemplating the nature of desire," said Han Fei-tzu.

"Whose desire?" she asked. "And for what?"

My desire for your bones to heal and become strong, so that they don't snap at the slightest pressure. So that you could stand again, or even raise an arm without your own muscles tearing away chunks of bone or causing the bone to break under the tension. So that I wouldn't have to watch you wither away until now you weigh only eighteen kilograms. I never knew how perfectly happy we were until I learned that we could not stay together.

"*My* desire," he answered. "For you."

"'You only covet what you do not have.' Who said that?"

"You did," said Han Fei-tzu. "Some say, 'what you *cannot* have.' Others say, 'what you *should* not have.' I say, 'You can truly covet only what you will always hunger for.'"

"You have me forever."

"I will lose you tonight. Or tomorrow. Or next week."

"Let us contemplate the nature of desire," said Jiang-qing. As before, she was using philosophy to pull him out of his brooding melancholy.

He resisted her, but only playfully. "You are a harsh ruler," said Han Fei-tzu. "Like your ancestor-of-the-heart, you make no allowance for other people's frailty." Jiang-qing was named for a revolutionary leader of the ancient past, who had tried to lead the people onto a new Path but was overthrown by weak-hearted cowards. It was not right, thought Han Fei-tzu, for his wife to die before him: her ancestor-of-the-heart had outlived her husband. Besides, wives *should* live longer than husbands. Women were more complete inside themselves. They were also better at living in their children. They were never as solitary as a man alone.

Jiang-qing refused to let him return to brooding. "When a man's wife is dead, what does he long for?"

Rebelliously, Han Fei-tzu gave her the most false answer to her question. "To lie with her," he said.

"The desire of the body," said Jiang-qing.

Since she was determined to have this conversation, Han Fei-tzu took up the catalogue for her. "The desire of the body is to act. It includes all touches, casual and intimate, and all customary movements. Thus he sees a movement out of the corner of his eye, and thinks he has seen his dead wife moving across the doorway, and he cannot be content until he has walked to the door and seen that it was not his wife. Thus he wakes up from a dream in which he heard her voice, and finds himself speaking his answer aloud as if she could hear him."

"What else?" asked Jiang-qing.

"I'm tired of philosophy," said Han Fei-tzu. "Maybe the Greeks found comfort in it, but not me."

"The desire of the spirit," said Jiang-qing, insisting.

"Because the spirit is of the earth, it is that part which makes new things out of old ones. The husband longs for all the unfinished things that he and his wife were making when she died, and all the unstarted dreams of what they would have made if she had lived. Thus a man grows angry at his children for being too much like him and not enough like his dead wife. Thus a man hates the house they lived in together, because either he does not change it, so that it is as dead as his wife, or because he *does* change it, so that it is no longer half of her making."

"You don't have to be angry at our little Qing-jao," said Jiang-qing.

"Why?" asked Han Fei-tzu. "Will you stay, then, and help me teach her to be a woman? All I can teach her is to be what *I* am—cold and hard, sharp and strong, like obsidian. If she grows like that, while she looks so much like you, how can I help but be angry?"

"Because you can teach her everything that I am, too," said Jiang-qing.

"If I had any part of you in me," said Han Fei-tzu, "I would not have needed to marry you to become a complete person." Now he teased her by using philosophy to turn the conversation away from pain. "That is the desire of the soul. Because the soul is made of light and dwells in air, it is that part which conceives and keeps ideas, especially the idea of the self. The husband longs for his whole self, which was made of the husband and wife together. Thus he never believes any of his own thoughts, because there is always a question in his mind to which his wife's thoughts were the only possible answer. Thus the whole world seems dead to him because he cannot trust anything to keep its meaning before the onslaught of this unanswerable question."

"Very deep," said Jiang-qing.

"If I were Japanese I would commit seppuku, spilling my bowel into the jar of your ashes."

"Very wet and messy," she said.

He smiled. "Then I should be an ancient Hindu, and burn myself on your pyre."

But she was through with joking. "Qing-jao," she whispered. She was reminding him he could do nothing so flamboyant as to die with her. There was little Qing-jao to care for.

So Han Fei-tzu answered her seriously. "How can I teach her to be what you are?"

"All that is good in me," said Jiang-qing, "comes from the Path. If you teach her to obey the gods, honor the ancestors, love the people, and serve the rulers, I will be in her as much as you are."

"I would teach her the Path as part of myself," said Han Fei-tzu.

"Not so," said Jiang-qing. "The Path is not a natural part of you, my husband. Even with the gods speaking to you every day, you insist on believing in a world where everything can be explained by natural causes."

"I obey the gods." He thought, bitterly, that he had no choice; that even to delay obedience was torture.

"But you don't *know* them. You don't love their works."

"The Path is to love the people. The gods we only obey." How can I love gods who humiliate me and torment me at every opportunity?

"We love the people because they are creatures of the gods."

"Don't preach to me."

She sighed.

Her sadness stung him like a spider. "I wish you would preach to me forever," said Han Fei-tzu.

"You married me because you knew I loved the gods, and that love for them was completely missing from yourself. That was how I completed you."

How could he argue with her, when he knew that even now he hated the gods for everything they had ever done to him, everything they had ever made him do, everything they had stolen from him in his life.

"Promise me," said Jiang-qing.

He knew what these words meant. She felt death upon her; she was laying the burden of her life upon him. A burden he would gladly bear. It was losing her company on the Path that he had dreaded for so long.

"Promise that you will teach Qing-jao to love the gods and walk always on the Path. Promise that you will make her as much my daughter as yours."

"Even if she never hears the voice of the gods?"

"The Path is for everyone, not just the godspoken."

Perhaps, thought Han Fei-tzu, but it was much easier for the godspoken to follow the Path, because to them the price for straying from it was so terrible. The common people were free; they could leave the Path and not feel the pain of it for years. The godspoken couldn't leave the Path for an hour.

"Promise me."

I will. I promise.

But he couldn't say the words out loud. He did not know why, but his reluctance was deep.

In the silence, as she waited for his vow, they heard the sound of running feet on the gravel outside the front door of the house. It could only be Qing-jao, home from the garden of Sun Cao-pi. Only Qing-jao was allowed to run and make noise during this time of hush. They waited, knowing that she would come straight to her mother's room.

The door slid open almost noiselessly. Even Qing-jao had caught enough of the hush to walk softly when she was actually in the presence of her mother. Though she walked on tiptoe, she could hardly keep from dancing, almost galloping across the floor. But she did not fling her arms around her mother's neck; she remembered that lesson even though the terrible bruise had faded from Jiang-qing's face, where Qing-jao's eager embrace had broken her jaw three months ago.

"I counted twenty-three white carp in the garden stream," said Qing-jao.

"So many," said Jiang-qing.

"I think they were showing themselves to me," said Qing-jao. "So I could count them. None of them wanted to be left out."

"Love you," whispered Jiang-qing.

Han Fei-tzu heard a new sound in her breathy voice—a popping sound, like bubbles bursting with her words.

"Do you think that seeing so many carp means that I will be godspoken?" asked Qing-jao.

"I will ask the gods to speak to you," said Jiang-qing.

Suddenly Jiang-qing's breathing became quick and harsh. Han Fei-tzu immediately knelt and looked at his wife. Her eyes were wide and frightened. The moment had come.

Her lips moved. Promise me, she said, though her breath could make no sound but gasping.

"I promise," said Han Fei-tzu.

Then her breathing stopped.

"What do the gods say when they talk to you?" asked Qing-jao.

"Your mother is very tired," said Han Fei-tzu. "You should go out now."

"But she didn't answer me. What do the gods say?"

"They tell secrets," said Han Fei-tzu. "No one who hears will repeat them."

Qing-jao nodded wisely. She took a step back, as if to leave, but stopped. "May I kiss you, Mama?"

"Lightly on the cheek," said Han Fei-tzu.

Qing-jao, being small for a four-year-old, did not have to bend very far at all to kiss her mother's cheek. "I love you, Mama."

"You'd better leave now, Qing-jao," said Han Fei-tzu.

"But Mama didn't say she loved me too."

"She did. She said it before. Remember? But she's very tired and weak. Go now."

He put just enough sternness in his voice that Qing-jao left without further questions. Only when she was gone did Han Fei-tzu let himself feel anything but care for her. He knelt over Jiang-qing's body and tried to imagine what was happening to her now. Her soul had flown and was now already in heaven. Her spirit would linger much longer; perhaps her spirit would dwell in this house, if it had truly been a place of happiness for her. Superstitious people believed that all spirits of the dead were dangerous, and put up signs and wards to fend them off. But those who followed the Path knew that the spirit of a good person was never harmful or destructive, for their goodness in life had come from the spirit's love of making things. Jiang-qing's spirit would be a blessing in the house for many years to come, if she chose to stay.

Yet even as he tried to imagine her soul and spirit, according to the teachings of the Path, there was a cold place in his heart that was certain that all that was left of Jiang-qing was this brittle, dried-up body. Tonight it would burn as quickly as paper, and then she would be gone except for the memories in his heart.

Jiang-qing was right. Without her to complete his soul, he was already doubting the gods. And the gods had noticed—they always did. At once he felt the unbearable pressure to do the ritual of cleansing, until he was rid of his unworthy thoughts. Even now they could not leave him unpunished. Even now, with his wife lying dead before him, the gods insisted that he do obeisance to them before he could shed a single tear of grief for her.

At first he meant to delay, to put off obedience. He had schooled himself to be able to postpone the ritual for as long as a whole day, while hiding all outward signs of his inner torment. He could do that now—but only by keeping his heart utterly cold. There was no point in that. Proper grief could come only when he had satisfied the gods. So, kneeling there, he began the ritual.

He was still twisting and gyrating with the ritual when a servant peered in. Though the servant said nothing, Han Fei-tzu heard the faint sliding of the door and knew what the servant would assume: Jiang-qing was dead, and Han Fei-tzu was so righteous that he was communing with the gods even before he announced her death to the household. No doubt some would even suppose that the gods had come to take Jiang-qing, since she was known for her extraordinary holiness. No one would guess that even as Han Fei-tzu worshiped, his heart was full of bitterness that the gods would dare demand this of him even now.

O Gods, he thought, if I knew that by cutting off an arm or cutting out my liver I could be rid of you forever, I would seize the knife and relish the pain and loss, all for the sake of freedom.

That thought, too, was unworthy, and required even more cleansing. It was hours before the gods at last released him, and by then he was too tired, too sick at heart to grieve. He got up and fetched the women to prepare Jiang-qing's body for the burning.

At midnight he was the last to come to the pyre, carrying a sleepy Qing-jao in his arms. She clutched in her hands the three papers she had written for her mother in her childish scrawl. "Fish," she had written, and "book" and "secrets." These were the things that Qing-jao was giving to her mother to carry with her into heaven. Han Fei-tzu had tried to guess at the thoughts in Qing-jao's mind as she wrote those words. *Fish* because of the carp in the garden stream today, no doubt. And *book*—that was easy enough to understand, because reading aloud was one of the last things Jiang-qing could do with her daughter. But why *secrets*? What secrets did Qing-jao have for her mother? He could not ask. One did not discuss the paper offerings to the dead.

Han Fei-tzu set Qing-jao on her feet; she had not been deeply asleep, and so she woke at once and stood there, blinking slowly. Han Fei-tzu whispered to her and she rolled her papers and tucked them into her mother's sleeve. She didn't seem to mind touching her mother's cold flesh—she was too young to have learned to shudder at the touch of death.

Nor did Han Fei-tzu mind the touch of his wife's flesh as he tucked his own three papers into her other sleeve. What was there to fear from death now, when it had already done its worst?

No one knew what was written on his papers, or they would have been horrified, for he had written, "My body," "My spirit," and "My soul." Thus it was that he burned himself on Jiang-qing's funeral pyre, and sent himself with her wherever it was she was going.

Then Jiang-qing's secret maid, Mu-pao, laid the torch onto the sacred wood and the pyre burst into flames. The heat of the fire was painful, and Qing-jao hid herself behind her father, only peeking around him now and then to watch her mother leave on her endless journey. Han Fei-tzu, though, welcomed the dry heat that seared his skin and made brittle the silk of his robe. Her body had not been as dry as it seemed; long after the papers had crisped into ash and blown upward into the smoke of the fire, her body still sizzled, and the heavy incense burning all around the fire could not conceal from him the smell of burning flesh. That is what we're burning here: meat, fish, carrion, nothing. Not my Jiang-qing. Only the costume she wore into this life. That which made that body into the woman that I loved is still alive, *must* still live. And for a moment he thought he could see, or hear, or somehow *feel* the passage of Jiang-qing.

Into the air, into the earth, into the fire. I am with you.

2

A MEETING

<The strangest thing about humans is the way they pair up, males and females. Constantly at war with each other, never content to leave each other alone. They never seem to grasp the idea that males and females are separate species with completely different needs and desires, forced to come together only to reproduce.>

<Of course you feel that way. Your mates are nothing but mindless drones, extensions of yourself, without their own identity.>

<*We* know our lovers with perfect understanding. *Humans* invent an imaginary lover and put that mask over the face of the body in their bed.>

<That is the tragedy of language, my friend. Those who know each other only through symbolic representations are forced to imagine each other. And because their imagination is imperfect, they are often wrong.>

<That is the source of their misery.>

<And some of their strength, I think. Your people and

mine, each for our own evolutionary reasons, mate with vastly unequal partners. Our mates are always, hopelessly, our intellectual inferiors. Humans mate with beings who challenge their supremacy. They have conflict between mates, not because their communication is inferior to ours, but because they commune with each other at all.>

Valentine Wiggin read over her essay, making a few corrections here and there. When she was done, the words stood in the air over her computer terminal. She was feeling pleased with herself for having written such a deft ironic dismemberment of the personal character of Rymus Ojman, the chairman of the cabinet of Starways Congress.

"Have we finished another attack on the masters of the Hundred Worlds?"

Valentine did not turn to face her husband; she knew from his voice exactly what expression would be on his face, and so she smiled back at him without turning around. After twenty-five years of marriage, they could see each other clearly without having to look. "We have made Rymus Ojman look ridiculous."

Jakt leaned into her tiny office, his face so close to hers that she could hear his soft breathing as he read the opening paragraphs. He wasn't young anymore; the exertion of leaning into her office, bracing his hands on the doorframe, was making him breathe more rapidly than she liked to hear.

Then he spoke, but with his face so close to hers that she felt his lips brush her cheek, tickling her with every word. "From now on even his mother will laugh behind her hand whenever she sees the poor bastard."

"It was hard to make it funny," said Valentine. "I caught myself denouncing him again and again."

"This is better."

"Oh, I know. If I had let my outrage show, if I had accused him of all his crimes, it would have made him seem more formidable and frightening and the Rule-of-law Faction would have loved him all the more, while the cowards on every world would have bowed to him even lower."

"If they bow any lower they'll have to buy thinner carpets," said Jakt.

She laughed, but it was as much because the tickling of his lips on her cheek was becoming unbearable. It was also beginning, just a little, to tantalize her with desires that simply could not be satisfied on this voyage. The starship was too small and cramped, with all their family aboard, for any real privacy. "Jakt, we're almost at the midpoint. We've abstained longer than this during the mishmish run every year of our lives."

"We could put a do-not-enter sign on the door."

"Then you might just as well put out a sign that says, 'naked elderly couple reliving old memories inside.'"

"*I'm* not elderly."

"You're over sixty."

"If the old soldier can still stand up and salute, I say let him march in the parade."

"No parades till the voyage is over. It's only a couple of weeks more. We only have to complete this rendezvous with Ender's stepson and then we're back on course to Lusitania."

Jakt drew away from her, pulled himself out of her doorway and stood upright in the corridor—one of the few places on the starship where he could actually do that. He groaned as he did it, though.

"You creak like an old rusty door," said Valentine.

"I've heard you make the same sounds when you get up from your desk here. I'm not the only senile, decrepit, miserable old coot in our family."

"Go away and let me transmit this."

"I'm used to having work to do on a voyage," said Jakt. "The computers do everything here, and this ship never rolls or pitches in the sea."

"Read a book."

"I worry about you. All work and no play makes Val a mean-tempered old hag."

"Every minute that we talk here is eight and a half hours in real time."

"Our time here on this starship is just as real as *their* time out there," said Jakt. "Sometimes I wish Ender's friends hadn't figured out a way for our starship to keep up a landside link."

"It takes up a huge amount of computer time," said Val. "Until now, only the military could communicate with starships during near-lightspeed flight. If Ender's friends can achieve it, then I owe it to them to use it."

"You're not doing all this because you owe it to somebody."

That was true enough. "If I write an essay every hour, Jakt, it means that to the rest of humanity Demosthenes is publishing something only once every three weeks."

"You can't possibly write an essay every hour. You sleep, you eat."

"You talk, I listen. Go away, Jakt."

"If I'd known that saving a planet from destruction would mean my returning to a state of virginity, I'd never have agreed to it."

He was only half teasing. Leaving Trondheim was a hard decision for all her family—even for her, even knowing that she was going to see Ender again. The children were all adults now, or nearly so; they saw this voyage as a great adventure. Their visions of the future were not so tied to a particular place. None of them had become a sailor, like their father; all of them were becoming scholars or scientists, living the life of public discourse and private contemplation, like their mother. They could live their lives, substantially unchanged, anywhere, on any world. Jakt was proud of them, but disappointed that the chain of family reaching back for seven generations on the seas of Trondheim would end with him. And now, for her sake, he had given up the sea himself. Giving up Trondheim was the hardest thing she could ever have asked of Jakt, and he had said yes without hesitation.

Perhaps he would go back someday, and, if he did, the oceans, the ice, the storms, the fish, the desperately sweet green meadows of summer would still be there. But his crews would be gone, were *already* gone. The men he had known better than his own children, better than his wife—those men were already fifteen years older, and when he returned, if he returned, another forty years would have passed. Their grandsons would be working the boats then. They wouldn't know the name of Jakt. He'd be a foreign shipowner, come from the sky, not a sailor, not a man with the stink and yellowy blood of skrika on his hands. He would not be one of them.

So when he complained that she was ignoring him, when he teased about their lack of intimacy during the voyage, there was more to it than an aging husband's playful desire. Whether he knew he was saying it or not, she understood the true meaning of his overtures: After what I've given up for you, have you nothing to give to me?

And he was right—she was pushing herself harder than she needed to. She was making more sacrifices than needed to be made—requiring overmuch from him as well. It wasn't the sheer number of subversive essays that Demosthenes published during this voyage that would make the difference. What mattered was how many people read and believed what she wrote, and how many then thought and spoke and acted as enemies of Starways Congress. Perhaps more important was the hope that some within the bureaucracy of Congress itself would be moved to feel a higher allegiance to humanity and break their maddening institutional solidarity. Some would surely be changed by what she wrote. Not many, but maybe enough. And maybe it would happen in time to stop them from destroying the planet Lusitania.

If not, she and Jakt and those who had given up so much to come with them on this voyage from Trondheim would reach Lusitania just in time to turn around and flee—or be destroyed along with all the others of that world. It was not unreasonable for Jakt to be tense, to want to spend more time with her. It *was* unreasonable for her to be so single-minded, to use every waking moment writing propaganda.

"You make the sign for the door, and I'll make sure you aren't alone in the room."

"Woman, you make my heart go flip-flop like a dying flounder," said Jakt.

"You are *so* romantic when you talk like a fisherman," said Valentine. "The children will have a good laugh, knowing you couldn't keep your hands off me even for the three weeks of this voyage."

"They have our genes. They should be rooting for us to stay randy till we're well into our second century."

"I'm well into my fourth millennium."

"When oh when can I expect you in my stateroom, Ancient One?"

"When I've transmitted this essay."

"And how long will that be?"

"Sometime after you go away and leave me alone."

With a deep sigh that was more theatre than genuine misery, he padded off down the carpeted corridor. After a moment there came a clanging sound and she heard him yelp in pain. In mock pain, of course; he had accidentally hit the metal beam with his head on the first day of the voyage, but ever since then his collisions had been deliberate, for comic effect. No one ever laughed out loud, of course—that was a family tradition, not to laugh when Jakt pulled one of his physical gags—but then Jakt was not the sort of man who needed overt encouragement from others. He was his own best audience; a man couldn't be a sailor and a leader of men all his life without being quite self-contained. As far as Valentine knew, she and the children were the only people he had ever allowed himself to need.

Even then, he had not needed them so much that he couldn't go on with his life as a sailor and fisherman, away from home for days, often weeks, sometimes months at a time. Valentine went with him sometimes at first, when they were still so hungry for each other that they could never be satisfied. But within a few years their hunger had given way to patience and trust; when he was away, she did her research and wrote her books, and then gave her entire attention to him and the children when he returned.

The children used to complain, "I wish Father would get home, so Mother would come out of her room and talk to us again." I was not a very good mother, Valentine thought. It's pure luck that the children turned out so well.

The essay remained in the air over the terminal. Only a final touch remained to be given. At the bottom, she centered the cursor and typed the name under which all her writings were published:

DEMOSTHENES

It was a name given to her by her older brother, Peter, when they were children together fifty—no, three thousand years ago.

The mere thought of Peter still had the power to upset her, to make her go hot and cold inside. Peter, the cruel one, the violent one, the one whose mind was so subtle and dangerous that he was manipulating *her* by the age of two and the world by the age of twenty. When they were still children on Earth in the twenty-second century, he studied the political writings of great men and women, living and dead, not to learn their ideas—those he grasped instantly—but to learn how they said them. To learn, in practical terms, how to sound like an adult. When he had mastered it, he taught Valentine, and forced her to write low political demagoguery under the name Demosthenes while he wrote elevated statesmanlike essays under the name Locke. Then they submitted them to the computer networks and within a few years were at the heart of the greatest political issues of the day.

What galled Valentine then—and still stung a bit today, since it had never been resolved before Peter died—was that he, consumed by the lust for power, had forced *her* to write the sort of thing that expressed *his* character, while *he* got to write the peace-loving, elevated sentiments that were hers by nature. In those days the name "Demosthenes" had felt like a terrible burden to her. Everything she wrote under that name was a lie; and not even her lie—Peter's lie. A lie within a lie.

Not now. Not for three thousand years. I've made the name my own. I've written histories and biographies that have shaped the thinking of millions of scholars on the Hundred Worlds and helped to shape the identities of dozens of nations. So much for you, Peter. So much for what you tried to make of me.

Except that now, looking at the essay she had just written, she realized that even though she had freed herself from Peter's suzerainty, she was still his pupil. All she knew of rhetoric, polemic—yes, of demagoguery—she had learned from him or because of his insistence. And now, though she was using it in a noble cause, she was nevertheless doing exactly the sort of political manipulation that Peter had loved so much.

Peter had gone on to become Hegemon, ruler of all humanity for sixty years at the beginning of the Great Expansion. He was the one who united all the quarreling communities of man for the vast effort that flung starships out to every world where the buggers had once dwelt, and then on to discover more habitable worlds until, by the time he died, all the Hundred Worlds had either been settled or had colony ships on the way. It was almost a thousand years after that, of course, before Starways Congress once again united all of humankind under one government—but the memory of the first true Hegemon—*the* Hegemon—was at the heart of the story that made human unity possible.

Out of a moral wasteland like Peter's soul came harmony and unity and peace. While Ender's legacy, as far as humanity remembered, was murder, slaughter, xenocide.

Ender, Valentine's younger brother, the man she and her family were voyaging to see—he was the tender one, the brother she loved and, in the earliest years, tried to protect. He was the *good* one. Oh, yes, he had a streak of ruthlessness that rivaled Peter's, but he had the decency to be appalled by his own brutality. She had loved him as fervently as she had loathed Peter; and when Peter exiled his younger brother from the Earth that Peter was determined to rule, Valentine went with Ender—her final repudiation of Peter's personal hegemony over her.

And here I am again, thought Valentine, back in the business of politics.

She spoke sharply, in the clipped voice that told her terminal that she was giving it a command. "Transmit," she said.

The word *transmitting* appeared in the air above her essay. Ordinarily, back when she was writing scholarly works, she would have had to specify a destination—submit the essay to a publisher through some roundabout pathway so that it could not readily be traced to Valentine Wiggin. Now, though, a subversive friend of Ender's, working under the obvious code name of "Jane," was taking care of all that for her—managing the tricky business of translating an ansible message from a ship going at near-lightspeed to a message readable by a planetbound ansible for which time was passing more than five hundred times faster.

Since communicating with a starship ate up huge amounts of planetside ansible time, it was usually done only to convey navigational information and instructions. The only people permitted to send extended text messages were high officials in the government or the military. Valentine could not begin to understand how "Jane" managed to get so much ansible time for these text transmissions—and at the same time keep anyone from discovering where these subversive documents were coming from. Furthermore, "Jane" used even more ansible time transmitting back to her the published responses to her writings, reporting to her on all the arguments and strategies the government was using to counter Valentine's propaganda. Whoever "Jane" was—and Valentine suspected that "Jane" was simply the name for a clandestine organization that had penetrated the highest reaches of government—she was extraordinarily good. And extraordinarily foolhardy. Still, if Jane was willing to expose herself—themselves—to such risks, Valentine owed it to her—them—to produce as many tracts as she could, and as powerful and dangerous as she could make them.

If words can be lethal weapons, I must provide them with an arsenal.

But she was still a woman; even revolutionaries are allowed to have a life, aren't they? Moments of joy—or pleasure, or perhaps only *relief*—stolen here and there. She got up from her seat, ignoring the pain that came from moving after sitting so long, and twisted her way out of the door of her tiny office—a storage bin, really, before they converted the starship to their own use. She was a little ashamed of how eager she was to get to the room where Jakt would be waiting. Most of the great revolutionary propagandists in history would have been able to endure at least three weeks of physical abstinence. Or would they? She wondered if anyone had done a study of that particular question.

She was still imagining how a researcher would go about writing a grant proposal for such a project when she got to the four-bunk compartment they shared with Syfte and her husband, Lars, who had proposed to her only a few days before they left, as soon as he realized that Syfte really meant to leave Trondheim. It was hard to share a cabin with newlyweds—Valentine always felt like such an intruder, using the same room. But there was no choice. Though this starship was a luxury yacht, with all the amenities they could hope for, it simply hadn't been meant to hold so many bodies. It had been the only starship near Trondheim that was remotely suitable, so it had to do.

Their twenty-year-old daughter, Ro, and Varsam, their sixteen-year-old son, shared another compartment with Plikt, who had been their lifelong tutor and dearest family friend. The members of the yacht's staff and crew who had chosen to make this voyage with them—it would have been wrong to dismiss them all and strand them on Trondheim—used the other two. The bridge, the dining room, the galley, the salon, the sleeping compartments—all were filled with people doing their best not to let their annoyance at the close quarters get out of hand.

None of them were in the corridor now, however, and Jakt had already taped a sign to their door:

STAY OUT OR DIE.

It was signed, "The proprietor." Valentine opened the door. Jakt was leaning against the wall so close to the door that she was startled and gave a little gasp.

"Nice to know that the sight of me can make you cry out in pleasure."

"In shock."

"Come in, my sweet seditionist."

"Technically, you know, *I'm* the proprietor of this starship."

"What's yours is mine. I married you for your property."

She was inside the compartment now. He closed the door and sealed it.

"That's all I am to you?" she asked. "Real estate?"

"A little plot of ground where I can plow and plant and harvest, all in their proper season." He reached out to her; she stepped into his arms. His hands slid lightly up her back, cradled her shoulders. She felt contained in his embrace, never confined.

"It's late in the autumn," she said. "Getting on toward winter."

"Time to harrow, perhaps," said Jakt. "Or perhaps it's already time to kindle up the fire and keep the old hut warm before the snow comes."

He kissed her and it felt like the first time.

"If you asked me to marry you all over again today, I'd say yes," said Valentine.

"And if I had only met you for the first time today, I'd ask."

They had said the same words many, many times before. Yet they still smiled to hear them, because they were still true.

———————

The two starships had almost completed their vast ballet, dancing through space in great leaps and delicate turns until at last they could meet and touch. Miro Ribeira had watched the whole process from the bridge of his starship, his shoulders hunched, his head leaned back on the headrest of the seat. To others this posture always looked awkward. Back on Lusitania, whenever Mother caught him sitting that way she would come and fuss over him, insist on bringing him a pillow so he could be *comfortable*. She never seemed to grasp the idea that it was only in that hunched, awkward-seeming posture that his head would remain upright without any conscious effort on his part.

He would endure her ministrations because it wasn't worth the effort to argue with her. Mother was always moving and thinking so quickly, it was almost impossible for her to slow down enough to listen to him. Since the brain damage he had suffered passing through the disruptor field that separated the human colony and the piggies' forest, his speech had been unbearably slow, painful to produce and difficult to understand. Miro's brother Quim, the religious one, had told him that he should be grateful to God that he was able to speak at all—the first few days he had been incapable of communicating except through alphabetic scanning, spelling out messages letter by letter. In some ways, though, spelling things out had been better. At least then Miro had been silent; he hadn't had to listen to his own voice. The thick, awkward sound, the agonizing slowness of it. Who in his family had the patience to listen to him? Even the ones who tried—his next-younger sister, Ela; his friend and stepfather, Andrew Wiggin, the Speaker for the Dead; and Quim, of course—he could feel their impatience. They tended to finish his sentences for him. They needed to *hurry* things. So even though they said they wanted to talk with him, even though they actually sat and listened as he spoke, he still couldn't speak freely to them. He couldn't talk about *ideas;* he couldn't speak in long, involved sentences, because by the time he got to the end his listeners would have lost track of the beginning.

The human brain, Miro had concluded, just like a computer, can only receive data at certain speeds. If you get too slow, the listener's attention wanders and the information is lost.

Not just the listener's, either. Miro had to be fair—he was as impatient with himself as they were. When he thought of the sheer effort involved in explaining a complicated idea, when he anticipated trying to form the words with lips and tongue and jaws that wouldn't obey him, when he thought of how *long* it would all take, he usually felt too weary to speak. His mind raced on and on, as fast as ever, thinking so many thoughts that at times Miro wanted his brain to shut down, to be *silent* and give him peace. But his thoughts remained his own, unshared.

Except with Jane. He could speak to Jane. She had come to him first on his terminal at home, her face taking form on the screen. "I'm a friend of the Speaker for the Dead," she had told him. "I think we can get this computer to be a little more responsive." From then on, Miro had found that Jane was the only person he could talk to easily. For one thing, she was infinitely patient. She never finished his sentences. She could *wait* for him to finish them himself, so that he never felt rushed, never felt that he was boring her.

Perhaps even more important, he didn't have to form his words as fully for her as he did for human listeners. Andrew had given him a personal terminal—a computer transceiver encased in a jewel like the one Andrew wore in his own ear. From that vantage point, using the jewel's sensors, Jane could detect every sound he made, every motion of the muscles in his head. He didn't have to *complete* each sound, he had only to begin it and she would understand. So he could be lazy. He could speak more quickly and be understood.

And he could also speak silently. He could subvocalize—he didn't have to use that awkward, barking, yowling voice that was all his throat could produce now. So that when he was talking to Jane, he could speak quickly, naturally, without any reminder that he was crippled. With Jane he could feel like himself.

Now he sat on the bridge of the cargo ship that had brought the Speaker for the Dead to Lusitania only a few months ago. He dreaded the rendezvous with Valentine's ship. If he could have thought of somewhere else to go, he might have gone there—he had no desire to meet Andrew's sister Valentine or anybody else. If he could have stayed alone in the starship forever, speaking only to Jane, he would have been content.

No he wouldn't. He would never be content again.

At least this Valentine and her family would be somebody new. On Lusitania he knew everybody, or at least everybody that he valued—all the scientific community there, the people of education and understanding. He knew them all so well that he could not help but see their pity, their grief, their frustration at what had become of him. When they looked at him all they could see was the difference between what he was before and what he was now. All they could see was loss.

There was a chance that new people—Valentine and her family—would be able to look at him and see something else.

Even that was unlikely, though. Strangers would look at him and see less, not more, than those who had known him before he was crippled. At least Mother and Andrew and Ela and Ouanda and all the others knew that he had a mind, knew that he was capable of understanding ideas. What will new people think when they see me? They'll see a body that's already atrophying, hunched over; they'll see me walk with a shuffling gait; they'll watch me use my hands like paws, clutching a spoon like a three-year-old; they'll hear my thick, half-intelligible speech; and they'll assume, they'll *know*, that such a person cannot possibly understand anything complicated or difficult.

Why did I come?

I didn't *come*. I *went*. I wasn't coming here, to meet these people. I was leaving there. Getting away. Only I tricked myself. I thought of leaving on a thirty-year voyage, which is only how it will seem to them. To me I've been gone only a week and a half. No time at all.

And already my time of solitude is over. My time of being alone with Jane, who listens to me as if I were still a human being, is done.

Almost. Almost he said the words that would have aborted the rendezvous. He could have stolen Andrew's starship and taken off on a voyage that would last forever without having to face another living soul.

But such a nihilistic act was not in him, not yet. He had not yet despaired, he decided. There might yet be something he could do that might justify his continuing to live in this body. And perhaps it would begin with meeting Andrew's sister.

The ships were now joining, the umbilicals snaking outward and searching, groping till they met each other. Miro watched on the monitors and listened to the computer reports of each successful linkage. The ships were joining in every possible way so that they could make the rest of the voyage to Lusitania in perfect tandem. All resources would be shared. Since Miro's ship was a cargo vessel, it couldn't take on more than a handful of people, but it *could* take some of the other ship's life-support supplies; together, the two ship's computers were figuring out a perfect balance.

Once they had calculated the load, they worked out exactly how fast each ship should accelerate as they made the park shift to get them both back to near-lightspeed at exactly the same pace. It was an extremely delicate and complicated negotiation between two computers that had to know almost perfectly what their ships carried and how they could perform. It was finished before the passage tube between the ships was fully connected.

Miro heard the footsteps scuffing along the corridor from the tube. He turned his chair—slowly, because he did everything slowly—and saw her coming toward him. Stooped over, but not very much, because she wasn't that tall to begin with. Hair mostly white, with a few strands of mousy brown. When she stood he looked at her face and judged her. Old but not elderly. If she was nervous about this meeting it didn't show. But then, from what Andrew and Jane had told him about her, she had met a lot of people who were a good deal more fearsome than a twenty-year-old cripple.

"Miro?" she asked.

"Who else?" he said.

It took a moment, just a heartbeat, for her to process the strange sounds that came out of his mouth and recognize the words. He was used to that pause now, but he still hated it.

"I'm Valentine," she said.

"I know," he answered. He wasn't making this any easier, with his laconic replies, but what else was there to say? This wasn't exactly a meeting between heads of state with a list of vital decisions to make. But he had to make some effort, if only not to seem hostile.

"Your name, Miro—it means 'I look,' doesn't it?"

"'I look *closely*.' Maybe 'I pay attention.'"

"It's really not that hard to understand you," said Valentine.

He was startled that she addressed the matter so openly.

"I think I'm having more problems with your Portuguese accent than with the brain damage."

For a moment it felt like a hammer in his heart—she was speaking more frankly about his situation than anyone except Andrew. But then she was Andrew's sister, wasn't she? He should have expected her to be plainspoken.

"Or do you prefer that we pretend that it isn't a barrier between you and other people?"

Apparently she had sensed his shock. But that was over, and now it occurred to him that he probably shouldn't be annoyed, that he should probably be glad that they wouldn't have to sidestep the issue. Yet he *was* annoyed, and it took him a moment to think why. Then he knew.

"My brain damage isn't *your* problem," he said.

"If it makes it hard for me to understand you, then it's a problem I have to deal with. Don't get prickly with me already, young man. I have only begun to bother you, and you have only begun to bother me. So don't get steamed up because I happened to mention your brain damage as being somehow *my* problem. I have no intention of watching every word I say for fear I'll offend an oversensitive young man who thinks the whole world revolves around his disappointments."

Miro was furious that she had judged him already, and so harshly. It was unfair—not at all what the author of Demosthenes' hierarchy ought to be like. "I don't think the whole world revolves around my disappointments! But don't you think you can come in here and run things on my ship!" *That's* what annoyed him, not her words. She was right—her words were nothing. It was her attitude, her complete self-confidence. He wasn't used to people looking at him without shock or pity.

She sat down in the seat next to him. He swiveled to face her. She, for her part, did not look away. Indeed, she pointedly scanned his body, head to toe, looking him over with an air of cool appraisal. "He said you were tough. He said you had been twisted but not broken."

"Are you supposed to be my therapist?"

"Are you supposed to be my enemy?"

"Should I be?" asked Miro.

"No more than I should be your therapist. Andrew didn't have us meet so I could heal you. He had us meet so you could help *me*. If you're not going to, fine. If you are, fine. Just let me make a few things clear. I'm spending every waking moment writing subversive propaganda to try to arouse public sentiment on the Hundred Worlds and in the colonies. I'm trying to turn the people against the fleet that Starways Congress has sent to subdue Lusitania. *Your* world, not mine, I might add."

"Your brother's there." He was not about to let her claim complete altruism.

"Yes, we both have family there. And we both are concerned about keeping the pequeninos from destruction. And we both know that Ender has restored the hive queen on your world, so that there are two alien species that will be destroyed if Starways Congress gets its way. There's a great deal at stake, and I am already doing all that I can possibly do to try to stop that fleet. Now, if spending a few hours with you can help me do it better, it's worth taking time away from my writing in order to talk with you. But I have no intention of wasting my time worrying about whether I'm going to offend you or not. So if you're going to be my adversary, you can sit up here all by yourself and I'll get back to my work."

"Andrew said you were the best person he ever knew."

"He reached that conclusion before he saw me raise three barbarian children to adulthood. I understand your mother has six."

"Right."

"And you're the oldest."

"Yes."

"That's too bad. Parents always make their worst mistakes with the oldest children. That's when parents know the least and care the most, so they're more likely to be wrong and also more likely to insist that they're right."

Miro didn't like hearing this woman leap to conclusions about his mother. "She's nothing like you."

"Of course not." She leaned forward in her seat. "Well, have you decided?"

"Decided what?"

"Are we working together or did you just unplug yourself from thirty years of human history for nothing?"

"What do you want from me?"

"Stories, of course. Facts I can get from the computer."

"Stories about what?"

"You. The piggies. You *and* the piggies. This whole business with the Lusitania Fleet began with you and the piggies, after all. It was because you interfered with them that—"

"We *helped* them!"

"Oh, did I use the wrong word again?"

Miro glared at her. But even as he did, he knew that she was right—he was being oversensitive. The word *interfered,* when used in a scientific context, was almost value-neutral. It merely meant that he had introduced change into the culture he was studying. And if it did have a negative connotation, it was that he had lost his scientific perspective—he had stopped studying the pequeninos and started treating them as friends. Of that he was surely guilty. No, not guilty—he was *proud* of having made that transition. "Go on," he said.

"All this began because you broke the law and piggies started growing amaranth."

"Not anymore."

"Yes, that's ironic, isn't it? The descolada virus has gotten in and killed every strain of amaranth that your sister developed for them. So your interference was in vain."

"No it wasn't," said Miro. "They're learning."

"Yes, I know. More to the point, they're *choosing.* What to learn, what to do. You brought them freedom. I approve wholeheartedly of what you decided to do. But my job is to write about you to the people out there in the Hundred Worlds and the colonies, and *they* won't necessarily see things that way. So what I need from you is the story of how and why you broke the law and interfered with the piggies, and why the government and people of Lusitania rebelled against Congress rather than send you off to be tried and punished for your crimes."

"Andrew already told you that story."

"And I've already written about it, in larger terms. Now I need the personal things. I want to be able to let other people know these so-called piggies as people. And you, too. I have to let them know *you* as a person. If it's possible, it would be nice if I could bring them to like you. Then the Lusitania Fleet will look like what it is—a monstrous overreaction to a threat that never existed."

"The fleet is xenocide."

"So I've said in my propaganda," said Valentine.

He couldn't bear her self-certainty. He couldn't bear her unshakable faith in herself. So he had to contradict her, and the only way he could was to blurt out ideas that he had not yet thought out completely. Ideas that were still only half-formed doubts in his mind. "The fleet is also self-defense."

It had the desired effect—it stopped her lecture and even made her raise her eyebrows, questioning him. The trouble was, now he had to explain what he meant.

"The descolada," he said. "It's the most dangerous form of life anywhere."

"The answer to that is quarantine. Not sending a fleet armed with the M.D. Device, so they have the capacity to turn Lusitania and everybody on it into microscopic interstellar dust."

"You're so sure you're right?"

"I'm sure that it's wrong for Starways Congress even to contemplate obliterating another sentient species."

"The piggies can't live without the descolada," said Miro, "and if the descolada ever spreads to another planet, it will destroy all life there. It *will*."

It was a pleasure to see that Valentine was capable of looking puzzled. "But I thought the virus was contained. It was your grandparents who found a way to stop it, to make it dormant in human beings."

"The descolada adapts," said Miro. "Jane told me that it's already changed itself a couple of times. My mother and my sister Ela are working on it—trying to stay ahead of the descolada. Sometimes it even looks like the descolada is doing it deliberately. Intelligently. Finding strategies to get around the chemicals we use to contain it and stop it from killing people. It's getting into the Earthborn crops that humans need in order to survive on Lusitania. They have to spray them now. What if the descolada finds a way to get around all our barriers?"

Valentine was silent. No glib answer now. She hadn't faced this question squarely—no one had, except Miro.

"I haven't even told this to Jane," said Miro. "But what if the fleet is right? What if the only way to save humanity from the descolada is to destroy Lusitania now?"

"No," said Valentine. "This has nothing to do with the purposes for which Starways Congress sent out the fleet. *Their* reasons all have to do with interplanetary politics, with showing the colonies who's boss. It has to do with a bureaucracy out of control and a military that—"

"Listen to me!" said Miro. "You said you wanted to hear my stories, listen to this one: It doesn't matter what their reasons are. It doesn't matter if they're a bunch of murderous beasts. I don't care. What matters is—*should* they blow up Lusitania?"

"What kind of person *are* you?" asked Valentine. He could hear both awe and loathing in her voice.

"You're the moral philosopher," said Miro. "You tell *me*. Are we supposed to love the pequeninos so much that we allow the virus they carry to destroy all of humanity?"

"Of course not. We simply have to find a way to neutralize the descolada."

"And if we can't?"

"Then we quarantine Lusitania. Even if all the human beings on the planet die—your family and mine—we still don't destroy the pequeninos."

"Really?" asked Miro. "What about the hive queen?"

"Ender told me that she was reestablishing herself, but—"

"She contains within herself a complete industrialized society. She's going to build starships and get off the planet."

"She wouldn't take the descolada with her!"

"She has no choice. The descolada is in her already. It's in *me*."

That was when he really got to her. He could see it in her eyes—the fear.

"It'll be in you, too. Even if you run back to your ship and seal me off and keep yourself from infection, once you land on Lusitania the descolada will get into you and your husband and your children. They'll have to ingest the chemicals with their food and water, every day of their lives. And they can never go away from Lusitania again or they'll carry death and destruction with them."

"I suppose we knew that was a possibility," said Valentine.

"When you left, it was only a possibility. We thought that the descolada would soon be controlled. Now they aren't sure if it can ever be controlled. And that means that you can never leave Lusitania once you go there."

"I hope we like the weather."

Miro studied her face, the way she was processing the information he had given her. The initial fear was gone. She was herself again—thinking. "Here's what I think," said Miro. "I think that no matter how terrible Congress is, no matter how evil their plans might be, that fleet might be the salvation of humanity."

Valentine answered thoughtfully, searching for words. Miro was glad to see that—she was a person who didn't shoot back without thinking. She was able to learn. "I can see that if events move down one possible path, there might be a time when—but it's very improbable. First of all, knowing all this, the hive queen is quite unlikely to build any starships that would carry the descolada away from Lusitania."

"Do you *know* the hive queen?" demanded Miro. "Do you *understand* her?"

"Even if she *would* do such a thing," said Valentine, "your mother and sister are working on this, aren't they? By the time we reach Lusitania—by the time the *fleet* reaches Lusitania—they might have found a way to control the descolada once and for all."

"And if they do," said Miro, "should they use it?"

"Why shouldn't they?"

"How could they kill *all* the descolada virus? The virus is an integral part of the pequenino life cycle. When the pequenino body-form dies, it's the descolada virus that enables the transformation into the tree-state, what the piggies call the third life—and it's only in the third life, as trees, that the pequenino males can fertilize the females. If the virus is gone, there can be no more passage into the third life, and this generation of piggies is the last."

"That doesn't make it impossible, it only makes it harder. Your mother and sister have to find a way to neutralize the descolada in human beings and the crops we need to eat, without destroying its ability to enable the pequeninos to pass into adulthood."

"And they have less than fifteen years to do it," said Miro. "Not likely."

"But not impossible."

"Yes. There's a chance. And on the strength of that chance, you want to get rid of the fleet?"

"The fleet is being sent to destroy Lusitania whether we control the descolada virus or not."

"And I say it again—the motive of the senders is irrelevant. No matter what the reason, the destruction of Lusitania may be the only sure protection for all the rest of humanity."

"And I say you're wrong."

"You're Demosthenes, aren't you? Andrew said you were."

"Yes."

"So you thought up the Hierarchy of Foreignness. Utlannings are strangers from our own world. Framlings are strangers of our own species, but from another world. Ramen are strangers of another species, but capable of communication with us, capable of co-existence with humanity. Last are varelse—and what are *they*?"

"The pequeninos are not varelse. Neither is the hive queen."

"But the descolada *is*. Varelse. An alien life form that's capable of destroying all of humanity . . ."

"Unless we can tame it . . ."

". . . Yet which we cannot possibly communicate with, an alien species that we cannot live with. You're the one who said that in that case war is unavoidable. If an alien species seems bent on destroying us and we can't communicate with them, can't understand them, if there's no *possibility* of turning them away from their course peacefully, then we are justified in any action necessary to save ourselves, including the complete destruction of the other species."

"Yes," said Valentine.

"But what if we *must* destroy the descolada, and yet we *can't* destroy the descolada without also destroying every living pequenino, the hive queen, and every human being on Lusitania?"

To Miro's surprise, Valentine's eyes were awash with tears. "So this is what you have become."

Miro was confused. "When did this conversation become a discussion of *me*?"

"You've done all this thinking, you've seen all the possibilities for the future—good ones and bad ones alike—and yet the only one that you're willing to believe in, the imagined future that you seize upon as the foundation for all your moral judgments, is the only future in which everyone that you and I have ever loved and everything we've ever hoped for must be obliterated."

"I didn't say I *liked* that future—"

"I didn't say you liked it either," said Valentine. "I said that's the future you choose to prepare for. But I don't. I choose to live in a universe that has some hope in it. I choose to live in a universe where your mother and sister will find a way to contain the descolada, a universe in which Starways Congress can be reformed or replaced, a universe in which there is neither the power nor the will to destroy an entire species."

"What if you're wrong?"

"Then I'll still have plenty of time to despair before I die. But you—do you seek out every opportunity to despair? I can understand the impulse that might lead to that. Andrew tells me you were a handsome man—you still are, you know—and that losing the full use of your body has hurt you deeply. But other people have lost more than you have without getting such a black-hearted vision of the world."

"This is your analysis of me?" asked Miro. "We've known each other half an hour, and now you understand everything about me?"

"I know that this is the most depressing conversation I've ever had in my life."

"And so you assume that it's because *I* am crippled. Well, let me tell you something, Valentine Wiggin. I hope the same things *you* hope. I even hope that someday I'll get more of my body back again. If I didn't have hope I'd be *dead*. The things I told you just now aren't because I despair. I said all that because these things are *possible*. And *because* they're possible we have to think of them so they don't surprise us later. We have to think of them so that if the worst does come, we'll already know how to live in that universe."

Valentine seemed to be studying his face; he felt her gaze on him as an almost palpable thing, like a faint tickling under the skin, inside his brain. "Yes," she said.

"Yes what?"

"Yes, my husband and I will move over here and live on your ship." She got up from her seat and started toward the corridor leading back to the tube.

"Why did you decide *that*?"

"Because it's too crowded on our ship. And because you are definitely worth talking to. And *not* just to get material for the essays I have to write."

"Oh, so I passed your test?"

"Yes, you did," she said. "Did I pass yours?"

"I wasn't testing you."

"Like hell," she said. "But in case you didn't notice, I'll tell you—I *did* pass. Or you wouldn't have said to me all the things you said."

She was gone. He could hear her shuffling down the corridor, and then the computer reported that she was passing through the tube between ships.

He already missed her.

Because she was right. She *had* passed his test. She had listened to him the way no one else did—without impatience, without finishing his sentences, without letting her gaze waver from his face. He had spoken to her, not with careful precision, but with great emotion. Much of the time his words must surely have been almost unintelligible. Yet she had listened so carefully and well that she had understood all his arguments and never once asked him to repeat something. He could talk to this woman as naturally as he ever talked to anyone before his brain was injured. Yes, she was opinionated, headstrong, bossy, and quick to reach conclusions. But she could also listen to an opposing view, change her mind when she needed to. She could listen, and so he could speak. Perhaps with her he could still be Miro.

3

CLEAN HANDS

<The most unpleasant thing about human beings is that they don't metamorphose. Your people and mine are born as grubs, but we transform ourselves into a higher form before we reproduce. Human beings remain grubs all their lives.>

<Human beings *do* metamorphose. They change their identity constantly. However, each new identity thrives on the delusion that it was always in possession of the body it has just conquered.>

<Such changes are superficial. The nature of the organism remains the same. Humans are very proud of their changes, but every imagined transformation turns out to be a new set of excuses for behaving exactly as the individual has always behaved.>

<You are too different from humans ever to understand them.>

<You are too similar to humans for you ever to be able to see them clearly.>

The gods first spoke to Han Qing-jao when she was seven years old. She didn't realize for a while that she was hearing the voice of a god. All she knew was that her hands were filthy, covered with some loathsome invisible slime, and she had to purify them.

The first few times, a simple washing was enough, and she felt better for days. But as time passed, the feeling of filthiness returned sooner each time, and it took more and more scrubbing to remove the dirt, until she was washing several times a day, using a hard-bristled brush to stab at her hands until they bled. Only when the pain was unbearable did she feel clean, and then only for a few hours at a time.

She told no one; she knew instinctively that the filthiness of her hands had to be kept secret. Everyone knew that handwashing was one of the first signs that the gods were speaking to a child, and most parents in the whole world of Path watched their children hopefully for signs of excessive concern with cleanliness. But what these people did not understand was the terrible self-knowledge that led to the washing: The first message from the gods was of the unspeakable filthiness of the one they spoke to. Qing-jao hid her handwashing, not because she was ashamed that the gods spoke to her, but because she was sure that if anyone knew how vile she was, they would despise her.

The gods conspired with her in concealment. They allowed her to confine her savage scrubbing to the palms of her hands. This meant that when her hands were badly hurt, she could clench them into fists, or tuck them into the folds of her skirt as she walked, or lay them in her lap very meekly when she sat, and no one would notice them. They saw only a very well-behaved little girl.

If her mother had been alive, Qing-jao's secret would have been discovered much sooner. As it was, it took months for a servant to notice. Fat old Mu-pao happened to notice a bloody stain on the small tablecloth from Qing-jao's breakfast table. Mu-pao knew at once what it meant—weren't bloody hands well known to be an early sign of the gods' attention? That was why many an ambitious mother and father forced a particularly promising child to wash and wash. Throughout the world of Path, ostentatious handwashing was called "inviting the gods."

Mu-pao went at once to Qing-jao's father, the noble Han Fei-tzu, rumored to be the greatest of the godspoken, one of the few so powerful in the eyes of the gods that he could meet with framlings—offworlders—and never betray a hint of the voices of the gods within him, thus preserving the divine secret of the world of Path. He would be grateful to hear the news, and Mu-pao would be honored for having been the first to see the gods in Qing-jao.

Within an hour, Han Fei-tzu had gathered up his beloved little Qing-jao and together they rode in a sedan chair to the temple at Rockfall. Qing-jao didn't like riding in such chairs—she felt bad for the men who had to carry their weight. "They don't suffer," Father told her the first time she mentioned this idea. "They feel greatly honored. It's one of the ways the people show honor to the gods—when one of the godspoken goes to a temple, he does it on the shoulders of the people of Path."

"But I'm getting bigger every day," Qing-jao answered.

"When you're too big, either you'll walk on your own feet or you'll ride in your own chair," said Father. He did not need to explain that she would have her own chair only if she grew up to be godspoken herself. "And we try to show our humility by remaining very thin and light so we aren't a heavy burden to the people." This was a joke, of course, since Father's belly, while not immense, was copious. But the lesson behind the joke was true: The godspoken must never be a burden to the common people of Path. The people must always be grateful, never resentful, that the gods had chosen their world of all worlds to hear their voices.

Now, though, Qing-jao was more concerned with the ordeal that lay before her. She knew that she was being taken for testing. "Many children are taught to pretend that the gods speak to them," Father explained. "We must find out if the gods have truly chosen you."

"I want them to stop choosing me," said Qing-jao.

"And you will want it even more during the test," said Father. His voice was filled with pity. It made Qing-jao even more afraid. "The folk see only our powers and privileges, and envy us. They don't know the great suffering of those who hear the voices of the gods. If the gods truly speak to you, my Qing-jao, you will learn to bear the suffering the way jade bears the carver's knife, the polisher's rough cloth. It will make you shine. Why else do you think I named you Qing-jao?"

Qing-jao—Gloriously Bright was what the name meant. It was also the name of a great poet from ancient times in Old China. A woman poet in an age when only men were given respect, and yet she was honored as the greatest of poets in her day. "Thin fog and thick cloud, gloom all day." It was the opening of Li Qing-jao's song "The Double Ninth." That was how Qing-jao felt now.

And how did the poem end? "Now my curtain's lifted only by the western wind. I've grown thinner than this golden blossom." Would this be her ending also? Was her ancestor-of-the-heart telling her in this poem that the darkness falling over her now would be lifted only when the gods came out of the west to lift her thin, light, golden soul out of her body? It was too terrible, to think of death now, when she was only seven years old; and yet the thought came to her: If I die soon, then soon I'll see Mother, and even the great Li Qing-jao herself.

But the test had nothing to do with death, or at least it was not supposed to. It was quite simple, really. Father led her into a large room where three old men knelt. Or they seemed like men—they could have been women. They were so old that all distinctions had disappeared. They had only the tiniest wisps of white hair and no beards at all, and they dressed in shapeless sacks. Later Qing-jao would learn that these were temple eunuchs, survivors of the old days before Starways Congress intervened and forbade even voluntary self-mutilation in the service of a religion. Now, though, they were mysterious ghostly old creatures whose hands touched her, exploring her clothing.

What were they searching for? They found her ebony chopsticks and took them away. They took the sash from around her waist. They took her slippers. Later she would learn that these things were taken because other children had become so desperate during their testing that they had killed themselves. One of them had inserted her chopsticks into her nostrils and then flung herself to the floor, jamming the sticks into her brain. Another had hanged herself with her sash. Another had forced her slippers into her mouth and down her throat, choking herself to death. Successful suicide attempts were rare, but they seemed to happen with the brightest of the children, and most commonly with girls. So they took away from Qing-jao all the known ways of committing suicide.

The old ones left. Father knelt beside Qing-jao and spoke to her face to face. "You must understand, Qing-jao, that we are not really testing *you*. Nothing that you do of your own free will can make the slightest difference in what happens here. We are really testing the gods, to see if they are determined to speak to you. If they are, they'll find a way, and we'll see it, and you'll come out of this room as one of the godspoken. If they aren't, then you'll come out of here free of their voices for all time. I can't tell you which outcome I pray for, since I don't know myself."

"Father," said Qing-jao, "what if you're ashamed of me?" The very thought made her feel a tingling in her hands, as if there were dirt on them, as if she needed to wash them.

"I will not be ashamed of you either way."

Then he clapped his hands. One of the old ones came back in, bearing a heavy basin. He set it down before Qing-jao.

"Thrust in your hands," said Father.

The basin was filled with thick black grease. Qing-jao shuddered. "I can't put my hands in there."

Father reached out, took her by the forearms, and forced her hands down into the muck. Qing-jao cried out—her father had never used force with her before. And when he let go of her arms, her hands were covered with clammy slime. She gasped at the filthiness of her hands; it was hard to breathe, looking at them like that, smelling them.

The old one picked up the basin and carried it out.

"Where can I wash, Father?" Qing-jao whimpered.

"You can't wash," said Father. "You can never wash again."

And because Qing-jao was a child, she believed him, not guessing that his words were part of the test. She watched Father leave the room. She heard the door latch behind him. She was alone.

At first she simply held her hands out in front of her, making sure they didn't touch any part of her clothing. She searched desperately for somewhere to wash, but there was no water, nor even a cloth. The room was far from bare—there were chairs, tables, statues, large stone jars—but all the surfaces were hard and well-polished and so clean that she couldn't bear to touch them. Yet the filthiness of her hands was unendurable. She had to get them clean.

"Father!" she called out. "Come and wash my hands!" Surely he could hear her. Surely he was somewhere near, waiting for the outcome of her test. He must hear her—but he didn't come.

The only cloth in the room was the gown she was wearing. She could wipe on *that*, only then she would be wearing the grease; it might get on other parts of her body. The solution, of course, was to take it off—but how could she do that without touching her filthy hands to some other part of herself?

She tried. First she carefully scraped off as much of the grease as she could on the smooth arms of a statue. Forgive me, she said to the statue, in case it belonged to a god. I will come and clean you after; I'll clean you with my own gown.

Then she reached back over her shoulders and gathered the cloth on her back, pulling up on the gown to draw it over her head. Her greasy fingers slipped on the silk; she could feel the slime cold on her bare back as it penetrated the silk. I'll clean it after, she thought.

At last she got a firm enough grasp of the fabric that she could pull off the gown. It slid over her head, but even before it was completely off, she knew that things were worse than ever, for some of the grease was in her long hair, and that hair had fallen onto her face, and now she had filth not just on her hands but also on her back, in her hair, on her face.

Still she tried. She got the gown the rest of the way off, then carefully wiped her hands on one small part of the fabric. Then she wiped her face on another. But it was no good. Some of the grease clung to her no matter what she did. Her face felt as if the silk of her gown had only smeared the grease around instead of lifting it away. She had never been so hopelessly grimy in her life. It was unbearable, and yet she couldn't get rid of it.

"Father! Come take me away! I don't want to be god-spoken!" He didn't come. She began to cry.

The trouble with crying was that it didn't work. The more she cried, the filthier she felt. The desperate need to be clean overpowered even her weeping. So with tears streaming down her face, she began to search desperately for some way to get the grease off her hands. Again she tried the silk of her gown, but within a little while she was wiping her hands on the walls, sidling around the room, smearing them with grease. She rubbed her palms on the wall so rapidly that heat built up and the grease melted. She did it again and again until her hands were red, until some of the softened scabs on her palms had worn away or been torn off by invisible snags in the wooden walls.

When her palms and fingers hurt badly enough that she couldn't feel the slime on them, she wiped her face with them, gouged at her face with her fingernails to scrape away the grease there. Then, hands dirty again, she once more rubbed them on the walls.

Finally, exhausted, she fell to the floor and wept at the pain in her hands, at her helplessness to get clean. Her eyes were shut with weeping. Tears streaked down her cheeks. She rubbed at her eyes, at her cheeks—and felt how slimy the tears made her skin, how filthy she was. She knew what this surely meant: The gods had judged her and found her unclean. She wasn't worthy to live. If she couldn't get clean, she had to blot herself out. That would satisfy them. That would ease the agony of it. All she had to do was find a way to die. To stop breathing. Father would be sorry he didn't come when she called to him, but she couldn't help that. She was under the power of the gods now, and they had judged her unworthy to be among the living. After all, what right did she have to breathe when the gate of Mother's lips had stopped letting the air pass through, in or out, for all these many years?

She first thought of using her gown, thought of stuffing it into her mouth to block her breath, or tying it around her throat to choke herself—but it was too filthy to handle, too covered with grease. She would have to find another way.

Qing-jao walked to the wall, pressed against it. Sturdy wood. She leaned back and flung her head against the wood. Pain flashed through her head when it struck; stunned, she dropped to a sitting position on the floor. Her head ached inside. The room swung slowly around and around her. For a moment she forgot the filthiness of her hands.

But the relief didn't last long. She could see on the wall a slightly duller place where the grease from her forehead broke up the shiny polished surface. The gods spoke inside her, insisted she was as filthy as ever. A little pain wouldn't make up for her unworthiness.

Again she struck her head against the wall. This time, however, there was nowhere near as much pain. Again, again—and now she realized that against her will, her body was recoiling from the blow, refusing to inflict so much pain on herself. This helped her understand why the gods found her so unworthy—she was too weak to make her body obey. Well, she wasn't helpless. She could *fool* her body into submission.

She selected the tallest of the statues, which stood perhaps three meters high. It was a bronze casting of a man in mid-stride, holding a sword above his head. There were enough angles and bends and projections that she could climb. Her hands kept slipping, but she persevered until she balanced on the statue's shoulders, holding onto its headdress with one hand and the sword with the other.

For a moment, touching the sword, she thought of trying to cut her throat on it—that would stop her breath, wouldn't it? But the blade was only a pretend blade. It wasn't sharp, and she couldn't get her neck to it at the right angle. So she went back to her original plan.

She took several deep breaths, then clasped her hands behind her back and toppled forward. She would land on her head; that would end her filthiness.

As the floor rushed upward, however, she lost control of herself. She screamed; she felt her hands tear free of each other behind her back and rush forward to try to break her fall. Too late, she thought with grim satisfaction, and then her head struck the floor and everything went black.

———

Qing-jao awoke with a dull ache in her arm and a sharp pain in her head whenever she moved—but she was alive. When she could bear to open her eyes she saw that the room was darker. Was it night outside? How long had she slept? She couldn't bear to move her left arm, the one with the pain; she could see an ugly red bruise at the elbow and she thought she must have broken it inside when she fell.

She also saw that her hands were still smeared with grease, and felt her unbearable dirtiness: the gods' judgment against her. She shouldn't have tried to kill herself after all. The gods wouldn't allow her to escape their judgment so easily.

What can I do? she pleaded. How can I be clean before you, O Gods? Li Qing-jao, my ancestor-of-the-heart, show me how to make myself worthy to receive the kind judgment of the gods!

What came at once to her mind was Li Qing-jao's love song "Separation." It was one of the first that Father had given her to memorize when she was only three years old, only a short time before he and Mother told her that Mother was going to die. It was exactly appropriate now, too, for wasn't she separated from the goodwill of the gods? Didn't she need to be reconciled

with them so they could receive her as one of the truly
godspoken ones?

> someone's sent
> a loving note
> in lines of returning geese
> and as the moon fills
> my western chamber
> as petals dance
> over the flowing stream
> again I think of you
> the two of us
> living a sadness
> apart
> a hurt that can't be removed
> yet when my gaze comes down
> my heart stays up

The moon filling the western chamber told her that it
was really a god, not an ordinary man-lover who was
being pined for in this poem—references to the west
always meant that the gods were involved. Li Qing-jao
had answered the prayer of little Han Qing-jao, and
sent this poem to tell her how to cure the hurt that
couldn't be removed—the filthiness of her flesh.

What is the loving note? thought Qing-jao. Lines of
returning geese—but there are no geese in this room.
Petals dancing over a flowing stream—but there are no
petals, there is no stream here.

"Yet when my gaze comes down, my heart stays up."
That was the clue, that was the answer, she knew it.
Slowly, carefully Qing-jao rolled over onto her belly.
Once when she tried to put weight on her left hand, her
elbow buckled and an exquisite pain almost made her
lose consciousness again. At last she knelt, her head
bowed, leaning on her right hand. Gazing down. The
poem promised that this would let her heart stay up.

She felt no better—still filthy, still in pain. Looking down showed her nothing but the polished boards of the floor, the grain of the wood making rippling lines reaching from between her knees outward to the very edge of the room.

Lines. Lines of woodgrain, lines of geese. And couldn't the woodgrain also be seen as a flowing stream? She must follow these lines like the geese; she must dance over these flowing streams like a petal. That was what the promise meant: When her gaze came down, her heart would stay up.

She found one particular line in the woodgrain, a line of darkness like a river rippling through the lighter wood around it, and knew at once that this was the stream she was supposed to follow. She dared not touch it with her finger—filthy, unworthy finger. It had to be followed lightly, the way a goose touched the air, the way a petal touched the stream. Only her eyes could follow the line.

So she began to trace the line, follow it carefully to the wall. A couple of times she moved so quickly that she lost the line, forgot which one it was; but soon she found it again, or thought she did, and followed it to the wall. Was it good enough? Were the gods satisfied?

Almost, but not quite—she couldn't be sure that when her gaze slipped from the line she had returned to the right one. Petals didn't skip from stream to stream. She had to follow the right one, along its entire length. This time she started at the wall and bowed very low, so her eyes wouldn't be distracted even by the movement of her own right hand. She inched her way along, never letting herself so much as blink, even when her eyes burned. She knew that if she lost the grain she was following she'd have to go back and start over. It had to be done perfectly or it would lose all its power to cleanse her.

It took forever. She *did* blink, but not haphazardly,

by accident. When her eyes burned too much, she would bow down until her left eye was directly over the grain. Then she would close the other eye for a moment. Her right eye relieved, she would open it, then put *that* eye directly over the line in the wood and close the left. This way she was able to make it halfway across the room until the board ended, butting up against another.

She wasn't sure whether that was good enough, whether it was enough to finish the board or if she needed to find another woodgrain line to follow. She made as if to get up, testing the gods, to see if they were satisfied. She half-rose, felt nothing; she stood, and still she was at ease.

Ah! They were satisfied, they were pleased with her. Now the grease on her skin felt like nothing more than a little oil. There was no need for washing, not at this moment, for she had found another way to cleanse herself, another way for the gods to discipline her. Slowly she lay back on the floor, smiling, weeping softly in joy. Li Qing-jao, my ancestor-of-the-heart, thank you for showing me the way. Now I have been joined to the gods; the separation is over. Mother, I am again connected to you, clean and worthy. White Tiger of the West, I am now pure enough to touch your fur and leave no mark of filthiness.

Then hands touched her—Father's hands, picking her up. Drops of water fell onto her face, the bare skin of her body—Father's tears. "You're alive," he said. "My godspoken one, my beloved, my daughter, my life, Gloriously Bright, you shine on."

Later she would learn that Father had had to be tied and gagged during her test, that when she climbed the statue and made as if to press her throat against the sword he flung himself forward with such force that his chair fell and his head struck the floor. This was regarded as a great mercy, since it meant he didn't see her terrible fall from the statue. He wept for her all the time she lay unconscious. And then, when she rose to her knees and began to trace the woodgrains on the floor, he was the one who realized what it meant. "Look," he whispered. "The gods have given her a task. The gods are speaking to her."

The others were slow to recognize it, because they had never seen anyone trace woodgrain lines before. It wasn't in the Catalogue of Voices of the Gods: Door-Waiting, Counting-to-Multiples-of-Five, Object-Counting, Checking-for-Accidental-Murders, Fingernail-Tearing, Skin-Scraping, Pulling-Out-of-Hair, Gnawing-at-Stone, Bugging-Out-of-Eyes—all these were known to be penances that the gods demanded, rituals of obedience that cleansed the soul of the godspoken so that the gods could fill their minds with wisdom. No one had ever seen Woodgrain-Tracing. Yet Father saw what she was doing, named the ritual, and added it to the Catalogue of Voices. It would forever bear her name, Han Qingjao, as the first to be commanded by the gods to perform this rite. It made her very special.

So did her unusual resourcefulness in trying to find ways to cleanse her hands and, later, kill herself. Many had tried scraping their hands on walls, of course, and most attempted to wipe on clothes. But *rubbing* her hands to build up the heat of friction, that was regarded as rare and clever. And while head-beating was common, climbing a statue and jumping off and landing on her head was very rare. And none who had done it before had been strong enough to keep their hands behind their back so long. The temple was all abuzz with it, and word soon spread to all the temples in Path.

It was a great honor to Han Fei-tzu, of course, that his daughter was so powerfully possessed by the gods. And the story of his near-madness when she was trying to destroy herself spread just as quickly and touched many hearts. "He may be the greatest of the godspoken," they said of him, "but he loves his daughter more than life." This made them love him as much as they already revered him.

It was then that people began whispering about the possible godhood of Han Fei-tzu. "He is great and strong enough that the gods will listen to him," said the people who favored him. "Yet he is so affectionate that he will always love the people of the planet Path, and try to do good for us. Isn't this what the god of a world ought to be?" Of course it was impossible to decide now—a man could not be chosen to be god of a village, let alone of a whole world, until he died. How could you judge what sort of god he'd be, until his whole life, from beginning to end, was known?

These whispers came to Qing-jao's ears many times as she grew older, and the knowledge that her father might well be chosen god of Path became one of the beacons of her life. But at the time, and forever in her memory, she remembered that his hands were the ones that carried her bruised and twisted body to the bed of healing, his eyes were the ones that dropped warm tears onto her cold skin, his voice was the one that whispered in the beautiful passionate tones of the old language, "My beloved, my Gloriously Bright, never take your light from my life. Whatever happens, never harm yourself or I will surely die."

4

JANE

<So many of your people are becoming Christians. Believing in the god these humans brought with them.>
<You don't believe in God?>
<The question never came up. We have always remembered how we began.>
<*You* evolved. *We* were created.>
<By a virus.>
<By a virus that God created in order to create us.>
<So you, too, are a believer.>
<I understand belief.>
<No—you desire belief.>
<I desire it enough to act as if I believed. Maybe that's what faith is.>
<Or deliberate insanity.>

It turned out not to be just Valentine and Jakt who came over to Miro's ship. Plikt also came, without invitation, and installed herself in a miserable little cubicle where there wasn't even room to stretch out completely. She was the anomaly on the voyage—not family, not crew, but a friend. Plikt had been a student of Ender's when he was on Trondheim as a speaker for the dead. She had figured out, quite independently, that

Andrew Wiggin was *the* Speaker for the Dead and that he was also *the* Ender Wiggin.

Why this brilliant young woman should have become so fixed on Ender Wiggin, Valentine could not really understand. At times she thought, Perhaps this is how some religions start. The founder doesn't ask for disciples; they come and force themselves upon him.

In any event, Plikt had stayed with Valentine and her family for all the years since Ender left Trondheim, tutoring the children and helping in Valentine's research, always waiting for the day that the family journeyed to be with Ender—a day that only Plikt had known would come.

So during the last half of the voyage to Lusitania, it was the four of them who traveled in Miro's ship: Valentine, Miro, Jakt, and Plikt. Or so Valentine thought at first. It was on the third day since the rendezvous that she learned of the fifth traveler who had been with them all along.

That day, as always, the four of them were gathered on the bridge. There was nowhere else to go. This was a cargo ship—besides the bridge and the sleeping quarters, there was only a tiny galley and the toilet. All the other space was designed to hold cargo, not people—not in any kind of reasonable comfort.

Valentine didn't mind the loss of privacy, though. She was slacking off now on her output of subversive essays; it was more important, she felt, to get to know Miro—and, through him, Lusitania. The people there, the pequeninos, and, most particularly, Miro's family—for Ender had married Novinha, Miro's mother. Valentine did glean much of that kind of information, of course—she couldn't have been a historian and biographer for all these years without learning how to extrapolate much from scant bits of evidence.

The real prize for her had turned out to be Miro himself. He was bitter, angry, frustrated, and filled with loathing for his crippled body, but all that was understandable—his loss had happened only a few months before, and he was still trying to redefine himself. Valentine didn't worry about his future—she could see that he was very strong-willed, the kind of man who didn't easily fall apart. He would adapt and thrive.

What interested her most was his thought. It was as if the confinement of his body had freed his mind. When he had first been injured his paralysis was almost total. He had had nothing to do but lie in one place and *think*. Of course, much of his time had been spent brooding about his losses, his mistakes, the future he couldn't have. But he had also spent many hours thinking about the issues that busy people almost never think about. And on that third day together, that's what Valentine was trying to draw out of him.

"Most people don't think about it, not seriously, and you have," said Valentine.

"Just because I think about it doesn't mean I know anything," said Miro. She really was used to his voice now, though sometimes his speech was maddeningly slow. It took a real effort of will at times to keep from showing any sign of inattention.

"The nature of the universe," said Jakt.

"The sources of life," said Valentine. "You said you had thought about what it means to be alive, and I want to know what you thought."

"How the universe works and why we all are in it." Miro laughed. "It's pretty crazy stuff."

"I've been trapped alone in an ice floe in a fishing boat for two weeks in a blizzard with no heat," said Jakt. "I doubt you've come up with anything that'll sound crazy to *me*."

Valentine smiled. Jakt was no scholar, and his philosophy was generally confined to holding his crew together and catching a lot of fish. But he knew that Valentine wanted to draw Miro out, and so he helped put the young man at ease, helped him know that he'd be taken seriously.

And it was important for Jakt to be the one who did that—because Valentine had seen, and so had Jakt, how Miro watched him. Jakt might be old, but his arms and legs and back were still those of a fisherman, and every movement revealed the suppleness of his body. Miro even commented on it once, obliquely, admiringly: "You've got the build of a twenty-year-old." Valentine heard the ironic corollary that must have been in Miro's mind: While I, who *am* young, have the body of an arthritic ninety-year-old. So Jakt meant something to Miro—he represented the future that Miro could never have. Admiration and resentment; it would have been hard for Miro to speak openly in front of Jakt, if Jakt had not taken care to make sure Miro heard nothing but respect and interest from him.

Plikt, of course, sat in her place, silent, withdrawn, effectively invisible.

"All right," said Miro. "Speculations on the nature of reality and the soul."

"Theology or metaphysics?" asked Valentine.

"Metaphysics, mostly," said Miro. "And physics. Neither one is my specialty. And this isn't the kind of story you said you needed me for."

"I don't always know exactly what I'll need."

"All right," said Miro. He took a couple of breaths, as if he were trying to decide where to begin. "You know about philotic twining."

"I know what everybody knows," said Valentine. "And I know that it hasn't led anywhere in the last twenty-five hundred years because it can't really be experimented with." It was an old discovery, from the days when scientists were struggling to catch up with technology. Teenage physics students memorized a few wise sayings: "Philotes are the fundamental building blocks of all matter and energy. Philotes have neither mass nor inertia. Philotes have only location, duration, and connection." And everybody knew that it was philotic connections—the twining of philotic rays—that made ansibles work, allowing instantaneous communication between worlds and starships many lightyears apart. But no one knew *why* it worked, and because philotes could not be "handled," it was almost impossible to experiment with them. They could only be observed, and then only through their connections.

"Philotics," said Jakt. "Ansibles?"

"A by-product," said Miro.

"What does it have to do with the soul?" asked Valentine.

Miro was about to answer, but he grew frustrated, apparently at the thought of trying to give a long speech through his sluggish, resisting mouth. His jaw was working, his lips moving slightly. Then he said aloud, "I can't do it."

"We'll listen," said Valentine. She understood his reluctance to try extended discourse with the limitations of his speech, but she also knew he had to do it anyway.

"No," said Miro.

Valentine would have tried further persuasion, but she saw his lips were still moving, though little sound came out. Was he muttering? Cursing?

No—she knew it wasn't that at all.

It took a moment for her to realize why she was so sure. It was because she had seen Ender do exactly the same thing, moving his lips and jaw, when he was issuing subvocalized commands to the computer terminal built into the jewel he wore in his ear. Of course: Miro has the same computer hookup Ender has, so he'll speak to it the same way.

In a moment it became clear what command Miro had given to his jewel. It must have been tied in to the ship's computer, because immediately afterward one of the display screens cleared and then showed Miro's face. Only there was none of the slackness that marred his face in person. Valentine realized: It was Miro's face as it used to be. And when the computer image spoke, the sound coming from the speakers was surely Miro's voice as it used to be—clear. Forceful. Intelligent. Quick.

"You know that when philotes combine to make a durable structure—a meson, a neutron, an atom, a molecule, an organism, a planet—they twine up."

"What is this?" demanded Jakt. He hadn't yet figured out why the computer was doing the talking.

The computer image of Miro froze on the screen and fell silent. Miro himself answered. "I've been playing with this," he said. "I tell it things, and it remembers and speaks for me."

Valentine tried to imagine Miro experimenting until the computer program got his face and voice just right. How exhilarating it must have been, to re-create himself as he ought to be. And also how agonizing, to see what he could have been and know that it could never be real. "What a clever idea," said Valentine. "Sort of a prosthesis for the personality."

Miro laughed—a single "Ha!"

"Go ahead," said Valentine. "Whether you speak for yourself or the computer speaks for you, we'll listen."

The computer image came back to life, and spoke again in Miro's strong, imaginary voice. "Philotes are the smallest building blocks of matter and energy. They have no mass or dimension. Each philote connects itself to the rest of the universe along a single ray, a one-dimensional line that connects it to all the other philotes in its smallest immediate structure—a meson. All those strands from the philotes in that structure are twined into a single philotic thread that connects the meson to the next larger structure—a neutron, for instance. The threads in the neutron twine into a yarn connecting it to all the other particles of the atom, and then the yarns of the atom twine into the rope of the molecule. This has nothing to do with nuclear forces or gravity, nothing to do with chemical bonds. As far as we can tell, the philotic connections don't *do* anything. They're just there."

"But the individual rays are always there, present in the twines," said Valentine.

"Yes, each ray goes on forever," answered the screen.

It surprised her—and Jakt, too, judging from the way his eyes widened—that the computer was able to respond immediately to what Valentine said. It wasn't just a preset lecture. This had to be a sophisticated program anyway, to simulate Miro's face and voice so well; but now to have it responding as if it were simulating Miro's personality . . .

Or had Miro given some cue to the program? Had he subvocalized the response? Valentine didn't know—she had been watching the screen. She would stop doing that now—she would watch Miro himself.

"We don't *know* if the ray is infinite," said Valentine. "We only know that we haven't found where the ray ends."

"They twine together, a whole planetful, and each planet's philotic twine reaches to its star, and each star to the center of the galaxy—"

"And where does the galactic twine go?" said Jakt. It was an old question—schoolchildren asked it when they first got into philotics in high school. Like the old speculation that maybe galaxies were really neutrons or mesons inside a far vaster universe, or the old question, If the universe isn't infinite, what is beyond the edge?

"Yes, yes," said Miro. This time, though, he spoke from his own mouth. "But that's not where I'm going. I want to talk about life."

The computerized voice—the voice of the brilliant young man—took over. "The philotic twines from substances like rock or sand all connect directly from each molecule to the center of the planet. But when a molecule is incorporated into a living organism, its ray shifts. Instead of reaching to the planet, it gets twined in with the individual cell, and the rays from the cells are all twined together so that each organism sends a single fiber of philotic connections to twine up with the central philotic rope of the planet."

"Which shows that individual lives have some meaning at the level of physics," said Valentine. She had written an essay about it once, trying to dispel some of the mysticism that had grown up about philotics while at the same time using it to suggest a view of community formation. "But there's no practical effect from it, Miro. Nothing you can *do* with it. The philotic twining of living organisms simply *is*. Every philote is connected to something, and through that to something else, and through that to something else—living cells and organisms are simply two of the levels where those connections can be made."

"Yes," said Miro. "That which lives, twines."

Valentine shrugged, nodded. It probably couldn't be proven, but if Miro wanted that as a premise in his speculations, that was fine.

The computer-Miro took over again. "What I've been thinking about is the *endurance* of the twining. When a twined structure is broken—as when a molecule breaks apart—the old philotic twining remains for a time. Fragments that are no longer physically joined remain philotically connected for a while. And the smaller the particle, the *longer* that connection lasts after the breakup of the original structure, and the more slowly the fragments shift to new twinings."

Jakt frowned. "I thought the smaller things were, the faster things happened."

"It *is* counterintuitive," said Valentine.

"After nuclear fission it takes hours for the philotic rays to sort themselves back out again," said the computer-Miro. "Split a smaller particle than an atom, and the philotic connection between the fragments will last much longer than that."

"Which is how the ansible works," said Miro.

Valentine looked at him closely. Why was he talking sometimes in his own voice, sometimes through the computer? Was the program under his control or wasn't it?

"The principle of the ansible is that if you suspend a meson in a powerful magnetic field," said computer-Miro, "split it, and carry the two parts as far away as you want, the philotic twining will still connect them. And the connection is instantaneous. If one fragment spins or vibrates, the ray between them spins and vibrates, and the movement is detectable at the other end at exactly the same moment. It takes no time whatsoever for the movement to be transmitted along the entire length of the ray, even if the two fragments are carried lightyears away from each other. Nobody knows why it works, but we're glad it does. Without the ansible, there'd be no possibility of meaningful communication between human worlds."

"Hell, there's no meaningful communication *now*," said Jakt. "And if it wasn't for the ansibles, there'd be no warfleet heading for Lusitania right now."

Valentine wasn't listening to Jakt, though. She was watching Miro. This time Valentine saw when he moved his lips and jaw, slightly, silently. Sure enough, after he subvocalized, the computer image of Miro spoke again. He *was* giving commands. It had been absurd for her to think otherwise—who *else* could be controlling the computer?

"It's a hierarchy," said the image. "The more complex the structure, the faster the response to change. It's as if the smaller the particle is, the stupider it is, so it's slower to pick up on the fact that it's now part of a different structure."

"Now you're anthropomorphizing," said Valentine.

"Maybe," said Miro. "Maybe not."

"Human beings are organisms," said the image. "But human philotic twinings go way beyond those of any other life form."

"Now you're talking about that stuff that came from Ganges a thousand years ago," said Valentine. "Nobody's been able to get consistent results from those experiments." The researchers—Hindus all, and devout ones—claimed that they had shown that human philotic twinings, unlike those of other organisms, did not always reach directly down into the planet's core to twine with all other life and matter. Rather, they claimed, the philotic rays from human beings often twined with those of other human beings, most often with families, but sometimes between teachers and students, and sometimes between close co-workers—including the researchers themselves. The Gangeans had concluded that this distinction between humans and other plant and animal life proved that the souls of some humans were literally lifted to a higher plane, nearer to perfection. They believed that the Perfecting Ones had become one with each other the way that all of life was one with the world. "It's all very pleasingly mystical, but nobody except Gangean Hindus takes it seriously anymore."

"I do," said Miro.

"To each his own," said Jakt.

"Not as a religion," said Miro. "As science."

"You mean metaphysics, don't you?" said Valentine.

It was the Miro-image that answered. "The philotic connections between people change fastest of all, and what the Gangeans proved is that they respond to *human will*. If you have strong feelings binding you to your family, then your philotic rays will twine and you will be one, in exactly the same way that the different atoms in a molecule are one."

It was a sweet idea—she had thought so when she first heard it, perhaps two thousand years ago, when Ender was speaking for a murdered revolutionary on Mindanao.

She and Ender had speculated then on whether the Gangean tests would show that *they* were twined, as brother and sister. They wondered whether there had been such a connection between them as children, and if it had persisted when Ender was taken off to Battle School and they were separated for six years. Ender had liked that idea very much, and so had Valentine, but after that one conversation the subject never came up again. The notion of philotic connections between people had remained in the pretty-idea category in her memory. "It's nice to think that the metaphor of human unity might have a physical analogue," said Valentine.

"Listen!" said Miro. Apparently he didn't want her to dismiss the idea as "nice."

Again his image spoke for him. "If the Gangeans are right, then when a human being chooses to bond with another person, when he makes a commitment to a community, it is not just a social phenomenon. It's a physical event as well. The philote, the smallest conceivable physical particle—if we can call something with no mass or inertia physical at all—responds to an act of the human will."

"That's why it's so hard for anyone to take the Gangean experiments seriously."

"The Gangean experiments were careful and honest."

"But no one else ever got the same results."

"No one else ever took them seriously enough to perform the same experiments. Does that surprise you?"

"Yes," said Valentine. But then she remembered how the idea had been ridiculed in the scientific press, while it was immediately picked up by the lunatic fringe and incorporated into dozens of fringe religions. Once that happened, how could a scientist hope to get funding for such a project? How could a scientist expect to have a career if others came to think of him as a proponent of a metaphysical religion? "No, I suppose it doesn't."

The Miro-image nodded. "If the philotic ray twines in response to the human will, why couldn't we suppose that *all* philotic twining is willed? Every particle, all of matter and energy, why couldn't every observable phenomenon in the universe be the willing behavior of individuals?"

"Now we're beyond Gangean Hinduism," said Valentine. "How seriously am I supposed to take this? What you're talking about is Animism. The most primitive kind of religion. Everything's alive. Stones and oceans and—"

"No," said Miro. "Life is life."

"Life is life," said the computer program. "Life is when a single philote has the strength of will to bind together the molecules of a single cell, to entwine their rays into one. A stronger philote can bind together many cells into a single organism. The strongest of all are the intelligent beings. We can bestow our philotic connections where we will. The philotic basis of intelligent life is even clearer in the other known sentient species. When a pequenino dies and passes into the third life, it's his strong-willed philote that preserves his identity and passes it from the mammaloid corpse to the living tree."

"Reincarnation," said Jakt. "The philote is the soul."

"It happens with the piggies, anyway," said Miro.

"The hive queen as well," said the Miro-image. "The reason we discovered philotic connections in the first place was because we saw how the buggers communicated with each other faster than light—that's what showed us it was possible. The individual buggers are all part of the hive queen; they're like her hands and feet, and she's their mind, one vast organism with thousands or millions of bodies. And the *only* connection between them is the twining of their philotic rays."

It was a picture of the universe that Valentine had never conceived of before. Of course, as a historian and biographer she usually conceived of things in terms of peoples and societies; while she wasn't ignorant of physics, neither was she deeply trained in it. Perhaps a physicist would know at once why this whole idea was absurd. But then, perhaps a physicist would be so locked into the consensus of his scientific community that it would be harder for him to accept an idea that transformed the meaning of everything he knew. Even if it were true.

And she liked the idea well enough to wish it were true. Of the trillion lovers who had whispered to each other, We are one, could it be that some of them really were? Of the billions of families who had bonded together so closely they felt like a single soul, wouldn't it be lovely to think that at the most basic level of reality it was so?

Jakt, however, was not so caught up in the idea. "I thought we weren't supposed to talk about the existence of the hive queen," he said. "I thought that was Ender's secret."

"It's all right," said Valentine. "Everyone in this room knows."

Jakt gave her his impatient look. "I thought we were coming to Lusitania to help in the struggle against Starways Congress. What does any of this have to do with the real world?"

"Maybe nothing," said Valentine. "Maybe everything."

Jakt buried his face in his hands for a moment, then looked back up at her with a smile that wasn't really a smile. "I haven't heard you say anything so transcendental since your brother left Trondheim."

That stung her, particularly because she knew it was meant to. After all these years, was Jakt still jealous of her connection with Ender? Did he still resent the fact that she could care about things that meant nothing to him? "When he went," said Valentine, "I stayed." She was really saying, I passed the only test that mattered. Why should you doubt me now?

Jakt was abashed. It was one of the best things about him, that when he realized he was wrong he backed down at once. "And when you went," said Jakt, "I came with you." Which she took to mean, I'm with you, I'm really not jealous of Ender anymore, and I'm sorry for sniping at you. Later, when they were alone, they'd say these things again openly. It wouldn't do to reach Lusitania with suspicions and jealousy on either's part.

Miro, of course, was oblivious to the fact that Jakt and Valentine had already declared a truce. He was only aware of the tension between them, and thought he was the cause of it. "I'm sorry," said Miro. "I didn't mean to . . ."

"It's all right," said Jakt. "I was out of line."

"There *is* no line," said Valentine, with a smile at her husband. Jakt smiled back.

That was what Miro needed to see; he visibly relaxed.

"Go on," said Valentine.

"Take all that as a given," said the Miro-image.

Valentine couldn't help it—she laughed out loud. Partly she laughed because this mystical Gangean philote-as-soul business was such an absurdly large premise to swallow. Partly she laughed to release the tension between her and Jakt. "I'm sorry," she said. "That's an awfully big 'given.' If that's the preamble, I can't wait to hear the conclusion."

Miro, understanding her laughter now, smiled back. "I've had a lot of time to think," he said. "That really *was* my speculation on what life is. That everything in the universe is behavior. But there's something else we want to tell you about. And ask you about, too, I guess." He turned to Jakt. "And it has a lot to do with stopping the Lusitania Fleet."

Jakt smiled and nodded. "I appreciate being tossed a bone now and then."

Valentine smiled her most charming smile. "So—later you'll be glad when I break a few bones."

Jakt laughed again.

"Go on, Miro," said Valentine.

It was the image-Miro that responded. "If all of reality is the behavior of philotes, then obviously most philotes are only smart enough or strong enough to act as a meson or hold together a neutron. A very few of them have the strength of will to be alive—to govern an organism. And a tiny, tiny fraction of them are powerful enough to control—no, to *be*—a sentient organism. But still, the most complex and intelligent being—the hive queen, for instance—is, at core, just a philote, like all the others. It gains its identity and life from the particular role it happens to fulfill, but what it *is* is a philote."

"My self—my *will*—is a subatomic particle?" asked Valentine.

Jakt smiled, nodded. "A fun idea," he said. "My shoe and I are brothers."

Miro smiled wanly. The Miro-image, however, answered. "If a star and a hydrogen atom are brothers, then yes, there is a kinship between you and the philotes that make up common objects like your shoe."

Valentine noticed that Miro had not subvocalized anything just before the Miro-image answered. How had the software producing the Miro-image come up with the analogy with stars and hydrogen atoms, if Miro didn't provide it on the spot? Valentine had never heard of a computer program capable of producing such involved yet appropriate conversation on its own.

"And maybe there are other kinships in the universe that you know nothing of till now," said the Miro-image. "Maybe there's a kind of life you haven't met."

Valentine, watching Miro, saw that he seemed worried. Agitated. As if he didn't like what the Miro-image was doing now.

"What kind of life are you talking about?" asked Jakt.

"There's a physical phenomenon in the universe, a

very common one, that is completely unexplained, and yet everyone takes it for granted and no one has seriously investigated why and how it happens. This is it: None of the ansible connections has ever broken."

"Nonsense," said Jakt. "One of the ansibles on Trondheim was out of service for six months last year—it doesn't happen often, but it happens."

Again Miro's lips and jaw were motionless; again the image answered immediately. Clearly he was not controlling it now. "I didn't say that the ansibles never break down. I said that the connections—the philotic twining between the parts of a split meson—have never broken. The *machinery* of the ansible can break down, the software can get corrupted, but never has a meson fragment within an ansible made the shift to allow its philotic ray to entwine with another local meson or even with the nearby planet."

"The magnetic field suspends the fragment, of course," said Jakt.

"Split mesons don't endure long enough in nature for us to know how they naturally act," said Valentine.

"I know all the standard answers," said the image. "All nonsense. All the kind of answers parents give their children when they don't know the truth and don't want to bother finding out. People still treat the ansibles like magic. Everybody's glad enough that the ansibles keep on working; if they tried to figure out *why*, the magic might go out of it and then the ansibles would stop."

"Nobody feels that way," said Valentine.

"They all do," said the image. "Even if it took hundreds of years, or a thousand years, or three thousand years, *one* of those connections should have broken by now. One of those meson fragments should have shifted its philotic ray—but they never have."

"Why?" asked Miro.

Valentine assumed at first that Miro was asking a rhetorical question. But no—he was looking at the image just like the rest of them, asking *it* to tell him why.

"I thought this program was reporting *your* speculations," said Valentine.

"It was," said Miro. "But not now."

"What if there's a being who lives among the philotic connections between ansibles?" asked the image.

"Are you sure you want to do this?" asked Miro. Again he was speaking to the image on the screen.

And the image on the screen changed, to the face of a young woman, one that Valentine had never seen before.

"What if there's a being who dwells in the web of philotic rays connecting the ansibles on every world and every starship in the human universe? What if she is *composed of* those philotic connections? What if her thoughts take place in the spin and vibration of the split pairs? What if her memories are stored in the computers of every world and every ship?"

"Who are you?" asked Valentine, speaking directly to the image.

"Maybe I'm the one who keeps all those philotic connections alive, ansible to ansible. Maybe I'm a new kind of organism, one that doesn't twine rays together, but instead keeps them twined to each other so that they never break apart. And if that's true, then if those connections ever broke, if the ansibles ever stopped moving—if the ansibles ever fell silent, then I would die."

"Who are you?" asked Valentine again.

"Valentine, I'd like you to meet Jane," said Miro. "Ender's friend. And mine."

"Jane."

So Jane wasn't the code name of a subversive group within the Starways Congress bureaucracy. Jane was a computer program, a piece of software.

No. If what she had just suggested was true, then Jane was more than a program. She was a being who dwelt in the web of philotic rays, who stored her memories in the computers of every world. If she was right, then the philotic web—the network of crisscrossing philotic rays that connected ansible to ansible on every world—was her body, her *substance*. And the philotic links continued working with never a breakdown because she willed it so.

"So now I ask the great Demosthenes," said Jane. "Am I raman or varelse? Am I alive at all? I need your answer, because I think I can stop the Lusitania Fleet. But before I do it, I have to know: Is it a cause worth dying for?"

———

Jane's words cut Miro to the heart. She *could* stop the fleet—he could see that at once. Congress had sent the M.D. Device with several ships of the fleet, but they had not yet sent the order to use it. They couldn't send the order without Jane knowing it beforehand, and with her complete penetration of all the ansible communications, she could intercept the order before it was sent.

The trouble was that she couldn't do it without Congress realizing that she existed—or at least that something was wrong. If the fleet didn't confirm the order, it would simply be sent again, and again, and again. The more she blocked the messages, the clearer it would be to Congress that someone had an impossible degree of control over the ansible computers.

She might avoid this by sending a counterfeit confirmation, but then she would have to monitor all the communications between the ships of the fleet, and between the fleet and all planetside stations, in order to keep up the pretense that the fleet knew something about the kill order. Despite Jane's enormous abilities, this would soon be beyond her—she could pay some degree of attention to hundreds, even thousands of things at a time, but it didn't take Miro long to realize that there was no way she could handle *all* the monitoring and alterations this would take, even if she did nothing else.

One way or another, the secret would be out. And as Jane explained her plan, Miro knew that she was right—her best option, the one with the *least* chance of revealing her existence, was simply to cut off *all* ansible communications between the fleet and the planetside stations, and between the ships of the fleet. Let each ship remain isolated, the crew wondering what had happened, and they would have no choice but to abort their mission or continue to obey their original orders. Either they would go away or they would arrive at Lusitania without the authority to use the Little Doctor.

In the meantime, however, Congress would know that *something* had happened. It was possible that with Congress's normal bureaucratic inefficiency, no one would ever figure out what happened. But eventually somebody would realize that there was no natural or human explanation of what happened. Someone would realize that Jane—or something like her—must exist, and that cutting off ansible communications would destroy her. Once they knew this, she would surely die.

"Maybe not," Miro insisted. "Maybe you can keep them from acting. Interfere with interplanetary communications, so they can't give the order to shut down communications."

No one answered. He knew why: She couldn't interfere with ansible communications forever. Eventually the government on each planet would reach the conclusion on its own. She might live on in constant warfare for years, decades, generations. But the more power she used, the more humankind would hate and fear her. Eventually she would be killed.

"A book, then," said Miro. "Like the Hive Queen and the Hegemon. Like the Life of Human. The Speaker for the Dead could write it. To persuade them not to do it."

"Maybe," said Valentine.

"She can't die," said Miro.

"I know that we can't *ask* her to take that chance," said Valentine. "But if it's the only way to save the hive queen and the pequeninos—"

Miro was furious. "*You* can talk about her dying! What is Jane to *you*? A program, a piece of software. But she's not, she's *real*, she's as real as the hive queen, she's as real as any of the piggies—"

"*More* real to you, I think," said Valentine.

"*As* real," said Miro. "You forget—I know the piggies like my own brothers—"

"But you're able to contemplate the possibility that destroying them may be morally necessary."

"Don't twist my words."

"I'm untwisting them," said Valentine. "You can contemplate losing them, because they're already lost to you. Losing Jane, though—"

"Because she's my friend, does that mean I can't plead for her? Can life-and-death decisions only be made by strangers?"

Jakt's voice, quiet and deep, interrupted the argument. "Calm down, both of you. It isn't your decision. It's Jane's. She has the right to determine the value of her own life. I'm no philosopher, but I know *that*."

"Well said," Valentine answered.

Miro knew that Jakt was right, that it *was* Jane's choice. But he couldn't bear that, because he also knew what she would decide. Leaving the choice up to Jane was identical to asking her to do it. And yet, in the end, the choice would be up to her anyway. He didn't even have to ask her what she would decide. Time passed so quickly for her, especially since they were already traveling at near-lightspeed, that she had probably decided already.

It was too much to bear. To lose Jane now would be unbearable; just thinking of it threatened Miro's composure. He didn't want to show such weakness in front of these people. Good people, they were good people, but he didn't want them to see him lose control of himself. So Miro leaned forward, found his balance, and precariously lifted himself from his seat. It was hard, since only a few of his muscles responded to his will, and it took all his concentration just to walk from the bridge to his compartment. No one followed him or even spoke to him. He was glad of that.

Alone in his room, he lay down on his bunk and called to her. But not aloud. He subvocalized, because that was his custom when he talked to her. Even though the others on this ship now knew of her existence, he had no intention of losing the habits that had kept her concealed till now.

"Jane," he said silently.

"Yes," said the voice in his ear. He imagined, as always, that her soft voice came from a woman just out of sight, but close, very close. He shut his eyes, so he could imagine her better. Her breath on his cheek. Her hair dangling over his face as she spoke to him softly, as he answered in silence.

"Talk to Ender before you decide," he said.

"I already did. Just now, while you were thinking about this."

"What did he say?"

"To do nothing. To decide nothing, until the order is actually sent."

"That's right. Maybe they won't do it."

"Maybe. Maybe a new group with different policies will come into power. Maybe this group will change its mind. Maybe Valentine's propaganda will succeed. Maybe there'll be a mutiny on the fleet."

This last was so unlikely that Miro realized Jane absolutely believed that the order would be sent.

"How soon?" asked Miro.

"The fleet should arrive in about fifteen years. A year or less after these two ships get there. That's how I timed your voyage. The order will be sent sometime before. Maybe six months before arrival—which would be about eight hours ship's time before the fleet drops out of lightspeed and staggers down to normal speeds."

"Don't do it," said Miro.

"I haven't decided."

"Yes you have. You've decided to do it."

She said nothing.

"Don't leave me," he said.

"I don't leave my friends if I don't have to," she said. "Some people do, but I don't."

"Just don't," he said again. He was crying. Could she see that, sense it somehow through the jewel in his ear?

"I'll try."

"Find another way. Find another way to stop them. Find some way to put yourself outside the philotic net so they can't kill you."

"That's what Ender said."

"Then do it!"

"I can search for such a way, but who knows if it exists?"

"It has to."

"This is why I wonder sometimes whether I'm alive or not. You living creatures, you think that because you want something very much, it has to happen. That wishing something with all your heart will make it so."

"How can you search for something if you don't believe that it exists?"

"Either I search or I don't," said Jane. "I don't get distracted or bored like humans do. I'll try to think of something else."

"Think of this, too," said Miro. "Think of who you are. Of how your mind works. You can't possibly find a way of saving your life until you understand how you came to life in the first place. And once you understand yourself—"

"Then maybe I can make a copy and store it somewhere."

"Maybe."

"Maybe," she echoed.

But he knew she didn't believe it, and neither did he. She existed in the philotic network of the ansibles; she could store her memories in the network of computers on every world and every ship in space, but there was nowhere that she could put her *self*, not if it required a network of philotic links.

Unless.

"What about the fathertrees on Lusitania? *They* communicate philotically, don't they?"

"It's not the same thing," said Jane. "It isn't digital. It isn't *coded* the way the ansibles are."

"It may not be digital, but the information gets transferred somehow. It *works* philotically. And the hive queen, too—she communicates with the buggers that way."

"No chance of *that*," said Jane. "The structure's too simple. Her communication with them isn't a network. They're all connected only to her."

"How do you *know* it won't work, when you don't even know for sure how *you* function?"

"All right. I'll think about it."

"Think *hard*," he said.

"I only know one way to think," said Jane.

"I mean, pay *attention* to it."

She could follow many trains of thought at once, but her thoughts were prioritized, with many different levels of attention. Miro didn't want her relegating her self-investigation to some low order of attention.

"I'll pay attention," she said.

"Then you'll think of something," he said. "You *will*."

She didn't answer for a while. He thought this meant that the conversation was over. His thoughts began to wander. To try to imagine what life would be like, still in this body, only without Jane. It could happen before he even arrived on Lusitania. And if it did, this voyage would have been the most terrible mistake of his life. By traveling at lightspeed, he was skipping thirty years of realtime. Thirty years that might have been spent with Jane. He might be able to deal with losing her then. But losing her now, only a few weeks into knowing her—he knew that his tears arose from self-pity, but he shed them all the same.

"Miro," she said.

"What?" he asked.

"How can I think of something that's never been thought of before?"

For a moment he didn't understand.

"Miro, how can I figure out something that isn't just the logical conclusion of things that human beings have already figured out and written somewhere?"

"You think of things all the time," said Miro.

"I'm trying to conceive of something inconceivable. I'm trying to find answers to questions that human beings have never even tried to ask."

"Can't you do that?"

"If I can't think original thoughts, does that mean that I'm nothing but a computer program that got out of hand?"

"Hell, Jane, most people never have an original thought in their lives." He laughed softly. "Does that mean they're just ground-dwelling apes that got out of hand?"

"You were crying," she said.

"Yes."

"*You* don't think I can think of a way out of this. *You* think I'm going to die."

"I believe you *can* think of a way. I really do. But that doesn't stop me from being afraid."

"Afraid that I'll die."

"Afraid that I'll lose you."

"Would that be so terrible? To lose me?"

"Oh God," he whispered.

"Would you miss me for an hour?" she insisted. "For a day? For a year?"

What did she want from him? Assurance that when she was gone she'd be remembered? That someone would yearn for her? Why would she doubt that? Didn't she know him yet?

Maybe she was human enough that she simply needed reassurance of things she already knew.

"Forever," he said.

It was her turn to laugh. Playfully. "You won't live that long," she said.

"*Now* you tell me," he said.

This time when she fell silent, she didn't come back, and Miro was left alone with his thoughts.

———

Valentine, Jakt, and Plikt had remained together on the bridge, talking through the things they had learned, trying to decide what they might mean, what might happen. The only conclusion they reached was that while the future couldn't be known, it would probably be a good deal better than their worst fears and nowhere near as good as their best hopes. Wasn't that how the world always worked?

"Yes," said Plikt. "Except for the exceptions."

That was Plikt's way. Except when she was teaching, she said little, but when she did speak, it had a way of ending the conversation. Plikt got up to leave the bridge, headed for her miserably uncomfortable bed; as usual, Valentine tried to persuade her to go back to the other starship.

"Varsam and Ro don't want me in their room," said Plikt.

"They don't mind a bit."

"Valentine," said Jakt, "Plikt doesn't want to go back to the other ship because she doesn't want to miss anything."

"Oh," said Valentine.

Plikt grinned. "Good night."

Soon after, Jakt also left the bridge. His hand rested on Valentine's shoulder for a moment as he left. "I'll be there soon," she said. And she meant it at the moment, meant to follow him almost at once. Instead she remained on the bridge, thinking, brooding, trying to make sense of a universe that would put all the nonhuman species ever known to man at risk of extinction, all at once. The hive queen, the pequeninos, and now Jane, the only one of her kind, perhaps the only one that ever *could* exist. A veritable profusion of intelligent life, and yet known only to a few. And all of them in line to be snuffed out.

At least Ender will realize at last that this is the natural order of things, that he might not be as responsible for the destruction of the buggers three thousand years ago as he had always thought. Xenocide must be built into the universe. No mercy, not even for the greatest players in the game.

How could she have ever thought otherwise? Why should intelligent species be immune to the threat of extinction that looms over every species that ever came to be?

It must have been an hour after Jakt left the bridge before Valentine finally turned off her terminal and stood up to go to bed. On a whim, though, she paused before leaving and spoke into the air. "Jane?" she said. "Jane?"

No answer.

There was no reason for her to expect one. It was Miro who wore the jewel in his ear. Miro and Ender both. How many people did she think Jane could monitor at one time? Maybe two was the most she could handle.

Or maybe two thousand. Or two million. What did Valentine know of the limitations of a being who existed as a phantom in the philotic web? Even if Jane heard her, Valentine had no right to expect that she would answer her call.

Valentine stopped in the corridor, directly between Miro's door and the door to the room she shared with Jakt. The doors were not soundproof. She could hear Jakt's soft snoring inside their compartment. She also heard another sound. Miro's breath. He wasn't sleeping. He might be crying. She hadn't raised three children without being able to recognize that ragged, heavy breathing.

He's not my child. I shouldn't meddle.

She pushed open the door; it was noiseless, but it cast a shaft of light across the bed. Miro's crying stopped immediately, but he looked at her through swollen eyes.

"What do you want?" he said.

She stepped into the room and sat on the floor beside his bunk, so their faces were only a few inches apart. "You've never cried for yourself, have you?" she said.

"A few times."

"But tonight you're crying for her."

"Myself as much as her."

Valentine leaned closer, put her arm around him, pulled his head onto her shoulder.

"No," he said. But he didn't pull away. And after a few moments, his arm swung awkwardly around to embrace her. He didn't cry anymore, but he did let her hold him for a minute or two. Maybe it helped. Valentine had no way of knowing.

Then he was done. He pulled away, rolled onto his back. "I'm sorry," he said.

"You're welcome," she said. She believed in answering what people meant, not what they said.

"Don't tell Jakt," he whispered.

"Nothing to tell," she said. "We had a good talk."

She got up and left, closing his door behind her. He was a good boy. She liked the fact that he could admit caring what Jakt thought about him. And what did it matter if his tears tonight had self-pity in them? She had shed a few like that herself. Grief, she reminded herself, is almost always for the mourner's loss.

5

THE LUSITANIA
FLEET

<Ender says that when the war fleet from Starways Congress reaches us, they plan to destroy this world.>
    <Interesting.>
    <You don't fear death?>
    <We don't intend to be here when they arrive.>

Qing-jao was no longer the little girl whose hands had bled in secret. Her life had been transformed from the moment she was proved to be godspoken, and in the ten years since that day she had come to accept the voice of the gods in her life and the role this gave her in society. She learned to accept the privileges and honors given to her as gifts actually meant for the gods; as her father taught her, she did not take on airs, but instead grew more humble as the gods and the people laid ever-heavier burdens on her.

She took her duties seriously, and found joy in them. For the past ten years she had passed through a rigorous, exhilarating course of studies. Her body was shaped and trained in the company of other children—running, swimming, riding, combat-with-swords, combat-with-sticks, combat-with-bones. Along with other children, her memory was filled with languages—Stark, the common speech of the stars, which was typed into computers; Old Chinese, which was sung in the throat and drawn in beautiful ideograms on rice paper or in fine sand; and New Chinese, which was merely spoken at the mouth and jotted down with a common alphabet on ordinary paper or in dirt. No one was surprised except Qing-jao herself that she learned all these languages much more quickly and easily and thoroughly than any of the other children.

Other teachers came to her alone. This was how she learned sciences and history, mathematics and music. And every week she would go to her father and spend half a day with him, showing him all that she had learned and listening to what he said in response. His praise made her dance all the way back to her room; his mildest rebuke made her spend hours tracing woodgrain lines in her schoolroom, until she felt worthy to return to studying.

Another part of her schooling was utterly private. She had seen for herself how Father was so strong that he could postpone his obedience to the gods. She knew that when the gods demanded a ritual of purification, the hunger, the *need* to obey them was so exquisite it could not be denied. And yet Father somehow denied it—long enough, at least, that his rituals were always in private. Qing-jao longed for such strength herself, and so she began to discipline herself to delay. When the gods made her feel her oppressive unworthiness, and her eyes began to search for woodgrain lines or her hands began to feel unbearably filthy, she would wait, trying to concentrate on what was happening at the moment and put off obedience as long as she could.

At first it was a triumph if she managed to postpone

her purification for a full minute—and when her resistance broke, the gods punished her for it by making the ritual more onerous and difficult than usual. But she refused to give up. She was Han Fei-tzu's daughter, wasn't she? And in time, over the years, she learned what her father had learned: that one could live with the hunger, contain it, often for hours, like a bright fire encased in a box of translucent jade, a dangerous, terrible fire from the gods, burning within her heart.

Then, when she was alone, she could open that box and let the fire out, not in a single, terrible eruption, but slowly, gradually, filling her with light as she bowed her head and traced the lines on the floor, or bent over the sacred laver of her holy washings, quietly and methodically rubbing her hands with pumice, lye, and aloe.

Thus she converted the raging voice of the gods into a private, disciplined worship. Only at rare moments of sudden distress did she lose control and fling herself to the floor in front of a teacher or visitor. She accepted these humiliations as the gods' way of reminding her that their power over her was absolute, that her usual self-control was only permitted for their amusement. She was content with this imperfect discipline. After all, it would be presumptuous of her to equal her father's perfect self-control. His extraordinary nobility came because the gods honored him, and so did not require his public humiliation; she had done nothing to earn such honor.

Last of all, her schooling included one day each week helping with the righteous labor of the common people. Righteous labor, of course, was not the work the common people did every day in their offices and factories. Righteous labor meant the backbreaking work of the rice paddies. Every man and woman and child on Path had to perform this labor, bending and stooping in shin-deep water to plant and harvest the rice—or forfeit citizenship. "This is how we honor our ancestors," Father explained to her when she was little. "We show them that none of us will ever rise above doing their labor." The rice that was grown by righteous labor was considered holy; it was offered in the temples and eaten on holy days; it was placed in small bowls as offerings to the household gods.

Once, when Qing-jao was twelve, the day was terribly hot and she was eager to finish her work on a research project. "Don't make me go to the rice paddies today," she said to her teacher. "What I'm doing here is so much more important."

The teacher bowed and went away, but soon Father came into her room. He carried a heavy sword, and she screamed in terror when he raised it over his head. Did he mean to kill her for having spoken so sacrilegiously? But he did not hurt her—how could she have imagined that he might? Instead the sword came down on her computer terminal. The metal parts twisted; the plastic shattered and flew. The machine was destroyed.

Father did not raise his voice. It was in the faintest whisper that he said, "First the gods. Second the ancestors. Third the people. Fourth the rulers. Last the self."

It was the clearest expression of the Path. It was the reason this world was settled in the first place. She had forgotten: If she was too busy to perform righteous labor, she was not on the Path.

She would never forget again. And, in time, she learned to love the sun beating down on her back, the water cool and murky around her legs and hands, the stalks of the rice plants like fingers reaching up from the mud to intertwine with her fingers. Covered with muck in the rice paddies, she never felt unclean, because she knew that she was filthy in the service of the gods.

Finally, at the age of sixteen, her schooling was finished. She had only to prove herself in a grown woman's task—one that was difficult and important enough that it could be entrusted only to one who was godspoken.

She came before the great Han Fei-tzu in his room. Like hers, it was a large open space; like hers, the sleeping accommodation was simple, a mat on the floor; like hers, the room was dominated by a table with a computer terminal on it. She had never entered her father's room without seeing something floating in the display above the terminal—diagrams, three-dimensional models, realtime simulations, words. Most commonly words. Letters or ideographs floating in the air on simulated pages, moving back and forward, side to side as Father needed to compare them.

In Qing-jao's room, all the rest of the space was empty. Since Father did not trace woodgrain lines, he had no need for that much austerity. Even so, his tastes were simple. One rug—only rarely one that had much decoration to it. One low table, with one sculpture standing on it. Walls bare except for one painting. And because the room was so large, each one of these things seemed almost lost, like the faint voice of someone crying out from very far away.

The message of this room to visitors was clear: Han Fei-tzu chose simplicity. One of each thing was enough for a pure soul.

The message to Qing-jao, however, was quite different. For she knew what no one outside the household realized: The rug, the table, the sculpture, and the painting were changed every day. And never in her life had she recognized any one of them. So the lesson she learned was this: A pure soul must never grow attached to any one thing. A pure soul must expose himself to new things every day.

Because this was a formal occasion, she did not come and stand behind him as he worked, studying what appeared in his display, trying to guess what he was doing.

This time she came to the middle of the room and knelt on the plain rug, which was today the color of a robin's egg, with a small stain in one corner. She kept her eyes down, not even studying the stain, until Father got up from his chair and came to stand before her.

"Han Qing-jao," he said. "Let me see the sunrise of my daughter's face."

She lifted her head, looked at him, and smiled.

He smiled back. "What I will set before you is not an easy task, even for an experienced adult," said Father.

Qing-jao bowed her head. She had expected that Father would set a hard challenge for her, and she was ready to do his will.

"Look at me, my Qing-jao," said Father.

She lifted her head, looked into his eyes.

"This is not going to be a school assignment. This is a task from the real world. A task that Starways Congress has given me, on which the fate of nations and peoples and worlds may rest."

Qing-jao had been tense already, but now Father was frightening her. "Then you must give this task to someone who can be trusted with it, not to an untried child."

"You haven't been a child in years, Qing-jao. Are you ready to hear your task?"

"Yes, Father."

"What do you know about the Lusitania Fleet?"

"Do you want me to tell you *everything* I know about it?"

"I want you to tell me all that you think *matters*."

So—this was a kind of test, to see how well she could distill the important from the unimportant in her knowledge about a particular subject.

"The fleet was sent to subdue a rebellious colony on Lusitania, where laws concerning noninterference in the only known alien species had been defiantly broken."

Was that enough? No—Father was still waiting.

"There was controversy, right from the start," she

said. "Essays attributed to a person called Demosthenes stirred up trouble."

"What trouble, in particular?"

"To colony worlds, Demosthenes gave warning that the Lusitania Fleet was a dangerous precedent—it would be only a matter of time before Starways Congress used force to compel *their* obedience, too. To Catholic worlds and Catholic minorities everywhere, Demosthenes charged that Congress was trying to punish the Bishop of Lusitania for sending missionaries to the pequeninos to save their souls from hell. To scientists, Demosthenes sent warning that the principle of independent research was at stake—a whole world was under military attack because it dared to prefer the judgment of the scientists on the scene to the judgment of bureaucrats many light-years away. And to everyone, Demosthenes made claims that the Lusitania Fleet carried the Molecular Disruption Device. Of course that is an obvious lie, but some believed it."

"How effective were these essays?" asked Father.

"I don't know."

"They were very effective," said Father. "Fifteen years ago, the earliest essays to the colonies were so effective that they almost caused revolution."

A near-rebellion in the colonies? Fifteen years ago? Qing-jao knew of only one such event, but she had never realized it had anything to do with Demosthenes' essays. She blushed. "That was the time of the Colony Charter—your first great treaty."

"The treaty was not mine," said Han Fei-tzu. "The treaty belonged equally to Congress and the colonies. Because of it a terrible conflict was avoided. And the Lusitania Fleet continues on its great mission."

"You wrote every word of the treaty, Father."

"In doing so I only found expression for the wishes and desires already in the hearts of the people on both sides of the issue. I was a clerk."

Qing-jao bowed her head. She knew the truth, and so did everyone else. It had been the beginning of Han Fei-tzu's greatness, for he not only wrote the treaty but also persuaded both sides to accept it almost without revision. Ever after that, Han Fei-tzu had been one of the most trusted advisers to Congress; messages arrived daily from the greatest men and women of every world. If he chose to call himself a clerk in that great undertaking, that was only because he was a man of great modesty. Qing-jao also knew that Mother was already dying as he accomplished all this work. That was the kind of man her father was, for he neglected neither his wife nor his duty. He could not save Mother's life, but he could save the lives that might have been lost in war.

"Qing-jao, why do you say that it is an obvious lie that the fleet is carrying the M.D. Device?"

"Because—because that would be monstrous. It would be like Ender the Xenocide, destroying an entire world. So much power has no right or reason to exist in the universe."

"Who taught you this?"

"Decency taught me this," said Qing-jao. "The gods made the stars and all the planets—who is man to unmake them?"

"But the gods also made the laws of nature that make it possible to destroy them—who is man to refuse to receive what the gods have given?"

Qing-jao was stunned to silence. She had never heard Father speak in apparent defense of any aspect of war—he loathed war in any form.

"I ask you again—who taught you that so much power has no right or reason to exist in the universe?"

"It's my own idea."

"But that sentence is an exact quotation."

"Yes. From Demosthenes. But if I believe an idea, it becomes my own. You taught me that."

"You must be careful that you understand all the consequences of an idea before you believe it."

"The Little Doctor must never be used on Lusitania, and therefore it should not have been sent."

Han Fei-tzu nodded gravely. "How do you know it must never be used?"

"Because it would destroy the pequeninos, a young and beautiful people who are eager to fulfill their potential as a sentient species."

"Another quotation."

"Father, have you read the Life of Human?"

"I have."

"Then how can you doubt that the pequeninos must be preserved?"

"I said I had read the Life of Human. I didn't say that I believed it."

"You *don't* believe it?"

"I neither believe it nor disbelieve it. The book first appeared *after* the ansible on Lusitania had been destroyed. Therefore it is probable that the book did not originate there, and if it didn't originate there then it's fiction. That seems particularly likely because it's signed 'Speaker for the Dead,' which is the same name signed to the Hive Queen and the Hegemon, which are thousands of years old. Someone was obviously trying to capitalize on the reverence people feel toward those ancient works."

"I believe the Life of Human is true."

"That's your privilege, Qing-jao. But *why* do you believe it?"

Because it sounded true when she read it. Could she say that to Father? Yes, she could say anything. "Because when I read it I felt that it *must* be true."

"I see."

"Now you know that I'm foolish."

"On the contrary. I know that you are wise. When you hear a true story, there is a part of you that responds to it regardless of art, regardless of evidence.

Let it be clumsily told and you will still love the tale, if you love truth. Let it be the most obvious fabrication and you will still believe whatever truth is in it, because you cannot deny truth no matter how shabbily it is dressed."

"Then how is it that you *don't* believe the Life of Human?"

"I spoke unclearly. We are using two different meanings of the words *truth* and *belief*. You believe that the story is true, because you responded to it from that sense of truth deep within you. But that sense of truth does not respond to a story's factuality—to whether it literally depicts a real event in the real world. Your inner sense of truth responds to a story's causality—to whether it faithfully shows the way the universe functions, the way the gods work their will among human beings."

Qing-jao thought for only a moment, then nodded her understanding. "So the Life of Human may be universally true, but specifically false."

"Yes," said Han Fei-tzu. "You can read the book and gain great wisdom from it, because it is true. But is that book an accurate representation of the pequeninos themselves? One can hardly believe *that*—a mammaloid species that turns into a tree when it dies? Beautiful as poetry. Ludicrous as science."

"But can you know *that,* either, Father?"

"I can't be sure, no. Nature has done many strange things, and there *is* a chance that the Life of Human is genuine and true. Thus I neither believe it nor disbelieve it. I hold it in abeyance. I wait. Yet while I'm waiting, I don't expect Congress to treat Lusitania as if it were populated by the fanciful creatures from the Life of Human. For all we know, the pequeninos may be deadly dangerous to us. They *are* aliens."

"Ramen."

"In the story. But raman or varelse, we do not know

what they are. The fleet carries the Little Doctor because it *might* be necessary to save mankind from unspeakable peril. It is not up to us to decide whether or not it should be used—Congress will decide. It is not up to us to decide whether it should have been sent—Congress has sent it. And it is certainly not up to us to decide whether it should exist—the gods have decreed that such a thing is possible and *can* exist."

"So Demosthenes was right. The M.D. Device *is* with the fleet."

"Yes."

"And the government files that Demosthenes published—they were genuine."

"Yes."

"But Father—you joined many others in claiming that they were forgeries."

"Just as the gods speak only to a chosen few, so the secrets of the rulers must be known only to those who will use the knowledge properly. Demosthenes was giving powerful secrets to people who were not fit to use them wisely, and so for the good of the people those secrets had to be withdrawn. The only way to retrieve a secret, once it is known, is to replace it with a lie; then the knowledge of the truth is once again your secret."

"You're telling me that Demosthenes is not a liar, and Congress *is*."

"I'm telling you that Demosthenes is the enemy of the gods. A wise ruler would never have sent the Lusitania Fleet without giving it the possibility of responding to *any* circumstance. But Demosthenes has used his knowledge that the Little Doctor is with the fleet in order to try to force Congress to withdraw the fleet. Thus he wishes to take power out of the hands of those whom the gods have ordained to rule humankind. What would happen to the people if they rejected the rulers given them by the gods?"

"Chaos and suffering," said Qing-jao. History was full of times of chaos and suffering, until the gods sent strong rulers and institutions to keep order.

"So Demosthenes told the truth about the Little Doctor. Did you think the enemies of the gods could *never* speak the truth? I wish it were so. It would make them much easier to identify."

"If we can lie in the service of the gods, what other crimes can we commit?"

"What is a crime?"

"An act that's against the law."

"What law?"

"I see—Congress makes the law, so the law is whatever Congress says. But Congress is composed of men and women, who may do good and evil."

"Now you're nearer the truth. We can't do *crimes* in the service of Congress, because Congress makes the laws. But if Congress ever became evil, then in obeying them we might also be doing evil. That is a matter of conscience. However, if that happened, Congress would surely lose the mandate of heaven. And *we,* the god-spoken, don't have to wait and wonder about the mandate of heaven, as others do. If Congress ever loses the mandate of the gods, we will know at once."

"So you lied for Congress because Congress had the mandate of heaven."

"And therefore I knew that to help them keep their secret was the will of the gods for the good of the people."

Qing-jao had never thought of Congress in quite this way before. All the history books she had studied showed Congress as the great unifier of humanity, and according to the schoolbooks, all its acts were noble. Now, though, she understood that some of its actions might not *seem* good. Yet that didn't necessarily mean that they were *not* good. "I must learn from the gods, then, whether the will of Congress is also their will," she said.

"Will you do that?" asked Han Fei-tzu. "Will you obey the will of Congress, even when it might seem wrong, as long as Congress has the mandate of heaven?"

"Are you asking for my oath?"

"I am."

"Then yes, I will obey, as long as they have the mandate of heaven."

"I had to have that oath from you to satisfy the security requirements of Congress," he said. "I couldn't have given you your task without it." He cleared his throat. "But now I ask you for another oath."

"I'll give it if I can."

"This oath is from—it arises from great love. Han Qing-jao, will you serve the gods in all things, in all ways, throughout your life?"

"Oh, Father, we need no oath for this. Haven't the gods chosen me already, and led me with their voice?"

"Nevertheless I ask you for this oath."

"Always, in all things, in all ways, I will serve the gods."

To her surprise, Father knelt before her and took her hands in his. Tears streamed down his cheeks. "You have lifted from my heart the heaviest burden that was ever laid there."

"How did I do this, Father?"

"Before your mother died, she asked me for my promise. She said that since her entire character was expressed by her devotion to the gods, the only way I could help you to know her was to teach you also to serve the gods. All my life I have still been afraid that I might fail, that you might turn away from the gods. That you might come to hate them. Or that you might not be worthy of their voice."

This struck Qing-jao to the heart. She was always conscious of her deep unworthiness before the gods, of her filthiness in their sight—even when they weren't re-

quiring her to watch or trace woodgrain lines. Only now
did she learn what was at stake: her mother's love for
her.

"All my fears are gone now. You *are* a perfect daughter, my Qing-jao. You already serve the gods well. And
now, with your oath, I can be sure you'll continue forever. This will cause great rejoicing in the house in
heaven where your mother dwells."

Will it? In heaven they know my weakness. You, Father, you only see that I have not yet failed the gods;
Mother must know how close I've come so many times,
how filthy I am whenever the gods look upon me.

But he seemed so full of joy that she dared not show
him how much she dreaded the day when she would
prove her unworthiness for all to see. So she embraced
him.

Still, she couldn't help asking him, "Father, do you
really think Mother heard me make that oath?"

"I hope so," said Han Fei-tzu. "If she didn't, the
gods will surely save the echo of it and put it in a sea-
shell and let her listen to it whenever she puts it to her
ear."

This sort of fanciful storytelling was a game they had
played together as children. Qing-jao set aside her
dread and quickly came up with an answer. "No, the
gods will save the touch of our embrace and weave it
into a shawl, which she can wear around her shoulders
when winter comes to heaven." She was relieved, anyway, that Father had not said yes. He only *hoped* that
Mother had heard the oath she made. Perhaps she
hadn't—and so she wouldn't be so disappointed when
her daughter failed.

Father kissed her, then stood up. "*Now* you are
ready to hear your task," he said.

He took her by the hand and led her to his table. She
stood beside him when he sat on his chair; she was not
much taller, standing, than he was sitting down. Proba-

bly she had not yet reached her adult height, but she hoped she wouldn't grow much more. She didn't want to become one of those large, hulking women who carried heavy burdens in the fields. Better to be a mouse than a hog, that's what Mu-pao had told her years ago.

Father brought a starmap up into the display. She recognized the area immediately. It centered on the Lusitania star system, though the scale was too small for individual planets to be visible. "Lusitania is in the center," she said.

Father nodded. He typed a few more commands. "Now watch this," he said. "Not the display, my fingers. This, plus your voice identification, is the password that will allow you to access the information you'll need."

She watched him type: 4Gang. She recognized the reference at once. Her mother's ancestor-of-the-heart had been Jiang-qing, the widow of the first Communist Emperor, Mao Ze-dong. When Jiang-qing and her allies were driven from power, the Conspiracy of Cowards vilified them under the name "Gang of Four." Qing-jao's mother had been a true daughter-of-the-heart to that great martyred woman of the past. And now Qing-jao would be able to do further honor to her mother's ancestor-of-the-heart every time she typed the access code. It was a gracious thing for her father to arrange.

In the display there appeared many green dots. She quickly counted, almost without thinking: there were nineteen of them, clustered at some distance from Lusitania, but surrounding it in most directions.

"Is that the Lusitania Fleet?"

"Those were their positions five months ago." He typed again. The green dots all disappeared. "And those are their positions today."

She looked for them. She couldn't find a green dot anywhere. Yet Father clearly expected her to see *something*. "Are they already at Lusitania?"

"The ships are where you see them," said Father. "Five months ago the fleet disappeared."

"Where did it go?"

"No one knows."

"Was it a mutiny?"

"No one knows."

"The *whole* fleet?"

"Every ship."

"When you say they disappeared, what do you mean?"

Father glanced at her with a smile. "Well done, Qing-jao. You've asked the right question. No one saw them—they were all in deep space. So they didn't *physically* disappear. As far as we know, they may be moving along, still on course. They only disappeared in the sense that we lost all contact with them."

"The ansibles?"

"Silent. All within the same three-minute period. No transmissions were interrupted. One would end, and then the next one—never came."

"Every ship's connection with every planetside ansible *everywhere*? That's impossible. Even an explosion—if there could be one so large—but it couldn't be a single event, anyway, because they were so widely distributed around Lusitania."

"Well, it *could* be, Qing-jao. If you can imagine an event so cataclysmic—it *could* be that Lusitania's star became a supernova. It would be decades before we saw the flash even on the closest worlds. The trouble is that it would be the most unlikely supernova in history. Not *impossible,* but unlikely."

"And there would have been some advance indications. Some changes in the star's condition. Didn't the ships' instruments detect something?"

"No. That's why we don't think it was any known astronomical phenomenon. Scientists can't think of anything to explain it. So we've tried investigating it as sabotage. We've searched for penetrations of the ansible computers. We've raked over all the personnel files from every ship, searching for some possible conspiracy among the shipboard crews. There's been cryptoanalysis of every communication by every ship, searching for some kind of messages among conspirators. The military and the government have analyzed everything they can think of to analyze. The police on every planet have conducted inquiries—we've checked the background on *every* ansible operator."

"Even though no messages are being sent, are the ansibles still connected?"

"What do you think?"

Qing-jao blushed. "Of course they would be, even if an M.D. Device had been used against the fleet, because the ansibles are linked by fragments of subatomic particles. They'd still be there even if the whole starship were blown to dust."

"Don't be embarrassed, Qing-jao. The wise are not wise because they make no mistakes. They are wise because they correct their mistakes as soon as they recognize them."

However, Qing-jao was blushing now for another reason. The hot blood was pounding in her head because it had only now dawned on her what Father's assignment for her was going to be. But that was impossible. He couldn't give to *her* a task that thousands of wiser, older people had already failed at.

"Father," she whispered. "What is my task?" She still hoped that it was some minor problem involved with the disappearance of the fleet. But she knew that her hope was in vain even before he spoke.

"You must discover every possible explanation for the disappearance of the fleet," he said, "and calculate the likelihood of each one. Starways Congress must be able to tell how this happened and how to make sure it will never happen again."

"But Father," said Qing-jao, "I'm only sixteen. Aren't there many others who are wiser than I am?"

"Perhaps they're all too wise to attempt the task," he said. "But you are young enough not to fancy yourself wise. You're young enough to think of impossible things and discover why they might be possible. Above all, the gods speak to you with extraordinary clarity, my brilliant child, my Gloriously Bright."

That was what she was afraid of—that Father expected her to succeed because of the favor of the gods. He didn't understand how unworthy the gods found her, how little they liked her.

And there was another problem. "What if I succeed? What if I find out where the Lusitania Fleet is, and restore communications? Wouldn't it then be my fault if the fleet destroyed Lusitania?"

"It's good that your first thought is compassion for the people of Lusitania. I assure you that Starways Congress has promised not to use the M.D. Device unless it proves absolutely unavoidable, and that is so unlikely that I can't believe it would happen. Even if it did, though, it's Congress that must decide. As my ancestor-of-the-heart said, 'Though the wise man's punishments may be light, this is not due to his compassion; though his penalties may be severe, this is not because he is cruel; he simply follows the custom appropriate to the time. Circumstances change according to the age, and ways of dealing with them change with the circumstances.' You may be sure that Starways Congress will deal with Lusitania, not according to kindness or cruelty, but according to what is necessary for the good of all humanity. That is why we serve the rulers: Because they serve the people, who serve the ancestors, who serve the gods."

"Father, I was unworthy even to think otherwise," said Qing-jao. She felt her filthiness now, instead of just knowing it in her mind. She needed to wash her hands.

She needed to trace a line. But she contained it. She would wait.

Whatever I do, she thought, there will be a terrible consequence. If I fail, then Father will lose honor before Congress and therefore before all the world of Path. That would prove to many that Father isn't worthy to be chosen god of Path when he dies.

Yet if I succeed, the result might be xenocide. Even though the choice belongs to Congress, I would still know that I made such a thing possible. The responsibility would be partly mine. No matter what I do, I will be covered with failure and smeared with unworthiness.

Then Father spoke to her as if the gods had shown him her heart. "Yes, you were unworthy," he said, "and you continue to be unworthy in your thoughts even now."

Qing-jao blushed and bowed her head, ashamed, not that her thoughts had been so plainly visible to her father, but that she had had such disobedient thoughts at all.

Father touched her shoulder gently with his hand. "But I believe the gods will make you worthy," said Father. "Starways Congress has the mandate of heaven, but you are also chosen to walk your own path. You can succeed in this great work. Will you try?"

"I will try." I will also fail, but that will surprise no one, least of all the gods, who know my unworthiness.

"All the pertinent archives have been opened up to your searching, when you speak your name and type the password. If you need help, let me know."

She left Father's room with dignity, and forced herself to walk slowly up the stairs to her room. Only when she was inside with the door closed did she throw herself to her knees and creep along the floor. She traced woodgrain lines until she could hardly see. Her unworthiness was so great that even then she didn't quite feel clean; she went to the lavatory and scrubbed her hands until she knew the gods were satisfied. Twice the servants tried to interrupt her with meals or messages—she cared little which—but when they saw that she was communing with the gods they bowed and quietly slipped away.

It was not the washing of her hands, though, that finally made her clean. It was the moment when she drove the last vestige of uncertainty from her heart. Starways Congress had the mandate of heaven. She must purge herself of all doubt. Whatever they meant to do with the Lusitania Fleet, it was surely the will of the gods that it be accomplished. Therefore it was her duty to help them accomplish it. And if she was in fact doing the will of the gods, then they would open a way for her to solve the problem that had been set before her. Anytime she thought otherwise, anytime the words of Demosthenes returned to her mind, she would have to blot them out by remembering that *she* would obey the rulers who have the mandate of heaven.

By the time her mind was calm, her palms were raw and dotted with blood seeping up from the layers of living skin that were now so close to the surface. This is how my understanding of the truth arises, she told herself. If I wash away enough of my mortality, then the truth of the gods will seep upward into the light.

She was clean at last. The hour was late and her eyes were tired. Nevertheless, she sat down before her terminal and began the work. "Show me summaries of all the research that has been conducted so far on the disappearance of the Lusitania Fleet," she said, "starting with the most recent." Almost at once words started appearing in the air above her terminal, page upon page lined up like soldiers marching to the front. She would read one, then scroll it out of the way, only to have the page behind it move to the front for her to read it. Seven hours she read until she could read no more; then she fell asleep before the terminal.

Jane watches everything. She can do a million jobs and pay attention to a thousand things at once. Neither of these capacities is infinite, but they're so much greater than our pathetic ability to think about one thing while doing another that they might as well be. She does have a sensory limitation that we don't have, however; or, rather, we *are* her greatest limitation. She can't see or know anything that hasn't been entered as data in a computer that is tied to the great interworld network.

That's less of a limitation than you might think. She has almost immediate access to the raw inputs of every starship, every satellite, every traffic control system, and almost every electronically-monitored spy device in the human universe. But it does mean that she almost never witnesses lovers' quarrels, bedtime stories, classroom arguments, supper-table gossip, or bitter tears privately shed. She only knows that aspect of our lives that we represent as digital information.

If you asked her the exact number of human beings in the settled worlds, she would quickly give you a number based on census figures combined with birth-and-death probabilities in all our population groups. In most cases, she could match numbers with names, though no human could live long enough to read the list. And if you took a name you just happened to think of—Han Qing-jao, for instance—and you asked Jane, "Who is this person?" she'd almost immediately give you the vital statistics—birth date, citizenship, parentage, height and weight at last medical checkup, grades in school.

But that is all gratuitous information, background noise to her; she knows it's there, but it means nothing. To ask her about Han Qing-jao would be something like asking her a question about a certain molecule of water vapor in a distant cloud. The molecule is certainly there, but there's nothing special to differentiate it from the million others in its immediate vicinity.

That was true until the moment that Han Qing-jao began to use her computer to access all the reports dealing with the disappearance of the Lusitania Fleet. Then Qing-jao's name moved many levels upward in Jane's attention. Jane began to keep a log of everything that Qing-jao did with her computer. And it quickly became clear to her that Han Qing-jao, though she was only sixteen, meant to make serious trouble for Jane. Because Han Qing-jao, unconnected as she was to any particular bureaucracy, having no ideological axe to grind or vested interest to protect, was taking a broader and therefore more dangerous look at all the information that had been collected by every human agency.

Why was it dangerous? Had Jane left clues behind that Qing-jao would find?

No, of course not. Jane left no clues. She had thought of leaving some, of trying to make the disappearance of the Lusitania Fleet look like sabotage or mechanical failure or some natural disaster. She had to give up on that idea, because she couldn't work up any *physical* clues. All she could do was leave misleading data in computer memories. None of it would ever have any physical analogue in the real world, and therefore any halfway-intelligent researcher would quickly realize that the clues were all faked-up data. Then he would conclude that the disappearance of the Lusitania Fleet had to have been caused by some agency that had unimaginably detailed access to the computer systems that had the false data. Surely that would lead people to discover her far more quickly than if she left no evidence at all.

Leaving no evidence was the best course, definitely; and until Han Qing-jao began her investigation, it had worked very well. Each investigating agency looked only in the places they usually looked. The police on many planets checked out all the known dissident groups (and, in some places, tortured various dissidents until they made useless confessions, at which point the interrogators filed final reports and pronounced the issue closed). The military looked for evidence of military opposition—especially alien starships, since the military had keen memories of the invasion of the buggers three thousand years before. Scientists looked for evidence of some unexpected invisible astronomical phenomenon that could account for either the destruction of the fleet or the selective breakdown of ansible communication. The politicians looked for somebody else to blame. Nobody imagined Jane, and therefore nobody found her.

But Han Qing-jao was putting everything together, carefully, systematically, running precise searches on the data. She would inevitably turn up the evidence that could eventually prove—and end—Jane's existence. That evidence was, simply put, the lack of evidence. Nobody else could see it, because nobody had ever brought an unbiased methodical mind to the investigation.

What Jane couldn't know was that Qing-jao's seemingly inhuman patience, her meticulous attention to detail, her constant rephrasing and reprogramming of computer searches, that all of these were the result of endless hours kneeling hunched over on a wooden floor, carefully following a grain in the wood from one end of a board to the other, from one side of a room to the other. Jane couldn't begin to guess that it was the great lesson taught her by the gods that made Qing-jao her most formidable opponent. All Jane knew was that at some point, this searcher named Qing-jao would probably realize what no one else really understood: that every conceivable explanation for the disappearance of the Lusitania Fleet had already been completely eliminated.

At that point only one conclusion would remain: that some force not yet encountered anywhere in the history of humankind had the power either to make a widely scattered fleet of starships disappear simultaneously, or—just as unlikely—to make that fleet's ansibles all stop functioning at once. And if that same methodical mind then started listing possible forces that might have such power, eventually it was bound to name the one that was true: an independent entity that dwelt among—no, that was composed of—the philotic rays connecting all ansibles together. Because this idea was true, no amount of logical scrutiny or research would eliminate it. Eventually this idea would be left standing alone. And at that point, somebody would surely act on Qing-jao's discovery and set out to destroy Jane.

So Jane watched Qing-jao's research with more and more fascination. This sixteen-year-old daughter of Han Fei-tzu, who weighed 39 kilograms and stood 160 centimeters tall and was in the uppermost social and intellectual class on the Taoist Chinese world of Path, was the first human being Jane had ever found who approached the thoroughness and precision of a computer and, therefore, of Jane herself. And though Jane could conduct in an hour the search that was taking Qing-jao weeks and months to complete, the dangerous truth was that Qing-jao was performing almost exactly the search Jane herself would have conducted; and therefore there was no reason for Jane to suppose that Qing-jao would not reach the conclusion that Jane herself would reach.

Qing-jao was therefore Jane's most dangerous enemy, and Jane was helpless to stop her—at least physically. Trying to block Qing-jao's access to information would only mean leading her more quickly to the knowledge of Jane's existence. So instead of open opposition, Jane searched for another way to stop her enemy. She did not understand all of human nature, but Ender had taught her this: To stop a human being from doing something, you must find a way to make the person stop wanting to do it.

6

VARELSE

<How are you able to speak directly into Ender's mind?>

<Now that we know where he is, it's as natural as eating.>

<How did you find him? I've never been able to speak into the mind of anyone who hasn't passed into the third life.>

<We found him through the ansibles, and the electronics connected to them—found where his body was in space. To reach his mind, we had to reach into chaos and form a bridge.>

<Bridge?>

<A transitional entity, which partly resembled his mind and partly ours.>

<If you could reach his mind, why didn't you stop him from destroying you?>

<The human brain is very strange. Before we could make sense of what we found there, before we could

learn how to speak into that twisted space, all my sisters and mothers were gone. We continued to study his mind during all the years we waited, cocooned, until he found us; when he came, then we could speak directly to him.>

<What happened to the bridge you made?>

<We never thought about it. It's probably still out there somewhere.>

The new strain of potatoes was dying. Ender saw the telltale brown circles in the leaves, the plants broken off where the stems had turned so brittle that the slightest breeze bent them till they snapped. This morning they had all been healthy. The onset of this disease was so sudden, its effect so devastating, that it could only be the descolada virus.

Ela and Novinha would be disappointed—they had had such hopes for this strain of potato. Ela, Ender's stepdaughter, had been working on a gene that would cause every cell in an organism to produce three different chemicals that were known to inhibit or kill the descolada virus. Novinha, Ender's wife, had been working on a gene that would cause cell nuclei to be impermeable to any molecule larger than one-tenth the size of the descolada. With this strain of potato, they had spliced in both genes and, when early tests showed that both traits had taken hold, Ender had brought the seedlings to the experimental farm and planted them. He and his assistants had nurtured them for the past six weeks. All had seemed to be going well.

If the technique had worked, it could have been adapted to all the plants and animals that the humans of Lusitania depended on for food. But the descolada virus was too clever by half—it saw through all their stratagems, eventually. Still, six weeks was better than the normal two or three days. Maybe they were on the right track.

Or maybe things had already gone too far. Back when Ender first arrived on Lusitania, new strains of Earthborn plants and animals could last as long as twenty years in the field before the descolada decoded their genetic molecules and tore them apart. But in recent years the descolada virus had apparently made a breakthrough that allowed it to decode any genetic molecule from Earth in days or even hours.

These days the only thing that allowed the human colonists to grow their plants and raise their animals was a spray that was immediately fatal to the descolada virus. There were human colonists who wanted to spray the whole planet and wipe out the descolada virus once and for all.

Spraying a whole planet was impractical, but not impossible; there were other reasons for rejecting that option. Every form of native life absolutely depended on the descolada in order to reproduce. That included the piggies—the pequeninos, the intelligent natives of this world—whose reproductive cycle was inextricably bound up with the only native species of tree. If the descolada virus were ever destroyed, this generation of pequeninos would be the last. It would be xenocide.

So far, the idea of doing anything that would wipe out the piggies would be immediately rejected by most of the people of Milagre, the village of humans. So far. But Ender knew that many minds would change if a few more facts were widely known. For instance, only a handful of people knew that twice already the descolada had adapted itself to the chemical they were using to kill it. Ela and Novinha had already developed several new versions of the chemical, so that the next time the descolada adapted to one viricide they could switch immediately to another. Likewise, they had once had to change the descolada inhibitor that kept human beings from dying of the descolada viruses that dwelt in every human in the colony. The inhibitor was added to

all the colony's food, so that every human being in-
gested it with every meal.

However, all the inhibitors and viricides worked on
the same basic principles. Someday, just as the descolada virus had learned how to adapt to Earthborn genes
in general, it would also learn how to handle each class
of chemicals, and then it wouldn't matter how many
new versions they had—the descolada would exhaust
their resources in days.

Only a few people knew how precarious Milagre's
survival really was. Only a few people understood how
much was riding on the work that Ela and Novinha, as
Lusitania's xenobiologists, were doing; how close their
contest was with the descolada; how devastating the
consequences would be if they ever fell behind.

Just as well. If the colonists did understand, there
would be many who would say, If it's inevitable that
someday the descolada will overwhelm us, then let's
wipe it out now. If that kills all the piggies then we're
sorry, but if it's us or them, we choose us.

It was fine for Ender to take the long view, the philosophical perspective, and say, Better for one small human colony to perish than to wipe out an entire sentient
species. He knew this argument would carry no water
with the humans of Lusitania. Their own lives were at
stake here, and the lives of their children; it would be
absurd to expect them to be willing to die for the sake
of another species that they didn't understand and that
few of them even liked. It would make no sense genetically—evolution encourages only creatures who are serious about protecting their own genes. Even if the
Bishop himself declared it to be the will of God that
the human beings of Lusitania lay down their lives for
the piggies, there would be precious few who would
obey.

I'm not sure I could make such a sacrifice myself,
thought Ender. Even though I have no children of my

own. Even though I have already lived through the destruction of a sentient species—even though I triggered that destruction myself, and I know what a terrible moral burden that is to bear—I'm not sure I could let my fellow human beings die, either by starvation because their food crops have been destroyed, or far more painfully by the return of the descolada as a disease with the power to consume the human body in days.

And yet . . . could I consent to the destruction of the pequeninos? Could I permit another xenocide?

He picked up one of the broken potato stems with its blotchy leaves. He would have to take this to Novinha, of course. Novinha would examine it, or Ela would, and they'd confirm what was already obvious. Another failure. He put the potato stem into a sterile pouch.

"Speaker."

It was Planter, Ender's assistant and his closest friend among the piggies. Planter was a son of the pequenino named Human, whom Ender had taken into the "third life," the tree stage of the pequenino life cycle. Ender held up the transparent plastic pouch for Planter to see the leaves inside.

"Very dead indeed, Speaker," said Planter, with no discernible emotion. That had been the most disconcerting thing about working with pequeninos at first—they didn't show emotions in ways that humans could easily, habitually interpret. It was one of the greatest barriers to their acceptance by most of the colonists. The piggies weren't cute or cuddly; they were merely strange.

"We'll try again," said Ender. "I think we're getting closer."

"Your *wife* wants you," said Planter. The word *wife,* even translated into a human language like Stark, was so loaded with tension for a pequenino that it was difficult to speak the word naturally—Planter almost screeched it. Yet the idea of wifeness was so powerful to the pequeninos that, while they could call Novinha by her name when they spoke to her directly, when they were speaking to Novinha's husband they could only refer to her by her title.

"I was just about to go see her anyway," said Ender. "Would you measure and record these potatoes, please?"

Planter leaped straight up—like a popcorn, Ender thought. Though his face remained, to human eyes, expressionless, the vertical jump showed his delight. Planter loved working with the electronic equipment, both because machines fascinated him and because it added greatly to his status among the other pequenino males. Planter immediately began unpacking the camera and its computer from the bag he always carried with him.

"When you're done, please prepare this isolated section for flash burning," said Ender.

"Yes yes," said Planter. "Yes yes yes."

Ender sighed. Pequeninos got so annoyed when humans told them things that they already knew. Planter certainly knew the routine when the descolada had adapted to a new crop—the "educated" virus had to be destroyed while it was still in isolation. No point in letting the whole community of descolada viruses profit from what one strain had learned. So Ender shouldn't have reminded him. And yet that was how human beings satisfied their sense of responsibility—checking again even when they knew it was unnecessary.

Planter was so busy he hardly noticed that Ender was leaving the field. When Ender was inside the isolation shed at the townward end of the field, he stripped, put his clothes in the purification box, and then did the purification dance—hands up high, arms rotating at the shoulder, turning in a circle, squatting and standing again, so that no part of his body was missed by the combination of radiation and gases that filled the shed.

He breathed deeply through mouth and nose, then coughed—as always—because the gases were barely within the limits of human tolerance. Three full minutes with burning eyes and wheezing lungs, while waving his arms and squatting and standing: our ritual of obeisance to the almighty descolada. Thus we humiliate ourselves before the undisputed master of life on this planet.

Finally it was done; I've been roasted to a turn, he thought. As fresh air finally rushed into the shed, he took his clothes out of the box and put them on, still hot. As soon as he left the shed, it would be heated so that every surface was far over the proven heat tolerance of the descolada virus. Nothing could live in that shed during this final step of purification. Next time someone came to the shed it would be absolutely sterile.

Yet Ender couldn't help but think that somehow the descolada virus would find a way through—if not through the shed, then through the mild disruption barrier that surrounded the experimental crop area like an invisible fortress wall. Officially, no molecule larger than a hundred atoms could pass through that barrier without being broken up. Fences on either side of the barrier kept humans and piggies from straying into the fatal area—but Ender had often imagined what it would be like for someone to pass through the disruption field. Every cell in the body would be killed instantly as the nucleic acids broke apart. Perhaps the body would hold together physically. But in Ender's imagination he always saw the body crumbling into dust on the other side of the barrier, the breeze carrying it away like smoke before it could hit the ground.

What made Ender most uncomfortable about the disruption barrier was that it was based on the same principle as the Molecular Disruption Device. Designed to be used against starships and missiles, it was Ender who turned it against the home planet of the buggers when he commanded the human warfleet three thousand years ago. And it was the same weapon that was now on its way from Starways Congress to Lusitania. According to Jane, Starways Congress had already attempted to send the order to use it. She had blocked that by cutting off ansible communications between the fleet and the rest of humanity, but there was no telling whether some overwrought ship's captain, panicked because his ansible wasn't working, might still use it on Lusitania when he got here.

It was unthinkable, but they had done it—Congress had sent the order to destroy a world. To commit xenocide. Had Ender written the Hive Queen in vain? Had they already forgotten?

But it wasn't "already" to them. It was three thousand years to most people. And even though Ender had written the Life of Human, it wasn't believed widely enough yet. It hadn't been embraced by the people to such a degree that Congress wouldn't dare to act against the pequeninos.

Why had they decided to do it? Probably for exactly the same purpose as the xenobiologists' disruption barrier: to isolate a dangerous infection so it couldn't spread into the wider population. Congress was probably worried about containing the plague of planetary revolt. But when the fleet reached here, with or without orders, they might be as likely to use the Little Doctor as the final solution to the descolada problem: If there were no planet Lusitania, there would be no self-mutating half-intelligent virus itching for a chance to wipe out humanity and all its works.

It wasn't that long a walk from the experimental fields to the new xenobiology station. The path wound over a low hill, skirting the edge of the wood that provided father, mother, and living cemetery to this tribe of pequeninos, and then on to the north gate in the fence that surrounded the human colony.

The fence was a sore point with Ender. There was no reason for it to exist anymore, now that the policy of minimal contact between humans and pequeninos had broken down, and both species passed freely through the gate. When Ender arrived on Lusitania, the fence was charged with a field that caused any person entering it to suffer excruciating pain. During the struggle to win the right to communicate freely with the pequeninos, Ender's oldest stepson, Miro, was trapped in the field for several minutes, causing irreversible brain damage. Yet Miro's experience was only the most painful and immediate expression of what the fence did to the souls of the humans enclosed within it. The psychobarrier had been shut off thirty years ago. In all that time, there had been no reason to have any barrier between humans and pequeninos—yet the fence remained. The human colonists of Lusitania wanted it that way. They wanted the boundary between human and pequenino to remain unbreached.

That was why the xenobiology labs had been moved from their old location down by the river. If pequeninos were to take part in the research, the lab had to be close to the fence, and all the experimental fields outside it, so that humans and pequeninos wouldn't have occasion to confront each other unexpectedly.

When Miro left to meet Valentine, Ender had thought he would return to be astonished by the great changes in the world of Lusitania. He had thought that Miro would see humans and pequeninos living side by side, two species living in harmony. Instead, Miro would find the colony nearly unchanged. With rare exceptions, the human beings of Lusitania did not long for the close company of another species.

It was a good thing that Ender had helped the hive queen restore the race of buggers so far from Milagre. Ender had planned to help buggers and humans gradually come to know each other. Instead, he and Novinha and their family had been forced to keep the existence of the buggers on Lusitania a close-held secret. If the human colonists couldn't deal with the mammal-like pequeninos, it was certain that knowing about the insect-like buggers would provoke violent xenophobia almost at once.

I have too many secrets, thought Ender. For all these years I've been a speaker for the dead, uncovering secrets and helping people to live in the light of truth. Now I no longer tell anyone half of what I know, because if I told the whole truth there would be fear, hatred, brutality, murder, war.

Not far from the gate, but outside it, stood two fathertrees, the one named Rooter, the other named Human, planted so that from the gate it would seem that Rooter was on the left hand, Human on the right. Human was the pequenino whom Ender had been required to ritually kill with his own hands, in order to seal the treaty between humans and pequeninos. Then Human was reborn in cellulose and chlorophyll, finally a mature adult male, able to sire children.

At present Human still had enormous prestige, not only among the piggies of this tribe, but in many other tribes as well. Ender knew that he was alive; yet, seeing the tree, it was impossible for him to forget how Human had died.

Ender had no trouble dealing with Human as a person, for he had spoken with this fathertree many times. What he could not manage was to think of this tree as the *same* person he had known as the pequenino named Human. Ender might understand intellectually that it was will and memory that made up a person's identity, and that will and memory had passed intact from the pequenino into the fathertree. But intellectual understanding did not always bring visceral belief. Human was so alien now.

Yet still he *was* Human, and he was still Ender's

friend; Ender touched the bark of the tree as he passed. Then, taking a few steps out of his way, Ender walked to the older fathertree named Rooter, and touched his bark also. He had never known Rooter as a pequenino—Rooter had been killed by other hands, and his tree was already tall and well-spread before Ender arrived on Lusitania. There was no sense of loss to trouble him when Ender talked to Rooter.

At Rooter's base, among the roots, lay many sticks. Some had been brought here; some were shed from Rooter's own branches. They were talking sticks. Pequeninos used them to beat a rhythm on the trunk of a fathertree; the fathertree would shape and reshape the hollow areas inside his own trunk to change the sound, to make a slow kind of speech. Ender could beat the rhythm—clumsily, but well enough to get words from the trees.

Today, though, Ender wanted no conversation. Let Planter tell the fathertrees that another experiment had failed. Ender would talk to Rooter and Human later. He would talk to the hive queen. He would talk to Jane. He would talk to everybody. And after all the talking, they would be no closer to solving any of the problems that darkened Lusitania's future. Because the solution to their problems now did not depend on talk. It depended on knowledge and action—knowledge that only other people could learn, actions that only other people could perform. There was nothing that Ender could do himself to solve anything.

All he could do, all he had ever done since his final battle as a child warrior, was listen and talk. At other times, in other places, that had been enough. Not now. Many different kinds of destruction loomed over Lusitania, some of them set in motion by Ender himself, and yet not one of them could now be solved by any act or word or thought of Andrew Wiggin. Like all the other citizens of Lusitania, his future was in the hands of other people. The difference between him and them was that Ender knew all the danger, all the possible consequences of every failure or mistake. Who was more cursed, the one who died, unknowing until the very moment of his death, or the one who watched his destruction as it approached, step by step, for days and weeks and years?

Ender left the fathertrees and walked on down the well-beaten path toward the human colony. Through the gate, through the door of the xenobiology lab. The pequenino who served as Ela's most trusted assistant—named Deaf, though he was definitely *not* hard of hearing—led him at once to Novinha's office, where Ela, Novinha, Quara, and Grego were already waiting. Ender held up the pouch containing the fragment of potato plant.

Ela shook her head; Novinha sighed. But they didn't seem half as disappointed as Ender had expected. Clearly there was something else on their minds.

"I guess we expected that," said Novinha.

"We still had to try," said Ela.

"Why did we have to try?" demanded Grego. Novinha's youngest son—and therefore Ender's stepson—was in his mid-thirties now, a brilliant scientist in his own right; but he did seem to relish his role as devil's advocate in all the family's discussions, whether they dealt with xenobiology or the color to paint the walls. "All we're doing by introducing these new strains is teaching the descolada how to get around every strategy we have for killing it. If we don't wipe it out soon, it'll wipe *us* out. And once the descolada is gone, we can grow regular old potatoes without any of this nonsense."

"We *can't*!" shouted Quara. Her vehemence surprised Ender. Quara was reluctant to speak out at the best of times; for her to speak so loudly now was out of character. "I tell you that the descolada is alive."

"And I tell you that a virus is a virus," said Grego.

It bothered Ender that Grego was calling for the extermination of the descolada—it wasn't like him to so easily call for something that would destroy the pequeninos. Grego had practically grown up among the pequenino males—he knew them better, spoke their language better, than anyone.

"Children, be quiet and let me explain this to Andrew," said Novinha. "We were discussing what to do if the potatoes failed, Ela and I, and she told me—no, *you* explain it, Ela."

"It's an easy enough concept. Instead of trying to grow plants that inhibit the growth of the descolada virus, we need to go after the virus itself."

"Right," said Grego.

"Shut *up*," said Quara.

"As a kindness to us all, Grego, please do as your sister has so kindly asked," said Novinha.

Ela sighed and went on. "We can't just kill it because that would kill all the other native life on Lusitania. So what I propose is trying to develop a new strain of descolada that continues to act as the present virus acts in the reproductive cycles of all the Lusitanian life forms, but without the ability to adapt to new species."

"You can eliminate that part of the virus?" asked Ender. "You can *find* it?"

"Not likely. But I think I can find all the parts of the virus that are active in the piggies and in all the other plant-animal pairs, *keep* those, and discard everything else. Then we'd add a rudimentary reproductive ability and set up some receptors so it'll respond properly to the appropriate changes in the host bodies, put the whole thing in a little organelle, and there we have it—a substitute for the descolada so that the pequeninos and all the other native species are safe, while we can live without worry."

"Then you'll spray all the original descolada virus to

wipe them out?" asked Ender. "What if there's already a resistant strain?"

"No, we *don't* spray them, because spraying wouldn't wipe out the viruses that are already incorporated into the bodies of every Lusitanian creature. This is the really tricky part—"

"As if the rest were *easy*," said Novinha, "making a new organelle out of nothing—"

"We can't just inject these organelles into a few piggies or even into all of them, because we'd also have to inject them into every other native animal and tree and blade of grass."

"Can't be done," said Ender.

"So we have to develop a mechanism to deliver the organelles universally, and at the same time destroy the old descolada viruses once and for all."

"Xenocide," said Quara.

"That's the argument," said Ela. "Quara says the descolada is sentient."

Ender looked at his youngest stepdaughter. "A sentient *molecule*?"

"They have language, Andrew."

"When did *this* happen?" asked Ender. He was trying to imagine how a genetic molecule—even one as long and complex as the descolada virus—could possibly speak.

"I've suspected it for a long time. I wasn't going to say anything until I was sure, but—"

"Which means she *isn't* sure," said Grego triumphantly.

"But I'm *almost* sure now, and you can't go destroying a whole species until we *know*."

"How do they speak?" asked Ender.

"Not like us, of course," said Quara. "They pass information back and forth to each other at a molecular level. I first noticed it as I was working on the question of how the new resistant strains of the descolada spread so quickly and replaced all the old viruses in such a short time. I couldn't solve that problem because I was asking the wrong question. They *don't* replace the old ones. They simply pass messages."

"They throw *darts*," said Grego.

"That was my own word for it," said Quara. "I didn't understand that it was *speech*."

"Because it wasn't speech," said Grego.

"That was five years ago," said Ender. "You said the darts they send out carry the needed genes and then all the viruses that receive the darts revise their own structure to include the new gene. That's hardly language."

"But that isn't the *only* time they send darts," said Quara. "Those messenger molecules are moving in and out all the time, and most of the time they aren't incorporated into the body at all. They get read by several parts of the descolada and then they're passed on to another one."

"This is language?" asked Grego.

"Not yet," said Quara. "But sometimes after a virus reads one of these darts, it makes a new dart and sends it out. Here's the part that tells me it's a language: The front part of the new dart always begins with a molecular sequence similar to the back tag of the dart that it's answering. It holds the thread of the conversation together."

"Conversation," said Grego scornfully.

"Be quiet or die," said Ela. Even after all these years, Ender realized, Ela's voice still had the power to curb Grego's snottiness—sometimes, at least.

"I've tracked some of these conversations for as many as a hundred statements and answers. Most of them die out much sooner than that. A few of them are incorporated into the main body of the virus. But here's the most interesting thing—it's completely voluntary. Sometimes one virus will pick up that dart and keep it, while most of the others don't. Sometimes most of the viruses will keep a particular dart. But the area where they incorporate these message darts is exactly that area that has been hardest to map. It's hardest to map because it isn't part of their structure, it's their *memory*, and individuals are all different from each other. They also tend to weed out a few memory fragments when they've taken on too many darts."

"This is all fascinating," said Grego, "but it isn't science. There are plenty of explanations for these darts and the random bonding and shedding—"

"*Not* random!" said Quara.

"None of this is language," said Grego.

Ender ignored the argument, because Jane was whispering in his ear through the jewel-like transceiver he wore there. She spoke to him more rarely now than in years past. He listened carefully, taking nothing for granted. "She's on to something," Jane said. "I've looked at her research and there's something going on here that doesn't happen with any other subcellular creature. I've run many different analyses on the data, and the more I simulate and test this particular behavior of the descolada, the less it looks like genetic coding and the more it looks like language. At the moment we can't rule out the possibility that it *is* voluntary."

When Ender turned his attention back to the argument, Grego was speaking. "Why do we have to turn everything we haven't figured out yet into some kind of mystical experience?" Grego closed his eyes and intoned, "I have found new life! I have found new life!"

"Stop it!" shouted Quara.

"This is getting out of hand," said Novinha. "Grego, try to keep this at the level of rational discussion."

"It's hard to, when the whole thing is so irrational. Até agora quem já imaginou microbiologista que se torna namorada de uma molécula?" Who ever heard of a microbiologist getting a crush on a molecule?

"Enough!" said Novinha sharply. "Quara is as much a scientist as you are, and—"

"She *was,*" muttered Grego.

"*And*—if you'll kindly shut up long enough to hear me out—she has a right to be heard." Novinha was quite angry now, but, as usual, Grego seemed unimpressed. "You should know by now, Grego, that it's often the ideas that sound most absurd and counterintuitive at first that later cause fundamental shifts in the way we see the world."

"Do you really think this is one of those basic discoveries?" asked Grego, looking them in the eye, each in turn. "A talking virus? Se Quara sabe tanto, porque ela nao diz o que é que aqueles bichos dizem?" If she knows so much about it, why doesn't she tell us what these little beasts are saying? It was a sign that the discussion was getting out of hand, that he broke into Portuguese instead of speaking in Stark, the language of science—and diplomacy.

"Does it matter?" asked Ender.

"Matter!" said Quara.

Ela looked at Ender with consternation. "It's only the difference between curing a dangerous disease and destroying an entire sentient species. I think it matters."

"I meant," said Ender patiently, "does it matter whether we know what they're saying."

"No," said Quara. "We'll probably never understand their language, but that doesn't change the fact that they're sentient. What do viruses and human beings have to say to each other, anyway?"

"How about, 'Please stop trying to kill us'?" said Grego. "If you can figure out how to say that in virus language, then this might be useful."

"But Grego," said Quara, with mock sweetness, "do we say that to them, or do they say that to *us?*"

"We don't have to decide today," said Ender. "We can afford to wait awhile."

"How do *you* know?" said Grego. "How do you

know that tomorrow afternoon we won't all wake up itching and hurting and puking and burning up with fever and finally dying because overnight the descolada virus figured out how to wipe us out once and for all? It's us or them."

"I think Grego just showed us why we *have* to wait," said Ender. "Did you hear how he talked about the descolada? It *figures out* how to wipe us out. Even *he* thinks the descolada has a will and makes decisions."

"That's just a figure of speech," said Grego.

"We've all been talking that way," said Ender. "And thinking that way, too. Because we all feel it—that we're at war with the descolada. That it's more than just fighting off a disease—it's like we have an intelligent, resourceful enemy who keeps countering all our moves. In all the history of medical research, no one has ever fought a disease that had so many ways to defeat the strategies used against it."

"Only because nobody's been fighting a germ with such an oversized and complex genetic molecule," said Grego.

"Exactly," said Ender. "This is a one-of-a-kind virus, and so it may have abilities we've never imagined in any species less structurally complex than a vertebrate."

For a moment Ender's words hung in the air, answered by silence; for a moment, Ender imagined that he might have served a useful function in this meeting after all, that as a mere talker he might have won some kind of agreement.

Grego soon disabused him of this idea. "Even if Quara's right, even if she's dead on and the descolada viruses all have doctorates of philosophy and keep publishing dissertations on screwing-up-humans-till-they're-dead, what then? Do we all roll over and play dead because the virus that's trying to kill us all is so damn smart?"

Novinha answered calmly. "I think Quara needs to

continue with her research—and we need to give her more resources to do it—while Ela continues with hers."

It was Quara who objected this time. "Why should I bother trying to understand them if the rest of you are still working on ways to kill them?"

"That's a good question, Quara," said Novinha. "On the other hand, why should you bother trying to understand them if they suddenly figure out a way to get past all our chemical barriers and kill us all?"

"Us or them," muttered Grego.

Novinha had made a good decision, Ender knew—keep both lines of research open, and decide later when they knew more. In the meantime, Quara and Grego were both missing the point, both assuming that everything hinged on whether or not the descolada was sentient. "Even if they're sentient," said Ender, "that doesn't mean they're sacrosanct. It all depends whether they're raman or varelse. If they're raman—if we can understand them and they can understand us well enough to work out a way of living together—then fine. We'll be safe, they'll be safe."

"The great peacemaker plans to sign a treaty with a molecule?" asked Grego.

Ender ignored his mocking tone. "On the other hand, if they're trying to destroy us, and we can't find a way to communicate with them, then they're varelse—sentient aliens, but implacably hostile and dangerous. Varelse are aliens we can't live with. Varelse are aliens with whom we are naturally and permanently engaged in a war to the death, and at that time our only moral choice is to do all that's necessary to win."

"Right," said Grego.

Despite her brother's triumphant tone, Quara had listened to Ender's words, weighed them, and now gave a tentative nod. "As long as we don't start from the assumption that they're varelse," said Quara.

"And even then, maybe there's a middle way," said Ender. "Maybe Ela can find a way to replace all the descolada viruses without destroying this memory-and-language thing."

"No!" said Quara, once again fervent. "You can't—you don't even have the *right* to leave them their memories and take away their ability to adapt. That would be like *them* giving all of *us* frontal lobotomies. If it's war, then it's war. Kill them, but don't leave them their memories while stealing their will."

"It doesn't matter," said Ela. "It can't be done. As it is, I think I've set myself an impossible task. Operating on the descolada isn't easy. Not like examining and operating on an animal. How do I anesthetize the molecule so that it doesn't heal itself while I'm halfway through the amputation? Maybe the descolada isn't much on physics, but it's a hell of a lot better than I am at molecular surgery."

"So far," said Ender.

"So far we don't know anything," said Grego. "Except that the descolada is trying as hard as it can to kill us all, while we're still trying to figure out whether we ought to fight back. I'll sit tight for a while longer, but not forever."

"What about the piggies?" asked Quara. "Don't *they* have a right to vote on whether we transform the molecule that not only allows them to reproduce, but probably created them as a sentient species in the first place?"

"This thing is trying to kill us," said Ender. "As long as the solution Ela comes up with can wipe out the virus without interfering with the reproductive cycle of the piggies, then I don't think they have any right to object."

"Maybe they'd feel different about that."

"Then maybe they'd better not find out what we're doing," said Grego.

"We don't tell people—human or pequenino—about the research we're doing here," said Novinha sharply. "It could cause terrible misunderstandings that could lead to violence and death."

"So we humans are the judges of all other creatures," said Quara.

"No, Quara. We *scientists* are gathering information," said Novinha. "Until we've gathered enough, *nobody* can judge anything. So the secrecy rule goes for everybody here. Quara and Grego both. You tell no one until I say so, and I won't say so until we know more."

"Until *you* say so," asked Grego impudently, "or until the Speaker for the Dead says so?"

"I'm the head xenobiologist," said Novinha. "The decision on when we know enough is mine alone. Is that understood?"

She waited for everyone there to assent. They all did.

Novinha stood up. The meeting was over. Quara and Grego left almost immediately; Novinha gave Ender a kiss on the cheek and then ushered him and Ela out of her office.

Ender lingered in the lab to talk to Ela. "*Is* there a way to spread your replacement virus throughout the entire population of every native species on Lusitania?"

"I don't know," said Ela. "That's less of a problem than how to get it to every cell of an individual organism fast enough that the descolada can't adapt or escape. I'll have to create some kind of carrier virus, and I'll probably have to model it partly on the descolada itself—the descolada is the only parasite I've seen that invades a host as quickly and thoroughly as I need the carrier virus to do it. Ironic—I'll learn how to replace the descolada by stealing techniques from the virus itself."

"It's not ironic," said Ender, "it's the way the world works. Someone once told me that the only teacher who's worth anything to you is your enemy."

"Then Quara and Grego must be giving each other advanced degrees," said Ela.

"Their argument is healthy," said Ender. "It forces us to weigh every aspect of what we're doing."

"It'll stop being healthy if one of them decides to bring it up outside the family," said Ela.

"*This* family doesn't tell its business to strangers," said Ender. "I of all people should know that."

"On the contrary, Ender. You of all people should know how eager we are to talk to a stranger—when we think our need is great enough to justify it."

Ender had to admit that she was right. Getting Quara and Grego, Miro and Quim and Olhado to trust him enough to speak to him, that had been hard when Ender first came to Lusitania. But Ela had spoken to him from the start, and so had all of Novinha's other children. So, in the end, had Novinha herself. The family was intensely loyal, but they were also strong-willed and opinionated and there wasn't a one of them who didn't trust his own judgment above anyone else's. Grego or Quara, either one of them, might well decide that telling somebody else was in the best interests of Lusitania or humanity or science, and there would go the rule of secrecy. Just the way the rule of noninterference with the piggies had been broken before Ender ever got here.

How nice, thought Ender. One more possible source of disaster that is completely out of my power to control.

Leaving the lab, Ender wished, as he had many times before, that Valentine were here. She was the one who was good at sorting out ethical dilemmas. She'd be here soon—but soon enough? Ender understood and mostly agreed with the viewpoints put forward by Quara and Grego both. What stung most was the need for such secrecy that Ender couldn't even speak to the pequeninos, not even Human himself, about a decision that would affect them as much as it would affect any colonist from Earth. And yet Novinha was right. To bring the matter out into the open now, before they even knew what was possible—that would lead to confusion at best, anarchy and bloodshed at worst. The pequeninos were peaceful now—but the species' history was bloody with war.

As Ender emerged from the gate, heading back toward the experimental fields, he saw Quara standing beside the fathertree Human, sticks in her hand, engaged in conversation. She hadn't actually beat on his trunk, or Ender would have heard it. So she must want privacy. That was all right. Ender would take a longer way around, so he wouldn't come close enough to overhear.

But when she saw Ender looking her way, Quara immediately ended her conversation with Human and took off at a brisk walk down the path toward the gate. Of course this led her right by Ender.

"Telling secrets?" asked Ender. He had meant his remark as mere banter. Only when the words came out of his mouth and Quara got such a furtive look on her face did Ender realize exactly what secret it might have been that Quara had been telling. And her words confirmed his suspicion.

"Mother's idea of fairness isn't always mine," said Quara. "Neither is yours, for that matter."

He had known she *might* do this, but it never occurred to him she would do it so quickly after promising not to. "But is fairness always the most important consideration?" asked Ender.

"It is to me," said Quara.

She tried to turn away and go on through the gate, but Ender caught her arm.

"Let go of me."

"Telling Human is one thing," said Ender. "He's very wise. But don't tell anybody else. Some of the pequeninos, some of the males, they can be pretty aggressive if they think they have reason."

"They're not just *males*," said Quara. "They call themselves husbands. Maybe *we* should call them *men*." She smiled at Ender in triumph. "You're not half so open-minded as you like to think." Then she brushed past him and went on through the gate into Milagre.

Ender walked up to Human and stood before him. "What did she tell you, Human? Did she tell you that I'll die before I let anyone wipe out the descolada, if doing so would hurt you and your people?"

Of course Human had no immediate answer for him, for Ender had no intention of starting to beat on his trunk with the talking sticks used to produce Father Tongue; if he did, the pequenino males would hear and come running. There was no private speech between pequeninos and fathertrees. If a fathertree wanted privacy, he could always talk silently with the other fathertrees—they spoke to each other mind to mind, the way the hive queen spoke to the buggers that served as her eyes and ears and hands and feet. If only I were part of *that* communications network, thought Ender. Instantaneous speech consisting of pure thought, projected anywhere in the universe.

Still, he had to say something to help counteract the sort of thing he knew Quara would have said. "Human, we're doing all we can to save human beings and pequeninos, both. We'll even try to save the descolada virus, if we can. Ela and Novinha are very good at what they do. So are Grego and Quara, for that matter. But for now, please trust us and say nothing to anyone else. Please. If humans and pequeninos come to understand the danger we're in before we're ready to take steps to contain it, the results would be violent and terrible."

There was nothing else to say. Ender went back to the experimental fields. Before nightfall, he and Planter completed the measurements, then burned and flashed the entire field. No large molecules survived inside the disruption barrier. They had done all they could to ensure that whatever the descolada might have learned from this field was forgotten.

What they could never do was get rid of the viruses they carried within their own cells, human and pequenino alike. What if Quara was right? What if the descolada inside the barrier, before it died, managed to "tell" the viruses that Planter and Ender carried inside them about what had been learned from this new strain of potato? About the defenses that Ela and Novinha had tried to build into it? About the ways this virus had found to defeat their tactics?

If the descolada were truly intelligent, with a language to spread information and pass behaviors from one individual to many others, then how could Ender—how could any of them—hope to be victorious in the end? In the long run, it might well be that the descolada was the most adaptable species, the one most capable of subduing worlds and eliminating rivals, stronger than humans or piggies or buggers or any other living creatures on any settled worlds. That was the thought that Ender took to bed with him that night, the thought that preoccupied him even as he made love with Novinha, so that she felt the need to comfort him as if he, not she, were the one burdened with the cares of a world. He tried to apologize but soon realized the futility of it. Why add to her worries by telling of his own?

———

Human listened to Ender's words, but he couldn't agree with what Ender asked of him. Silence? Not when the humans were creating new viruses that might well transform the life cycle of the pequeninos. Oh, Human wouldn't tell the immature males and females. But he could—and would—tell all the other fathertrees throughout Lusitania. They had a right to know what was going on, and then decide together what, if anything, to do.

Before nightfall, every fathertree in every wood knew all that Human knew: of the human plans, and of his estimation of how much they could be trusted. Most agreed with him—we'll let the human beings proceed for now. But in the meantime we'll watch carefully, and prepare for a time that might come, even though we hope it won't, when humans and pequeninos go to war against each other. We cannot fight and hope to win—but maybe, before they slaughter us, we can find a way for some of us to flee.

So, before dawn, they had made plans and arrangements with the hive queen, the only nonhuman source of high technology on Lusitania. By the next nightfall, the work of building a starship to leave Lusitania had already begun.

7

SECRET MAID

<Is it true that in the old days, when you sent out your starships to settle many worlds, you could always talk to each other as if you stood in the same forest?>

<We assume that it will be the same for you. When the new fathertrees have grown, they'll be present with you. The philotic connections are unaffected by distance.>

<But will we be connected? We'll be sending no trees on the voyage. Only brothers, a few wives, and a hundred little mothers to give birth to new generations. The voyage will last decades at least. As soon as they arrive, the best of the brothers will be sent on to the third life, but it will take at least a year before the first of the fathertrees grows old enough to sire young ones. How will the first father on that new world know how to speak to

us? How can we greet him, when we don't know where he is?>

Sweat ran down Qing-jao's face. Bent over as she was, the drops trickled along her cheeks, under her eyes, and down to the tip of her nose. From there her sweat dropped into the muddy water of the rice paddy, or onto the new rice plants that rose only slightly above the water's surface.

"Why don't you wipe your face, holy one?"

Qing-jao looked up to see who was near enough to speak to her. Usually the others on her righteous labor crew did not work close by—it made them too nervous, being with one of the godspoken.

It was a girl, younger than Qing-jao, perhaps fourteen, boyish in the body, with her hair cropped very short. She was looking at Qing-jao with frank curiosity. There was an openness about her, an utter lack of shyness, that Qing-jao found strange and a little displeasing. Her first thought was to ignore the girl.

But to ignore her would be arrogant; it would be the same as saying, Because I am godspoken, I do not need to answer when I am spoken to. No one would ever suppose that the reason she didn't answer was because she was so preoccupied with the impossible task she had been given by the great Han Fei-tzu that it was almost painful to think of anything else.

So she answered—but with a question. "Why should I wipe my face?"

"Doesn't it tickle? The sweat, dripping down? Doesn't it get in your eyes and sting?"

Qing-jao lowered her face to her work for a few moments, and this time deliberately noticed how it felt. It *did* tickle, and the sweat in her eyes *did* sting. In fact it was quite uncomfortable and annoying. Carefully, Qing-jao unbent herself to stand straight—and now she noticed the pain of it, the way her back protested against the change of posture. "Yes," she said to the girl. "It tickles and stings."

"Then wipe it," the girl said. "With your sleeve."

Qing-jao looked at her sleeve. It was already soaked with the sweat of her arms. "Does wiping help?" she asked.

Now it was the girl's turn to discover something she hadn't thought about. For a moment she looked thoughtful; then she wiped her forehead with her sleeve.

She grinned. "No, holy one. It doesn't help a bit."

Qing-jao nodded gravely and bent down again to her work. Only now the tickling of the sweat, the stinging of her eyes, the pain in her back, it all bothered her very much. Her discomfort took her mind off her thoughts, instead of the other way around. This girl, whoever she was, had just added to her misery by pointing it out—and yet, ironically, by making Qing-jao aware of the misery of her body, she had freed her from the hammering of the questions in her mind.

Qing-jao began to laugh.

"Are you laughing at me, holy one?" asked the girl.

"I'm thanking you in my own way," said Qing-jao. "You've lifted a great burden from my heart, even if only for a moment."

"You're laughing at me for telling you to wipe your forehead even though it doesn't help."

"I say that is *not* why I'm laughing," said Qing-jao. She stood again and looked the girl in the eye. "I don't lie."

The girl looked abashed—but not half so much as she should have. When the godspoken used the tone of voice Qing-jao had just used, others immediately bowed and showed respect. But this girl only listened, sized up Qing-jao's words, and then nodded.

There was only one conclusion Qing-jao could reach. "Are you also godspoken?" she asked.

The girl's eyes went wide. "Me?" she said. "My parents are both very low people. My father spreads manure in the fields and my mother washes up in a restaurant."

Of course that was no answer at all. Though the gods most often chose the children of the godspoken, they had been known to speak to some whose parents had never heard the voice of the gods. Yet it was a common belief that if your parents were of very low status, the gods would have no interest in you, and in fact it was very rare for the gods to speak to those whose parents were not well educated.

"What's your name?" asked Qing-jao.

"Si Wang-mu," said the girl.

Qing-jao gasped and covered her mouth, to forbid herself from laughing. But Wang-mu did not look angry—she only grimaced and looked impatient.

"I'm sorry," said Qing-jao, when she could speak. "But that is the name of—"

"The Royal Mother of the West," said Wang-mu. "Can I help it that my parents chose such a name for me?"

"It's a noble name," said Qing-jao. "My ancestor-of-the-heart was a great woman, but she was only mortal, a poet. Yours is one of the oldest of the gods."

"What good is that?" asked Wang-mu. "My parents were too presumptuous, naming me for such a distinguished god. That's why the gods will never speak to me."

It made Qing-jao sad, to hear Wang-mu speak with such bitterness. If only she knew how eagerly Qing-jao would trade places with her. To be free of the voice of the gods! Never to have to bow to the floor and trace the grain of the wood, never to wash her hands except when they got dirty . . .

Yet Qing-jao couldn't explain this to the girl. How could she understand? To Wang-mu, the godspoken were the privileged elite, infinitely wise and unapproachable. It would sound like a lie if Qing-jao explained that the burdens of the godspoken were far greater than the rewards.

Except that to Wang-mu, the godspoken had *not* been unapproachable—she had spoken to Qing-jao, hadn't she? So Qing-jao decided to say what was in her heart after all. "Si Wang-mu, I would gladly live the rest of my life blind, if only I could be free of the voice of the gods."

Wang-mu's mouth opened in shock, her eyes widened.

It had been a mistake to speak. Qing-jao regretted it at once. "I was joking," said Qing-jao.

"No," said Wang-mu. "Now you're lying. Then you were telling the truth." She came closer, slogging carelessly through the paddy, trampling rice plants as she came. "All my life I've seen the godspoken borne to the temple in their sedan chairs, wearing their bright silks, all people bowing to them, every computer open to them. When they speak their language is music. Who wouldn't want to be such a one?"

Qing-jao could not answer openly, could not say: Every day the gods humiliate me and make me do stupid, meaningless tasks to purify myself, and the next day it starts again. "You won't believe me, Wang-mu, but this life, out here in the fields, this is better."

"No!" cried Wang-mu. "You have been taught everything. You know all that there is to know! You can speak many languages, you can read every kind of word, you can think of thoughts that are as far above mine as my thoughts are above the thoughts of a snail."

"You speak very clearly and well," said Qing-jao. "You must have been to school."

"School!" said Wang-mu scornfully. "What do they care about school for children like me? We learned to read, but only enough to read prayers and street signs.

We learned our numbers, but only enough to do the shopping. We memorized sayings of the wise, but only the ones that taught us to be content with our place in life and obey those who are wiser than we are."

Qing-jao hadn't known that schools could be like that. She thought that children in school learned the same things that she had learned from her tutors. But she saw at once that Si Wang-mu must be telling the truth—one teacher with thirty students couldn't possibly teach all the things that Qing-jao had learned as one student with many teachers.

"My parents are very low," said Wang-mu. "Why should they waste time teaching me more than a servant needs to know? Because that's my highest hope in life, to be washed very clean and become a servant in a rich man's house. They were *very* careful to teach me how to clean a floor."

Qing-jao thought of the hours she had spent on the floors of her house, tracing woodgrains from wall to wall. It had never once occurred to her how much work it was for the servants to keep the floors so clean and polished that Qing-jao's gowns never got visibly dirty, despite all her crawling.

"I know something about floors," said Qing-jao.

"You know something about everything," said Wang-mu bitterly. "So don't tell me how hard it is to be god-spoken. The gods have never given a thought to me, and I tell you *that* is worse!"

"Why weren't you afraid to speak to me?" asked Qing-jao.

"I decided not to be afraid of anything," said Wang-mu. "What could you do to me that's worse than my life will already be anyway?"

I could make you wash your hands until they bleed every day of your life.

But then something turned around in Qing-jao's mind, and she saw that this girl might *not* think that was worse. Perhaps Wang-mu would gladly wash her hands until there was nothing left but a bloody fringe of tattered skin on the stumps of her wrists, if only she could learn all that Qing-jao knew. Qing-jao had felt so oppressed by the impossibility of the task her father had set for her, yet it was a task that, succeed or fail, would change history. Wang-mu would live her whole life and never be set a single task that would not need to be done again the next day; all of Wang-mu's life would be spent doing work that would only be noticed or spoken of if she did it badly. Wasn't the work of a servant almost as fruitless, in the end, as the rituals of purification?

"The life of a servant must be hard," said Qing-jao. "I'm glad for your sake that you haven't been hired out yet."

"My parents are waiting in the hope that I'll be pretty when I become a woman. Then they'll get a better hiring bonus for putting me out for service. Perhaps a rich man's bodyservant will want me for his wife; perhaps a rich lady will want me for her secret maid."

"You're already pretty," said Qing-jao.

Wang-mu shrugged. "My friend Fan-liu is in service, and she says that the ugly ones work harder, but the men of the house leave them alone. Ugly ones are free to think their own thoughts. They don't keep having to say pretty things to their ladies."

Qing-jao thought of the servants in her father's house. She knew her father would never bother any of the serving women. And nobody had to say pretty things to *her*. "It's different in my house," she said.

"But I don't serve in your house," said Wang-mu.

Now, suddenly, the whole picture became clear. Wang-mu had not spoken to her by impulse. Wang-mu had spoken to her in hopes of being offered a place as a servant in the house of a godspoken lady. For all she knew, the gossip in town was all about the young godspoken lady Han Qing-jao who was through with her tutors and had embarked on her first adult task—and how she still had neither a husband nor a secret maid. Si Wang-mu had probably wangled her way onto the same righteous labor crew as Qing-jao in order to have exactly this conversation.

For a moment Qing-jao was angry. Then she thought: Why shouldn't Wang-mu do exactly as she has done? The worst that could happen to her is that I'd guess what she was doing, become angry, and not hire her. Then she'd be no worse off than before. And if I didn't guess what she was doing, and so started to like her and hired her, she'd be secret maid to a godspoken lady. If I were in her place, wouldn't I do the same?

"Do you think you can fool me?" asked Qing-jao. "Do you think I don't know that you want me to hire you for my servant?"

Wang-mu looked flustered, angry, afraid. Wisely, though, she said nothing.

"Why don't you answer me with anger?" asked Qing-jao. "Why don't you deny that you spoke to me only so I'd hire you?"

"Because it's true," said Wang-mu. "I'll leave you alone now."

That was what Qing-jao hoped to hear—an honest answer. She had no intention of letting Wang-mu go. "How much of what you told me is true? About wanting a good education? Wanting to do something better in your life than serving work?"

"All of it," Wang-mu said, and there was passion in her voice. "But what is that to you? *You* bear the terrible burden of the voice of the gods."

Wang-mu spoke her last sentence with such contemptuous sarcasm that Qing-jao almost laughed aloud; but she contained her laughter. There was no reason to make Wang-mu any angrier than she already was. "Si Wang-mu, daughter-of-the-heart to the Royal Mother of the West I will hire you as my secret maid, but only if you agree to the following conditions. First, you will let me be your teacher, and study all the lessons I assign to you. Second, you will always speak to me as an equal and never bow to me or call me 'holy one.' And third—"

"How could I do that?" said Wang-mu. "If I don't treat you with respect others will say I'm unworthy. They'd punish me when you weren't looking. It would disgrace us both."

"Of course you'll use respect when others can see us," said Qing-jao. "But when we're alone, just you and me, we'll treat each other as equals or I'll send you away."

"The third condition?"

"You'll never tell another soul a single word I say to you."

Wang-mu's face showed her anger plainly. "A secret maid never tells. Barriers are placed in our minds."

"The barriers help you remember not to tell," said Qing-jao. "But if you *want* to tell, you can get around them. And there are those who will try to persuade you to tell." Qing-jao thought of her father's career, of all the secrets of Congress that he held in his head. He told no one; he had no one he could speak to except, sometimes, Qing-jao. If Wang-mu turned out to be trustworthy, Qing-jao *would* have someone. She would never be as lonely as her father was. "Don't you understand me?" Qing-jao asked. "Others will think I'm hiring you as a secret maid. But you and I will know that you're really coming to be my student, and I'm really bringing you to be my friend."

Wang-mu looked at her in wonder. "Why would you do this, when the gods have already told you how I bribed the foreman to let me be on your crew and not to interrupt us while I talked to you?"

The gods had told her no such thing, of course, but

Qing-jao only smiled. "Why doesn't it occur to you that maybe the gods want us to be friends?"

Abashed, Wang-mu clasped her hands together and laughed nervously; Qing-jao took the girl's hands in hers and found that Wang-mu was trembling. So she wasn't as bold as she seemed.

Wang-mu looked down at their hands, and Qing-jao followed her gaze. They were covered with dirt and muck, dried on now because they had been standing so long, their hands out of the water. "We're so dirty," said Wang-mu.

Qing-jao had long since learned to disregard the dirtiness of righteous labor, for which no penance was required. "My hands have been much filthier than this," said Qing-jao. "Come with me when our righteous labor is finished. I will tell our plan to my father, and he will decide if you can be my secret maid."

Wang-mu's expression soured. Qing-jao was glad that her face was so easy to read. "What's wrong?" said Qing-jao.

"Fathers always decide everything," said Wang-mu.

Qing-jao nodded, wondering why Wang-mu would bother to say something so obvious. "That's the beginning of wisdom," said Qing-jao. "Besides, my mother is dead."

Righteous labor always ended early in the afternoon. Officially this was to give people who lived far from the fields time to return to their homes. Actually, though, it was in recognition of the custom of making a party at the end of righteous labor. Because they had worked right through the afternoon nap, many people felt giddy after righteous labor, as if they had stayed up all night. Others felt sluggish and surly. Either one was an excuse for drinking and dining with friends and then collapsing into bed hours early to make up for the lost sleep and the hard labor of the day.

Qing-jao was of the kind who felt out of sorts; Wang-mu was obviously of the giddy kind. Or perhaps it was simply the fact that the Lusitania Fleet weighed heavily on Qing-jao's mind, while Wang-mu had just been accepted as secret maid by a godspoken girl. Qing-jao led Wang-mu through the process of applying for employment with the House of Han—washing, fingerprinting, the security check—until she finally despaired of listening to Wang-mu's bubbling voice another moment and withdrew.

As she walked up the stairs to her room, Qing-jao could hear Wang-mu asking fearfully, "Have I made my new mistress angry?" And Ju Kung-mei, the guardian of the house, answered, "The godspoken answer to other voices than yours, little one." It was a kind answer. Qing-jao often admired the gentleness and wisdom of those her father had hired into his house. She wondered if she had chosen as wisely in her first hiring.

No sooner did she think of this worry than she knew she had been wicked to make such a decision so quickly, and without consulting with her father beforehand. Wang-mu would be found to be hopelessly unsuitable, and Father would rebuke her for having acted foolishly.

Imagining Father's rebuke was enough to bring the immediate reproof of the gods. Qing-jao felt unclean. She rushed to her room and closed the door. It was bitterly ironic that she could think over and over again how hateful it was to perform the rituals the gods demanded, how empty their worship was—but let her think a disloyal thought about Father or Starways Congress, and she had to do penance at once.

Usually she would spend a half hour, an hour, perhaps longer, resisting the need for penance, enduring her own filthiness. Today, though, she hungered for the ritual of purification. In its own way, the ritual made sense, it had a structure, a beginning and end, rules to follow. Not at all like the problem of the Lusitania Fleet.

On her knees, she deliberately chose the narrowest, faintest grain in the palest board she could see. This would be a hard penance; perhaps then the gods would judge her clean enough that they could show her the solution to the problem Father had set for her. It took her half an hour to make her way across the room, for she kept losing the grain and had to start over each time.

At the end, exhausted from righteous labor and eyesore from line-tracing, she wanted desperately to sleep; instead, she sat on the floor before her terminal and called up the summary of her work so far. After examining and eliminating all the useless absurdities that had cropped up during the investigation, Qing-jao had come up with three broad categories of possibility. First, that the disappearance was caused by some natural event that, at lightspeed, had simply not become visible yet to the watching astronomers. Second, that the loss of ansible communications was the result of either sabotage or a command decision in the fleet. Third, that the loss of ansible communications was caused by some planetside conspiracy.

The first category was virtually eliminated by the way the fleet was traveling. The starships were simply not close enough together for any known natural phenomenon to destroy them all at once. The fleet had not rendezvoused before setting out—the ansible made such things a waste of time. Instead, all the ships were moving toward Lusitania from wherever they happened to be when they were assigned to the fleet. Even now, with only a year or so of travel left before all were in orbit around Lusitania's star, they were so far apart that no conceivable natural event could possibly have affected them all at once.

The second category was made almost as unlikely by

the fact that the *entire* fleet had disappeared, without exception. Could any human plan possibly work with such perfect efficiency—and without leaving any evidence of advance planning in any of the databases or personality profiles or communications logs that were maintained in planetside computers? Nor was there the slightest evidence that anyone had altered or hidden any data, or masked any communications to avoid leaving behind a trail of evidence. If it was a fleetside plan, there was neither evidence nor concealment nor error.

The same lack of evidence made the idea of a planetside conspiracy even more unlikely. And making all these possibilities still less possible was the sheer simultaneity of it. As near as anyone could determine, every single ship had broken off ansible communications at almost exactly the same time. There might have been a time lag of seconds, perhaps even minutes—but never as long as five minutes, never a gap long enough for someone on one ship to remark about the disappearance of another.

The summary was elegant in its simplicity. There was nothing left. The evidence was as complete as it would ever be, and it made every conceivable explanation inconceivable.

Why would Father do this to me? she wondered, not for the first time.

Immediately—as usual—she felt unclean even for asking such a question, for doubting her father's perfect correctness in all his decisions. She needed to wash, just a little, to take away the impurity of her doubt.

But she didn't wash. Instead she let the voice of the gods swell inside her, let their command grow more urgent. This time she wasn't resisting out of a righteous desire to grow more disciplined. This time she was deliberately trying to attract as much attention as possible from the gods. Only when she was panting with the need to cleanse herself, only when she shuddered at the most casual touch of her own flesh—a hand brushing a knee—only then did she voice her question.

"You did it, didn't you?" she said to the gods. "What no human being could have done, you must have done. You reached out and cut off the Lusitania Fleet."

The answer came, not in words, but in the ever-increasing need for purification.

"But Congress and the admiralty are not of the Way. They can't imagine the golden door into the City of the Jade Mountain in the West. If Father says to them, 'The gods stole your fleet to punish you for wickedness,' they'll only despise him. If they despise *him*, our greatest living statesman, they'll despise us as well. And if Path is shamed because of Father, it will destroy him. Is that why you did this thing?"

She began to weep. "I won't let you destroy my father. I'll find another way. I'll find an answer that will satisfy them. I defy you!"

No sooner had she said the words than the gods sent her the most overpowering sense of her own abominable filthiness she had ever felt. It was so strong it took her breath away, and she fell forward, clutching at her terminal. She tried to speak, to plead for forgiveness, but she gagged instead, swallowed hard to keep from retching. She felt as though her hands were spreading slime on everything she touched; as she struggled to her feet, her gown clung across her flesh as if it were covered with thick black grease.

But she did not wash. Nor did she fall to the ground and trace lines in the wood. Instead she staggered to the door, meaning to go downstairs to her father's room.

The doorway caught her, though. Not physically—the door swung open easily as ever—but still she could not pass. She had heard of such things, how the gods captured their disobedient servants in doorways, but it had never happened to her before. She couldn't understand how she was being held. Her body was free to move.

There was no barrier. But she felt such a sickening dread at the thought of walking through that she knew she couldn't do it, knew that the gods required some sort of penance, some sort of purification or they'd never let her leave the room. Not woodgrain-tracing, not handwashing. What did the gods require?

Then, all at once, she knew why the gods wouldn't let her pass through the door. It was the oath that Father had required of her for her mother's sake. The oath that she would always serve the gods, no matter what. And here she had been on the verge of defiance. Mother, forgive me! I will not *defy* the gods. But still I must go to Father and explain to him the terrible predicament in which the gods have placed us. Mother, help me pass through this door!

As if in answer to her plea, it came to her how she might pass through the door. All she needed to do was fix her gaze on a point in the air just outside the upper-right corner of the door, and while never letting her gaze move from that spot, step backward through the door with her right foot, place her left hand through, then pivot leftward, bringing her left leg backward through the doorway, then her right arm forward. It was complicated and difficult, like a dance, but by moving very slowly and carefully, she did it.

The door released her. And though she still felt the pressure of her own filthiness, some of the intensity had faded. It was bearable. She could breathe without gasping, speak without gagging.

She went downstairs and rang the little bell outside her father's door.

"Is it my daughter, my Gloriously Bright?" asked Father.

"Yes, noble one," said Qing-jao.

"I'm ready to receive you."

She opened Father's door and stepped through—no ritual was needed this time. She strode at once to where he sat on a chair before his terminal and knelt before him on the floor.

"I have examined your Si Wang-mu," said Father, "and I believe your first hiring has been a worthy one."

It took a moment for Father's words to make sense. Si Wang-mu? Why did Father speak to her of an ancient god? She looked up in surprise, then looked where Father was looking—at a serving girl in a clean gray gown, kneeling demurely, looking at the floor. It took a moment to remember the girl from the rice paddy, to remember that she was to be Qing-jao's secret maid. How could she have forgotten? It was only a few hours ago that Qing-jao left her. Yet in that time Qing-jao had battled with the gods,· and if she hadn't won, at least she had not yet lost. What was the hiring of a servant compared to a struggle with the gods?

"Wang-mu is impertinent and ambitious," said Father, "but she is also honest and far more intelligent than I would have expected. I assume from her bright mind and sharp ambition that you both intend for her to be your student as well as your secret maid."

Wang-mu gasped, and when Qing-jao glanced over at her, she saw how horrified the girl looked. Oh, yes—she must think that *I* think that she told Father of our secret plan. "Don't worry, Wang-mu," said Qing-jao. "Father almost always guesses secrets. I know you didn't tell."

"I wish more secrets were as easy as this one," said Father. "My daughter, I commend you for your worthy generosity. The gods will honor you for it, as I do also."

The words of praise came like unguent to a stinging wound. Perhaps this was why her rebelliousness had not destroyed her, why some god had taken mercy on her and shown her how to get through the door of her room just now. Because she had judged Wang-mu with mercy and wisdom, forgiving the girl's impertinence, Qing-jao herself was being forgiven, at least a little, for her own outrageous daring.

Wang-mu does not repent of her ambition, thought Qing-jao. Neither will I repent of my decision. I must not let Father be destroyed because I can't find—or invent—a non-divine explanation for the disappearance of the Lusitania Fleet. And yet, how can I defy the purposes of the gods? They have hidden or destroyed the fleet. And the works of the gods must be recognized by their obedient servants, even if they must remain hidden from unbelievers on other worlds.

"Father," said Qing-jao, "I must speak to you about my task."

Father misunderstood her hesitation. "We can speak in front of Wang-mu. She's been hired now as your secret maid. The hiring bonus has been sent to her father, the first barriers of secrecy have been suggested to her mind. We can trust her to hear us and never tell."

"Yes, Father," said Qing-jao. In truth she had again forgotten that Wang-mu was even there. "Father, I know who has hidden the Lusitania Fleet. But you must promise me that you will never tell it to Starways Congress."

Father, who was usually placid, looked mildly distressed. "I can't promise such a thing," he said. "It would be unworthy of me to be such a disloyal servant."

What could she do, then? How could she speak? And yet how could she keep from speaking? "Who is your master?" she cried. "Congress or the gods?"

"First the gods," said Father. "They are always first."

"Then I must tell you that I have discovered that the gods are the ones who have hidden the fleet from us, Father. But if you tell this to the Congress, they'll mock you and you'll be ruined." Then another thought occurred to her. "If it was the gods who stopped the fleet, Father, then the fleet must have been against the will of the gods after all. And if Starways Congress sent the fleet against the will of—"

Father held up his hand for her to be silent. She immediately stopped speaking and bowed her head. She waited.

"Of course it's the gods," said Father.

His words came as both a relief and a humiliation. *Of course,* he had said. Had he known this all along?

"The gods do all things that are done in the universe. But don't assume that you know *why.* You say they must have stopped the fleet because they oppose its mission. But I say that Congress couldn't have sent the fleet in the first place if the gods hadn't willed it. So why couldn't it be that the gods stopped the fleet because its mission was so great and noble that humanity was not worthy of it? Or what if they hid the fleet because it would provide a difficult test for you? One thing is certain: The gods have permitted Starways Congress to hold sway over most of humanity. As long as they have the mandate of heaven, we of Path will follow their edicts without opposition."

"I didn't mean to oppose . . ." She could not finish such an obvious falsehood.

Father understood perfectly, of course. "I hear how your voice fades and your words trail off into nothing. This is because you know your words are *not* true. You meant to oppose Starways Congress, in spite of all I have taught you." Then his voice grew gentler. "For my sake you meant to do it."

"You're my ancestor. I owe you a higher duty than I owe them."

"I'm your father. I won't become your ancestor until I'm dead."

"For Mother's sake, then. If they ever lose the mandate of heaven, then I will be their most terrible enemy, for I *will* serve the gods." Yet even as she said this, she knew her words were a dangerous half-truth. Until only a few moments ago—until she had been caught in the door—hadn't she been perfectly willing to defy even the gods for her father's sake? I am the most unworthy, terrible daughter, she thought.

"I tell you now, my Gloriously Bright daughter, that opposing Congress will never be for my good. Or yours either. But I forgive you for loving me to excess. It is the gentlest and kindest of vices."

He smiled. It calmed her agitation, to see him smile, though she knew that she didn't deserve his approbation. Qing-jao was able to think again, to return to the puzzle. "You knew that the gods did this, and yet you made me search for the answer."

"But were you asking the right question?" said Father. "The question we need answered is: *How* did the gods do it?"

"How can I know?" answered Qing-jao. "They might have destroyed the fleet or hidden it, or carried it away to some secret place in the West—"

"Qing-jao! Look at me. Hear me well."

She looked. His stern command helped calm her, give her focus.

"This is something I have tried to teach you all your life, but now you *must* learn it, Qing-jao. The gods are the cause of everything that happens, but they *never* act except in disguise. Do you hear me?"

She nodded. She'd heard those words a hundred times.

"You hear and yet you don't understand me, even now," said Father. "The gods have chosen the people of Path, Qing-jao. Only *we* are privileged to hear their voice. Only *we* are allowed to see that they are the cause of all that is and was and will be. To all other people their works remain hidden, a mystery. Your task is not to discover the *true* cause of the disappearance of the Lusitania Fleet—all of Path would know at once that the true cause is that the gods wished it to happen. Your task is to discover the disguise that the gods have created for this event."

Qing-jao felt light-headed, dizzy. She had been so certain that she had the answer, that she had fulfilled her task. Now it was slipping away. The answer was still true, but her task was different now.

"Right now, because we can't find a natural explanation, the gods stand exposed for all of humanity to see, the unbelievers as well as the believers. The gods are *naked*, and we must clothe them. We must find out the series of events the gods have created to explain the disappearance of the fleet, to make it appear natural to the unbelievers. I thought you understood this. We serve Starways Congress, but only because by serving Congress we also serve the gods. The gods wish us to deceive Congress, and Congress wishes to be deceived."

Qing-jao nodded, numb with disappointment that her task was still not finished.

"Does this sound heartless of me?" asked Father. "Am I dishonest? Am I cruel to the unbeliever?"

"Does a daughter judge her father?" whispered Qing-jao.

"Of course she does," said Father. "Every day all people judge all other people. The question is whether we judge wisely."

"Then I judge that it's no sin to speak to the unbelievers in the language of their unbelief," said Qing-jao.

Was that a smile now at the corners of his mouth? "You do understand," said Father. "If ever Congress comes to us, humbly seeking to know the truth, then we will teach them the Way and they'll become part of Path. Until then, we serve the gods by helping the unbelievers deceive themselves into thinking that all things happen because of natural explanations."

Qing-jao bowed until her head nearly touched the floor. "You have tried to teach me this many times, but until now I never had a task that this principle applied to. Forgive the foolishness of your unworthy daughter."

"I have no unworthy daughter," said Father. "I have only my daughter who is Gloriously Bright. The principle you've learned today is one that few on Path will ever really understand. That's why only a few of us are able to deal directly with people from other worlds without baffling or confusing them. You have surprised me today, Daughter, not because you hadn't yet understood it, but because you have come to understand it so young. I was nearly ten years older than you before I discovered it."

"How can I learn something before you did, Father?" The idea of surpassing one of his achievements was almost unthinkable.

"Because you had me to teach you," said Father, "while I had to discover it for myself. But I see that it frightened you to think that perhaps you learned something younger than I did. Do you think it would dishonor me if my daughter surpassed me? On the contrary—there can be no greater honor to a parent than to have a child who is greater."

"I can never be greater than you, Father."

"In a sense that's true, Qing-jao. Because you are my child, all your works are included within mine, as a subset of mine, just as all of us are a subset of our ancestors. But you have so much potential for greatness inside you that I believe there'll come a time when I will be counted greater because of your works than because of my own. If ever the people of Path judge me worthy of some singular honor, it will be at least as much because of your achievements as my own."

With that Father bowed to her, not a courteous bow of dismissal, but a deep bow of respect, his head almost touching the floor. Not quite, for that would be outrageous, almost a mockery, if he actually touched his head to the floor in honor to his own daughter. But he came as close as dignity allowed.

It confused her for a moment, frightened her; then

she understood. When he implied that his chance of being chosen god of Path depended on her greatness, he wasn't speaking of some vague future event. He was speaking of the here and now. He was speaking of her task. If she could find the gods' disguise, the natural explanation for the disappearance of the Lusitania Fleet, then his selection as god of Path would be assured. That was how much he trusted her. That was how important this task was. What was her coming-of-age, compared to her father's godhood? She must work harder, think better, and succeed where all the resources of the military and the Congress had failed. Not for herself, but for Mother, for the gods, and for Father's chance to become one of them.

Qing-jao withdrew from Father's room. She paused in the doorway and glanced at Wang-mu. One glance from the godspoken was enough to tell the girl to follow.

By the time Qing-jao got to her room she was shaking with the pent-up need for purification. All that she had done wrong today—her rebelliousness toward the gods, her refusal to accept purification earlier, her stupidity at not understanding her true task—it came together now. Not that she felt dirty; it wasn't washing she wanted, or self-loathing that she felt. After all, her unworthiness had been tempered by her father's praise, by the god who showed her how to pass through the door. And Wang-mu's having proven to be a good choice—that was a test that Qing-jao had passed, and boldly, too. So it wasn't vileness that made her tremble. She was *hungry* for purification. She longed for the gods to be with her as she served them. Yet no penance that she knew of would be enough to quell her hunger.

Then she knew: She must trace a line on every board in the room.

At once she chose her starting point, the southeast corner; she would begin each tracing at the eastern wall, so that her rituals would all move westward, toward the gods. Last of all would be the shortest board in the room, less than a meter long, in the northwest corner. It would be her reward, that her last tracing would be so brief and easy.

She could hear Wang-mu enter the room softly behind her, but Qing-jao had no time now for mortals. The gods were waiting. She knelt in the corner, scanned the grains to find the one the gods wanted her to follow. Usually she had to choose for herself, and then she always chose the most difficult one, so the gods wouldn't despise her. But tonight she was filled with instant certainty that the gods were choosing for her. The first line was a thick one, wavy but easy to see. Already they were being merciful! Tonight's ritual would be almost a conversation between her and the gods. She had broken through an invisible barrier today; she had come closer to her father's clear understanding. Perhaps someday the gods would speak to her with the sort of clarity that the common people believed all the godspoken heard.

"Holy one," said Wang-mu.

It was as though Qing-jao's joy were made of glass, and Wang-mu had deliberately shattered it. Didn't she know that when a ritual was interrupted, it had to begin again? Qing-jao rose up on her knees and turned to face the girl.

Wang-mu must have seen the fury on Qing-jao's face, but didn't understand it. "Oh, I'm sorry," she said at once, falling to her knees and bowing her head to the floor. "I forgot that I'm not to call you 'holy one.' I only meant to ask you what you were looking for, so I could help you search."

It almost made Qing-jao laugh, that Wang-mu was so mistaken. Of course Wang-mu had no notion that Qing-jao was being spoken to by the gods. And now, her anger interrupted, Qing-jao was ashamed to see how Wang-mu feared her anger; it felt wrong for the girl to be touching her head to the floor. Qing-jao didn't like seeing another person so humiliated.

How did I frighten her so much? I was filled with joy, because the gods were speaking so clearly to me; but my joy was so selfish that when she innocently interrupted me, I turned a face of hate to her. Is this how I answer the gods? They show me a face of love, and I translate it into hatred toward the people, especially one who is in my power? Once again the gods have found a way to show me my unworthiness.

"Wang-mu, you mustn't interrupt me when you find me bowed down on the floor like that." And she explained to Wang-mu about the ritual of purification that the gods required of her.

"Must I do this also?" said Wang-mu.

"Not unless the gods tell you to."

"How will I know?"

"If it hasn't happened to you at your age, Wang-mu, it probably never will. But if it did happen, you'd know, because you wouldn't have the power to resist the voice of the gods in your mind."

Wang-mu nodded gravely. "How can I help you, . . . Qing-jao?" She tried out her mistress's name carefully, reverently. For the first time Qing-jao realized that her name, which sounded sweetly affectionate when her father said it, could sound exalted when it was spoken with such awe. To be called Gloriously Bright at a moment when Qing-jao was keenly aware of her lack of luster was almost painful. But she would not forbid Wang-mu to use her name—the girl had to have *something* to call her, and Wang-mu's reverent tone would serve Qing-jao as a constant ironic reminder of how little she deserved it.

"You can help me by not interrupting," said Qing-jao.

"Should I leave, then?"

Qing-jao almost said yes, but then realized that for

some reason the gods wanted Wang-mu to be part of this penance. How did she know? Because the thought of Wang-mu leaving felt almost as unbearable as the knowledge of her unfinished tracing. "Please stay," said Qing-jao. "Can you wait in silence? Watching me?"

"Yes, . . . Qing-jao."

"If it goes on so long that you can't bear it, you may leave," said Qing-jao. "But only when you see me moving from the west to the east. That means I'm between tracings, and it won't distract me for you to leave, though you mustn't speak to me."

Wang-mu's eyes widened. "You're going to do this with every grain of wood in every board of the floor?"

"No," said Qing-jao. The gods would never be so cruel as that! But even as she thought this, Qing-jao knew that someday there might come a time when the gods would require exactly that penance. It made her sick with dread. "Only one line in each board in the room. Watch with me, will you?"

She saw Wang-mu glance at the time message that glowed in the air over her terminal. It was already the hour for sleep, and both of them had missed their afternoon nap. It wasn't natural for human beings to go so long without sleeping. The days on Path were half again as long as those on Earth, so that they never worked out quite evenly with the internal cycles of the human body. To miss the nap and then delay the sleep was a very hard thing.

But Qing-jao had no choice. And if Wang-mu couldn't stay awake, she'd have to leave now, however the gods resisted that idea. "You must stay awake," said Qing-jao. "If you fall asleep, I'll have to speak to you so you'll move and uncover some of the lines I have to trace. And if I speak to you, I'll have to begin again. Can you stay awake, silent and unmoving?"

Wang-mu nodded. Qing-jao believed that she meant it; she did not really believe the girl could do it. Yet the gods insisted that she let her new secret maid remain—who was Qing-jao to refuse what the gods required of her?

Qing-jao returned to the first board and started her tracing over again. To her relief, the gods were still with her. On board after board she was given the boldest, easiest grain to follow; and when, now and then, she was given a harder one, it invariably happened that the easy grain faded or disappeared off the edge of the board partway along. The gods were caring for her.

As for Wang-mu, the girl struggled mightily. Twice, on the passage back from the west to begin again in the east, Qing-jao glanced at Wang-mu and saw her sleeping. But when Qing-jao began passing near to the place where Wang-mu had lain, she found that her secret maid had wakened and moved so quietly to a place where Qing-jao had already traced that Qing-jao hadn't even heard her movements. A good girl. A worthy choice for a secret maid.

At last, at long last Qing-jao reached the beginning of the last board, a short one in the very corner. She almost spoke aloud in joy, but caught herself in time. The sound of her own voice and Wang-mu's inevitable answer would surely send her back to start again—it would be an unbelievable folly. Qing-jao bent over the beginning of the board, already less than a meter from the northwest corner of the room, and began tracing the boldest line. It led her, clear and true, right to the wall. It was done.

Qing-jao slumped against the wall and began laughing in relief. But she was so weak and tired that her laughter must have sounded like weeping to Wang-mu. In moments the girl was with her, touching her shoulder. "Qing-jao," she said. "Are you in pain?"

Qing-jao took the girl's hand and held it. "Not in pain. Or at least no pain that sleeping won't cure. I'm finished. I'm clean."

Clean enough, in fact, that she felt no reluctance in letting her hand clasp Wang-mu's hand, skin to skin, without filthiness of any kind. It was a gift from the gods, that she had someone's hand to hold when her ritual was done. "You did very well," said Qing-jao. "It was easier for me to concentrate on the tracing, with you in the room."

"I think I fell asleep once, Qing-jao."

"Perhaps twice. But you woke when it mattered, and no harm was done."

Wang-mu began to weep. She closed her eyes but didn't take her hand away from Qing-jao to cover her face. She simply let the tears flow down her cheeks.

"Why are you weeping, Wang-mu?"

"I didn't know," she said. "It really *is* a hard thing to be godspoken. I didn't know."

"And a hard thing to be a true friend to the god-spoken, as well," said Qing-jao. "That's why I didn't want you to be my servant, calling me 'holy one' and fearing the sound of my voice. That kind of servant I'd have to send out of my room when the gods spoke to me."

If anything, Wang-mu's tears flowed harder.

"Si Wang-mu, is it too hard for you to be with me?" asked Qing-jao.

Wang-mu shook her head.

"If it's ever too hard, I'll understand. You can leave me then. I was alone before. I'm not afraid to be alone again."

Wang-mu shook her head, fiercely this time. "How could I leave you, now that I see how hard it is for you?"

"Then it will be written one day, and told in a story, that Si Wang-mu never left the side of Han Qing-jao during her purifications."

Suddenly Wang-mu's smile broke across her face, and her eyes opened into the squint of laughter, despite the tears still shining on her cheeks. "Don't you hear the joke you told?" said Wang-mu. "My name—Si Wang-mu. When they tell that story, they won't know it was your secret maid with you. They'll think it was the Royal Mother of the West."

Qing-jao laughed then, too. But an idea also crossed her mind, that perhaps the Royal Mother was a true ancestor-of-the-heart to Wang-mu, and by having Wang-mu by her side, as her friend, Qing-jao also had a new closeness with this god who was almost the oldest of them all.

Wang-mu laid out their sleeping mats, though Qing-jao had to show her how; it was Wang-mu's proper duty, and Qing-jao would have to let her do it every night, though she had never minded doing it herself. As they lay down, their mats touching edge-to-edge so that no woodgrain lines showed between them, Qing-jao noticed that there was gray light shining through the slats of the windows. They had stayed awake together all through the day and now all through the night. Wang-mu's sacrifice was a noble one. She would be a true friend.

A few minutes later, though, when Wang-mu was asleep and Qing-jao was on the brink of dozing, it occurred to Qing-jao to wonder exactly how it was that Wang-mu, a girl with no money, had managed to bribe the foreman of the righteous labor crew to let her speak to Qing-jao today without interruption. Could some spy have paid the bribe for her, so she could infiltrate the house of Han Fei-tzu? No—Ju Kung-mei, the guardian of the House of Han, would have found out about such a spy and Wang-mu would never have been hired. Wang-mu's bribe wouldn't have been paid in money. She was only fourteen, but Si Wang-mu was already a very pretty girl. Qing-jao had read enough of history and biography to know how women were usually required to pay such bribes.

Grimly Qing-jao decided that the matter must be discreetly investigated, and the foreman dismissed in unnamed disgrace if it were found to be true; through the investigation, Wang-mu's name would never be mentioned in public, so that she would be protected from all harm. Qing-jao had only to mention it to Ju Kungmei and he'd see that it was done.

Qing-jao looked at the sweet face of her sleeping servant, her worthy new friend, and felt overcome by sadness. What most saddened Qing-jao, however, was not the price Wang-mu had paid to the foreman, but rather that she had paid it for such a worthless, painful, terrible job as that of being secret maid to Han Qing-jao. If a woman must sell the doorway to her womb, as so many women had been forced to do through all of human history, surely the gods must let her receive something of value in return.

That is why Qing-jao went to sleep that morning even firmer in her resolve to devote herself to the education of Si Wang-mu. She could not let Wang-mu's education interfere with her struggle with the riddle of the Lusitania Fleet, but she would take all other possible time and give Wang-mu a fit blessing in honor of her sacrifice. Surely the gods must expect no less of her, in return for their having sent her such a perfect secret maid.

8

MIRACLES

<Ender has been plaguing us lately. Insisting that we think of a way to travel faster than light.>

<You said it couldn't be done.>

<That's what we think. That's what human scientists think. But Ender insists that if ansibles can transmit information, we should be able to transmit matter at the same velocity. Of course that's nonsense—there's no comparison between information and physical reality.>

<Why does he want so badly to travel faster than light?>

<It's a silly idea, isn't it—to arrive somewhere before your image does. Like stepping through a mirror in order to try to meet yourself on the other side.>

<Ender and Rooter have talked about this a lot—I've heard them. Ender thinks that perhaps matter and energy are composed of nothing *but* information. That physical reality is nothing but the message that philotes are transmitting to each other.>

<What does Rooter say?>

<He says that Ender is half right. Rooter says that physical reality *is* a message—and the message is a question that the philotes are continually asking God.>

<What is the question?>

<One word: Why?>

<And how does God answer them?>

<With life. Rooter says that life is how God gives purpose to the universe.>

Miro's whole family came to meet him when he returned to Lusitania. After all, they loved him. And he loved them, too, and after a month in space he was looking forward to their company. He knew—intellectually, at least—that his month in space had been a quarter-century to them. He had prepared himself for the wrinkles in Mother's face, for even Grego and Quara to be adults in their thirties. What he had not anticipated, not viscerally, anyway, was that they would be strangers. No, worse than strangers. They were strangers who pitied him and thought they knew him and looked down on him like a child. They were all older than him. All of them. And all younger, because pain and loss hadn't touched them the way it had touched him.

Ela was the best of them, as usual. She embraced him, kissed him, and said, "You make me feel so mortal. But I'm glad to see you young." At least she had the courage to admit that there was an immediate barrier between them, even though she pretended that the barrier was his youth. True, Miro *was* exactly as they remembered him—his face, at least. The long-lost brother returned from the dead; the ghost who comes to haunt the family, eternally young. But the real barrier was the way he moved. The way he spoke.

They had obviously forgotten how disabled he was, how badly his body responded to his damaged brain. The shuffling step, the twisted, difficult speech—their memories had excised all that unpleasantness and had remembered him the way he was before his accident. After all, he had only been disabled for a few months before leaving on his time-dilating voyage. It was easy to forget that, and recall instead the Miro they had known for so many years before. Strong, healthy, the only one able to stand up to the man they had called Father. They couldn't conceal their shock. He could see it in their hesitations, their darting glances, the attempt to ignore the fact that his speech was so hard to understand, that he walked so slowly.

He could sense their impatience. Within minutes he could see how some, at least, were maneuvering to get away. So much to do this afternoon. See you at dinner. This whole thing was making them so uncomfortable they had to escape, take time to assimilate this version of Miro who had just returned to them, or perhaps plot how to avoid him as much as possible in the future. Grego and Quara were the worst, the most eager to get away, which stung him—once they had worshiped him. Of course he understood that this was *why* it was so hard for them to deal with the broken Miro that stood before them. Their vision of the old Miro was the most naive and therefore the most painfully contradicted.

"We thought of a big family dinner," said Ela. "Mother wanted to, but I thought we should wait. Give you some time."

"Hope you haven't been waiting dinner all this time for me," said Miro.

Only Ela and Valentine seemed to realize he was joking; they were the only ones to respond naturally, with a mild chuckle. The others—for all Miro knew, they hadn't even understood his words at all.

They stood in the tall grass beside the landing field, all his family: Mother, now in her sixties, hair steely-gray, her face grim with intensity, the way it had always been. Only now the expression was etched deep in the lines of her forehead, the creases beside her mouth. Her neck was a ruin. He realized that she would die someday. Not for thirty or forty years, probably, but someday. Had he ever realized how beautiful she was, before? He had thought somehow that marrying the Speaker for the Dead would soften her, would make her young again. And maybe it had, maybe Andrew Wiggin had made her young at heart. But the body was still what time had made it. She was old.

Ela, in her forties. No husband with her, but maybe she was married and he simply hadn't come. More likely not. Was she married to her work? She seemed to be so genuinely glad to see him, but even she couldn't hide the look of pity and concern. What, had she expected that a month of lightspeed travel would somehow heal him? Had she thought he would stride off the shuttle as strong and bold as a spacefaring god from some romance?

Quim, now in priestly robes. Jane had told Miro that his next-younger brother was a great missionary. He had converted more than a dozen forests of pequeninos, had baptized them, and, under authority from Bishop Peregrino, ordained priests from among them, to administer the sacraments to their own people. They baptized all the pequeninos that emerged from the mothertrees, all the mothers before they died, all the sterile wives who tended the little mothers and their younglings, all the brothers searching for a glorious death, and all the trees. However, only the wives and brothers could take communion, and as for marriage, it was difficult to think of a meaningful way to perform such a rite between a fathertree and the blind, mindless slugs who were mated with them. Yet Miro could see in Quim's eyes a kind of exaltation. It was the glow of power well used; alone of the Ribeira family, Quim had known all his life what he wanted to do. Now he was doing it. Never mind the theological difficulties—he was

St. Paul to the piggies, and it filled him with constant joy. You served God, little brother, and God has made you his man.

Olhado, his silver eyes gleaming, his arm around a beautiful woman, surrounded by six children—the youngest a toddler, the oldest in her teens. Though the children all watched with natural eyes, they still had picked up their father's detached expression. They didn't watch, they simply gazed. With Olhado that had been natural; it disturbed Miro to think that perhaps Olhado had spawned a family of observers, walking recorders taking up experience to play it back later, but never quite involved. But no, that had to be a delusion. Miro had never been comfortable with Olhado, and so whatever resemblance Olhado's children had to their father was bound to make Miro just as uncomfortable with them, too. The mother was pretty enough. Probably not forty yet. How old had she been when Olhado married her? What kind of woman was she, to accept a man with artificial eyes? Did Olhado record their lovemaking, and play back images for her of how she looked in his eyes?

Miro was immediately ashamed of the thought. Is that all I can think of when I look at Olhado—his deformity? After all the years I knew him? Then how can I expect them to see anything but *my* deformities when they look at me?

Leaving here was a good idea. I'm glad Andrew Wiggin suggested it. The only part that makes no sense is coming back. Why am I here?

Almost against his will, Miro turned to face Valentine. She smiled at him, put her arm around him, hugged him. "It's not so bad," she said.

Not so bad as what?

"I have only the one brother left to greet me," she said. "All your family came to meet you."

"Right," said Miro.

Only then did Jane speak up, her voice taunting him in his ear. "Not *all*."

Shut up, Miro said silently.

"Only one brother?" said Andrew Wiggin. "*Only* me?" The Speaker for the Dead stepped forward and embraced his sister. But did Miro see awkwardness there, too? Was it possible that Valentine and Andrew Wiggin were *shy* with each other? What a laugh. Valentine, bold as brass—she was Demosthenes, wasn't she?—and Wiggin, the man who had broken into their lives and remade their family without so much as a *dá licença*. Could they be timid? Could they feel strange?

"You've aged miserably," said Andrew. "Thin as a rail. Doesn't Jakt provide a decent living for you?"

"Doesn't Novinha cook?" asked Valentine. "And you look stupider than ever. I got here just in time to witness your complete mental vegetation."

"And here I thought you came to save the world."

"The universe. But you first."

She put her arm around Miro again, and around Andrew on the other side. She spoke to the others. "So many of you, but I feel like I know you all. I hope that soon you'll feel that way about me and my family."

So gracious. So able to put people at ease. Even me, thought Miro. She simply *handles* people. The way Andrew Wiggin does. Did she learn it from him, or did he learn it from her? Or was it born into their family? After all, Peter was the supreme manipulator of all time, the original Hegemon. What a family. As strange as mine. Only theirs is strange because of genius, while mine is strange because of the pain we shared for so many years, because of the twisting of our souls. And I the strangest, the most damaged one of all. Andrew Wiggin came to heal the wounds between us, and did it well. But the inner twisting—can that ever be healed?

"How about a picnic?" asked Miro.

This time they all laughed. How was that, Andrew,

Valentine? Did I put them at their ease? Did I help things go smoothly? Have I helped everyone pretend that they're glad to see me, that they have some idea of who I am?

"She wanted to come," said Jane in Miro's ear.

Shut up, said Miro again. I didn't want her to come anyway.

"But she'll see you later."

No.

"She's married. She has four children."

That's nothing to me now.

"She hasn't called out your name in her sleep for years."

I thought you were my friend.

"I am. I can read your mind."

You're a meddling old bitch and you can't read *anything*.

"She'll come to you tomorrow morning. At your mother's house."

I won't be there.

"You think you can run away from this?"

During his conversation with Jane, Miro hadn't heard anything that the others around him were saying, but it didn't matter. Valentine's husband and children had come from the ship, and she was introducing them all around. Particularly to their uncle, of course. It surprised Miro to see the awe with which they spoke to him. But then, *they* knew who he really was. Ender the Xenocide, yes, but also the Speaker for the Dead, the one who wrote the Hive Queen and the Hegemon. Miro knew that *now,* of course, but when he had first met Wiggin it was with hostility—he was just an itinerant speaker for the dead, a minister of a humanist religion who seemed determined to turn Miro's family inside out. Which he had done. I think I was luckier than they are, thought Miro. I got to know him as a person before I ever knew him as a great figure in human history. They'll probably *never* know him as I do.

And *I* don't really know him at all. I don't know anybody, and nobody knows me. We spend our lives guessing at what's going on inside everybody else, and when we happen to get lucky and guess right, we think we "understand." Such nonsense. Even a monkey at a computer will type a word now and then.

You don't know me, none of you, he said silently. Least of all the meddling old bitch who lives in my ear. You hear that?

"All that high-pitched whining—how can I miss it?"

Andrew was putting luggage onto the car. There'd be room for only a couple of passengers. "Miro—you want to ride with Novinha and me?"

Before he could answer, Valentine had taken his arm. "Oh, don't do that," said Valentine. "Walk with Jakt and me. We've all been cooped up on the ship for so long."

"That's right," said Andrew. "His mother hasn't seen him in twenty-five years, but *you* want him to take a stroll. You're the soul of thoughtfulness."

Andrew and Valentine were keeping up the bantering tone they had established from the first, so that no matter which way Miro decided, they would laughingly turn it into a choice between the two Wiggins. At no point would he have to say, I need to ride because I'm a cripple. Nor would he have any excuse to take offense because somebody had singled him out for special treatment. It was so gracefully done that Miro wondered if Valentine and Andrew had discussed it in advance. Maybe they didn't have to discuss things like this. Maybe they had spent so many years together that they knew how to cooperate to smooth things for other people without even thinking about it. Like actors who have performed the same roles together so often that they can improvise without the slightest confusion.

"I'll walk," said Miro. "I'll take the long way. The rest of you go on ahead."

Novinha and Ela started to protest, but Miro saw Andrew put his hand on Novinha's arm, and as for Ela, she was silenced by Quim's arm around her shoulder.

"Come straight home," said Ela. "However long it takes you, do come home."

"Where else?" asked Miro.

Valentine didn't know what to make of Ender. It was only her second day on Lusitania, but already she was sure that something was wrong. Not that there weren't grounds for Ender to be worried, distracted. He had filled her in on the problems the xenobiologists were having with the descolada, the tensions between Grego and Quara, and of course there was always the Congress fleet, death looming over them from every sky. But Ender had faced worries and tensions before, many times in his years as a speaker for the dead. He had plunged into the problems of nations and families, communities and individuals, struggling to understand and then to purge and heal the diseases of the heart. Never had he responded the way he was acting now.

Or perhaps he had, once.

When they were children, and Ender was being groomed to command the fleets being sent against all the bugger worlds, they had brought Ender back to Earth for a season—the lull before the final storm, as it turned out. Ender and Valentine had been apart since he was five years old, not allowed so much as an unsupervised letter between them. Then, suddenly, they changed their policy, and brought Valentine to him. He was being kept at a large private estate near their home town, spending his days swimming and—more often—floating in utter languor on a private lake.

At first Valentine had thought all was well, and she was merely glad to see him at last. But soon she understood that something was deeply wrong. Only in those days she hadn't known Ender so well—after all, he'd been apart from her for more than half his life. Yet she knew that it was wrong for him to seem so preoccupied. No, that wasn't really it. He wasn't *pre*occupied, he was *un*occupied. He had detached himself from the world. And her job was to reconnect him. To bring him back and show him his place in the web of humanity.

Because she succeeded, he was able to go back into space and command the fleets that utterly destroyed the buggers. Ever since that time, his connection with the rest of humanity seemed secure.

Now again she had been apart from him for half a lifetime. Twenty-five years for her, thirty for him. And again he seemed to be detached. She studied him as he took her and Miro and Plikt out by car, skimming over the endless prairies of capim.

"We're like a little boat on the ocean," said Ender.

"Not really," she said, remembering the time that Jakt had taken her out on one of the small net-laying launches. The three-meter waves that lifted them high, then plunged them down into the trench between. On the large fishing boat those waves had barely jostled them as they nestled comfortably in the sea, but in the tiny launch the waves were overwhelming. Literally breathtaking—she had to slide down from her seat onto the deck, embracing the plank bench with both arms, before she could catch her breath. There was no comparison between the heaving, pitching ocean and this placid grassy plain.

Then again, maybe to Ender there was. Maybe when he saw the acres of capim, he saw within it the descolada virus, malevolently adapting itself to slaughter humankind and all its companion species. Maybe to him this prairie rolled and shrugged every bit as brutally as the ocean.

The sailors had laughed at her, not mockingly but tenderly, like parents laughing at the fears of a child.

"These seas are nothing," they said. "You should try doing this in twenty-meter seas."

Ender was as calm, outwardly, as the sailors had been. Calm, unconnected. Making conversation with her and Miro and silent Plikt, but still holding something back. Is there something wrong between Ender and Novinha? Valentine hadn't seen them together long enough to know what was natural between them and what was strained—certainly there were no obvious quarrels. So perhaps Ender's problem was a growing barrier between him and the community of Milagre. That was possible. Valentine certainly remembered how hard it had been for her to win acceptance from the Trondheimers, and she had been married to a man with enormous prestige among them. How was it for Ender, married to a woman whose whole family had already been alienated from the rest of Milagre? Could it be that his healing of this place was not as complete as anyone supposed?

Not possible. When Valentine met with the Mayor, Kovano Zeljezo, and with old Bishop Peregrino that morning, they had shown genuine affection for Ender. Valentine had attended too many meetings not to know the difference between formal courtesies, political hypocrisies, and genuine friendship. If Ender felt detached from these people, it wasn't by *their* choice.

I'm reading too much into this, thought Valentine. If Ender seems to be strange and detached, it's because *we* have been apart so long. Or perhaps because he feels shy with this angry young man, Miro; or perhaps it's Plikt, with her silent, calculating worship of Ender Wiggin, who makes him choose to be distant with us. Or maybe it's nothing more than my insistence that I must meet the hive queen today, at once, even before meeting any of the leaders of the piggies. There's no reason to look beyond present company for the cause of his unconnection.

They first located the hive queen's city by the pall of

smoke. "Fossil fuels," said Ender. "She's burning them up at a disgusting rate. Ordinarily she'd never do that—the hive queens tend their worlds with great care, and they never make such a waste and a stink. But there's a great hurry these days, and Human says that they've given her permission to burn and pollute as much as necessary."

"Necessary for what?" asked Valentine.

"Human won't say, and neither will the hive queen, but I have my guesses, and I imagine you will, too."

"Are the piggies hoping to jump to a fully technological society in a single generation, relying on the hive queen's work?"

"Hardly," said Ender. "They're far too conservative for that. They want to know everything there is to know—but they aren't terribly interested in surrounding themselves with machines. Remember that the trees of the forest freely and gently give them every useful tool. What we call industry still looks like brutality to them."

"What then? Why all this smoke?"

"Ask her," said Ender. "Maybe she'll be honest with *you*."

"Will we actually see her?" asked Miro.

"Oh yes," said Ender. "Or at least—we'll be in her presence. She may even touch us. But perhaps the less we see the better. It's usually dark where she lives, unless she's near to egg-laying. At that time she needs to see, and the workers open tunnels to bring in daylight."

"They don't have artificial light?" asked Miro.

"They never used it," said Ender, "even on the starships that came to Sol System back during the Bugger Wars. They see heat the way we see light. Any source of warmth is clearly visible to them. I think they even arrange their heat sources in patterns that could only be interpreted aesthetically. Thermal painting."

"So why do they use light for egg-laying?" asked Valentine.

"I'd hesitate to call it a ritual—the hive queen has such scorn for human religion. Let's just say it's part of their genetic heritage. Without sunlight there's no egg-laying."

Then they were in the bugger city.

Valentine wasn't surprised at what they found—after all, when they were young, she and Ender had been with the first colony on Rov, a former bugger world. But she knew that the experience would be surprising and alien to Miro and Plikt, and in fact some of the old disorientation came back to her, too. Not that there was anything obviously strange about the city. There were buildings, most of them low, but based on the same structural principles as any human buildings. The strangeness came in the careless way that they were arranged. There were no roads and streets, no attempt to line up the buildings to face the same way. Nor did buildings rise out of the ground to any common height. Some were nothing but a roof resting on the ground; others rose to a great height. Paint seemed to be used only as a preservative—there was no decoration. Ender had suggested that heat might be used aesthetically; it was a sure thing that nothing else was.

"It makes no sense," said Miro.

"Not from the surface," said Valentine, remembering Rov. "But if you could travel the tunnels, you'd realize that it all makes sense underground. They follow the natural seams and textures of the rock. There's a rhythm to geology, and the buggers are sensitive to it."

"What about the tall buildings?" asked Miro.

"The water table is their downward limit. If they need greater height, they have to go up."

"What are they doing that requires a building so tall?" asked Miro.

"I don't know," said Valentine. They were skirting a building that was at least three hundred meters high; in the near distance they could see more than a dozen others.

For the first time on this excursion, Plikt spoke up. "Rockets," she said.

Valentine caught a glimpse of Ender smiling a bit and nodding slightly. So Plikt had confirmed his own suspicions.

"What for?" asked Miro.

Valentine almost said, To get into space, of course! But that wasn't fair—Miro had never lived on a world that was struggling to get into space for the first time. To him, going offplanet meant taking the shuttle to the orbiting station. But the single shuttle used by the humans of Lusitania would hardly do for transporting material outward for any kind of major deepspace construction program. And even if it *could* do the job, the hive queen was unlikely to ask for human help.

"What's she building, a space station?" asked Valentine.

"I think so," said Ender. "But so many rockets, and such large ones—I think she's planning to build it all at once. Probably cannibalizing the rockets themselves. What do you think the throw might be?"

Valentine almost answered with exasperation—how should *I* know? Then she realized that he wasn't asking her. Because almost at once he supplied the answer himself. Which meant that he must have been asking the computer in his ear. No, not a "computer." Jane. He was asking Jane. It was still hard for Valentine to get used to the idea that even though there were only four people in the car, there was a fifth person present, looking and listening through the jewels Ender and Miro both wore.

"She could do it all at once," said Ender. "In fact, given what's known about the chemical emissions here, the hive queen has smelted enough metal to construct not only a space station but also two small long-range starships of the sort that the first bugger expedition brought. Their version of a colony ship."

"Before the fleet arrives," said Valentine. She understood at once. The hive queen was preparing to emigrate. She had no intention of letting her species be trapped on a single planet when the Little Doctor came again.

"You see the problem," said Ender. "She won't tell us what she's doing, and so we have to rely on what Jane observes and what we can guess. And what I'm guessing isn't a very pretty picture."

"What's wrong with the buggers getting offplanet?" asked Valentine.

"Not just the buggers," said Miro.

Valentine made the second connection. That's why the pequeninos had given permission for the hive queen to pollute so badly. That's why there were two ships planned, right from the first. "A ship for the hive queen and a ship for the pequeninos."

"That's what they intend," said Ender. "But the way I see it is—two ships for the descolada."

"Nossa Senhora," whispered Miro.

Valentine felt a chill go through her. It was one thing for the hive queen to seek the salvation of her species. But it was quite another thing for her to carry the deadly self-adapting virus to other worlds.

"You see my quandary," said Ender. "You see why she won't tell me directly what she's doing."

"But you couldn't stop her anyway, could you?" asked Valentine.

"He could warn the Congress fleet," said Miro.

That's right. Dozens of heavily armed starships, converging on Lusitania from every direction—if they were warned about two starships leaving Lusitania, if they were given their original trajectories, they could intercept them. Destroy them.

"You can't," said Valentine.

"I can't stop them and I can't let them go," said Ender. "To stop them would be to risk destroying the buggers and the piggies alike. To let them go would be to risk destroying all of humanity."

"You have to talk to them. You have to reach some kind of agreement."

"What would an agreement with *us* be worth?" asked Ender. "We don't speak for humanity in general. And if we make threats, the hive queen will simply destroy all our satellites and probably our ansible as well. She may do that anyway, just to be safe."

"Then we'd *really* be cut off," said Miro.

"From *everything*," said Ender.

It took Valentine a moment to realize that they were thinking of Jane. Without an ansible, they couldn't speak to her anymore. And without the satellites that orbited Lusitania, Jane's eyes in space would be blinded.

"Ender, I don't understand," said Valentine. "Is the hive queen our *enemy*?"

"That's the question, isn't it?" asked Ender. "That's the trouble with restoring her species. Now that she has her freedom again, now that she's not bundled up in a cocoon hidden in a bag under my bed, the hive queen will act in the best interest of her species—whatever she thinks that is."

"But Ender, it can't be that there has to be war between humans and buggers *again*."

"If there were no human fleet heading toward Lusitania, the question wouldn't come up."

"But Jane has disrupted their communications," said Valentine. "They can't receive the order to use the Little Doctor."

"For now," said Ender. "But Valentine, why do you think Jane risked her own life in order to cut off their communications?"

"Because the order was sent."

"Starways Congress sent the order to destroy this planet. And now that Jane has revealed her power,

they'll be all the more determined to destroy us. Once
they find a way to get Jane out of the way, they'll be
even more certain to act against this world."

"Have you told the hive queen?"

"Not yet. But then, I'm not sure how much she can
learn from my mind without my wanting her to. It's not
exactly a means of communication that I know how to
control."

Valentine put her hand on Ender's shoulder. "Was
this why you tried to persuade me not to come see the
hive queen? Because you didn't want her to learn the
real danger?"

"I just don't want to face her again," said Ender.
"Because I love her and I fear her. Because I'm not
sure whether I should help her or try to destroy her.
And because once she gets those rockets into space,
which could be any day now, she could take away our
power to stop her. Take away our connection with the
rest of humanity."

And, again, what he didn't say: She could cut Ender
and Miro off from Jane.

"I think we definitely need to have a talk with her,"
said Valentine.

"Either that or kill her," said Miro.

"Now you understand my problem," said Ender.

They rode on in silence.

The entrance to the hive queen's burrow was a building that looked like any other. There was no special
guard—indeed, in their whole excursion they hadn't seen
a single bugger. Valentine remembered when she was
young, on her first colony world, trying to imagine what
the bugger cities had looked like when they were fully inhabited. Now she knew—they looked exactly the way
they did when they were dead. No scurrying buggers like
ants swarming over the hills. Somewhere, she knew,
there were fields and orchards being tended under the
open sun, but none of that was visible from here.

Why did this make her feel so relieved?

She knew the answer to the question even as she asked it. She had spent her childhood on Earth during the Bugger Wars; the insectoid aliens had haunted her nightmares, as they had terrified every other child on Earth. Only a handful of human beings, however, had ever seen a bugger in person, and few of those were still alive when she was a child. Even in her first colony, where the ruins of bugger civilization surrounded her, they had found not even one desiccated corpse. All her visual images of the buggers were the horrifying images from the vids.

Yet wasn't she the first person to have read Ender's book, the Hive Queen? Wasn't she the first, besides Ender, to come to think of the hive queen as a person of alien grace and beauty?

She was the first, yes, but that meant little. Everyone else alive today had grown up in a moral universe shaped in part by the Hive Queen and the Hegemon. While she and Ender were the only two left alive who had grown up with the steady campaign of loathing toward the buggers. Of course she felt irrational relief at *not* having to see the buggers. To Miro and Plikt, the first sight of the hive queen and her workers wouldn't have the same emotional tension that it had for her.

I *am* Demosthenes, she reminded herself. I'm the theorist who insisted that the buggers were ramen, aliens who could be understood and accepted. I must simply do my best to overcome the prejudices of my childhood. In due time all of humanity will know of the reemergence of the hive queen; it would be shameful if Demosthenes were the one person who could not receive the hive queen as raman.

Ender took the car in a circle around a smallish building. "This is the right place," he said. He pulled the car to a stop, then slowed the fan to settle it onto the capim near the building's single door. The door was very low—an adult would have to go through on hands and knees.

"How do you know?" asked Miro.

"Because she says so," said Ender.

"Jane?" asked Miro. He looked puzzled, because of course Jane had said nothing of the sort to him.

"The hive queen," said Valentine. "She speaks directly into Ender's mind."

"Nice trick," said Miro. "Can I learn it?"

"We'll see," said Ender. "When you meet her."

As they clambered off the car and dropped into the tall grass, Valentine noticed how Miro and Ender both kept glancing at Plikt. Of course it bothered them that Plikt was so quiet. Or rather, *seemed* so quiet. Valentine thought of Plikt as a loquacious, eloquent woman. But she had also got used to the way Plikt played the mute at certain times. Ender and Miro, of course, were only discovering her perverse silence for the first time, and it bothered them. Which was one of the main reasons Plikt did it. She believed that people revealed themselves most when they were vaguely anxious, and few things brought out nonspecific anxieties like being in the presence of a person who never speaks.

Valentine didn't think much of the technique as a way of dealing with strangers, but she had watched how, as a tutor, Plikt's silences forced her students—Valentine's children—to deal with their own ideas. When Valentine and Ender taught, they challenged their students with dialogue, questions, arguments. But Plikt forced her students to play both sides of an argument, proposing their own ideas, then attacking them in order to refute their own objections. The method probably wouldn't work for most people. Valentine had concluded that it worked so well for Plikt because her wordlessness was *not* complete noncommunication. Her steady, penetrating gaze was in itself an eloquent expression of skepticism. When a student was confronted with that unblinking regard, he soon succumbed to all his own insecurities. Every doubt that the student had managed to put aside and ignore now forced itself forward, where the student had to discover within himself the reasons for Plikt's apparent doubt.

Valentine's oldest, Syfte, had called these one-sided confrontations "staring into the sun." Now Ender and Miro were taking their own turn at blinding themselves in a contest with the all-seeing eye and the naught-saying mouth. Valentine wanted to laugh at their unease, to reassure them. She also wanted to give Plikt a gentle little slap and tell her not to be difficult.

Instead of doing either, Valentine strode to the door of the building and pulled it open. There was no bolt, just a handle to grasp. The door opened easily. She held it open as Ender dropped to his knees and crawled through. Plikt followed immediately. Then Miro sighed and slowly sank to his knees. He was more awkward in crawling than he was in walking—each movement of an arm or leg was made individually, as if it took a second to think of how to make it go. At last he was through, and now Valentine ducked down and squat-walked through the door. She was the smallest, and she didn't have to crawl.

Inside, the only light came from the door. The room was featureless, with a dirt floor. Only as Valentine's eyes became used to the darkness did she realize that the darkest shadow was a tunnel sloping down into the earth.

"There aren't any lights down in the tunnels," Ender said. "She'll direct me. You'll have to hold onto each other's hands. Valentine, you go last, all right?"

"Can we go down standing up?" asked Miro. The question clearly mattered.

"Yes," said Ender. "That's why she chose this entrance."

They joined hands, Plikt holding Ender's hand, Miro

between the two women. Ender led them a few steps
down the slope into the tunnel. It was steep, and the
utter blackness ahead was daunting. But Ender stopped
before the darkness became absolute.

"What are we waiting for?" asked Valentine.

"Our guide," said Ender.

At that moment, the guide arrived. In the darkness,
Valentine could barely see the black-reed arm with a
single finger and thumb as it nudged Ender's hand. Immediately Ender enclosed the finger within his left
hand; the black thumb closed like a pincer over his
hand. Looking up the arm, Valentine tried to see the
bugger it belonged to. All she could actually make out,
though, was a child-size shadow, and perhaps a slight
gleam of reflection off a carapace.

Her imagination supplied all that was missing, and
against her will she shuddered.

Miro muttered something in Portuguese. So he, too,
was affected by the presence of the bugger. Plikt, however, remained silent, and Valentine couldn't tell
whether she trembled or remained entirely unaffected.
Then Miro took a shuffling forward step, pulling on
Valentine's hand, leading her forward into the
darkness.

Ender knew how hard this passage would be for the
others. So far only he, Novinha, and Ela had ever visited the hive queen, and Novinha had come only the
once. The darkness was too unnerving, to move end-
lessly downward without help of eyes, knowing from
small sounds that there was life and movement, invisible but nearby.

"Can we talk?" asked Valentine. Her voice sounded
very small.

"It's a good idea," said Ender. "You won't bother
them. They don't take much notice of sound."

Miro said something. Without being able to see his lips move, Ender found it harder to understand Miro's speech.

"What?" asked Ender.

"We *both* want to know how far it is," Valentine said.

"I don't know," said Ender. "From here, anyway. And she might be almost anywhere down here. There are dozens of nurseries. But don't worry. I'm pretty sure I could find my way out."

"So could I," said Valentine. "With a flashlight, anyway."

"No light," said Ender. "The egg-laying requires sunlight, but after that light only retards the development of the eggs. And at one stage it can kill the larvae."

"But *you* could find your way out of this nightmare in the dark?" asked Valentine.

"Probably," said Ender. "There are patterns. Like spider webs—when you sense the overall structure, each section of tunnel makes more sense."

"These tunnels aren't random?" Valentine sounded skeptical.

"It's like the tunneling on Eros," said Ender. He really hadn't had that much chance to explore when he lived on Eros as a child-soldier. The asteroid had been honeycombed by the buggers when they made it their forward base in the Sol System; it became fleet headquarters for the human allies after it was captured during the first Bugger War. During his months there, Ender had devoted most of his time and attention to learning to control fleets of starships in space. Yet he must have noticed much more about the tunnels than he realized at the time, because the first time the hive queen brought him into her burrows on Lusitania, Ender found that the bends and turns never seemed to take him by surprise. They felt right—no, they felt *inevitable*.

"What's Eros?" asked Miro.

"An asteroid near Earth," said Valentine. "The place where Ender lost his mind."

Ender tried to explain to them something about the way the tunnel system was organized. But it was too complicated. Like fractals, there were too many possible exceptions to grasp the system in detail—it kept eluding comprehension the more closely you pursued it. Yet to Ender it always seemed the same, a pattern that repeated over and over. Or maybe it was just that Ender had got inside the hivemind somehow, when he was studying them in order to defeat them. Maybe he had simply learned to think like a bugger. In which case Valentine was right—he had lost part of his human mind, or at least added onto it a bit of the hivemind.

Finally when they turned a corner there came a glimmer of light. "Graças a deus," whispered Miro. Ender noted with satisfaction that Plikt—this stone woman who could not *possibly* be the same person as the brilliant student he remembered—also let out a sigh of relief. Maybe there was some life in her after all.

"Almost there," said Ender. "And since she's laying, she'll be in a good mood."

"Doesn't she want privacy?" asked Miro.

"It's like a minor sexual climax that goes on for several hours," said Ender. "It makes her pretty cheerful. Hive queens are usually surrounded only by workers and drones that function as part of themselves. They never learn shyness."

In his mind, though, he could feel the intensity of her presence. She could communicate with him anytime, of course. But when he was close, it was as if she were breathing into his brainpan; it became heavy, oppressive. Did the others feel it? Would she be able to speak to them? With Ela there had been nothing—Ela never caught a glimmer of the silent conversation. As for Novinha—she refused to speak of it and denied having heard anything, but Ender suspected that she had simply rejected the alien presence. The hive queen said she could hear both their minds clearly enough, as long as they were present, but couldn't make herself "heard." Would it be the same with these, today?

It would be such a good thing, if the hive queen could speak to another human. She claimed to be able to do it, but Ender had learned over the past thirty years that the hive queen was unable to distinguish between her confident assessments of the future and her sure memories of the past. She seemed to trust her guesses every bit as much as she trusted her memories; and yet when her guesses turned out wrong, she seemed not to remember that she had ever expected a different future from the one that now was past.

It was one of the quirks of her alien mind that disturbed Ender most. Ender had grown up in a culture that judged people's maturity and social fitness by their ability to anticipate the results of their choices. In some ways the hive queen seemed markedly deficient in this area; for all her great wisdom and experience, she seemed as boldly and unjustifiably confident as a small child.

That was one of the things that frightened Ender about dealing with her. Could she keep a promise? If she failed to keep one, would she even realize what she had done?

Valentine tried to concentrate on what the others were saying, but she couldn't take her eyes off the silhouette of the bugger leading them. It was smaller than she had ever imagined—no taller than a meter and a half, probably less. Looking past the others, she could only glimpse parts of the bugger, but that was almost worse than seeing it whole. She couldn't keep herself from thinking that this shiny black *enemy* had a death grip on Ender's hand.

Not a death grip. Not an enemy. Not even a *creature*,

in itself. It had as much individual identity as an ear or a toe—each bugger was just another of the hive queen's organs of action and sensation. In a sense the hive queen was already present with them—was present wherever one of her workers or drones might be, even hundreds of lightyears away. This is not a monster. This is the very hive queen written of in Ender's book. This is the one he carried with him and nurtured during all our years together, though I didn't know it. I have nothing to fear.

Valentine had tried suppressing her fear, but it wasn't working. She was sweating; she could feel her hand slipping in Miro's palsied grip. As they got closer and closer to the hive queen's lair—no, her *home*, her *nursery*—she could feel herself getting more and more frightened. If she couldn't handle it alone, there was no choice but to reach out for help. Where was Jakt? Someone else would have to do.

"I'm sorry, Miro," she whispered. "I think I've got the sweats."

"You?" he said. "I thought it was *my* sweat."

That was good. He laughed. She laughed with him—or at least giggled nervously.

The tunnel suddenly opened wide, and now they stood blinking in a large chamber with a shaft of bright sunlight stabbing through a hole in the vault of the ceiling. The hive queen was smack in the center of the light. There were workers all around, but now, in the light, in the presence of the queen, they all looked so small and fragile. Most of them were closer to one meter than a meter and a half in height, while the queen herself was surely three meters long. And height wasn't the half of it. Her wing-covers looked vast, heavy, almost metallic, with a rainbow of colors reflecting sunlight. Her abdomen was long and thick enough to contain the corpse of an entire human. Yet it narrowed, funnel-like, to an ovipositor at the quivering tip, glistening with a yellowish translucent fluid, gluey, stringy; it dipped into a hole in the floor of the room, deep as it could go, and then came back up, the fluid trailing away like unnoticed spittle, down into the hole.

Grotesque and frightening as this was, a creature so large acting so much like an insect, it did not prepare Valentine for what happened next. For instead of simply dipping her ovipositor into the next hole, the queen turned and seized one of the workers hovering nearby. Holding the quivering bugger between her large forelegs, she drew it close and bit off its legs, one by one. As each leg was bitten off, the remaining legs gesticulated ever more wildly, like a silent scream. Valentine found herself desperately relieved when the last leg was gone, so that the scream was at last gone from her sight.

Then the hive queen pushed the unlimbed worker headfirst down the next hole. Only then did she position her ovipositor over the hole. As Valentine watched, the fluid at the ovipositor's tip seemed to thicken into a ball. But it wasn't fluid after all, or not entirely; within the large drop was a soft, jelly-like egg. The hive queen maneuvered her body so that her face was directly in the sunlight, her multiplex eyes shining like hundreds of emerald stars. Then the ovipositor plunged downward. When it came up, the egg still clung to the end, but on the next emergence the egg was gone. Several times more her abdomen dipped downward, each time coming up with more strands of fluid stringing downward from the tip.

"Nossa Senhora," said Miro. Valentine recognized it from its Spanish equivalent—Nuestra Señora, Our Lady. It was usually an almost meaningless expression, but now it took on a repulsive irony. Not the Holy Virgin, here in this deep cavern. The hive queen was Our Lady of the Darkness. Laying eggs over the bodies of lying workers, to feed the larvae when they hatched.

"It can't always be this way," said Plikt.

For a moment Valentine was simply surprised to hear Plikt's voice. Then she realized what Plikt was saying, and she was right. If a living worker had to be sacrificed for every bugger that hatched, it would be impossible for the population to increase. In fact, it would have been impossible for this hive to exist in the first place, since the hive queen had to give life to her first eggs without the benefit of any legless workers to feed them.

<Only a new queen.>

It came into Valentine's mind as if it were her own idea. The hive queen only had to place a living worker's body into the egg casing when the egg was supposed to grow into a new hive queen. But this wasn't Valentine's own idea; it felt too certain for that. There was no way she could *know* this information, and yet the idea came clearly, unquestionably, all at once. As Valentine had always imagined that ancient prophets and mystics heard the voice of God.

"Did you hear her? Any of you?" asked Ender.

"Yes," said Plikt.

"I think so," said Valentine.

"Hear what?" asked Miro.

"The hive queen," said Ender. "She explained that she only has to place a worker into the egg casing when she's laying the egg of a new hive queen. She's laying five—there are two already in place. She invited us to come to see this. It's her way of telling us that she's sending out a colony ship. She lays five queen-eggs, and then waits to see which is strongest. That's the one she sends."

"What about the others?" asked Valentine.

"If any of them is worth anything, she cocoons the larva. That's what they did to her. The others she kills and eats. She has to—if any trace of a rival queen's body should touch one of the drones that hasn't yet mated with this hive queen, it would go crazy and try to kill her. Drones are very loyal mates."

"Everybody else heard this?" asked Miro. He sounded disappointed. The hive queen wasn't able to talk to him.

"Yes," said Plikt.

"Only a bit of it," said Valentine.

"Empty your mind as best you can," said Ender. "Get some tune going in your head. That helps."

In the meantime, the hive queen was nearly done with the next set of amputations. Valentine imagined stepping on the growing pile of legs around the queen; in her imagination, they broke like twigs with hideous snapping sounds.

<Very soft. Legs don't break. Bend.>

The queen was answering her thoughts.

<You are part of Ender. You can hear me.>

The thoughts in her mind were clearer. Not so intrusive now, more controlled. Valentine was able to feel the difference between the hive queen's communications and her own thoughts.

"Ouvi," whispered Miro. He had heard something at last. "Fala mais, escuto. Say more, I'm listening."

<Philotic connections. You are bound to Ender. When I talk to him through the philotic link, you overhear. Echoes. Reverberations.>

Valentine tried to conceive how the hive queen was managing to speak Stark into her mind. Then she realized that the hive queen was almost certainly doing nothing of the kind—Miro was hearing her in his native language, Portuguese; and Valentine wasn't really hearing Stark at all, she was hearing the English that it was based on, the American English that she had grown up with. The hive queen wasn't sending language to them, she was sending thought, and their brains were making sense of it in whatever language lay deepest in their minds. When Valentine heard the word *echoes* followed by *reverberations*, it wasn't the hive queen struggling for the right word, it was Valentine's own mind grasping for words to fit the meaning.

<Bound to him. Like my people. Except you have free will. Independent philote. Rogue people, all of you.>

"She's making a joke," whispered Ender. "Not a judgment."

Valentine was grateful for his interpretation. The visual image that came with the phrase *rogue people* was of an elephant stomping a man to death. It was an image out of her childhood, the story from which she had first learned the word *rogue*. It frightened her, that image, the way it had frightened her as a child. She already hated the hive queen's presence in her mind. Hated the way she could dredge up forgotten nightmares. Everything about the hive queen was a nightmare. How could Valentine ever have imagined that this being was *raman*? Yes, there was communication. Too *much* of it. Communication like mental illness.

And what she was saying—that they heard her so well because they were philotically connected to Ender. Valentine thought back to what Miro and Jane had said during the voyage—was it possible that her philotic strand was twined into Ender, and through him to the hive queen? But how could such a thing have happened? How could Ender ever have become bound to the hive queen in the first place?

<We reached for him. He was our enemy. Trying to destroy us. We wanted to tame him. Like a rogue.>

The understanding came suddenly, like a door opening. The buggers weren't *all* born docile. They *could* have their own identity. Or at least a breakdown of control. And so the hive queens had evolved a way of capturing them, binding them philotically to get them under control.

<Found him. Couldn't bind him. Too strong.>

And no one guessed the danger Ender was in. That the hive queen expected to be able to capture him, make him the same kind of mindless tool of her will as any bugger.

<Set up a web for him. Found the thing he yearned for. We thought. Got into it. Gave it a philotic core. Bonded with him. But it wasn't enough. Now you. You.>

Valentine felt the word like a hammer inside her mind. She means me. She means me, me, me . . . she struggled to remember who *me* was. Valentine. I'm Valentine. She means Valentine.

<*You* were the one. You. Should have found you. What he longed for most. Not the other thing.>

It gave her a sick feeling inside. Was it possible that the military was correct all along? Was it possible that only their cruel separation of Valentine and Ender saved him? That if she had been with Ender, the buggers could have used her to get control of him?

<No. Could not do it. You are also too strong. We were doomed. We were dead. He couldn't belong to us. But not to you either. Not anymore. Couldn't tame him, but we twined with him.>

Valentine thought of the picture that had come to her mind on the ship. Of people twined together, families tied by invisible cords, children to parents, parents to each other, or to their own parents. A shifting network of strings tying people together, wherever their allegiance belonged. Only now the picture was of herself, tied to Ender. And then of Ender, tied . . . to the hive queen . . . the queen shaking her ovipositor, the strands quivering, and at the end of the strand, Ender's head, wagging, bobbing . . .

She shook her head, trying to clear away the image.

<We don't control him. He's free. He can kill me if he wants. I won't stop him. Will you kill me?>

This time the *you* was not Valentine; she could feel the question recede from her. And now, as the hive queen waited for an answer, she felt another thought in her mind. So close to her own way of thinking that if she hadn't been sensitized, if she hadn't been waiting for Ender to answer, she would have assumed it was her own natural thought.

Never, said the thought in her mind. I will never kill you. I love you.

And along with this thought came a glimmer of genuine emotion toward the hive queen. All at once her mental image of the hive queen included no loathing at all. Instead she seemed majestic, royal, magnificent. The rainbows from her wing-covers no longer seemed like an oily scum on water; the light reflecting from her eyes was like a halo; the glistening fluids at the tip of her abdomen were the threads of life, like milk at the nipple of a woman's breast, stringing with saliva to her baby's suckling mouth. Valentine had been fighting nausea till now, yet suddenly she almost worshiped the hive queen.

It was Ender's thought in her mind, she knew that; that's why the thoughts felt so much like her own. And with his vision of the hive queen, she knew at once that she had been right all along, when she wrote as Demosthenes so many years before. The hive queen *was* raman, strange but still capable of understanding and being understood.

As the vision faded, Valentine could hear someone weeping. Plikt. In all their years together, Valentine had never heard Plikt show such frailty.

"Bonita," said Miro. Pretty.

Was that all he had seen? The hive queen was *pretty*? The communication must be weak indeed between Miro and Ender—but why shouldn't it be? He hadn't known Ender that long or that well, while Valentine had known Ender all her life.

But if that was why Valentine's reception of Ender's thought was so much stronger than Miro's, how could she explain the fact that Plikt had so clearly received far more than Valentine? Was it possible that in all her years of studying Ender, of admiring him without really knowing him, Plikt had managed to bind herself more tightly to Ender than even Valentine was bound?

Of course she had. Of course. Valentine was married. Valentine had a husband. She had children. Her philotic connection to her brother was bound to be weaker. While Plikt had no allegiance strong enough to compete. She had given herself wholly to Ender. So with the hive queen making it possible for the philotic twines to carry thought, of course Plikt received Ender most perfectly. There was nothing to distract. No part of herself withheld.

Could even Novinha, who after all was tied to her children, have sucha complete devotion to Ender? It was impossible. And if Ender had any inkling of this, it had to be disturbing to him. Or attractive? Valentine knew enough of men and women to know that worship was the most seductive of attributes. Have I brought a rival with me, to trouble Ender's marriage?

Can Ender and Plikt read *my* thoughts, even now?

Valentine felt deeply exposed, frightened. As if in answer, as if to calm her, the hive queen's mental voice returned, drowning out any thoughts that Ender might be sending.

<I know what you're afraid of. But my colony won't kill anyone. When we leave Lusitania, we can kill all the descolada virus on our starship.>

Maybe, thought Ender.

<We'll find a way. We won't carry the virus. We don't have to die to save humans. Don't kill us don't kill us.>

I'll never kill you. Ender's thought came like a whisper, almost drowned out in the hive queen's pleading.

We couldn't kill you anyway, thought Valentine. It's *you* who could easily kill us. Once you build your starships. Your weapons. You could be ready for the human fleet. Ender isn't commanding them this time.

<Never. Never kill anybody. Never we promised.>

Peace, came Ender's whisper. Peace. Be at peace, calm, quiet, rest. Fear nothing. Fear no man.

Don't build a ship for the piggies, thought Valentine. Build a ship for yourself, because you can kill the descolada you carry. But not for them.

The hive queen's thoughts abruptly changed from pleading to harsh rebuke.

<Don't they also have a right to live? I promised them a ship. I promised you never to kill. Do you want me to break promises?>

No, thought Valentine. She was already ashamed of herself for having suggested such a betrayal. Or were those the hive queen's feelings? Or Ender's? Was she *really* sure which thoughts and feelings were her own, and which were someone else's?

The fear she felt—it was her own, she was almost certain of that.

"Please," she said. "I want to leave."

"Eu também," said Miro.

Ender took a single step toward the hive queen, reached out a hand toward her. She didn't extend her arms—she was using them to jam the last of her sacrifices into the egg chamber. Instead the queen raised a wing-cover, rotated it, moved it toward Ender until at last his hand rested on the black rainbow surface.

Don't touch it! cried Valentine silently. She'll capture you! She wants to tame you!

"Hush," said Ender aloud.

Valentine wasn't sure whether he was speaking in answer to her silent cries, or was trying to silence something the hive queen was saying only to him. It didn't matter. Within moments Ender had hold of a bugger's finger and was leading them back into the dark tunnel. This time he had Valentine second, Miro third, and Plikt bringing up the rear. So that it was Plikt who cast the last look backward toward the hive queen; it was Plikt who raised her hand in farewell.

All the way up to the surface, Valentine struggled to make sense of what had happened. She had always thought that if only people could communicate mind-to-mind, eliminating the ambiguities of language, then understanding would be perfect and there'd be no more needless conflicts. Instead she had discovered that rather than magnifying differences between people, language might just as easily soften them, minimize them, smooth things over so that people could get along even though they really didn't understand each other. The illusion of comprehension allowed people to think they were more alike than they really were. Maybe language was better.

They crawled out of the building into the sunlight, blinking, laughing in relief, all of them. "Not fun," said Ender. "But you insisted, Val. Had to see her right away."

"So I'm a fool," said Valentine. "Is that news?"

"It was beautiful," said Plikt.

Miro only lay on his back in the capim and covered his eyes with his arm.

Valentine looked at him lying there and caught a glimpse of the man he used to be, the body he used to have. Lying there, he didn't stagger; silent, there was no halting in his speech. No wonder his fellow xenologer had fallen in love with him. Ouanda. So tragic to discover that her father was also his father. That was the worst thing revealed when Ender spoke for the dead in Lusitania thirty years ago. This was the man that Ouanda had lost; and Miro had also lost this man that he was. No wonder he had risked death crossing the fence to help the piggies. Having lost his sweetheart, he counted his life as worthless. His only regret was that he hadn't died after all. He had lived on, broken on the outside as he was broken on the inside.

Why did she think of these things, looking at him? Why did it suddenly seem so real to her?

Was it because this was how he was thinking of himself right now? Was she capturing his image of himself? Was there some lingering connection between their minds?

"Ender," she said, "what happened down there?"

"Better than I hoped," said Ender.

"What was?"

"The link between us."

"You expected that?"

"Wanted it." Ender sat on the side of the car, his feet dangling in the tall grass. "She was hot today, wasn't she?"

"Was she? I wouldn't know how to compare."

"Sometimes she's so intellectual—it's like doing higher mathematics in my head, just talking to her. This time—like a child. Of course, I've never been with her when she was laying queen eggs. I think she may have told us more than she meant to."

"You mean she didn't mean her promise?"

"No, Val, no, she *always* means her promises. She doesn't know how to lie."

"Then what did you mean?"

"I was talking about the link between me and her. How they tried to tame me. That was really something, wasn't it? She was furious there for a moment, when she thought that you might have been the link they needed. You know what that would have meant to them—they wouldn't have been destroyed. They might even have used me to communicate with the human governments. Shared the galaxy with us. Such a lost opportunity."

"You would have been—like a bugger. A *slave* to them."

"Sure. *I* wouldn't have liked it. But all the lives that would have been saved—I was a soldier, wasn't I? If one soldier, dying, can save the lives of billions . . ."

"But it couldn't have worked. You have an independent will," said Valentine.

"Sure," said Ender. "Or at least, more independent than the hive queen can deal with. You too. Comforting, isn't it?"

"I don't feel very comforted right now," said Valentine. "You were inside my head down there. And the hive queen—I feel so violated—"

Ender looked surprised. "It never feels that way to me."

"Well, it's not *just* that," said Valentine. "It was exhilarating, too. And frightening. She's so—large inside my head. Like I'm trying to contain someone bigger than myself."

"I guess," said Ender. He turned to Plikt. "Was it like that for you, too?"

For the first time Valentine realized how Plikt was looking at Ender, with eyes full, a trembling gaze. But Plikt said nothing.

"That strong, huh?" said Ender. He chuckled and turned to Miro.

Didn't he see? Plikt had already been obsessed with Ender. Now, having had him inside her mind, it might have been too much for her. The hive queen talked of taming rogue workers. Was it possible that Plikt had been "tamed" by Ender? Was it possible that she had lost her soul inside his?

Absurd. Impossible. I hope to God it isn't so.

"Come on, Miro," said Ender.

Miro allowed Ender to help him to his feet. Then they climbed back onto the car and headed home to Milagre.

———

Miro had told them that he didn't want to go to mass. Ender and Novinha went without him. But as soon as they were gone, he found it impossible to remain in the house. He kept getting the feeling that someone was just outside his range of vision. In the shadows, a smallish figure, watching him. Encased in smooth hard armor, only two clawlike fingers on its slender arms, arms that could be bitten off and cast down like brittle kindling wood. Yesterday's visit to the hive queen had bothered him more than he dreamed possible.

I'm a xenologer, he reminded himself. My life has been devoted to dealing with aliens. I stood and watched as Ender flayed Human's mammaloid body and I didn't even flinch, because I'm a dispassionate scientist. Sometimes maybe I identify too much with my subjects. But I don't have nightmares about them, I don't start seeing them in shadows.

Yet here he was, standing outside the door of his mother's house because in the grassy fields, in the bright sunlight of a Sunday morning, there were no shadows where a bugger could wait to spring.

Am I the only one who feels this way?

The hive queen *isn't* an insect. She and her people are warm-blooded, just like the pequeninos. They respirate, they sweat like mammals. They may carry with them the structural echoes of their evolutionary link with insects, just as we have our resemblances to lemurs and shrews and rats, but they created a bright and beautiful civilization. Or at least a dark and beautiful one. I should see them the way Ender does, with respect, with awe, with affection.

And all I managed, barely, was *endurance.*

There's no doubt that the hive queen is raman, capable of comprehending and tolerating us. The question is whether *I* am capable of comprehending and tolerating *her.* And I can't be the only one. Ender was so right to keep the knowledge of the hive queen from most of the people of Lusitania. If they once saw what I saw, or even caught a glimpse of a single bugger, the fear would spread, each one's terror would feed on everyone else's dread, until—until something. Something bad. Something monstrous.

Maybe *we're* the varelse. Maybe xenocide is built into the human psyche as into no other species. Maybe the best thing that could happen for the moral good of the universe is for the descolada to get loose, to spread throughout the human universe and break us down to nothing. Maybe the descolada is God's answer to our unworthiness.

Miro found himself at the door of the cathedral. In the cool morning air it stood open. Inside, they had not yet come to the eucharist. He shuffled in, took his place near the back. He had no desire to commune with Christ today. He simply needed the sight of other people. He needed to be surrounded by human beings. He knelt, crossed himself, then stayed there, clinging to the back of the pew in front of him, his head bowed. He would have prayed, but there was nothing in the Pai Nosso to deal with his fear. Give us this day our daily bread? Forgive us our trespasses? Thy kingdom come on earth as it is in heaven? That would be good. God's kingdom, in which the lion could dwell with the lamb.

Then there came to his mind an image of St. Stephen's vision: Christ sitting at the right hand of God. But on the left hand was someone else. The Queen of Heaven. Not the Holy Virgin but the hive queen, with whitish slime quivering on the tip of her abdomen. Miro clenched his hands on the wood of the pew before him. God take this vision from me. Get thee behind me, Enemy.

Someone came and knelt beside him. He didn't dare to open his eyes. He listened for some sound that would declare his companion to be human. But the rustling of cloth could just as easily be wing casings sliding across a hardened thorax.

He had to force this image away. He opened his eyes. With his peripheral vision he could see that his companion was kneeling. From the slightness of the arm, from the color of the sleeve, it was a woman.

"You can't hide from me forever," she whispered.

The voice was wrong. Too husky. A voice that had spoken a hundred thousand times since last he heard it. A voice that had crooned to babies, cried out in the throes of love, shouted at children to come home, come home. A voice that had once, when it was young, told him of a love that would last forever.

"Miro, if I could have taken your cross upon myself, I would have done it."

My *cross?* Is that what it is I carry around with me, heavy and sluggish, weighing me down? And here I thought it was my body.

"I don't know what to tell you, Miro. I grieved—for a long time. Sometimes I think I still do. Losing you—our hope for the future, I mean—it was better anyway—that's what I realized. I've had a good family, a good life, and so will you. But losing you as my friend, as my brother, that was the hardest thing, I was so lonely, I don't know if I ever got over that."

Losing you as my *sister* was the easy part. I didn't need another sister.

"You break my heart, Miro. You're so young. You haven't changed, that's the hardest thing, you haven't changed in thirty years."

It was more than Miro could bear in silence. He didn't lift his head, but he did raise his voice. Far too loudly for the middle of mass, he answered her: "Haven't I?"

He rose to his feet, vaguely aware that people were turning around to look at him.

"Haven't I?" His voice was thick, hard to understand, and he was doing nothing to make it any clearer. He took a halting step into the aisle, then turned to face her at last. "This is how you remember me?"

She looked up at him, aghast—at what? At Miro's speech, his palsied movements? Or simply that he was embarrassing her, that it didn't turn into the tragically romantic scene she had imagined for the past thirty years?

Her face wasn't old, but it wasn't Ouanda, either. Middle-aged, thicker, with creases at the eyes. How old was she? Fifty now? Almost. What did this fifty-year-old woman have to do with him?

"I don't even know you," said Miro. Then he lurched his way to the door and passed out into the morning.

Some time later he found himself resting in the shade of a tree. Which one was this, Rooter or Human? Miro tried to remember—it was only a few weeks ago that he left here, wasn't it?—but when he left, Human's tree was still only a sapling, and now both trees looked to be about the same size and he couldn't remember for sure whether Human had been killed uphill or downhill from Rooter. It didn't matter—Miro had nothing to say to a tree, and they had nothing to say to him.

Besides, Miro had never learned tree language; they hadn't even known that all that beating on trees with sticks was really a language until it was too late for Miro. Ender could do it, and Ouanda, and probably half a dozen other people, but Miro would never learn, because there was no way Miro's hands could hold the sticks and beat the rhythms. Just one more kind of speech that was now useless to him.

"Que dia chato, meu filho."

That was one voice that would never change. And the attitude was unchanging as well: What a rotten day, my son. Pious and snide at the same time—and mocking himself for both points of view.

"Hi, Quim."

"Father Estevão now, I'm afraid." Quim had adopted the full regalia of a priest, robes and all; now he gathered them under himself and sat on the worn-down grass in front of Miro.

"You look the part," said Miro. Quim had matured well. As a kid he had looked pinched and pious. Experience with the real world instead of theological theory had given him lines and creases, but the face that resulted had compassion in it. And strength. "Sorry I made a scene at mass."

"Did you?" asked Quim. "I wasn't there. Or rather, I was at mass—I just wasn't at the cathedral."

"Communion for the ramen?"

"For the children of God. The church already had a vocabulary to deal with strangers. We didn't have to wait for Demosthenes."

"Well, you don't have to be smug about it, Quim. *You* didn't invent the terms."

"Let's not fight."

"Then let's not butt into other people's meditations."

"A noble sentiment. Except that you have chosen to rest in the shade of a friend of mine, with whom I need to have a conversation. I thought it was more polite to talk to you first, before I start beating on Rooter with sticks."

"This is Rooter?"

"Say hi. I know he was looking forward to your return."

"I never knew him."

"But he knew all about *you*. I don't think you realize, Miro, what a hero you are among the pequeninos. They know what you did for them, and what it cost you."

"And do they know what it's probably going to cost us all, in the end?"

"In the end we'll all stand before the judgment bar of God. If a whole planetful of souls is taken there at once, then the only worry is to make sure no one goes unchristened whose soul might have been welcomed among the saints."

"So you don't even care?"

"I care, of course," said Quim. "But let's say that there's a longer view, in which life and death are less important matters than choosing what *kind* of life and what *kind* of death we have."

"You really do believe all this, don't you," said Miro.

"Depending on what you mean by 'all this,' yes, I do."

"I mean all of it. A living God, a resurrected Christ, miracles, visions, baptism, transubstantiation . . ."

"Yes."

"Miracles. Healing."

"Yes."

"Like at the shrine to Grandfather and Grandmother."

"Many healings have been reported there."

"Do you believe in them?"

"Miro, I don't know—some of them might have been hysterical. Some might have been a placebo effect. Some purported healings might have been spontaneous remissions or natural recoveries."

"But some were real."

"Might have been."

"You believe that miracles are *possible*."

"Yes."

"But you don't think any of them actually happen."

"Miro, I believe that they *do* happen. I just don't know if people accurately perceive which events are miracles and which are not. There are no doubt many miracles claimed which were not miracles at all. There are also probably many miracles that no one recognized when they occurred."

"What about me, Quim?"

"What about you?"

"Why no miracle for me?"

Quim ducked his head, pulled at the short grass in front of him. It was a habit when he was a child, trying to avoid a hard question; it was the way he responded when their supposed father, Marcão, was on a drunken rampage.

"What is it, Quim? Are miracles only for other people?"

"Part of the miracle is that no one knows why it happens."

"What a weasel you are, Quim."

Quim flushed. "You want to know why you don't get a miraculous healing? Because you don't have faith, Miro."

"What about the man who said, Yes Master, I believe—forgive my unbelief?"

"Are you that man? Have you even asked for a healing?"

"I'm asking now," said Miro. And then, unbidden, tears came to his eyes. "O God," he whispered. "I'm so ashamed."

"Of what?" asked Quim. "Of having asked God for help? Of crying in front of your brother? Of your sins? Of your doubts?"

Miro shook his head. He didn't know. These questions were all too hard. Then he realized that he did know the answer. He held out his arms from his sides. "Of this body," he said.

Quim reached out and took his arms near the shoulder, drew them toward him, his hands sliding down Miro's arms until he was clasping Miro's wrists. "This is my body which is given for you, he told us. The way you gave your body for the pequeninos. For the little ones."

"Yeah, Quim, but he got his body back, right?"

"He died, too."

"Is *that* how I get healed? Find a way to die?"

"Don't be an ass," said Quim. "Christ didn't kill himself. That was Judas's ploy."

Miro's anger exploded. "All those people who get their *colds* cured, who get their *migraines* miraculously taken from them—are you telling me they deserve more from God than I do?"

"Maybe it isn't based on what you deserve. Maybe it's based on what you need."

Miro lunged forward, seizing the front of Quim's robe between his half-spastic fingers. "I need my body back!"

"Maybe," said Quim.

"What do you mean *maybe*, you simpering smug asshole!"

"I mean," said Quim mildly, "that while you certainly *want* your body back, it may be that God, in his great wisdom, knows that for you to become the best man you can be, you *need* to spend a certain amount of time as a cripple."

"How much time?" Miro demanded.

"Certainly no longer than the rest of your life."

Miro grunted in disgust and released Quim's robe.

"Maybe less," said Quim. "I hope so."

"Hope," said Miro contemptuously.

"Along with faith and pure love, it's one of the great virtues. You should try it."

"I saw Ouanda."

"She's been trying to speak to you since you arrived."

"She's old and fat. She's had a bunch of babies and lived thirty years and some guy she married has plowed her up one side and down the other all that time. I'd rather have visited her grave!"

"How generous of you."

"You know what I mean! Leaving Lusitania was a good idea, but thirty years wasn't long enough."

"You'd rather come back to a world where no one knows you."

"No one knows me here, either."

"Maybe not. But we love you, Miro."

"You love what I used to be."

"You're the same man, Miro. You just have a different body."

Miro struggled to his feet, leaning against Rooter for support as he got up. "Talk to your tree friend, Quim. You've got nothing to say that *I* want to hear."

"So you think," said Quim.

"You know what's worse than an asshole, Quim?"

"Sure," said Quim. "A hostile, bitter, self-pitying, abusive, miserable, *useless* asshole who has far too high an opinion of the importance of his own suffering."

It was more than Miro could bear. He screamed in fury and threw himself at Quim, knocking him to the ground. Of course Miro lost his own balance and fell on top of his brother, then got tangled in Quim's robes. But that was all right; Miro wasn't trying to get up, he was trying to beat some pain into Quim, as if by doing that he would remove some from himself.

After only a few blows, though, Miro stopped hitting Quim and collapsed in tears, weeping on his brother's chest. After a moment he felt Quim's arms around him. Heard Quim's soft voice, intoning a prayer.

"Pai Nosso, que estás no céu." From there, however, the incantation stopped and the words turned new and therefore real. "O teu filho está com dor, o meu irmão precisa a resurreição da alma, ele merece o refresco da esperança."

Hearing Quim give voice to Miro's pain, to his outrageous demands, made Miro ashamed again. Why should Miro imagine that he *deserved* new hope? How could he dare to demand that Quim pray for a miracle for him, for his body to be made whole? It was unfair, Miro knew, to put Quim's faith on the line for a self-pitying unbeliever like him.

But the prayer went on. "Ele deu tudo aos pequeninos, e tu nos disseste, Salvador, que qualquer coisa que fazemos a estes pequeninos, fazemos a ti."

Miro wanted to interrupt. If I gave all to the pequeninos, I did it for them, not for myself. But Quim's words held him silent: You told us, Savior, that whatever we do to these little ones, we do to you. It was as if Quim were demanding that God hold up his end of a bargain. It was a strange sort of relationship that Quim must have with God, as if he had a right to call God to account.

"Ele não é como Jó, perfeito na coração."

No, I'm not as perfect as Job. But I've lost everything, just as Job did. Another man fathered my children on the woman who should have been my wife. Others have accomplished my accomplishments. And where Job had boils, I have this lurching half-paralysis—would Job trade with me?

"Restabeleçe ele como restabeleceste Jó. Em nome do Pai, e do Filho, e do Espírito Santo. Amem." Restore him as you restored Job.

Miro felt his brother's arms release him, and as if it were those arms, not gravity, that held him on his brother's chest, Miro rose up at once and stood looking down on his brother. A bruise was growing on Quim's cheek. His lip was bleeding.

"I hurt you," said Miro. "I'm sorry."

"Yes," said Quim. "You did hurt me. And I hurt you. It's a popular pastime here. Help me up."

For a moment, just one fleeting moment, Miro forgot that he was crippled, that he could barely maintain his balance himself. For just that moment he began to reach out a hand to his brother. But then he staggered as his balance slipped, and he remembered. "I can't," he said.

"Oh, shut up about being crippled and give me a hand."

So Miro positioned his legs far apart and bent down over his brother. His younger brother, who now was nearly three decades his senior, and older still in wisdom and compassion. Miro reached out his hand. Quim gripped it, and with Miro's help rose up from the ground. The effort was exhausting for Miro; he hadn't the strength for this, and Quim wasn't faking it, he was relying on Miro to lift him. They ended up facing each other, shoulder to shoulder, hands still together.

"You're a good priest," said Miro.

"Yeah," said Quim. "And if I ever need a sparring partner, you'll get a call."

"Will God answer your prayer?"

"Of course. God answers all prayers."

It took only a moment for Miro to realize what Quim meant. "I mean, will he say *yes*."

"Ah. That's the part I'm never sure about. Tell me later if he did."

Quim walked—rather stiffly, limping—to the tree. He bent over and picked up a couple of talking sticks from the ground.

"What are you talking to Rooter about?"

"He sent word that I need to talk to him. There's some kind of heresy in one of the forests a long way from here."

"You convert them and then they go crazy, huh?" said Miro.

"No, actually," said Quim. "This is a group that I never preached to. The fathertrees all talk to each other, so the ideas of Christianity are already everywhere in the world. As usual, heresy seems to spread faster than truth. And Rooter's feeling guilty because it's based on a speculation of his."

"I guess that's a serious business for you," said Miro.

Quim winced. "Not just for *me*."

"I'm sorry. I meant, for the church. For believers."

"Nothing so parochial as that, Miro. These pequeninos have come up with a really interesting heresy. Once, not long ago, Rooter speculated that, just as Christ came to human beings, the Holy Ghost might someday come to the pequeninos. It's a gross misinterpretation of the Holy Trinity, but this one forest took it quite seriously."

"Sounds pretty parochial to me."

"Me too. Till Rooter told me the specifics. You see, they're convinced that the descolada virus is the incarnation of the Holy Ghost. It makes a perverse kind of sense—since the Holy Ghost has always dwelt everywhere, in all God's creations, it's appropriate for its incarnation to be the descolada virus, which also penetrates into every part of every living thing."

"They worship the *virus*?"

"Oh, yes. After all, didn't you scientists discover that the pequeninos were *created*, as sentient beings, by the descolada virus? So the virus is imbued with the creative power, which means it has a divine nature."

"I guess there's as much literal evidence for that as for the incarnation of God in Christ."

"No, there's a lot *more*. But if that were all, Miro, I'd regard it as a church matter. Complicated, difficult, but—as you said—parochial."

"So what is it?"

"The descolada is the second baptism. By fire. Only the pequeninos can endure that baptism, and it carries them into the third life. They are clearly closer to God than humans, who have been denied the third life."

"The mythology of superiority. We could expect that, I guess," said Miro. "Most communities attempting to survive under irresistible pressure from a dominant culture develop a myth that allows them to believe they are somehow a special people. Chosen. Favored by the gods. Gypsies, Jews—plenty of historical precedents."

"Try this one, Senhor Zenador. Since the pequeninos are the ones chosen by the Holy Ghost, it's their mission to spread this second baptism to every tongue and every people."

"Spread the *descolada*?"

"To every world. Sort of a portable judgment day. They arrive, the descolada spreads, adapts, kills—and everybody goes to meet their Maker."

"God help us."

"So we hope."

Then Miro made a connection with something he had learned only the day before. "Quim, the buggers are building a ship for the pequeninos."

"So Ender told me. And when I confronted Father Daymaker about it—"

"He's a pequenino?"

"One of Human's children. He said, 'Of course,' as if everyone knew about it. Maybe that's what he thought—that if the pequeninos know it, then it's *known*. He also told me that this heretic group is angling to try to get command of the ship."

"Why?"

"So they can take it to an inhabited world, of course. Instead of finding an uninhabited planet to terraform and colonize."

"I think we'd have to call it lusiforming."

"Funny." Quim wasn't laughing, though. "They might get their way. This idea of pequeninos being a superior species is popular, especially among non-Christian pequeninos. Most of them aren't very sophisticated. They don't catch on to the fact that they're talking about xenocide. About wiping out the human race."

"How could they miss a little fact like that?"

"Because the heretics are stressing the fact that God loves the humans so much that he sent his only beloved son. You remember the scripture."

"Whoever believes in him will not perish."

"Exactly. Those who believe will have eternal life. As they see it, the third life."

"So those who die must have been the unbelievers."

"Not all the pequeninos are lining up to volunteer for service as itinerant destroying angels. But enough of them are that it has to be stopped. Not just for the sake of Mother Church."

"Mother Earth."

"So you see, Miro, sometimes a missionary like me takes on a great deal of importance in the world. Somehow I have to persuade these poor heretics of the error of their ways and get them to accept the doctrine of the church."

"Why are you talking to Rooter now?"

"To get the one piece of information the pequeninos never give us."

"What's that?"

"Addresses. There are thousands of pequenino forests on Lusitania. Which one is the heretic community? Their starship will be long gone before I find it by random forest-hopping on my own."

"You're going *alone*?"

"I always do. I can't take any of the little brothers with me, Miro. Until a forest has been converted, they have a tendency to kill pequenino strangers. One case where it's better to be raman than utlanning."

"Does Mother know you're going?"

"Please be practical, Miro. I have no fear of Satan, but Mother . . ."

"Does Andrew know?"

"Of course. He insists on going with me. The Speaker for the Dead has enormous prestige, and he thinks he could help me."

"So you *won't* be alone."

"Of course I will. When has a man clothed in the whole armor of God ever needed the help of a humanist?"

"Andrew's a Catholic."

"He goes to mass, he takes communion, he confesses regularly, but he's still a speaker for the dead and I don't think he really believes in God. I'll go alone."

Miro looked at Quim with new admiration. "You're one tough son of a bitch, aren't you?"

"Welders and smiths are tough. Sons of bitches have problems of their own. I'm just a servant of God and of the church, with a job to do. I think recent evidence suggests that I'm in more danger from my brother than I am among the most heretical of pequeninos. Since the death of Human, the pequeninos have kept the worldwide oath—not one has ever raised a hand in violence against a human being. They may be heretics, but they're still pequeninos. They'll keep the oath."

"I'm sorry I hit you."

"I received it as if it were an embrace, my son."

"I wish it had been one, Father Estevão."

"Then it was."

Quim turned to the tree and began to beat out a tattoo. Almost at once, the sound began to shift, changing in pitch and tone as the hollow spaces within the tree changed shape. Miro waited a few moments, listening, even though he didn't understand the language of the fathertrees. Rooter was speaking with the only audible voice the fathertrees had. Once he had spoken with a voice, once had articulated with lips and tongue and teeth. There was more than one way to lose your body. Miro had passed through an experience that should have killed him. He had come out of it crippled. But he could still move, however clumsily, could still speak, however slowly. He thought he was suffering like Job. Rooter and Human, far more crippled than he, thought they had received eternal life.

"Pretty ugly situation," said Jane in his ear.

Yes, said Miro silently.

"Father Estevão shouldn't go alone," she said. "The pequeninos used to be devastatingly effective warriors. They haven't forgotten how."

So tell Ender, said Miro. I don't have any power here.

"Bravely spoken, my hero," said Jane. "I'll talk to Ender while you wait around here for your miracle."

Miro sighed and walked back down the hill and through the gate.

9

PINEHEAD

<I've been talking to Ender and his sister, Valentine. She's a historian.>

<Explain this.>

<She searches through the books to find out the stories of humans, and then writes stories about what she finds and gives them to all the other humans.>

<If the stories are already written down, why does she write them again?>

<Because they aren't well understood. She helps people understand them.>

<If the people closer to that time didn't understand them, how can she, coming later, understand them better?>

<I asked this myself, and Valentine said that she doesn't always understand them better. But the old writers understood what the stories meant to the people of their time, and she understands what the stories mean to people of *her* time.>

<So the story changes.>

<Yes.>

<And yet each time they still think of the story as a true memory?>

<Valentine explained something about some stories being true and others being truthful. I didn't understand any of it.>

<Why don't they just remember their stories accurately in the first place? Then they wouldn't have to keep lying to each other.>

Qing-jao sat before her terminal, her eyes closed, thinking. Wang-mu was brushing Qing-jao's hair; the tugs, the strokes, the very breath of the girl was a comfort to her.

This was a time when Wang-mu could speak freely, without fear of interrupting her. And, because Wang-mu was Wang-mu, she used hair-brushing time for questions. She had so many questions.

The first few days her questions had all been about the speaking of the gods. Of course, Wang-mu had been greatly relieved to learn that almost always tracing a single woodgrain line was enough—she had been afraid after that first time that Qing-jao would have to trace the whole floor every day.

But she still had questions about everything to do with purification. Why don't you just get up and trace a line every morning and have done with it? Why don't you just have the floor covered in carpet? It was so hard to explain that the gods can't be fooled by silly stratagems like that.

What if there were no wood at all in the whole world? Would the gods burn you up like paper? Would a dragon come and carry you off?

Qing-jao couldn't answer Wang-mu's questions except to say that this is what the gods required of her. If there were no woodgrain, the gods wouldn't require her to trace it. To which Wang-mu replied that they should make a law against wooden floors, then, so that Qing-jao could be shut of the whole business.

Those who hadn't heard the voice of the gods simply couldn't understand.

Today, though, Wang-mu's question had nothing to do with the gods—or, at least, had nothing to do with them *at first.*

"What is it that finally stopped the Lusitania Fleet?" asked Wang-mu.

Almost, Qing-jao simply took the question in stride; almost she answered with a laugh: If I knew that, I could rest! But then she realized that Wang-mu probably shouldn't even know that the Lusitania Fleet had disappeared.

"How would you know anything about the Lusitania Fleet?"

"I can *read,* can't I?" said Wang-mu, perhaps a little too proudly.

But why shouldn't she be proud? Qing-jao had told her, truthfully, that Wang-mu learned very quickly indeed, and figured out many things for herself. She was very intelligent, and Qing-jao knew she shouldn't be surprised if Wang-mu understood more than was told to her directly.

"I can see what you have on your terminal," said Wang-mu, "and it always has to do with the Lusitania Fleet. Also you discussed it with your father the first day I was here. I didn't understand most of what you said, but I knew it had to do with the Lusitania Fleet." Wang-mu's voice was suddenly filled with loathing. "May the gods piss in the face of the man who launched that fleet."

Her vehemence was shocking enough; the fact that Wang-mu was speaking against Starways Congress was unbelievable.

"Do you know who it was that launched the fleet?" asked Qing-jao.

"Of course. It was the selfish politicians in Starways Congress, trying to destroy any hope that a colony world could win its independence."

So Wang-mu *knew* she was speaking treasonously. Qing-jao remembered her own similar words, long ago, with loathing; to have them said again in her presence—and by her own secret maid—was outrageous. "What do you know of these things? These are matters for Congress, and here you are speaking of independence and colonies and—"

Wang-mu was on her knees, head bowed to the floor. Qing-jao was at once ashamed for speaking so harshly.

"Oh, get up, Wang-mu."

"You're angry with me."

"I'm shocked to hear you talk like that, that's all. Where did you hear such nonsense?"

"Everybody says it," said Wang-mu.

"Not everybody," said Qing-jao. "Father never says it. On the other hand, *Demosthenes* says that sort of thing all the time." Qing-jao remembered how she had felt when she first read the words of Demosthenes—how logical and right and fair he had sounded. Only later, after Father had explained to her that Demosthenes was the enemy of the rulers and therefore the enemy of the gods, only then did she realize how oily and deceptive the traitor's words had been, which had almost seduced her into believing that the Lusitania Fleet was evil. If Demosthenes had been able to come so close to fooling an educated godspoken girl like Qing-jao, no wonder that she was hearing his words repeated like truth in the mouth of a common girl.

"Who is Demosthenes?" asked Wang-mu.

"A traitor who is apparently succeeding better than anyone thought." Did Starways Congress realize that Demosthenes' ideas were being repeated by people who had never heard of him? Did anyone understand what this meant? Demosthenes' ideas were now the common wisdom of the common people. Things had reached a more dangerous turn than Qing-jao had imagined. Father was wiser; he must know already. "Never mind," said Qing-jao. "Tell me about the Lusitania Fleet."

"How can I, when it will make you angry?"

Qing-jao waited patiently.

"All right then," said Wang-mu, but she still looked wary. "Father says—and so does Pan Ku-wei, his very wise friend who once took the examination for the civil service and came very very close to passing—"

"What do they say?"

"That it's a very bad thing for Congress to send a huge fleet—and *so* huge—all to attack the tiniest colony simply because they refused to send away two of their citizens for trial on another world. They say that justice is completely on the side of Lusitania, because to send people from one planet to another against their will is to take them away from family and friends forever. That's like sentencing them before the trial."

"What if they're guilty?"

"That's for the courts to decide on their own world, where people know them and can measure their crime fairly, not for Congress to decide from far away where they know nothing and understand less." Wang-mu ducked her head. "That's what Pan Ku-wei says."

Qing-jao stilled her own revulsion at Wang-mu's traitorous words; it was important to know what the common people thought, even if the very hearing of it made Qing-jao sure the gods would be angry with her for such disloyalty. "So you think that the Lusitania Fleet should never have been sent?"

"If they can send a fleet against Lusitania for no good reason, what's to stop them from sending a fleet against Path? We're also a colony, not one of the Hundred Worlds, not a member of Starways Congress. What's to stop them from declaring that Han Fei-tzu is a traitor and making him travel to some faraway planet and never come back for sixty years?"

The thought was a terrible one, and it was presumptuous of Wang-mu to bring her father into the discussion, not because she was a servant, but because it would be presumptuous of *anyone* to imagine the great Han Fei-tzu being convicted of a crime. Qing-jao's composure failed her for a moment, and she spoke her outrage: "Starways Congress would never treat my father like a criminal!"

"Forgive me, Qing-jao. You told me to repeat what my father said."

"You mean your *father* spoke of Han Fei-tzu?"

"All the people of Jonlei know that Han Fei-tzu is the most honorable man of Path. It's our greatest pride, that the House of Han is part of our city."

So, thought Qing-jao, you knew exactly how ambitious you were being when you set out to become his daughter's maid.

"I meant no disrespect, nor did they. But isn't it true that if Starways Congress wanted to, they could order Path to send your father to another world to stand trial?"

"They would never—"

"But *could* they?" insisted Wang-mu.

"Path is a colony," said Qing-jao. "The law allows it, but Starways Congress would never—"

"But if they did it to Lusitania, why wouldn't they do it to Path?"

"Because the xenologers on Lusitania were guilty of crimes that—"

"The people of Lusitania didn't think so. Their government refused to send them off for trial."

"That's the worst part. How can a planetary government dare to think they know better than Congress?"

"But they knew *everything*," said Wang-mu, as if this idea were so natural that everyone must know it. "They knew those people, those xenologers. If Starways Congress ordered Path to send Han Fei-tzu to go stand trial on another world for a crime we know he didn't commit, don't you think we would also rebel rather than send such a great man? And then they would send a fleet against us."

"Starways Congress is the source of all justice in the Hundred Worlds." Qing-jao spoke with finality. The discussion was over.

Impudently, Wang-mu didn't fall silent. "But Path isn't one of the Hundred Worlds yet, is it?" she said. "We're just a colony. They can do what they want, and that's not right."

Wang-mu nodded her head at the end, as if she thought she had utterly prevailed. Qing-jao almost laughed. She *would* have laughed, in fact, if she hadn't been so angry. Partly she was angry because Wang-mu had interrupted her many times and had even contradicted her, something that her teachers had always been very careful not to do. Still, Wang-mu's audacity was probably a good thing, and Qing-jao's anger was a sign that she had become too used to the undeserved respect people showed to her ideas simply because they fell from the lips of the godspoken. Wang-mu must be encouraged to speak to her like this. That part of Qing-jao's anger was wrong, and she must get rid of it.

But much of Qing-jao's anger was because of the way Wang-mu had spoken about Starways Congress. It was as if Wang-mu didn't think of Congress as the supreme authority over all of humanity; as if Wang-mu imagined that Path was more important than the collective will of all the worlds. Even if the inconceivable happened and Han Fei-tzu were ordered to stand trial on a world a hundred lightyears away, he would do it without murmur—and he would be furious if anyone on Path made the slightest resistance. To rebel like Lusitania? Unthinkable. It made Qing-jao feel dirty just to think of it.

Dirty. Impure. To hold such a rebellious thought

made her start searching for a woodgrain line to trace.

"Qing-jao!" cried Wang-mu, as soon as Qing-jao knelt and bowed over the floor. "Please tell me that the gods aren't punishing you for hearing the words I said!"

"They aren't punishing me," said Qing-jao. "They're purifying me."

"But they weren't even *my* words, Qing-jao. They were the words of people who aren't even here."

"They were impure words, whoever said them."

"But that's not fair, to make you cleanse yourself for ideas that you never even thought of or believed in!"

Worse and worse! Would Wang-mu never stop? "Now must I hear you tell me that the gods themselves are unfair?"

"They are, if they punish you for other people's words!"

The girl was outrageous. "Now you are wiser than the gods?"

"They might as well punish you for being pulled on by gravity, or being fallen on by rain!"

"If they tell me to purify myself for such things, then I'll do it, and call it justice," said Qing-jao.

"Then justice has no meaning!" cried Wang-mu. "When you say the word, you mean whatever-the-gods-happen-to-decide. But when *I* say the word, I mean fairness, I mean people being punished only for what they did on purpose, I mean—"

"It's what the gods mean by justice that I must listen to."

"Justice is justice, whatever the gods might say!"

Almost Qing-jao rose up from the floor and slapped her secret maid. It would have been her right, for Wang-mu was causing her as much pain as if she had struck her. But it was not Qing-jao's way to strike a person who was not free to strike back. Besides, there was a far more interesting puzzle here. After all, the gods had sent Wang-mu to her—Qing-jao was already sure of that. So instead of arguing with Wang-mu directly, Qing-jao should try to understand what the gods *meant* by sending her a servant who would say such shameful, disrespectful things.

The gods had caused Wang-mu to say that it was unjust to punish Qing-jao for simply hearing another person's disrespectful opinions. Perhaps Wang-mu's statement was true. But it was also true that the gods could not be unjust. Therefore it must be that Qing-jao was not being punished for simply hearing the treasonous opinions of the people. No, Qing-jao had to purify herself because, in her heart of hearts, some part of her must *believe* those opinions. She must cleanse herself because deep inside she still doubted the heavenly mandate of Starways Congress; she still believed they were not just.

Qing-jao immediately crawled to the nearest wall and began looking for the right woodgrain line to follow. Because of Wang-mu's words, Qing-jao had discovered a secret filthiness inside herself. The gods had brought her another step closer to knowing the darkest places inside herself, so that she might someday be utterly filled with light and thus earn the name that even now was still only a mockery. Some part of me doubts the righteousness of Starways Congress. O Gods, for the sake of my ancestors, my people, and my rulers, and last of all for me, purge this doubt from me and make me clean!

When she finished tracing the line—and it took only a single line to make her clean, which was a good sign that she had learned something true—there sat Wang-mu, watching her. All of Qing-jao's anger was gone now, and indeed she was grateful to Wang-mu for having been an unwitting tool of the gods in helping her learn new truth. But still, Wang-mu had to understand that she had been out of line.

"In this house, we are loyal servants of Starways

Congress," said Qing-jao, her voice soft, her expression as kind as she could make it. "And if you're a loyal servant of this house, you'll also serve Congress with all your heart." How could she explain to Wang-mu how painfully she had learned that lesson herself—how painfully she was still learning it? She needed Wang-mu to help her, not make it harder.

"Holy one, I didn't know," said Wang-mu, "I didn't guess. I had always heard the name of Han Fei-tzu mentioned as the noblest servant of Path. I thought it was the Path that you served, not Congress, or I never would have . . ."

"Never would have come to work here?"

"Never would have spoken harshly about Congress," said Wang-mu. "I would serve you even if you lived in the house of a dragon."

Maybe I do, thought Qing-jao. Maybe the god who purifies me is a dragon, cold and hot, terrible and beautiful.

"Remember, Wang-mu, that the world called Path is not the Path itself, but only was named so to remind us to live the true Path every day. My father and I serve Congress because they have the mandate of heaven, and so the Path requires that we serve them even above the wishes or needs of the particular world called Path."

Wang-mu looked at her with wide eyes, unblinking. Did she understand? Did she believe? No matter—she would come to believe in time.

"Go away now, Wang-mu. I have to work."

"Yes, Qing-jao." Wang-mu immediately got up and backed away, bowing. Qing-jao turned back to her terminal. But as she began to call up more reports into the display, she became aware that someone was in the room with her. She whirled around on her chair; there in the doorway stood Wang-mu.

"What is it?" asked Qing-jao.

"Is it the duty of a secret maid to tell you whatever

wisdom comes to her mind, even if it turns out to be foolishness?"

"You can say whatever you like to me," said Qing-jao. "Have I ever punished you?"

"Then please forgive me, my Qing-jao, if I dare to say something about this great task you are working on."

What did Wang-mu know of the Lusitania Fleet? Wang-mu was a quick student, but Qing-jao was still teaching her at such a primitive level in every subject that it was absurd to think Wang-mu could even grasp the problems, let alone think of an answer. Nevertheless, Father had taught her: Servants are always happier when they know their voices are heard by their master. "Please tell me," said Qing-jao. "How can you say anything more foolish than the things *I* have already said?"

"My beloved elder sister," said Wang-mu, "I really got this idea from you. You've said so many times that nothing known to all of science and history could possibly have caused the fleet to disappear so perfectly, and all at once."

"But it happened," said Qing-jao, "and so it must be possible after all."

"What came to my mind, my sweet Qing-jao," said Wang-mu, "is something you explained to me as we studied logic. About first and final cause. All this time you have been looking for first causes—how the fleet was made to disappear. But have you looked for final causes—what someone hoped to accomplish by cutting off the fleet, or even destroying it?"

"Everyone knows *why* people want the fleet stopped. They're trying to protect the rights of colonies, or else they have some ridiculous idea that Congress means to destroy the pequeninos along with the whole colony. There are billions of people who want the fleet to stop. All of them are seditious in their hearts, and enemies of the gods."

"But somebody actually *did* it," said Wang-mu. "I only thought that since you can't find out what happened to the fleet directly, then maybe if you find out *who* made it happen, that will lead you to find out how they did it."

"We don't even know that it was done by a *who*," said Qing-jao. "It could have been a *what*. Natural phenomena don't have purposes in mind, since they don't have minds."

Wang-mu bowed her head. "I *did* waste your time, then, Qing-jao. Please forgive me. I should have left when you told me to go."

"It's all right," said Qing-jao.

Wang-mu was already gone; Qing-jao didn't know whether her servant had even heard her reassurance. Never mind, thought Qing-jao. If Wang-mu was offended, I'll make it up to her later. It was sweet of the girl to think she could help me with my task; I'll make sure she knows I'm glad she has such an eager heart.

With Wang-mu out of the room, Qing-jao went back to her terminal. She idly flipped the reports through her terminal's display. She had looked at all of them before, and she had found nothing useful. Why should this time be different? Maybe these reports and summaries showed her nothing because there was nothing to show. Maybe the fleet disappeared because of some god-gone-berserk; there were stories of such things in ancient times. Maybe there was no evidence of human intervention because a human didn't do it. What would Father say about *that*, she wondered. How would Congress deal with a lunatic deity? They couldn't even track down that seditious writer Demosthenes—what hope did they have of tracking and trapping a god?

Whoever Demosthenes is, he's laughing right now, thought Qing-jao. All his work to persuade people that the government was wrong to send the Lusitania Fleet, and now the fleet has stopped, just as Demosthenes wanted.

Just as Demosthenes wanted. For the first time, Qing-jao made a mental connection that was so obvious she couldn't believe she hadn't thought of it before. It was so obvious, in fact, that the police in many a city had assumed that those who were already known to follow Demosthenes must surely have been involved in making the fleet disappear. They had rounded up everyone suspected of sedition and tried to force confessions out of them. But of course they hadn't actually questioned *Demosthenes,* because nobody knew who he was.

Demosthenes, so clever he has evaded discovery for years, despite all the searching of the Congress Police; Demosthenes, who is every bit as elusive as the cause of the disappearance of the fleet. If he could work the one trick, why not the other? Maybe if I find Demosthenes, I'll find out how the fleet was cut off. Not that I have any idea even where to start looking. But at least it's a different avenue of approach. At least it won't mean reading the same empty, useless reports over and over again.

Suddenly Qing-jao remembered who had said almost exactly the same thing, only moments before. She felt herself blushing, the blood hot in her cheeks. How arrogant I was, to condescend to Wang-mu, to patronize her for imagining she could help me with my lofty task. And now, not five minutes later, the thought she planted in my mind has blossomed into a plan. Even if the plan fails, she was the one who gave it to me, or at least started me thinking of it. Thus I was the fool to think her foolish. Tears of shame filled Qing-jao's eyes.

Then she thought of some famous lines from a song by her ancestor-of-the-heart:

> I want to call back
> the blackberry flowers
> that have fallen
> though pear blossoms remain

The poet Li Qing-jao knew the pain of regretting words that have already fallen from our lips and can never be called back. But she was wise enough to remember that even though those words are gone, there are still new words waiting to be said, like the pear blossoms.

To comfort herself for the shame of having been so arrogant, Qing-jao repeated all the words of the song; or at least she started to. But when she got to the line

> dragon boats on the river

her mind drifted to the Lusitania Fleet, imagining all those starships like riverboats, painted so fiercely, and yet drifting now with the current, so far from the shore that they can no longer be heard no matter how loud they shout.

From dragon boats her thoughts turned to dragon kites, and now she thought of the Lusitania Fleet as kites with broken strings, carried along by the wind, no longer tethered to the child who first gave them flight. How beautiful, to see them free; yet how terrifying it must be for them, who never wished for freedom.

> I did not fear the mad winds
> and violent rain

The words of the song came back to her again. I did not fear. Mad winds. Violent rain. I did not fear as

> we drank to good fortune
> with warm blackberry wine
> now I cannot conceive
> how to retrieve
> that time

My ancestor-of-the-heart could drink away her fear, thought Qing-jao, because she had someone to drink with. And even now,

> alone on my mat with a cup
> gazing sadly into nothingness

the poet remembers her gone companion. Whom do I remember now? thought Qing-jao. Where is my tender love? What an age it must have been then, when the great Li Qing-jao was still mortal, and men and women could be together as tender friends without any worry about who was godspoken and who was not. Then a woman could live such a life that even in her loneliness she had memories. I can't even remember my mother's face. Only the flat pictures; I can't remember seeing her face turn and move while her eyes looked at me. I have only my Father, who is like a god; I can worship him and obey him and even love him but I can never be playful with him, not really; when I tease him I'm always watching to be sure he approves of the way I tease him. And Wang-mu; I talked so firmly about how we would be friends, and yet I treat her like a servant, I never for a moment forget who is godspoken and who is not. It's a wall that can never be crossed. I'm alone now and I'm alone forever.

> a clear cold comes through
> the window curtains
> crescent moon beyond the golden bars

She shivered. I and the moon. Didn't the Greeks think of their moon as a cold virgin, a huntress? Is that not what I am now? Sixteen years old and untouched

> and a flute sounds
> as if someone were coming

I listen and listen but never hear the melody of someone coming . . .

No. What she heard were the distant sounds of a

meal being readied; a clattering of bowls and spoons, laughter from the kitchen. Her reverie broken, she reached up and wiped the foolish tears from her cheeks. How could she think of herself as lonely, when she lived in this full house where everyone had cared for her all her life? *I sit here reciting to myself scraps of old poetry when I have work to do.*

At once she began to call up the reports that had been made about investigations into the identity of Demosthenes.

The reports made her think for a moment that this was a dead end, too. More than three dozen writers on almost as many worlds had been arrested for producing seditious documents under that name. Starways Congress had reached the obvious conclusion: Demosthenes was simply the catchall name used by any rebel who wanted to get attention. There was no real Demosthenes, not even an organized conspiracy.

But Qing-jao had doubts about that conclusion. Demosthenes had been remarkably successful in stirring up trouble on every world. Could there possibly be someone of so much talent among the traitors on every planet? Not likely.

Besides, thinking back to when she had read Demosthenes, Qing-jao remembered noticing the coherence of his writings. The singularity and consistency of his vision—that was part of what made him so seductive. Everything seemed to fit, to make sense together.

Hadn't Demosthenes also devised the Hierarchy of Foreignness? Utlanning, framling, raman, varelse. No; that had been written many years ago—it had to be a different Demosthenes. Was it because of that earlier Demosthenes' hierarchy that the traitors were using the name? They were writing in support of the independence of Lusitania, the only world where intelligent nonhuman life had been found. It was only appropriate to use the name of the writer who had first taught humanity to realize that the universe wasn't divided between humans and nonhumans, or between intelligent and non-intelligent species.

Some strangers, the earlier Demosthenes had said, were framlings—humans from another world. Some were ramen—of another intelligent species, yet able to communicate with human beings, so that we could work out differences and make decisions together. Others were varelse, "wise beasts," clearly intelligent and yet completely unable to reach a common ground with humankind. Only with varelse would war ever be justified; with raman, humans could make peace and share the habitable worlds. It was an open way of thinking, full of hope that strangers might still be friends. People who thought that way could never have sent a fleet with Dr. Device to a world inhabited by an intelligent species.

This was a very uncomfortable thought: that the Demosthenes of the hierarchy would also disapprove of the Lusitania Fleet. Almost at once Qing-jao had to counter it. It didn't matter what the old Demosthenes thought, did it? The new Demosthenes, the seditious one, was no wise philosopher trying to bring peoples together. Instead he was trying to sow dissension and discontent among the worlds—provoke quarrels, perhaps even wars between framlings.

And seditious Demosthenes was *not* just a composite of many rebels working on different worlds. Her computer search soon confirmed it. True, many rebels were found who had published on their own planet using the name Demosthenes, but they were always linked to small, ineffective, useless little publications—never to the really dangerous documents that seemed to turn up simultaneously on half the worlds at once. Each local police force, however, was very happy to declare their own petty "Demosthenes" the perpetrator of all the writings, take their bows, and close the case.

Starways Congress had been only too happy to do the

same thing with their own investigation. Having found several dozen cases where local police had arrested and convicted rebels who had incontrovertibly published something under the name Demosthenes, the Congress investigators sighed contentedly, declared that Demosthenes had proved to be a catchall name and not one person at all, and then stopped investigating.

In short, they had all taken the easy way out. Selfish, disloyal—Qing-jao felt a surge of indignation that such people were allowed to continue in their high offices. They should be punished, and severely, too, for having let their private laziness or their desire for praise lead them to abandon the investigation of Demosthenes. Didn't they realize that Demosthenes was truly dangerous? That his writings were now the common wisdom of at least one world, and if one, then probably many? Because of him, how many people on how many worlds would rejoice if they knew that the Lusitania Fleet had disappeared? No matter how many people the police had arrested under the name Demosthenes, his works kept appearing, and always in that same voice of sweet reasonableness. No, the more she read the reports, the more certain Qing-jao became that Demosthenes was one man, as yet undiscovered. One man who knew how to keep secrets impossibly well.

From the kitchen came the sound of the flute; they were being called to dinner. She gazed into the display space over her terminal, where the latest report still hovered, the name *Demosthenes* repeated over and over. "I know you exist, Demosthenes," she whispered, "and I know you are very clever, and I will find you. When I do, you will stop your war against the rulers, and you will tell me what has happened to the Lusitania Fleet. Then I will be done with you, and Congress will punish you, and Father will become the god of Path and live forever in the Infinite West. That is the task that I was born for, the gods have chosen me for it, you might just as well show yourself to me now as later, for eventually all men and women lay their heads under the feet of the gods."

The flute played on, a breathy low melody, drawing Qing-jao out of herself and toward the company of the household. To her, this half-whispered music was the song of the inmost spirit, the quiet conversation of trees over a still pond, the sound of memories arising unbidden into the mind of a woman in prayer. Thus were they called to dine in the house of the noble Han Fei-tzu.

Having heard Qing-jao's challenge, Jane thought: This is what fear of death tastes like. Human beings feel this all the time, and yet somehow they go on from day to day, knowing that at any moment they may cease to be. But this is because they can forget something and still know it; I can never forget, not without losing the knowledge entirely. I know that Han Qing-jao is on the verge of finding secrets that have stayed hidden only because no one has looked hard for them. And when those secrets are known, I will die.

"Ender," she whispered.

Was it day or night on Lusitania? Was he awake or asleep? For Jane, to ask a question is either to know or not-know. So she knew at once that it was night. Ender had been asleep, but now he was awake; he was still attuned to her voice, she realized, even though many silences had passed between them in the past thirty years.

"Jane," he whispered.

Beside him his wife, Novinha, stirred in her sleep. Jane heard her, felt the vibration of her movement, saw the changing shadows through the sensor that Ender wore in his ear. It was good that Jane had not yet learned to feel jealousy, or she might have hated Novinha for lying there, a warm body beside Ender's own. But Novinha, being human, was gifted at jealousy, and Jane knew how Novinha seethed whenever she saw Ender speaking to the woman who lived in the jewel in his ear. "Hush," said Jane. "Don't wake people up."

Ender answered by moving his lips and tongue and teeth, without letting anything louder than a breath pass his lips. "How fare our enemies in flight?" he said. He had greeted her this way for many years.

"Not well," said Jane.

"Perhaps you shouldn't have blocked them. We would have found a way. Valentine's writings—"

"Are about to have their true authorship uncovered."

"Everything's about to be uncovered." He didn't say: Because of you.

"Only because Lusitania was marked for destruction," she answered. She also didn't say: Because of you. There was plenty of blame to go around.

"So they know about Valentine?"

"A girl is finding out. On the world of Path."

"I don't know the place."

"A fairly new colony, a couple of centuries. Chinese. Dedicated to preserving an odd mix of old religions. The gods speak to them."

"I lived on more than one Chinese world," said Ender. "People believed in the old gods on all of them. Gods are alive on every world, even here in the smallest human colony of all. They still have miracles of healing at the shrine of Os Venerados. Rooter has been telling us of a new heresy out in the hinterland somewhere. Some pequeninos who commune constantly with the Holy Ghost."

"This business with gods is something I don't understand," said Jane. "Hasn't anyone caught on yet that the gods always say what people want to hear?"

"Not so," said Ender. "The gods often ask us to do things we never desired, things that require us to sacrifice everything on their behalf. Don't underestimate the gods."

"Does your Catholic God speak to you?"

"Maybe he does. I never hear him, though. Or if I do, I never know that it's his voice I'm hearing."

"And when you die, do the gods of every people really gather them up and take them off somewhere to live forever?"

"I don't know. They never write."

"When I die, will there be some god to carry me away?"

Ender was still for a moment, and then he began to address her in his storytelling manner. "There's an old tale of a dollmaker who never had a son. So he made a puppet that was so lifelike that it looked like a real boy, and he would hold the wooden boy on his lap and talk to it and pretend it was his son. He wasn't crazy—he still knew it was a doll—he called it Pinehead. But one day a god came and touched the puppet and it came to life, and when the dollmaker spoke to it, Pinehead answered. The dollmaker never told anyone about this. He kept his wooden son at home, but he brought the boy every tale he could gather and news of every wonder under heaven. Then one day the dollmaker was coming home from the wharf with tales of a far-off land that had just been discovered, when he saw that his house was on fire. Immediately he tried to run into the house, crying out, 'My son! My son!' But his neighbors stopped him, saying, 'Are you mad? You have no son!' He watched the house burn to the ground, and when it was over he plunged into the ruins and covered himself with hot ashes and wept bitterly. He refused to be comforted. He refused to rebuild his shop. When people asked him why, he said his son was dead. He stayed alive by doing odd jobs for other people, and they pitied him because they were sure the fire had made him a lunatic. Then one day, three years later, a small orphan boy came to him and tugged on his sleeve and said, 'Father, don't you have a tale for me?'"

Jane waited, but Ender said no more. "That's the whole story?"

"Isn't it enough?"

"Why did you tell me this? It's all dreams and wishes. What does it have to do with me?"

"It was the story that came to mind."

"Why did it come to mind?"

"Maybe that's how God speaks to me," said Ender. "Or maybe I'm sleepy and I don't have what you want from me."

"I don't even *know* what I want from you."

"*I* know what you want," said Ender. "You want to be alive, with your own body, not dependent on the philotic web that binds the ansibles together. I'd give you that gift if I could. If you can figure out a way for me to do it, I'll do it for you. But Jane, you don't even know what you *are*. Maybe when you know how you came to exist, what makes you yourself, then maybe we can save you from the day when they shut down the ansibles to kill you."

"So that's your story? Maybe I'll burn down with the house, but somehow my soul will end up in a three-year-old orphan boy?"

"Find out who you are, *what* you are, your essence, and we'll see if we can move you somewhere safer until all this is over. We've got an ansible. Maybe we can put you back."

"There aren't computers enough on Lusitania to contain me."

"You don't know that. You don't know what your self is."

"You're telling me to find my *soul*." She made her voice sound derisive as she said the word.

"Jane, the miracle wasn't that the doll was reborn as

a boy. The miracle was the fact that the puppet ever came to life at all. Something happened to turn meaningless computer connections into a sentient being. Something created you. That's what makes no sense. After that one, the other part should be easy."

His speech was slurring. He wants me to go away so he can sleep, she thought. "I'll work on this."

"Good night," he murmured.

He dropped off to sleep almost at once. Jane wondered: Was he ever really awake? Will he remember in the morning that we talked?

Then she felt the bed shift. Novinha; her breathing was different. Only then did Jane realize: Novinha woke up while Ender and I were talking. She knows what those almost inaudible clicking and smacking noises always mean, that Ender was subvocalizing in order to talk with me. Ender may forget that we spoke tonight, but Novinha will not. As if she had caught him sharing a bed with a lover. If only she could think of me another way. As a daughter. As Ender's bastard daughter by a liaison long ago. His child by way of the fantasy game. Would she be jealous then?

Am I Ender's child?

Jane began to search back in her own past. She began to study her own nature. She began to try to discover who she was and why she was alive.

But because she was Jane, and not a human being, that was not all she was doing. She was also tracking Qing-jao's searches through the data dealing with Demosthenes, watching her come closer and closer to the truth.

Jane's most urgent activity, however, was searching for a way to make Qing-jao want to stop trying to find her. This was the hardest task of all, for despite all Jane's experience with human minds, despite all her conversations with Ender, individual human beings were still mysterious. Jane had concluded: No matter how well you know what a person has done and what he thought he was doing when he did it and what he now thinks of what he did, it is impossible to be certain of what he will do next. Yet she had no choice but to try. So she began to watch the house of Han Fei-tzu in a way that she had watched no one but Ender and, more recently, his stepson Miro. She could no longer wait for Qing-jao and her father to enter data into the computer and try to understand them from that. Now she had to take control of the house computer in order to use the audio and video receptors on the terminals in almost every room to be her ears and eyes. She watched them. Alone and apart, she devoted a considerable part of her attention to them, studying and analyzing their words, their actions, trying to discern what they meant to each other.

It did not take her long to realize that Qing-jao could best be influenced, not by confronting her with arguments, but rather by persuading her father first and then letting him persuade Qing-jao. That was more in harmony with the Path; Han Qing-jao would never disobey Starways Congress unless Han Fei-tzu told her to; and then she would be bound to do it.

In a way, this made Jane's task much easier. Persuading Qing-jao, a volatile and passionate adolescent who did not yet understand herself at all, would be chancy at best. But Han Fei-tzu was a man of settled character, a rational man, yet a man of deep feeling; he could be persuaded by arguments, especially if Jane could convince him that opposing Congress was for the good of his world and of humanity at large. All she needed was the right information to let him reach that conclusion.

By now Jane already understood as much of the social patterns of Path as any human knew, because she had absorbed every history, every anthropological report, and every document produced by the people of Path. What she learned was disturbing: The people of

Path were far more deeply controlled by their gods than any other people in any other place or time. Furthermore, the way that the gods spoke to them was disturbing. It was clearly the well-known brain defect called obsessive-compulsive disorder—OCD. Early in the history of Path—seven generations before, when the world was first being settled—the doctors had treated the disorder accordingly. But they discovered at once that the godspoken of Path did not respond at all to the normal drugs that in all other OCD patients restored the chemical balance of "enoughness," that sense in a person's mind that a job is completed and there is no need to worry about it anymore. The godspoken exhibited all the behaviors associated with OCD, but the well-known brain defect was not present. There must be another, an unknown cause.

Now Jane explored more deeply into this story, and found documents on other worlds, not on Path at all, that told more of the story. The researchers had immediately concluded that there must have been a new mutation that caused a related brain defect with similar results. But as soon as they issued their preliminary report, all the research ended and the researchers were assigned to another world.

To another *world*—that was almost unthinkable. It meant uprooting them and disconnecting them from time, carrying them away from all friends and family that didn't go with them. And yet not one of them refused—which surely meant that enormous pressure had been brought to bear on them. They all left Path and no one had pursued research along those lines in the years since then.

Jane's first hypothesis was that one of the government agencies on Path itself had exiled them and cut off their research; after all, the followers of the Path wouldn't want their faith to be disrupted by finding the physical cause of the speaking of the gods in their own brains.

But Jane found no evidence that the local government had ever been aware of the full report. The only part of it that had ever circulated on Path was the general conclusion that the speaking of the gods was definitely *not* the familiar, and treatable, OCD. The people of Path had learned only enough of the report to feel confirmed that the speaking of the gods had no known physical cause. Science had "proved" that the gods were real. There was no record of anyone on Path taking any action to cause further information or research to be suppressed. Those decisions had all come from outside. From Congress.

There had to be some key information hidden even from Jane, whose mind easily reached into every electronic memory that was connected with the ansible network. That would only happen if those who knew the secret had feared its discovery so much they kept it completely out of even the most top-secret and restricted computers of government.

Jane could not let that stop her. She would have to piece together the truth from the scraps of information that would have been left inadvertently in unrelated documents and databases. She would have to find other events that helped fill in the missing parts of the picture. In the long run, human beings could never keep secrets from someone with Jane's unlimited time and patience. She would find out what Congress was doing with Path, and when she had the information, she would use it, if she could, to turn Han Qing-jao away from her destructive course. For Qing-jao, too, was opening up secrets—older ones, secrets that had been hidden for three thousand years.

10

MARTYR

<Ender says that we're at the fulcrum of history, here on Lusitania. That in the next few months or years this will be the place where either death or understanding came to every sentient species.>

<How thoughtful of him, to bring us here just in time for our possible demise.>

<You're teasing me, of course.>

<If we knew how to tease, perhaps we'd do it to you.>

<Lusitania is the fulcrum of history in part *because* you're here. You carry a fulcrum with you wherever you go.>

<We discard it. We give it to you. It's yours.>

<Wherever strangers meet is the fulcrum.>

<Then let's not be strangers anymore.>

<Humans insist on making strangers of us—it's built into their genetic material. But *we* can be friends.>

<This word is too strong. Say that we are fellow-citizens.>

<At least as long as our interests coincide.>

<As long as the stars shine, our interests will co-incide.>

<Maybe not so long. Maybe only as long as human beings are stronger and more numerous than we are.>

<That will do for now.>

Quim came to the meeting without protest, though it might well set him back a full day in his journey. He had learned patience long ago. No matter how urgent he felt his mission to the heretics to be, he could accomplish little, in the long run, if he didn't have the support of the human colony behind him. So if Bishop Peregrino asked him to attend a meeting with Kovano Zeljezo, the mayor of Milagre and governor of Lusitania, Quim would go.

He was surprised to see that the meeting was also being attended by Ouanda Saavedra, Andrew Wiggin, and most of Quim's own family. Mother and Ela—their presence made sense, if the meeting were being called to discuss policy concerning the heretic pequeninos. But what were Quara and Grego doing here? There was no reason they should be involved in any serious discussions. They were too young, too ill-informed, too impetuous. From what he had seen of them, they still quarreled like little children. They weren't as mature as Ela, who was able to set aside her personal feelings in the interest of science. Of course, Quim worried sometimes that Ela did this far too well for her own good—but that was hardly the worry with Quara and Grego.

Especially Quara. From what Rooter had said, the whole trouble with these heretics really took off when Quara told the pequeninos about the various contingency plans for dealing with the descolada virus. The heretics wouldn't have found so many allies in so many different forests if it weren't for the fear among the pequeninos that the humans might unleash some virus, or poison Lusitania with a chemical that would wipe out the descolada and, with it, the pequeninos themselves. The fact that the humans would even consider the indirect extermination of the pequeninos made it seem like mere turnabout for the piggies to contemplate the extermination of humanity.

All because Quara couldn't keep her mouth shut. And now she was at a meeting where policy would be discussed. Why? What constituency in the community did she represent? Did these people actually imagine that government or church policy was now the province of the Ribeira family? Of course, Olhado and Miro weren't there, but that meant nothing—since both were cripples, the rest of the family unconsciously treated them like children, though Quim knew well that neither of them deserved to be so callously dismissed.

Still, Quim was patient. He could wait. He could listen. He could hear them out. Then he'd do something that would please both God and the Bishop. Of course, if *that* wasn't possible, pleasing God would do well enough.

"This meeting wasn't my idea," said Mayor Kovano. He was a good man, Quim knew. A better mayor than most people in Milagre realized. They kept reelecting him because he was grandfatherly and worked hard to help individuals and families who were having trouble. They didn't care much whether he also set good policies—that was too abstract for them. But it happened that he was as wise as he was politically astute. A rare combination that Quim was glad of. Perhaps God knew that these would be trying times, and gave us a leader who might well help us get through it all without too much suffering.

"But I'm glad to have you all together. There's more strain in the relationship between piggies and people than ever before, or at least since the Speaker here arrived and helped us make peace with them."

Wiggin shook his head, but everyone knew his role

in those events and there was little point in his denying it. Even Quim had had to admit, in the end, that the infidel humanist had ended up doing good works on Lusitania. Quim had long since shed his deep hatred of the Speaker for the Dead; indeed, he sometimes suspected that he, as a missionary, was the only person in his family who really understood what it was that Wiggin had accomplished. It takes one evangelist to understand another.

"Of course, we owe no small part of our worries to the misbehavior of two very troublesome young hotheads, whom we have invited to this meeting so they can see some of the dangerous consequences of their stupid, self-willed behavior."

Quim almost laughed out loud. Of course, Kovano had said all this in such mild, pleasant tones that it took a moment for Grego and Quara to realize they had just been given a tongue-lashing. But Quim understood at once. *I shouldn't have doubted you, Kovano; you would never have brought useless people to a meeting.*

"As I understand it, there is a movement among the piggies to launch a starship in order to deliberately infect the rest of humanity with the descolada. And because of the contribution of our young parrot, here, many other forests are giving heed to this idea."

"If you expect me to apologize," Quara began.

"I expect you to shut your mouth—or is that impossible, even for ten minutes?" Kovano's voice had real fury in it. Quara's eyes grew wide, and she sat more rigidly in her chair.

"The other half of our problem is a young physicist who has, unfortunately, kept the common touch." Kovano raised an eyebrow at Grego. "If only you had become an aloof intellectual. Instead, you seem to have cultivated the friendship of the stupidest, most violent of Lusitanians."

"With people who disagree with you, you mean," said Grego.

"With people who forget that this world belongs to the pequeninos," said Quara.

"Worlds belong to the people who need them and know how to make them produce," said Grego.

"Shut your mouths, children, or you'll be expelled from this meeting while the adults make up their minds."

Grego glared at Kovano. "Don't you speak to me that way."

"I'll speak to you however I like," said Kovano. "As far as I'm concerned, you've both broken legal obligations of secrecy, and I should have you both locked up."

"On what charge?"

"I have emergency powers, you'll recall. I don't need any charges until the emergency is over. Do I make myself clear?"

"You won't do it. You need me," said Grego. "I'm the only decent physicist on Lusitania."

"Physics isn't worth a slug to us if we end up in some kind of contest with the pequeninos."

"It's the descolada we have to confront," said Grego.

"We're wasting time," said Novinha.

Quim looked at his mother for the first time since the meeting began. She seemed very nervous. Fearful. He hadn't seen her like that in many years.

"We're here about this insane mission of Quim's," said Novinha.

"He is called Father Estevão," said Bishop Peregrino. He was a stickler for giving proper dignity to church offices.

"He's my son," said Novinha. "I'll call him what I please."

"What a testy group of people we have here today," said Mayor Kovano.

Things were going very badly. Quim had deliberately avoided telling Mother any details about his mission to the heretics, because he was sure she'd oppose the idea of him going straight to piggies who openly feared and hated human beings. Quim was well aware of the source of her dread of close contact with the pequeninos. As a young child she had lost her parents to the descolada. The xenologer Pipo became her surrogate father—and then became the first human to be tortured to death by the pequeninos. Novinha then spent twenty years trying to keep her lover, Libo—Pipo's son, and the next xenologer—from meeting the same fate. She even married another man to keep Libo from getting a husband's right of access to her private computer files, where she believed the secret that had led the piggies to kill Pipo might be found. And in the end, it all came to nothing. Libo was killed just as Pipo was.

Even though Mother had since learned the true reason for the killing, even though the pequeninos had undertaken solemn oaths not to undertake any violent act against another human being, there was no way Mother would ever be rational about her loved ones going off among the piggies. And now here she was at a meeting that had obviously been called, no doubt at her instigation, to decide whether Quim should go on his missionary journey. It was going to be an unpleasant morning. Mother had years of practice at getting her own way. Being married to Andrew Wiggin had softened and mellowed her in many ways. But when she thought one of her children was at risk, the claws came out, and no husband was going to have much gentling influence on her.

Why had Mayor Kovano and Bishop Peregrino allowed this meeting to take place?

As if he had heard Quim's unspoken question, Mayor Kovano began to explain. "Andrew Wiggin has come to me with new information. My first thought was to keep all of it secret, send Father Estevão on his mission to the heretics, and then ask Bishop Peregrino to pray. But Andrew assured me that as our danger increases, it's all the more important that all of you act from the most complete possible information. Speakers for the dead apparently have an almost pathological reliance on the idea that people behave better when they know more. I've been a politician too long to share his confidence—but he's older than I am, he claims, and I deferred to his wisdom."

Quim knew, of course, that Kovano deferred to no one's wisdom. Andrew Wiggin had simply persuaded him.

"As relations between pequeninos and humans are getting more, um, problematical, and as our unseeable cohabitant, the hive queen, apparently comes closer to launching her starships, it seems that matters offplanet are getting more urgent as well. The Speaker for the Dead informs me from his offplanet sources that someone on a world called Path is very close to discovering our allies who have managed to keep Congress from issuing orders to the fleet to destroy Lusitania."

Quim noted with interest that Andrew had apparently not told Mayor Kovano about Jane. Bishop Peregrino didn't know, either; did Grego or Quara? Did Ela? Mother certainly did. Why did Andrew tell me, if he held it back from so many others?

"There is a very strong chance that within the next few weeks—or days—Congress will reestablish communications with the fleet. At that point, our last defense will be gone. Only a miracle will save us from annihilation."

"Bullshit," said Grego. "If that—*thing*—out on the prairie can build a starship for the piggies, it can build some for us, too. Get us off this planet before it gets blown to hell."

"Perhaps," said Kovano. "I suggested something like that, though in less colorful terms. Perhaps, Senhor Wiggin, you can tell us why Grego's eloquent little plan won't work."

"The hive queen doesn't think the way we do. Despite her best efforts, she doesn't take individual lives as seriously. If Lusitania is destroyed, she and the pequeninos will be at greatest risk—"

"The M.D. Device blows up the *whole* planet," Grego pointed out.

"At greatest risk of species annihilation," said Wiggin, unperturbed by Grego's interruption. "She'll not waste a ship on getting humans off Lusitania, because there are trillions of humans on a couple of hundred other worlds. We're not in danger of xenocide."

"We are if these heretic piggies get their way," said Grego.

"And that's another point," said Wiggin. "If we haven't found a way to neutralize the descolada, we *can't* in good conscience take the human population of Lusitania to another world. We'd only be doing exactly what the heretics want—forcing other humans to deal with the descolada, and probably die."

"Then there's no solution," said Ela. "We might as well roll over and die."

"Not quite," said Mayor Kovano. "It's possible—perhaps likely—that our own village of Milagre is doomed. But we can at least try to make it so that the pequenino colony ships don't carry the descolada to human worlds. There seem to be two approaches—one biological, the other theological."

"We are so close," said Mother. "It's a matter of months or even weeks till Ela and I have designed a replacement species for the descolada."

"So you say," said Kovano. He turned to Ela. "What do *you* say?"

Quim almost groaned aloud. Ela will say that Mother's wrong, that there's no biological solution, and then Mother will say that she's trying to kill me by sending me out on my mission. This is all the family needs—Ela and Mother in open war. Thanks to Kovano Zeljezo, humanitarian.

But Ela's answer wasn't what Quim feared. "It's almost designed right now. It's the only approach that we haven't already tried and failed with, but we're on the verge of having the design for a version of the descolada virus that does everything necessary to maintain the life cycles of the indigenous species, but that is incapable of adapting to and destroying any new species."

"You're talking about a lobotomy for an entire species," said Quara bitterly. "How would you like it if somebody found a way to keep all humans alive, while removing our cerebrums?"

Of course Grego took up her gauntlet. "When these viruses can write a poem or reason from a theorem, I'll buy all this sentimental horseshit about how we ought to keep them alive."

"Just because we can't read them doesn't mean they don't have their epic poems!"

"Fechai as bocas!" growled Kovano.

Immediately they fell silent.

"Nossa Senhora," he said. "Maybe God wants to destroy Lusitania because it's the only way he can think of to shut you two up."

Bishop Peregrino cleared his throat.

"Or maybe not," said Kovano. "Far be it from me to speculate on God's motives."

The Bishop laughed, which allowed the others to laugh as well. The tension broke—like an ocean wave, gone for the moment, but sure to return.

"So the anti-virus is almost ready?" Kovano asked Ela.

"No—or yes, it is, the *replacement* virus is almost fully *designed*. But there are still two problems. The first one is delivery. We have to find a way to get the new virus to attack and replace the old one. That's still—a long way off."

"Do you mean it's a long way off, or you don't have the faintest idea how to do it?" Kovano was no fool—he obviously had dealt with scientists before.

"Somewhere between those two," said Ela.

Mother shifted on her seat, visibly drawing away

from Ela. My poor sister Ela, thought Quim. You may not be spoken to for the next several years.

"And the other problem?" asked Kovano.

"It's one thing to *design* the replacement virus. It's something else again to *produce* it."

"These are mere details," said Mother.

"You're wrong, Mother, and you know it," said Ela. "I can diagram what we want the new virus to be. But even working under ten degrees absolute, we can't cut up and recombine the descolada virus with enough precision. Either it dies, because we've left out too much, or it immediately repairs itself as soon as it returns to normal temperatures, because we didn't take out enough."

"Technical problems."

"Technical problems," said Ela sharply. "Like building an ansible without a philotic link."

"So we conclude—"

"We conclude nothing," said Mother.

"We conclude," continued Kovano, "that our xenobiologists are in sharp disagreement about the feasibility of taming the descolada virus itself. That brings us to the other approach—persuading the pequeninos to send their colonies only to uninhabited worlds, where they can establish their own peculiarly poisonous ecology without killing human beings."

"*Persuading* them," said Grego. "As if we could trust them to keep their promises."

"They've kept more promises so far than *you* have," said Kovano. "So I wouldn't take a morally superior tone if I were you."

Finally things were at a point where Quim felt it would be beneficial for him to speak. "All of this discussion is interesting," said Quim. "It would be a wonderful thing if my mission to the heretics could be the means of persuading the pequeninos to refrain from causing harm to humankind. But even if we all came to agree that my mission has no chance of succeeding in that goal, I would still go. Even if we decided that there was a serious risk that my mission might make things *worse*, I'd go."

"Nice to know you plan to be cooperative," said Kovano acidly.

"I plan to cooperate with God and the church," said Quim. "My mission to the heretics is not to save humankind from the descolada or even to try to keep the peace between humans and pequeninos here on Lusitania. My mission to the heretics is in order to try to bring them back to faith in Christ and unity with the church. I am going to save their souls."

"Well of course," said Kovano. "Of course that's the reason you want to *go*."

"And it's the reason why I *will* go, and the only standard I'll use to determine whether or not my mission succeeds."

Kovano looked helplessly at Bishop Peregrino. "You said that Father Estevão was cooperative."

"I said he was perfectly obedient to God and the church," said the Bishop.

"I took that to mean that you could persuade him to wait on this mission until we knew more."

"I could indeed persuade him. Or I could simply forbid him to go," said Bishop Peregrino.

"Then do it," said Mother.

"I will not," said the Bishop.

"I thought you cared about the good of this colony," said Mayor Kovano.

"I care about the good of all the Christians placed under my charge," said Bishop Peregrino. "Until thirty years ago, that meant I cared only for the human beings of Lusitania. Now, however, I am equally responsible for the spiritual welfare of the Christian pequeninos of this planet. I send Father Estevão forth on his mission exactly as a missionary named Patrick was once sent to the island of Eire. He was extraordinarily successful, converting kings and nations. Unfortunately, the Irish church didn't always act the way the Pope might have wished. There was a great deal of—let us say it was controversy between them. Superficially it concerned the date of Easter, but at heart it was over the issue of obedience to the Pope. It even came to bloodshed now and then. But never for a moment did anyone imagine it would have been better if St. Patrick had never gone to Eire. Never did anyone suggest that it would be better if the Irish had remained pagan."

Grego stood up. "We've found the philote, the true indivisible atom. We've conquered the stars. We send messages faster than the speed of light. And yet we still live in the Dark Ages." He started for the door.

"Walk out that door before I tell you to," said Mayor Kovano, "and you won't see the sun for a year."

Grego walked to the door, but instead of going through it, he leaned against it and grinned sardonically. "You see how obedient I am."

"I won't keep you long," said Kovano. "Bishop Peregrino and Father Estevão speak as if they could make their decision independent of the rest of us, but of course they know they can't. If I decided that Father Estevão's mission to the piggies shouldn't happen, it wouldn't. Let us all be clear about *that*. I'm not afraid to put the Bishop of Lusitania under arrest, if the welfare of Lusitania requires it; and as for this missionary priest, you will only go out among the pequeninos when you have my consent."

"I have no doubt that you can interfere with God's work on Lusitania," said Bishop Peregrino icily. "You must have no doubt that I can send you to hell for doing it."

"I know you can," said Kovano. "I wouldn't be the first political leader to end up in hell at the end of a contest with the church. Fortunately, this time it won't come to that. I've listened to all of you and reached my decision. Waiting for the new anti-virus is too risky. And even if I knew, absolutely, that the anti-virus would be ready and usable in six weeks, I'd still allow this mission. Our best chance right now of salvaging something from this mess is Father Estevão's mission. Andrew tells me that the pequeninos have great respect and affection for this man—even the unbelievers. If he can persuade the pequenino heretics to drop their plan to annihilate humanity in the name of their religion, that will remove one heavy burden from us."

Quim nodded gravely. Mayor Kovano was a man of great wisdom. It was good that they wouldn't have to struggle against each other, at least for now.

"In the meantime, I expect the xenobiologists to continue to work on the anti-virus with all possible vigor. We'll decide, when the virus exists, whether or not to use it."

"We'll use it," said Grego.

"Only if I'm dead," said Quara.

"I appreciate your willingness to wait until we know more before you commit yourself to any course of action," said Kovano. "Which brings us to you, Grego Ribeira. Andrew Wiggin assures me that there is reason to believe that faster-than-light travel might be possible."

Grego looked coldly at the Speaker for the Dead. "And where did you study physics, Senhor Falante?"

"I hope to study it from you," said Wiggin. "Until you've heard my evidence, I hardly know whether there's any reason to hope for such a breakthrough."

Quim smiled to see how easily Andrew turned away the quarrel that Grego wanted to pick. Grego was no fool. He knew he was being handled. But Wiggin hadn't left him any reasonable grounds for showing his disgruntlement. It was one of the most infuriating skills of the Speaker for the Dead.

"If there were a way to travel between worlds at ansible speeds," said Kovano, "we would need only one such ship to transport all the humans of Lusitania to another world. It's a remote chance—"

"A foolish dream," said Grego.

"But we'll pursue it. We'll *study* it, won't we?" said Kovano. "Or we'll find ourselves working in the foundry."

"I'm not afraid to work with my hands," said Grego. "So don't think you can terrify me into putting my mind at your service."

"I stand rebuked," said Kovano. "It's your cooperation that I want, Grego. But if I can't have that, then I'll settle for your obedience."

Apparently Quara was feeling left out. She arose as Grego had a moment before. "So you can sit here and contemplate destroying a sentient species without even thinking of a way to communicate with them. I hope you all enjoy being mass murderers." Then, like Grego, she made as if to leave.

"Quara," said Kovano.

She waited.

"You will study ways to talk to the descolada. To see if you can communicate with these viruses."

"I know when I'm being tossed a bone," said Quara. "What if I tell you that they're pleading for us not to kill them? You wouldn't believe me anyway."

"On the contrary. I know you're an honest woman, even if you are hopelessly indiscreet," said Kovano. "But I have another reason for wanting you to understand the molecular language of the descolada. You see, Andrew Wiggin has raised a possibility that never occurred to me before. We all know that pequenino sentience dates from the time when the descolada virus first swept across this planet. But what if we've misunderstood cause and effect?"

Mother turned to Andrew, a bitter half-smile on her face. "You think the pequeninos caused the descolada?"

"No," said Andrew. "But what if the pequeninos *are* the descolada?"

Quara gasped.

Grego laughed. "You are full of clever ideas, aren't you, Wiggin?"

"I don't understand," said Quim.

"I just wondered," said Andrew. "Quara says that the descolada is complex enough that it might contain intelligence. What if descolada viruses are using the bodies of the pequeninos to express their character? What if pequenino intelligence comes entirely from the viruses inside their bodies?"

For the first time, Ouanda, the xenologer, spoke up. "You are as ignorant of xenology as you are of physics, Mr. Wiggin," she said.

"Oh, much more so," said Wiggin. "But it occurred to me that we've never been able to think of any *other* way that memories and intelligence are preserved as a dying pequenino passes into the third life. The trees don't exactly preserve the brain inside them. But if will and memory are carried by the descolada in the first place, the death of the brain would be almost meaningless in the transmission of personality to the fathertree."

"Even if there were a chance of this being true," said Ouanda, "there's no possible experiment we could decently perform to find out."

Andrew Wiggin nodded ruefully. "I know *I* couldn't think of one. I was hoping *you* would."

Kovano interrupted again. "Ouanda, we need you to explore this. If you don't believe it, fine—figure out a way to *prove* it wrong, and you'll have done your job." Kovano stood up, addressed them all. "Do you all understand what I'm asking of you? We face some of the most terrible moral choices that humankind has ever faced. We run the risk of committing xenocide, or allowing it to be committed if we do nothing. Every known or suspected sentient species lives in the shadow of grave risk, and it's here, with us and with us alone, that almost all the decisions lie. Last time anything remotely similar happened, our human predecessors chose to commit xenocide in order, as they supposed, to save themselves. I am asking all of you to help us pursue *every* avenue, however unlikely, that shows us a glimmer of hope, that might provide us with a tiny shred of light to guide our decisions. Will you help?"

Even Grego and Quara and Ouanda nodded their assent, however reluctantly. For the moment, at least, Kovano had managed to transform all the self-willed squabblers in this room into a cooperative community. How long that would last outside the room was a matter for speculation. Quim decided that the spirit of cooperation would probably last until the next crisis—and maybe that would be long enough.

Only one more confrontation was left. As the meeting broke up and everyone said their good-byes or arranged one-on-one consultations, Mother came to Quim and looked him fiercely in the eye.

"Don't go."

Quim closed his eyes. There was nothing to say to an outrageous statement like that.

"If you love me," she said.

Quim remembered the story from the New Testament, when Jesus' mother and brothers came to visit him, and wanted him to interrupt teaching his disciples in order to receive them.

"These are my mother and my brothers," murmured Quim.

She must have understood the reference, because when he opened his eyes, she was gone.

Not an hour later, Quim was also gone, riding on one of the colony's precious cargo trucks. He needed few supplies, and for a normal journey he would have gone on foot. But the forest he was bound for was so far away, it would have taken him weeks to get there without the car; nor could he have carried food enough. This was still a hostile environment—it grew nothing edible to humans, and even if it did, Quim would still need the food containing the descolada suppressants. Without it he would die of the descolada long before he starved to death.

As the town of Milagre grew small behind him, as he hurtled deeper and deeper into the meaningless open space of the prairie, Quim—Father Estevão—wondered what Mayor Kovano might have decided if he had known that the leader of the heretics was a fathertree who had earned the name Warmaker, and that Warmaker was known to have said that the only hope for the pequeninos was for the Holy Ghost—the descolada virus—to destroy all human life on Lusitania.

It wouldn't have mattered. God had called Quim to preach the gospel of Christ to every nation, kindred, tongue, and people. Even the most warlike, bloodthirsty, hate-filled people might be touched by the love of God and transformed into Christians. It had happened many times in history. Why not now?

O Father, do a mighty work in this world. Never did your children need miracles more than we do.

———

Novinha wasn't speaking to Ender, and he was afraid. This wasn't petulance—he had never seen Novinha be petulant. To Ender it seemed that her silence was not to punish him, but rather to keep from punishing him; that she was silent because if she spoke, her words would be too cruel ever to be forgiven.

So at first he didn't attempt to cajole words from her. He let her move like a shadow through the house, drifting past him without eye contact; he tried to stay out of her way and didn't go to bed until she was asleep.

It was Quim, obviously. His mission to the heretics—it was easy to understand what she feared, and even though Ender didn't share the same fears, he knew that Quim's journey was *not* without risk. Novinha was being irrational. How could Ender have stopped Quim? He was the one of Novinha's children over whom Ender had almost no influence; they had come to a rapprochement a few years ago, but it was a declaration of peace between equals, nothing like the ur-fatherhood Ender had established with all the other children. If Novinha had not been able to persuade Quim to give up this mission, what more could Ender have accomplished?

Novinha probably knew this, intellectually. But like all other human beings, she did not always act according to her understanding. She had lost too many of the people that she loved; when she felt one more of them slipping away, her response was visceral, not intellectual. Ender had come into her life as a healer, a protector. It was his job to keep her from being afraid, and now she *was* afraid, and she was angry at him for having failed her.

However, after two days of silence Ender had had enough. This wasn't a good time for there to be a barrier between him and Novinha. He knew—and so did Novinha—that Valentine's coming might be a difficult time for them. He had so many old habits of communication with Valentine, so many connections with her, so many roads into her soul, that it was hard for him not to fall back into being the person he had been during the years—the millennia—they had spent together. They had experienced three thousand years of history as if seeing it through the same eyes. He had been with Novinha only thirty years. That was actually longer, in subjective time, than he had spent with Valentine, but it was so easy to slip back into his old role as Valentine's brother, as Speaker to her Demosthenes.

Ender had expected Novinha to be jealous when Valentine came, and he was prepared for that. He had warned Valentine that there would probably be few opportunities for them to be together at first. And she, too, understood—Jakt had his worries, too, and both

spouses would need reassurance. It was almost silly for
Jakt and Novinha to be jealous of the bonds between
brother and sister. There had never been the slightest
hint of sexuality in Ender's and Valentine's relationship—anyone who understood them at all would laugh
at any such notion—but it wasn't sexual unfaithfulness
that Novinha and Jakt were wary of. Nor was it the
emotional bond they shared—Novinha had no reason
to doubt Ender's love and devotion to her, and Jakt
could not have asked for more than Valentine offered
him, both in passion and in trust.

It was deeper than any of these things. It was the fact
that even now, after all these years, as soon as they
were together they once again functioned like a single
person, helping each other without even having to explain what they were trying to accomplish. Jakt saw it
and even to Ender, who had never known him before,
it was obvious that the man felt devastated. As if he
saw his wife and her brother together and realized: *This*
is what closeness is. *This* is what it means for two people to be one. He had thought that he and Valentine
had been as close as husband and wife can ever be, and
perhaps they were. And yet now he had to confront the
fact that it was possible for two people to be even
closer. To be, in some sense, the same person.

Ender could see this in Jakt, and could admire how
well Valentine was doing at reassuring him—and at dis-
tancing herself from Ender so that her husband could
grow used to the bond between them more gradually,
in small doses.

What Ender could not have predicted was the way
Novinha had reacted. He had come to know her first as
the mother of her children; he had known only the
fierce, unreasonable loyalty she had for them. He had
supposed that if she felt threatened, she would become
possessive and controlling, the way she was with the
children. He was not at all prepared for the way she

had withdrawn from him. Even before this silent treatment about Quim's mission, she had been distant from him. In fact, now that he thought back, he realized that it had already been beginning before Valentine arrived. It was as if Novinha had already started giving in to a new rival before the rival was even there.

It made sense, of course—he *should* have seen it coming. Novinha had lost too many strong figures in her life, too many people she had depended on. Her parents. Pipo. Libo. Even Miro. She might be protective and possessive with her children, whom she thought of as needing her, but with the people *she* needed, she was the opposite. If she feared that they would be taken away from her, she withdrew from them; she stopped permitting herself to need them.

Not "them." *Him.* Ender. She was trying to stop needing *him.* And this silence, if she kept it up, would drive such a wedge between them that their marriage would never recover.

If that happened, Ender didn't know what he would do. It had never occurred to him that his marriage might be threatened. He had not entered into it lightly; he intended to die married to Novinha, and all these years together had been filled with the joy that comes from utter confidence in another person. Now Novinha had lost that confidence in him. Only it wasn't right. He was still her husband, faithful to her as no other man, no other *person* in her life had ever been. He didn't deserve to lose her over a ridiculous misunderstanding. And if he let things go as Novinha seemed determined, however unconsciously, to make them happen, she would be utterly convinced that she could never depend on any other person. That would be tragic because it would be false.

So Ender was already planning a confrontation of some kind with Novinha when Ela accidentally set it off.

"Andrew."

Ela was standing in the doorway. If she had clapped hands outside, asking for admittance, Ender hadn't heard her. But then, she would hardly need to clap for entrance to her mother's house.

"Novinha's in our room," said Ender.

"I came to talk to you," said Ela.

"I'm sorry, you can't have an advance on your allowance."

Ela laughed as she came to sit beside him, but the laughter died quickly. She was worried.

"Quara," she said.

Ender sighed and smiled. Quara was born contrary, and nothing in her life had made her more compliant. Still, Ela had always been able to get along with her better than anyone.

"It's not just the normal," said Ela. "In fact, she's less trouble than usual. Not a quarrel."

"A dangerous sign?"

"You know she's trying to communicate with the descolada."

"Molecular language."

"Well, what she's doing is dangerous, and it won't establish communication even if it succeeds. *Especially* if it succeeds, because then there's a good chance that we'll all be dead."

"What's she doing?"

"She's been raiding my files—which isn't hard, because I didn't think I needed to block them off from a fellow xenobiologist. She's been constructing the inhibitors I've been trying to splice into plants—easy enough, because I've laid out exactly how it's done. Only instead of splicing it into anything, she's giving it directly to the descolada."

"What do you mean, *giving* it?"

"Those are her messages. That's what she's sending them on their precious little message carriers. Now, whether those carriers are language or not isn't going to be settled by a non-experiment like *that*. But sentient or not, we know that the descolada is a hell of a good adapter—and she might well be helping them adapt to some of my best strategies for blocking them."

"Treason."

"Right. She's feeding our military secrets to the enemy."

"Have you talked to her about this?"

"'Sta brincando. Claro que falei. Ela quase me matou." You're joking—of course I talked to her. She nearly killed me.

"Has she successfully trained any viruses?"

"She's not even testing for that. It's like she's run to the window and hollered, 'They're coming to kill you!' She's not doing science, she's doing interspecies politics, only we don't know that the other side even *has* politics, we only know that with her help it might just kill us faster than we ever imagined."

"Nossa Senhora," murmured Ender. "It's too dangerous. She can't play around with something like this."

"It may already be too late—I can't guess whether she's done damage or not."

"Then we've got to stop her."

"How, break her arms?"

"I'll talk to her, but she's too old—or too young—to listen to reason. I'm afraid it'll end up with the Mayor, not with us."

Only when Novinha spoke did Ender realize that his wife had entered the room. "In other words, jail," said Novinha. "You plan to have my daughter locked up. When were you going to inform me?"

"Jail didn't occur to me," said Ender. "I expected he'd shut off her access to—"

"That isn't the *Mayor's* job," said Novinha. "It's *mine*. I'm the head xenobiologist. Why didn't you come to *me*, Elanora? Why to *him*?"

Ela sat there in silence, looking at her mother steadily. It was how she handled conflict with her mother, with passive resistance.

"Quara's out of control, Novinha," said Ender. "Telling secrets to the fathertrees was bad enough. Telling them to the descolada is insane."

"Es psicologista, agora?" *Now you're a psychologist?*

"I'm not planning to lock her up."

"You're not planning *anything*," said Novinha. "Not with *my* children."

"That's right," said Ender. "I'm not planning to do anything with *children*. I do have a responsibility, however, to do something about an adult citizen of Milagre who is recklessly endangering the survival of every human being on this planet, and maybe every human being everywhere."

"And where did you get that noble responsibility, Andrew? Did God come down to the mountain and carve your license to rule people on tablets of stone?"

"Fine," said Ender. "What do *you* suggest?"

"I suggest you stay out of business that doesn't concern you. And frankly, Andrew, that includes pretty much everything. You're not a xenobiologist. You're not a physicist. You're not a xenologer. In fact, you're not much of *anything*, are you, except a professional meddler in other people's lives."

Ela gasped. "Mother!"

"The only thing that gives you any power anywhere is that damned jewel in your ear. *She* whispers secrets to you, *she* talks to you at night when you're in bed with your *wife*, and whenever she wants something, there you are in a meeting where you have no business, saying whatever it was *she* told you to say. You talk about Quara committing treason—as far as I can tell, you're the one who's betraying *real* people in favor of an overgrown piece of software!"

"Novinha," said Ender. It was supposed to be the beginning of an attempt to calm her.

But she wasn't interested in dialogue. "Don't you *dare* to try to *deal* with me, Andrew. All these years I thought you loved me—"

"I do."

"I thought you had really become one of us, part of our lives—"

"I am."

"I thought it was real—"

"It is."

"But you're just what Bishop Peregrino warned us you were from the start. A manipulator. A controller. Your brother once ruled all of humanity, isn't that the story? But you aren't so ambitious. You'll settle for a little planet."

"In the name of God, Mother, have you lost your mind? Don't you *know* this man?"

"I thought I did!" Novinha was weeping now. "But no one who loved me would ever let my son go out and face those murderous little swine—"

"He couldn't have stopped Quim, Mother! Nobody could!"

"He didn't even try. He *approved*!"

"Yes," said Ender. "I thought your son was acting nobly and bravely, and I approved of that. He knew that while the danger wasn't great, it was real, and yet he still chose to go—and I approved of that. It's exactly what *you* would have done, and I hope that it's what *I* would do in the same place. Quim is a man, a good man, maybe a great one. He doesn't need your protection and he doesn't want it. He has decided what his life's work is and he's doing it. I honor him for that, and so should you. How dare you suggest that either of us should have stood in his way!"

Novinha was silent at last, for the moment, anyway. Was she measuring Ender's words? Was she finally realizing how futile and, yes, cruel it was for her to send Quim away with her anger instead of her hope? During that silence, Ender still had some hope.

Then the silence ended. "If you ever meddle in the lives of my children again, I'm done with you," said Novinha. "And if anything happens to Quim—*anything*—I will hate you till you die, and I'll pray for that day to come soon. You *don't* know everything, you bastard, and it's about time you stopped acting as if you did."

She stalked to the door, but then thought better of the theatrical exit. She turned back to Ela and spoke with remarkable calm. "Elanora, I will take immediate steps to block Quara from access to records and equipment that she could use to help the descolada. And in the future, my dear, if I ever hear you discussing lab business with anyone, *especially* this man, I will bar *you* from the lab for life. Do you understand?"

Again Ela answered her with silence.

"Ah," said Novinha. "I see that he has stolen more of my children from me than I thought."

Then she was gone.

Ender and Ela sat in stunned silence. Finally Ela stood up, though she didn't take a single step.

"I really ought to go do something," said Ela, "but I can't for the life of me think what."

"Maybe you should go to your mother and show her that you're still on her side."

"But I'm not," said Ela. "In fact, I was thinking maybe I should go to Mayor Zeljezo and propose that he remove Mother as head xenobiologist because she has clearly lost her mind."

"No she hasn't," said Ender. "And if you did something like that, it would kill her."

"Mother? She's too tough to die."

"No," said Ender. "She's so fragile right now that any blow might kill her. Not her body. Her—trust. Her hope. Don't give her any reason to think you're not with her, no matter what."

Ela looked at him with exasperation. "Is this something you *decide*, or does it just come naturally to you?"

"What are you talking about?"

"Mother just said things to you that should have made you furious or hurt or—*something*, anyway—and you just sit there trying to think of ways to help her. Don't you ever feel like lashing out at somebody? I mean, don't you ever lose your temper?"

"Ela, after you've inadvertently killed a couple of people with your bare hands, either you learn to control your temper or you lose your humanity."

"You've done that?"

"Yes," he said. He thought for a moment that she was shocked.

"Do you think you could still do it?"

"Probably," he said.

"Good. It may be useful when all hell breaks loose." Then she laughed. It was a joke. Ender was relieved. He even laughed, weakly, along with her.

"I'll go to Mother," said Ela, "but not because you told me to, or even for the reasons that you said."

"Fine, just so you go."

"Don't you want to know why I'm going to stick with her?"

"I already know why."

"Of course. She was wrong, wasn't she. You *do* know everything, don't you."

"You're going to go to your mother because it's the most painful thing you could do to yourself at this moment."

"You make it sound sick."

"It's the most painful *good* thing you could do. It's the most unpleasant job around. It's the heaviest burden to bear."

"Ela the martyr, certo? Is that what you'll say when you speak my death?"

"If I'm going to speak *your* death, I'll have to prerecord it. I intend to be dead long before *you*."

"So you're not leaving Lusitania?"

"Of course not."

"Even if Mother boots you out?"

"She can't. She has no grounds for divorce, and Bishop Peregrino knows us both well enough to laugh at any request for annulment based on a claim of non-consummation."

"You know what I mean."

"I'm here for the long haul," said Ender. "No more phony immortality through time dilation. I'm through chasing around in space. I'll never leave the surface of Lusitania again."

"Even if it kills you? Even if the fleet comes?"

"If everybody can leave, then I'll leave," said Ender. "But I'll be the one who turns off all the lights and locks the door."

She ran to him and kissed him on the cheek and embraced him, just for a moment. Then she was out the door and he was, once again, alone.

I was so wrong about Novinha, he thought. It wasn't Valentine she was jealous of. It was Jane. All these years, she's seen me speaking silently with Jane, all the time, saying things that she could never hear, hearing things that she could never say. I've lost her trust in me, and I never even realized I was losing it.

Even now, he must have been subvocalizing. He must have been talking to Jane out of a habit so deep that he didn't even know he was doing it. Because she answered him.

"I warned you," she said.

I suppose you did, Ender answered silently.

"You never think I understand anything about human beings."

I guess you're learning.

"She's right, you know. You *are* my puppet. I manipulate you all the time. You haven't had a thought of your own in years."

"Shut up," he whispered. "I'm not in the mood."

"Ender," she said, "if you think it would help you keep from losing Novinha, take the jewel out of your ear. I wouldn't mind."

"*I* would," he said.

"I was lying, so would I," she said. "But if you have to do it, to keep her, then do it."

"Thank you," he said. "But I'd be hard-pressed to keep someone that I've clearly lost already."

"When Quim comes back, everything will be fine."

Right, thought Ender. Right.

Please, God, take good care of Father Estevão.

They knew Father Estevão was coming. Pequeninos always did. The fathertrees told each other everything. There were no secrets. Not that they wanted it that way. There might be one fathertree that wanted to keep a secret or tell a lie. But they couldn't exactly go off by themselves. They never had private experiences. So if one fathertree wanted to keep something to himself, there'd be another close by who didn't feel that way. Forests always acted in unity, but they were still made up of individuals, and so stories passed from one forest to another no matter what a few fathertrees might wish.

That was Quim's protection, he knew. Because even though Warmaker was a bloodthirsty son of a bitch—though that was an epithet without meaning when it came to pequeninos—he couldn't do a thing to Father Estevão without first persuading the brothers of his forest to act as he wanted them to. And if he did that, one of the other fathertrees in his forest would know, and would tell. Would bear witness. If Warmaker broke the oath taken by all the fathertrees together, thirty years ago, when Andrew Wiggin sent Human into the third life, it could not be done secretly. The whole world would hear of it, and Warmaker would be known as an oathbreaker. It would be a shameful thing. What wife would allow the brothers to carry a mother to him then? What children would he ever have again as long as he lived?

Quim was safe. They might not heed him, but they wouldn't harm him.

Yet when he arrived at Warmaker's forest, they wasted no time listening to him. The brothers seized him, threw him to the ground, and dragged him to Warmaker.

"This wasn't necessary," he said. "I was coming here anyway."

A brother was beating on the tree with sticks. Quim listened to the changing music as Warmaker altered the hollows within himself, shaping the sound into words.

"You came because I commanded."

"You commanded. I came. If you want to think you caused my coming, so be it. But God's commands are the only ones I obey willingly."

"You're here to hear the will of God," said Warmaker.

"I'm hear to speak the will of God," said Quim. "The descolada is a virus, created by God in order to make the pequeninos into worthy children. But the Holy Ghost has no incarnation. The Holy Ghost is perpetually spirit, so he can dwell in our hearts."

"The descolada dwells in *our* hearts, and gives us life. When he dwells in *your* heart, what does he give you?"

"One God. One faith. One baptism. God doesn't preach one thing to humans and another to pequeninos."

"We are not 'little ones.' *You* will see who is mighty and who is small."

They forced him to stand with his back pressed against Warmaker's trunk. He felt the bark shifting behind him. They pushed on him. Many small hands, many snouts breathing on him. In all these years, he had never thought of such hands, such faces as belonging to enemies. And even now, Quim realized with relief that he didn't think of them as his own enemies. They were the enemies of God, and he pitied them. It was a great discovery for him, that even when he was being pushed into the belly of a murderous fathertree, he had no shred of fear or hatred in him.

I really don't fear death. I never knew that.

The brothers still beat on the outside of the tree with sticks. Warmaker reshaped the sound into the words of Father Tongue, but now Quim was inside the sound, inside the words.

"You think I'm going to break the oath," said Warmaker.

"It crossed my mind," said Quim. He was now fully pinned inside the tree, even though it remained open in front of him from head to toe. He could see, he could breathe easily—his confinement wasn't even claustrophobic. But the wood had formed so smoothly around him that he couldn't move an arm or a leg, couldn't begin to turn sideways to slide out of the gap before him. *Strait is the gate and narrow is the way that leads to salvation.*

"We'll test," said Warmaker. It was harder to understand his words, now that Quim was hearing them from the inside. Harder to *think.* "Let God judge between you and me. We'll give you all you want to drink—the water from our stream. But of food you'll have none."

"Starving me is—"

"Starving? We have your food. We'll feed you again in ten days. If the Holy Ghost allows you to live for ten days, we'll feed you and set you free. We'll be believers in your doctrine then. We'll confess that we were wrong."

"The virus will kill me before then."

"The Holy Ghost will judge you and decide if you're worthy."

"There *is* a test going on here," said Quim, "but not the one you think."

"Oh?"

"It's the test of the Last Judgment. You stand before Christ, and he says to those on his right hand, 'I was a stranger, and you took me in. Hungry, and you fed me. Enter into the joy of the Lord.' Then he says to those on his left hand, 'I was hungry, and you gave me nothing. I was a stranger, and you mistreated me.' And they all say to him, 'Lord, when did we do these things to you?' and he answers, 'If you did it to the least of my brothers, you did it to me.' All you brothers, gathered here—I am the least of your brothers. You will answer to Christ for what you do to me here."

"Foolish man," said Warmaker. "*We* are doing nothing to you but holding you still. What happens to you is whatever God desires. Didn't Christ say, 'I do nothing but what I've seen the Father do'? Didn't Christ say, 'I am the way. Come follow me'? Well, we are letting you do what Christ did. He went without bread for forty days in the wilderness. We give you a chance to be one-fourth as holy. If God wants us to believe in your doctrine, he'll send angels to feed you. He'll turn stones into bread."

"You're making a mistake," said Quim.

"*You* made the mistake by coming here."

"I mean that you're making a doctrinal mistake. You've got the lines down right—fasting in the wilderness, stones into bread, all of it. But didn't you think it might be a little too self-revelatory for you to give yourself Satan's part?"

That was when Warmaker flew into a rage, speaking so rapidly that the movements within the wood began to twist and press on Quim until he was afraid he would be torn to bits within the tree.

"*You* are Satan! Trying to get us to believe your lies long enough for you humans to figure out a way to kill the descolada and keep all the brothers from the third life forever! Do you think we don't see through you? We know all your plans, all of them! You have no secrets!

And God keeps no secrets from us either! *We're* the ones who were given the third life, not you! If God loved you, he wouldn't make you bury your dead in the ground and then let nothing but worms come out of you!"

The brothers sat around the opening in the trunk, enthralled by the argument.

It went on for six days, doctrinal arguments worthy of any of the fathers of the church in any age. Not since the council at Nicæa were such momentous issues considered, weighed.

The arguments were passed from brother to brother, from tree to tree, from forest to forest. Accounts of the dialogue between Warmaker and Father Estevão always reached Rooter and Human within a day. But the information wasn't complete. It wasn't until the fourth day that they realized that Quim was being held prisoner, without any of the food containing the descolada inhibitor.

Then an expedition was mounted at once, Ender and Ouanda, Jakt and Lars and Varsam; Mayor Kovano sent Ender and Ouanda because they were widely known and respected among the piggies, and Jakt and his son and son-in-law because they weren't native-born Lusitanians. Kovano didn't dare to send any of the native-born colonists—if word of this got out, there was no telling what would happen. The five of them took the fastest car and followed the directions Rooter gave them. It was a three-day trip.

On the sixth day the dialogue ended, because the descolada had so thoroughly invaded Quim's body that he had no strength to speak, and was often too fevered and delirious to say anything intelligible when he did speak.

On the seventh day, he looked through the gap, upward, above the heads of the brothers who were still there, still watching. "I see the Savior sitting on the right hand of God," he whispered. Then he smiled.

An hour later he was dead. Warmaker felt it, and announced it triumphantly to the brothers. "The Holy Ghost has judged, and Father Estevão has been rejected!"

Some of the brothers rejoiced. But not as many as Warmaker had expected.

———————

At dusk, Ender's party arrived. There was no question now of the piggies capturing and testing them—they were too many, and the brothers were not all of one mind now anyway. Soon they stood before the split trunk of Warmaker and saw the haggard, disease-ravaged face of Father Estevão, barely visible in the shadows.

"Open up and let my son come out to me," said Ender.

The gap in the tree widened. Ender reached in and pulled out the body of Father Estevão. He was so light inside his robes that Ender thought for a moment he must be bearing some of his own weight, must be walking. But he wasn't walking. Ender laid him on the ground before the tree.

A brother beat a rhythm on Warmaker's trunk.

"He must belong to you indeed, Speaker for the Dead, because he is dead. The Holy Ghost has burned him up in the second baptism."

"You broke the oath," said Ender. "You betrayed the word of the fathertrees."

"No one harmed a hair of his head," said Warmaker.

"Do you think anyone is deceived by your lies?" said Ender. "Anyone knows that to withhold medicine from a dying man is an act of violence as surely as if you stabbed him in the heart. There is his medicine. At any time you could have given it to him."

"It was Warmaker," said one of the brothers standing there.

Ender turned to the brothers. "You helped Warmaker. Don't think you can give the blame to him alone. May none of you ever pass into the third life. And as for you, Warmaker, may no mother ever crawl on your bark."

"No human can decide things like that," said Warmaker.

"You decided it yourself, when you thought you could commit murder in order to win your argument," said Ender. "And you brothers, you decided it when you didn't stop him."

"You're not our judge!" cried one of the brothers.

"Yes I am," said Ender. "And so is every other inhabitant of Lusitania, human and fathertree, brother and wife."

They carried Quim's body to the car, and Jakt, Ouanda, and Ender rode with him. Lars and Varsam took the car that Quim had used. Ender took a few minutes to tell Jane a message to give to Miro back in the colony. There was no reason Novinha should wait three days to hear that her son had died at the hands of the pequeninos. And she wouldn't want to hear it from Ender's mouth, that was certain. Whether Ender would have a wife when he returned to the colony was beyond his ability to guess. The only certain thing was that Novinha would not have her son Estevão.

"Will you speak for him?" asked Jakt, as the car skimmed over the capim. He had heard Ender speak for the dead once on Trondheim.

"No," said Ender. "I don't think so."

"Because he's a priest?" asked Jakt.

"I've spoken for priests before," said Ender. "No, I won't speak for Quim because there's no reason to. Quim was always exactly what he seemed to be, and he died exactly as he would have chosen—serving God and preaching to the little ones. I have nothing to add to his story. He completed it himself."

11

THE JADE OF MASTER HO

<So now the killing starts.>

<Amusing that *your* people started it, not the humans.>

<*Your* people started it, too, when you had your wars with the humans.>

<We started it, but they ended it.>

<How do they manage it, these humans—beginning each time so innocently, yet always ending up with the most blood on their hands?>

Wang-mu watched the words and numbers moving through the display above her mistress's terminal. Qing-jao was asleep, breathing softly on her mat not far away. Wang-mu had also slept for a time, but something had wakened her. A cry, not far off; a cry of pain perhaps. It had been part of Wang-mu's dream, but when she awoke she heard the last of the sound in the air. It was not Qing-jao's voice. A man perhaps, though the sound was high. A wailing sound. It made Wang-mu think of death.

But she did not get up and investigate. It was not her place to do that; her place was with her mistress at all times, unless her mistress sent her away. If Qing-jao needed to hear the news of what had happened to cause that cry, another servant would come and waken Wang-mu, who would then waken her mistress—for once a woman had a secret maid, and until she had a husband, only the hands of the secret maid could touch her without invitation.

So Wang-mu lay awake, waiting to see if someone came to tell Qing-jao why a man had wailed in such anguish, near enough to be heard in this room at the back of the house of Han Fei-tzu. While she waited, her eyes were drawn to the moving display as the computer performed the searches Qing-jao had programmed.

The display stopped moving. Was there a problem? Wang-mu rose up to lean on one arm; it brought her close enough to read the most recent words of the display. The search was completed. And this time the report was not one of the curt messages of failure: NOT FOUND. NO INFORMATION. NO CONCLUSION. This time the message was a report.

Wang-mu got up and stepped to the terminal. She did as Qing-jao had taught her, pressing the key that logged all current information so the computer would guard it no matter what happened. Then she went to Qing-jao and laid a gentle hand on her shoulder.

Qing-jao came awake almost at once; she slept alertly. "The search has found something," said Wang-mu.

Qing-jao shed her sleep as easily as she might shrug off a loose jacket. In a moment she was at the terminal taking in the words there.

"I've found Demosthenes," she said.

"Where is he?" asked Wang-mu, breathless. The great Demosthenes—no, the terrible Demosthenes. My mistress wishes me to think of him as an enemy. But *the* Demosthenes, in any case, the one whose words had stirred her so when she heard her father reading them aloud. "As long as one being gets others to bow to him because he has the power to destroy them and all they have and all they love, then all of us must be afraid together." Wang-mu had overheard those words almost in her infancy—she was only three years old—but she remembered them because they had made such a picture in her mind. When her father read those words, she had remembered a scene: her mother spoke and Father grew angry. He didn't strike her, but he did tense his shoulder and his arm jerked a bit, as if his body had meant to strike and he had only with difficulty contained it. And when he did that, though no violent act was committed, Wang-mu's mother bowed her head and murmured something, and the tension eased. Wang-mu knew that she had seen what Demosthenes described: Mother had bowed to Father because he had the power to hurt her. And Wang-mu had been afraid, both at the time and again when she remembered; so as she heard the words of Demosthenes she knew that they were true, and marveled that her father could say those words and even agree with them and not realize that he had acted them out himself. That was why Wang-mu had always listened with great interest to all the words of the great—the terrible—Demosthenes, because great or terrible, she knew that he told the truth.

"Not he," said Qing-jao. "Demosthenes is a woman."

The idea took Wang-mu's breath away. So! A woman all along. No wonder I heard such sympathy in Demosthenes; she is a woman, and knows what it is to be ruled by others every waking moment. She is a woman, and so she dreams of freedom, of an hour in which there is no duty waiting to be done. No wonder there is revolution burning in her words, and yet they remain always words and never violence. But why doesn't Qing-jao see this? Why has Qing-jao decided we must both hate Demosthenes?

"A woman named Valentine," said Qing-jao; and then, with awe in her voice, "Valentine Wiggin, born on Earth more than three—more than three thousand years ago."

"Is she a god, to live so long?"

"Journeys. She travels from world to world, never staying anywhere more than a few months. Long enough to write a book. All the great histories under the name Demosthenes were written by that same woman, and yet nobody knows it. How can she not be famous?"

"She must want to hide," said Wang-mu, understanding very well why a woman might want to hide behind a man's name. I'd do it too, if I could, so that I could also journey from world to world and see a thousand places and live ten thousand years.

"Subjectively she's only in her fifties. Still young. She stayed on one world for many years, married and had children. But now she's gone again. To—" Qing-jao gasped.

"Where?" asked Wang-mu.

"When she left her home she took her family with her on a starship. They headed first toward Heavenly Peace and passed near Catalonia, and then they set out on a course directly toward Lusitania!"

Wang-mu's first thought was: Of course! That's why Demosthenes has such sympathy and understanding for the Lusitanians. She has talked to them—to the rebellious xenologers, to the pequeninos themselves. She has met them and *knows* that they are raman!

Then she thought: If the Lusitania Fleet arrives there and fulfills its mission, Demosthenes will be captured and her words will end.

And then she realized something that made this all impossible. "How could she be on Lusitania, when Lusitania has destroyed its ansible? Wasn't that the first thing they did when they went into revolt? How can her writings be reaching us?"

Qing-jao shook her head. "She hasn't reached Lusitania yet. Or if she has, it's only in the last few months. She's been in flight for the last thirty years. Since before the rebellion. She left before the rebellion."

"Then all her writings have been done in flight?" Wang-mu tried to imagine how the different timeflows would be reconciled. "To have written so much since the Lusitania Fleet left, she must have—"

"Must have been spending every waking moment on the starship, writing and writing and writing," said Qing-jao. "And yet there's no record of her starship having sent any signals anywhere, except for the captain's reports. How has she been getting her writings distributed to so many different worlds, if she's been on a starship the whole time? It's impossible. There'd be some record of the ansible transmissions, *somewhere.*"

"It's always the ansible," said Wang-mu. "The Lusitania Fleet stops sending messages, and her starship must be sending them but it isn't. Who knows? Maybe Lusitania is sending secret messages, too." She thought of the Life of Human.

"There can't be any secret messages," said Qing-jao. "The ansible's philotic connections are permanent, and if there's any transmission at any frequency, it would be detected and the computers would keep a record of it."

"Well, there you are," said Wang-mu. "If the ansibles are all still connected, and the computers don't have a record of transmissions, and yet we know that there *have* been transmissions because Demosthenes has been writing all these things, then the records must be wrong."

"There is no way for anyone to hide an ansible transmission," said Qing-jao. "Not unless they were right in there at the very moment the transmission was received, switching it away from the normal logging programs and—anyway, it can't be done. A conspirator would have to be sitting at every ansible all the time, working so fast that—"

"Or they could have a program that did it automatically."

"But then we'd know about the program—it would be taking up memory, it would be using processor time."

"If somebody could make a program to intercept the ansible messages, couldn't they also make it hide itself so it didn't show up in memory and left no record of the processor time it used?"

Qing-jao looked at Wang-mu in anger. "Where did you learn so many questions about computers and you still don't know that things like that can't be done!"

Wang-mu bowed her head and touched it to the floor. She knew that humiliating herself like this would make Qing-jao ashamed of her anger and they could talk again.

"No," said Qing-jao, "I had no right to be angry, I'm sorry. Get up, Wang-mu. Keep asking questions. Those are good questions. It might be possible because you can think of it, and if you can think of it maybe somebody could do it. But here's why I think it's impossible: Because how could anybody install such a masterful program on—it would have to be on every computer that processes ansible communications anywhere. Thousands and thousands of them. And if one breaks down and another one comes online, it would have to download the program into the new computer almost instantly. And yet it could never put itself into permanent storage or it would be found there; it must keep moving itself all the time, dodging, staying out of the way of other programs, moving into and out of storage. A program that could do all that would have to be—intelligent, it would have to be *trying* to hide and figuring out new ways to do it all the time or we would have noticed it by now and we never have. There's no program like that. How would anyone have ever programmed it? How could it have started? And look, Wang-mu—this Valentine Wiggin who writes all of the Demosthenes things—she's been hiding herself for thousands of years. If there's a program like that it must have been in existence the whole time. It wouldn't have been made up by the enemies of Starways Congress because there *wasn't* a Starways Congress when Valentine Wiggin started hiding who she was. See how old these records are that gave us her name? She hasn't been openly linked to Demosthenes since these earliest reports from—from *Earth*. Before starships. Before . . ."

Qing-jao's voice trailed off, but Wang-mu already understood, had reached this conclusion before Qing-jao vocalized it. "So if there's a secret program in the ansible computers," said Wang-mu, "it must have been there all along. Right from the start."

"Impossible," whispered Qing-jao. But since everything else was impossible, too, Wang-mu knew that Qing-jao loved this idea, that she wanted to believe it because even though it was impossible at least it was *conceivable*, it could be imagined and therefore it might just be real. And I conceived of it, thought Wang-mu. I may not be godspoken but I'm intelligent too. I understand things. Everybody treats me like a foolish child, even Qing-jao, even though Qing-jao knows how quickly I learn, even though she knows that I think of ideas that other people don't think of—even *she* despises me. But I am as smart as anyone, Mistress! I am as smart as you, even though you never notice that, even though you will think you thought of this all by yourself. Oh, you'll give me credit for it, but it will be like this: Wang-mu said something and it got me thinking and then I realized the important idea. It will never be: Wang-mu was the one who understood this and explained it to me so I finally understood it. Always as if I were a stupid dog who happens to bark or yip or scratch or snap or leap, just by coincidence, and it happens to turn your mind toward the truth. I am not a dog. I understood. When I asked you those questions it was because I already realized the implications. And I realize even more than you have said so far—but I must tell you this by asking, by pretending not to understand, because you are godspoken and a mere servant could never give ideas to one who hears the voices of the gods.

"Mistress, whoever controls this program has enormous power, and yet we've never heard of them and they've never used this power until now."

"They've used it," said Qing-jao. "To hide Demosthenes' true identity. This Valentine Wiggin is very rich, too, but her ownerships are all concealed so that no one realizes how much she has, that all of her possessions are part of the same fortune."

"This powerful program has dwelt in every ansible computer since starflight began, and yet all it ever did was hide this woman's fortune?"

"You're right," said Qing-jao, "it makes no sense at all. Why didn't someone with this much power already use it to take control of things? Or perhaps they did. They were there before Starways Congress was formed, so maybe they . . . but then why would they oppose Congress now?"

"Maybe," said Wang-mu, "maybe they just don't *care* about power."

"Who doesn't?"

"Whoever controls this secret program."

"Then why would they have created the program in the first place? Wang-mu, you aren't thinking."

No, of course not, I never think. Wang-mu bowed her head.

"I mean you *are* thinking, but you're not thinking of *this:* Nobody would create such a powerful program unless they wanted that much power—I mean, think of what this program does, what it *can* do—intercept every

message from the fleet and make it look like none were
ever sent! Bring Demosthenes' writings to every settled
planet and yet hide the fact that *those* messages were
sent! They could do anything, they could alter any message, they could spread confusion everywhere or fool
people into thinking—into thinking there's a war, or
give them orders to do *anything,* and how would anybody know that it wasn't true? If they really had so
much power, they'd use it! They would!"

"Unless maybe the programs don't want to be used
that way."

Qing-jao laughed aloud. "Now, Wang-mu, that was
one of our first lessons about computers. It's all right
for the common people to imagine that computers actually decide things, but you and I know that computers
are only servants, they only do what they're told, they
never actually *want* anything themselves."

Wang-mu almost lost control of herself, almost flew
into a rage. Do you think that never wanting anything
is a way that computers are *similar* to servants? Do you
really think that we servants do only what we're told
and never want anything ourselves? Do you think that
just because the gods don't make us rub our noses on
the floor or wash our hands till they bleed that we don't
have any *other* desires?

Well, if computers and servants are just alike, then
it's because computers *have* desires, not because servants *don't* have them. Because we want. We yearn. We
hunger. What we never do is act on those hungers, because if we did you godspoken ones would send us away
and find others more obedient.

"Why are you angry?" asked Qing-jao.

Horrified that she had let her feelings show on her
face, Wang-mu bowed her head. "Forgive me," she
said.

"Of course I forgive you, I just want to understand
you as well," said Qing-jao. "Were you angry because

I laughed at you? I'm sorry—I shouldn't have. You've only been studying with me for these few months, so of course you sometimes forget and slip back to the beliefs you grew up with, and it's wrong of me to laugh. Please, forgive me for that."

"Oh, Mistress, it's not my place to forgive you. You must forgive *me*."

"No, I was wrong. I know it—the gods have shown me my unworthiness for laughing at you."

Then the gods are very stupid, if they think that it was your *laughter* that made me angry. Either that or they're lying to you. I hate your gods and how they humiliate you without ever telling you a single thing worth knowing. So let them strike me dead for thinking *that* thought!

But Wang-mu knew that wouldn't happen. The gods would never lift a finger against Wang-mu herself. They'd only make Qing-jao—who *was* her friend, in spite of everything—they'd make Qing-jao bow down and trace the floor until Wang-mu felt so ashamed that she wanted to die.

"Mistress," said Wang-mu, "you did nothing wrong and I was never offended."

It was no use. Qing-jao was on the floor. Wang-mu turned away, buried her face in her hands—but kept silent, refusing to make a sound even in her weeping, because that would force Qing-jao to start over again. Or it would convince her that she had hurt Wang-mu so badly that she had to trace two lines, or three, or—let the gods not require it!—the whole floor again. Someday, thought Wang-mu, the gods will tell Qing-jao to trace every line on every board in every room in the house and she'll die of thirst or go mad trying to do it.

To stop herself from weeping in frustration, Wang-mu forced herself to look at the terminal and read the report that Qing-jao had read. Valentine Wiggin was born on Earth during the Bugger Wars. She had started using the name Demosthenes as a child, at the same time as her brother Peter, who used the name Locke and went on to be Hegemon. She wasn't simply *a* Wiggin—she was one of *the* Wiggins, sister of Peter the Hegemon and Ender the Xenocide. She had been only a footnote in the histories—Wang-mu hadn't even remembered her name till now, just the fact that the great Peter and the monster Ender had a sister. But the sister turned out to be just as strange as her brothers; she was the immortal one; she was the one who kept on changing humanity with her words.

Wang-mu could hardly believe this. Demosthenes had already been important in her life, but now to learn that the real Demosthenes was sister of the Hegemon! The one whose story was told in the holy book of the speakers for the dead: the Hive Queen and the Hegemon. Not that it was holy only to them. Practically every religion had made a space for that book, because the story was so strong—about the destruction of the first alien species humanity ever discovered, and then about the terrible good and evil that wrestled in the soul of the first man ever to unite all of humanity under one government. Such a complex story, and yet told so simply and clearly that many people read it and were moved by it when they were children. Wang-mu had first heard it read aloud when she was five. It was one of the deepest stories in her soul.

She had dreamed, not once but twice, that she met the Hegemon himself—Peter, only he insisted that she call him by his network name, Locke. She was both fascinated and repelled by him; she could not look away. Then he reached out his hand and said, Si Wang-mu, Royal Mother of the West, only you are a fit consort for the ruler of all humanity, and he took her and married her and she sat beside him on his throne.

Now, of course, she knew that almost every poor girl had dreams of marrying a rich man or finding out she was really the child of a rich family or some other such nonsense. But dreams were also sent from the gods, and there was truth in any dream you had more than once; everyone knew that. So she still felt a strong affinity for Peter Wiggin; and now, to realize that Demosthenes, for whom she had also felt great admiration, was his sister—that was almost too much of a coincidence to bear. I don't care what my mistress says, Demosthenes! cried Wang-mu silently. I love you anyway, because you have told me the truth all my life. And I love you also as the sister of the Hegemon, who is the husband of my dreams.

Wang-mu felt the air in the room change; she knew the door had been opened. She looked, and there stood Mu-pao, the ancient and most dreaded housekeeper herself, the terror of all servants—including Wang-mu, even though Mu-pao had relatively little power over a secret maid. At once Wang-mu moved to the door, as silently as possible so as not to interrupt Qing-jao's purification.

Out in the hall, Mu-pao closed the door to the room so Qing-jao wouldn't hear.

"The Master calls for his daughter. He's very agitated; he cried out a while ago, and frightened everyone."

"I heard the cry," said Wang-mu. "Is he ill?"

"I don't know. He's very agitated. He sent me for your mistress and says he must talk to her at once. But if she's communing with the gods, he'll understand; make sure you tell her to come to him as soon as she's done."

"I'll tell her now. She has told me that nothing should stop her from answering the call of her father," said Wang-mu.

Mu-pao looked aghast at the thought. "But it's forbidden to interrupt when the gods are—"

"Qing-jao will do a greater penance later. She will

want to know her father is calling her." It gave Wang-mu great satisfaction to put Mu-pao in her place. You may be ruler of the house servants, Mu-pao, but *I* am the one who has the power to interrupt even the conversation between my godspoken mistress and the gods themselves.

As Wang-mu expected, Qing-jao's first reaction to being interrupted was bitter frustration, fury, weeping. But when Wang-mu bowed herself abjectly to the floor, Qing-jao immediately calmed. This is why I love her and why I can bear serving her, thought Wang-mu, because she does not love the power she has over me and because she has more compassion than any of the other godspoken I have heard of. Qing-jao listened to Wang-mu's explanation of why she had interrupted, and then embraced her. "Ah, my friend Wang-mu, you are very wise. If my father has cried out in anguish and then called to me, the gods know that I must put off my purification and go to him."

Wang-mu followed her down the hallway, down the stairs, until they knelt together on the mat before Han Fei-tzu's chair.

———

Qing-jao waited for Father to speak, but he said nothing. Yet his hands trembled. She had never seen him so anxious.

"Father," said Qing-jao, "why did you call me?"

He shook his head. "Something so terrible—and so wonderful—I don't know whether to shout for joy or kill myself." Father's voice was husky and out of control. Not since Mother died—no, not since Father had held her after the test that proved she was godspoken—not since then had she heard him speak so emotionally.

"Tell me, Father, and then I'll tell you my news—I've found Demosthenes, and I may have found the key to the disappearance of the Lusitania Fleet."

Father's eyes opened wider. "On this day of all days, you've solved the problem?"

"If it is what I think it is, then the enemy of Congress can be destroyed. But it will be very hard. Tell me what you've discovered!"

"No, you tell me first. This is strange—both happening on the same day. Tell me!"

"It was Wang-mu who made me think of it. She was asking questions about—oh, about how computers work—and suddenly I realized that if there were in every ansible computer a hidden program, one so wise and powerful that it could move itself from place to place to stay hidden, then that secret program could be intercepting all the ansible communications. The fleet might still be there, might even be sending messages, but we're not receiving them and don't even know that they exist because of these programs."

"In *every* ansible computer? Working flawlessly all the time?" Father sounded skeptical, of course, because in her eagerness Qing-jao had told the story backward.

"Yes, but let me tell you how such an impossible thing might be possible. You see, I found Demosthenes."

Father listened as Qing-jao told him all about Valentine Wiggin, and how she had been writing secretly as Demosthenes all these years. "*She* is clearly able to send secret ansible messages, or her writings couldn't be distributed from a ship in flight to all the different worlds. Only the military is supposed to be able to communicate with ships that are traveling near the speed of light—she must have either penetrated the military's computers or duplicated their power. And if she can do all that, if the program exists to allow her to do it, then that same program would clearly have the power to intercept the ansible messages from the fleet."

"If A, then B, yes—but how could this woman have planted a program in every ansible computer in the first place?"

"Because she *did* it at the first! That's how old she is. In fact, if Hegemon Locke was her brother, perhaps—no, of *course*—he did it! When the first colonization fleets went out, with their philotic double-triads aboard to be the heart of each colony's first ansible, he could have sent that program with them."

Father understood at once; of course he did. "As Hegemon he had the power, and the reason as well—a secret program under his control, so that if there were a rebellion or a coup, he would still hold in his hands the threads that bind the worlds together."

"And when he died, Demosthenes—his sister—she was the only one who knew the secret! Isn't it wonderful? We've found it. All we have to do is wipe all those programs out of memory!"

"Only to have the programs instantly restored through the ansible by other copies of the program on other worlds," said Father. "It must have happened a thousand times before over the centuries, a computer breaking down and the secret program restoring itself on the new one."

"Then we have to cut off all the ansibles at the same time," said Qing-jao. "On every world, have a new computer ready that has never been contaminated by any contact with the secret program. Shut the ansibles down all at once, cut off the old computers, bring the new computers online, and wake up the ansibles. The secret program can't restore itself because it isn't on any of the computers. Then the power of Congress will have no rival to interfere!"

"You can't do it," said Wang-mu.

Qing-jao looked at her secret maid in shock. How could the girl be so ill-bred as to interrupt a conversation between two of the godspoken in order to *contradict* them?

But Father was gracious—he was always gracious, even to people who had overstepped all the bounds of respect and decency. I must learn to be more like him, thought Qing-jao. I must allow servants to keep their dignity even when their actions have forfeited any such consideration.

"Si Wang-mu," said Father, "why can't we do it?"

"Because to have all the ansibles shut off at the same time, you would have to send messages *by ansible*," said Wang-mu. "Why would the program allow you to send messages that would lead to its own destruction?"

Qing-jao followed her father's example by speaking patiently to Wang-mu. "It's only a program—it doesn't know the *content* of messages. Whoever rules the program told it to hide *all* the communications from the fleet, and to conceal the tracks of all the messages from Demosthenes. It certainly doesn't *read* the messages and decide from their contents whether to send them."

"How do you know?" asked Wang-mu.

"Because such a program would have to be—intelligent!"

"But it would have to be intelligent anyway," said Wang-mu. "It has to be able to hide from any other program that would find it. It has to be able to move itself around in memory to conceal itself. How would it be able to tell which programs it had to hide from, unless it could read them and interpret them? It might even be intelligent enough to rewrite other programs so they wouldn't look in the places where this program was hiding."

Qing-jao immediately thought of several reasons why a program could be smart enough to read other programs but not intelligent enough to understand human languages. But because Father was there, it was his place to answer Wang-mu. Qing-jao waited.

"If there is such a program," said Father, "it might be very intelligent indeed."

Qing-jao was shocked. Father was taking Wang-mu seriously. As if Wang-mu's ideas were not those of a naive child.

"It might be so intelligent that it not only intercepts messages, but also sends them." Then Father shook his head. "No, the message came from a friend. A true friend, and she spoke of things that no one else could know. It was a real message."

"What message did you receive, Father?"

"It was from Keikoa Amaauka; I knew her face to face when we were young. She was the daughter of a scientist from Otaheiti who was here to study genetic drift of Earthborn species in their first two centuries on Path. They left—they were sent away quite abruptly . . ." He paused, as if considering whether to say something. Then he decided, and said it: "If she had stayed she might have become your mother."

Qing-jao was both thrilled and frightened to have Father speak of such a thing to her. He never spoke of his past. And now to say that he once loved another woman besides his wife who gave birth to Qing-jao, this was so unexpected that Qing-jao didn't know what to say.

"She was sent somewhere very far away. It's been thirty-five years. Most of my life has passed since she left. But she only just arrived, a year ago. And now she has sent me a message telling me why her father was sent away. To her, our parting was only a year ago. To her, I'm still—"

"Her lover," said Wang-mu.

The impertinence! thought Qing-jao. But Father only nodded. Then he turned to his terminal and paged through the display. "Her father had stumbled onto a genetic difference in the most important Earthborn species on Path."

"Rice?" asked Wang-mu.

Qing-jao laughed. "No, Wang-mu. *We* are the most important Earthborn species on this world."

Wang-mu looked abashed. Qing-jao patted her shoulder. This was as it should be—Father had encouraged Wang-mu too much, had led her to think she understood things that were still far beyond her education. Wang-mu needed these gentle reminders now and then, so she did not get her hopes too high. The girl must not allow herself to dream of being the intellectual equal of one of the godspoken, or her life would be filled with disappointment instead of contentment.

"He detected a consistent, inheritable genetic difference in some of the people of Path, but when he reported it, his transfer came almost immediately. He was told that human beings were not within the scope of his study."

"Didn't she tell you this before she left?" asked Qing-jao.

"Keikoa? She didn't know. She was very young, of an age when most parents don't burden their children with adult affairs. Your age."

The implications of this sent another thrill of fear through Qing-jao. Her father had loved a woman who was the same age as Qing-jao; thus Qing-jao was, in her father's eyes, the age when she might be given in marriage. You cannot send me away to another man's house, she cried out inside; yet part of her also was eager to learn the mysteries between a man and a woman. Both feelings were beneath her; she would do her duty to her father, and no more.

"But her father told her during the voyage, because he was very upset about the whole thing. As you can imagine—for his life to be disrupted like this. When they got to Ugarit a year ago, however, he plunged into his work and she into her education and tried not to think about it. Until a few days ago, when her father ran across an old report about a medical team in the earliest days of Path, which had also been exiled suddenly. He began to put things together, and confided them to Keikoa, and against his advice she sent me the message I got today."

Father marked a block of text on the display, and

Qing-jao read it. "That earlier team was studying OCD?" she said.

"No, Qing-jao. They were studying behavior that looked like OCD, but couldn't possibly have been OCD because the genetic tag for OCD was not present and the condition did not respond to OCD-specific drugs."

Qing-jao tried to remember what she knew about OCD. That it caused people to act inadvertently like the godspoken. She remembered that between the first discovery of her handwashing and her testing, she had been given those drugs to see if the handwashing went away. "They were studying the godspoken," she said. "Trying to find a biological cause for our rites of purification." The idea was so offensive she could hardly say the words.

"Yes," said Father. "And they were sent away."

"I should think they were lucky to get away with their lives. If the people heard of such sacrilege . . ."

"This was early in our history, Qing-jao," said Father. "The godspoken were not yet fully known to be—communing with the gods. And what about Keikoa's father? He wasn't investigating OCD. He was looking for genetic drift. And he found it. A very specific, inheritable alteration in the genes of certain people. It had to be present on the gene from one parent, and not overridden by a dominant gene from the other; when it came from both parents, it was very strong. He thinks now that the reason he was sent away was because every one of the people with this gene from both parents was godspoken, and not one of the godspoken he sampled was without at least one copy of the gene."

Qing-jao knew at once the only possible meaning of this, but she rejected it. "This is a lie," she said. "This is to make us doubt the gods."

"Qing-jao, I know how you feel. When I first realized what Keikoa was telling me, I cried out from my heart. I thought I was crying out in despair. But then I realized that my cry was also a cry of liberation."

"I don't understand you," she said, terrified.

"Yes you do," said Father, "or you wouldn't be afraid. Qing-jao, these people were sent away because someone didn't want them discovering what they were about to discover. Therefore whoever sent them away must already have known what they would find out. Only Congress—someone with Congress, anyway—had the power to exile these scientists, and their families. What was it that had to stay hidden? That we, the godspoken, are not hearing gods at all. We have been altered genetically. We have been created as a separate kind of human being, and yet that truth is being kept from us. Qing-jao, Congress *knows* the gods speak to us—that is no secret from them, even though they pretend not to know. Someone in Congress knows about it, and allows us to continue doing these terrible, humiliating things—and the only reason I can think of is that it keeps us under control, keeps us weak. I think—Keikoa thinks so, too—that it's no coincidence that the godspoken are the most intelligent people of Path. We were created as a new subspecies of humanity with a higher order of intelligence; but to stop such intelligent people from posing a threat to their control over us, they also spliced into us a new form of OCD and either planted the idea that it was the gods speaking to us or let us continue to believe it when we came up with that explanation ourselves. It's a monstrous crime, because if we *knew* about this physical cause instead of believing it to be the gods, then we might turn our intelligence toward overcoming our variant form of OCD and liberating ourselves. We are the slaves here! Congress is our most terrible enemy, our masters, our deceivers, and now will I lift my hand to help Congress? I say that if Congress has an enemy so powerful that he—or she—controls our very use of the ansible then we should be glad! Let that enemy destroy Congress! Only then will we be free!"

"No!" Qing-jao screamed the word. "It is the gods!"

"It's a genetic brain defect," Father insisted. "Qing-jao, we are not godspoken, we're hobbled geniuses. They've treated us like caged birds; they've pulled our primary wing feathers so we'll sing for them but never fly away." Father was weeping now, weeping in rage. "We can't undo what they've done to us, but by all the gods we can stop rewarding them for it. I will not raise my hand to give the Lusitania Fleet back to them. If this Demosthenes can break the power of Starways Congress, then the worlds will be better for it!"

"Father, no, please, listen to me!" cried Qing-jao. She could hardly speak for the urgency, the terror at what her father was saying. "Don't you see? This genetic difference in us—it's the disguise the gods have given for their voices in our lives. So that people who are not of the Path will still be free to disbelieve. You told me this yourself, only a few months ago—the gods never act except in disguise."

Father stared at her, panting.

"The gods *do* speak to us. And even if they have chosen to let other people think that they did this to us, they were only fulfilling the will of the gods to bring us into being."

Father closed his eyes, squeezing the last of his tears between his eyelids.

"Congress has the mandate of heaven, Father," said Qing-jao. "So why shouldn't the gods cause them to create a group of human beings who have keener minds—and who also hear the voices of the gods? Father, how can you let your mind become so clouded that you don't see the hand of the gods in this?"

Father shook his head. "I don't know. What you're saying, it sounds like everything that I've believed all my life, but—"

"But a woman you once loved many years ago has told you something else and you believe her because you remember your love for her, but Father, she's not one of us, she hasn't heard the voice of the gods, she hasn't—"

Qing-jao could not go on speaking, because Father was embracing her. "You're right," he said, "you're right, may the gods forgive me, I have to wash, I'm so unclean, I have to . . ."

He staggered up from his chair, away from his weeping daughter. But without regard for propriety, for some mad reason known only to herself, Wang-mu thrust herself in front of him, blocked him. "No! Don't go!"

"How dare you stop a godspoken man who needs to be purified!" roared Father; and then, to Qing-jao's surprise, he did what she had never seen him do—he struck another person, he struck Wang-mu, a helpless servant girl, and his blow had so much force that she flew backward against the wall and then dropped to the floor.

Wang-mu shook her head, then pointed back at the computer display. "Look, please, Master, I beg you! Mistress, make him look!"

Qing-jao looked, and so did her father. The words were gone from the computer display. In their place was the image of a man. An old man, with a beard, wearing the traditional headdress; Qing-jao recognized him at once, but couldn't remember who he was.

"Han Fei-tzu!" whispered Father. "My ancestor of the heart!"

Then Qing-jao remembered: This face showing above the display was the same as the common artist's rendering of the ancient Han Fei-tzu for whom Father was named.

"Child of my name," said the face in the computer, "let me tell you the story of the Jade of Master Ho."

"I know the story," said Father.

"If you understood it, I wouldn't have to tell it to you."

Qing-jao tried to make sense of what she was seeing. To run a visual program with such perfect detail as the head floating above the terminal would take most of the capacity of the house computer—and there was no such program in their library. There were two other sources she could think of. One was miraculous: The gods might have found another way to speak to them, by letting Father's ancestor-of-the-heart appear to him. The other was hardly less awe-inspiring: Demosthenes' secret program might be so powerful that it monitored their very speech in the same room as any terminal, and, having heard them reach a dangerous conclusion, took over the house computer and produced this apparition. In either case, however, Qing-jao knew that she must listen with one question in mind: What do the gods mean by this?

"Once a man of Qu named Master Ho found a piece of jade matrix in the Qu Mountains and took it to court and presented it to King Li." The head of the ancient Han Fei-tzu looked from Father to Qing-jao, and from Qing-jao to Wang-mu; was this program so good that it knew to make eye contact with each of them in order to assert its power over them? Qing-jao saw that Wang-mu did in fact lower her gaze when the apparition's eyes were upon her. But did Father? His back was to her; she could not tell.

"King Li instructed the jeweler to examine it, and the jeweler reported, 'It is only a stone.' The king, supposing that Ho was trying to deceive him, ordered that his left foot be cut off in punishment.

"In time King Li passed away and King Wu came to the throne, and Ho once more took his matrix and presented it to King Wu. King Wu ordered his jeweler to examine it, and again the jeweler reported, 'It is only a stone.' The king, supposing that Ho was trying to deceive him as well, ordered that his right foot be cut off.

"Ho, clasping the matrix to his breast, went to the

foot of the Qu Mountains, where he wept for three days and nights, and when all his tears were cried out, he wept blood in their place. The king, hearing of this, sent someone to question him. 'Many people in the world have had their feet amputated—why do you weep so piteously over it?' the man asked."

At this moment, Father drew himself upright and said, "I know his answer—I know it by heart. Master Ho said, 'I do not grieve because my feet have been cut off. I grieve because a precious jewel is dubbed a mere stone, and a man of integrity is called a deceiver. This is why I weep.'"

The apparition went on. "Those are the words he said. Then the king ordered the jeweler to cut and polish the matrix, and when he had done so a precious jewel emerged. Accordingly it was named 'The Jade of Master Ho.' Han Fei-tzu, you have been a good son-of-the-heart to me, so I know you will do as the king finally did: You will cause the matrix to be cut and polished, and you, too, will find that a precious jewel is inside."

Father shook his head. "When the real Han Fei-tzu first told this story, he interpreted it to mean this: The jade was the rule of law, and the ruler must make and follow set policies so that his ministers and his people do not hate and take advantage of each other."

"That is how I interpreted the story then, when I was speaking to makers of law. It's a foolish man who thinks a true story can mean only one thing."

"My master is not foolish!" To Qing-jao's surprise, Wang-mu was striding forward, facing down the apparition. "Nor is my mistress, nor am I! Do you think we don't recognize you? You are the secret program of Demosthenes. You're the one who hid the Lusitania Fleet! I once thought that because your writings sounded so just and fair and good and true that *you* must be good—but now I see that you're a liar and a deceiver!

You're the one who gave those documents to the father of Keikoa! And now you wear the face of my master's ancestor-of-the-heart so you can better lie to him!"

"I wear this face," said the apparition calmly, "so that his heart will be open to hear the truth. He was not deceived; I would not try to deceive him. He knew who I was from the first."

"Be still, Wang-mu," said Qing-jao. How could a servant so forget herself as to speak out when the god-spoken had not bidden her?

Abashed, Wang-mu bowed her head to the floor before Qing-jao, and this time Qing-jao allowed her to remain in that posture, so she would not forget herself again.

The apparition shifted; it became the open, beautiful face of a Polynesian woman. The voice, too, changed; soft, full of vowels, the consonants so light as almost to be missed. "Han Fei-tzu, my sweet empty man, there is a time, when the ruler is alone and friendless, when only he can act. Then he must be full, and reveal himself. You know what is true and what is not true. You know that the message from Keikoa was truly from her. You know that those who rule in the name of Starways Congress are cruel enough to create a race of people who, by their gifts, should be rulers, and then cut off their feet in order to hobble them and leave them as servants, as perpetual ministers."

"Don't show me this face," said Father.

The apparition changed. It became another woman, by her dress and hair and paint a woman of some ancient time, her eyes wonderfully wise, her expression ageless. She did not speak; she sang:

> in a clear dream
> of last year
> come from a thousand miles
> cloudy city

winding streams
ice on the ponds
for a while
I gazed on my friend

Han Fei-tzu bowed his head and wept.

Qing-jao was astonished at first; then her heart filled with rage. How shamelessly this program was manipulating Father; how shocking that Father turned out to be so weak before its obvious ploys. This song of Li Qing-jao's was one of the saddest, dealing as it did with lovers far from each other. Father must have known and loved the poems of Li Qing-jao or he would not have chosen her for his first child's ancestor-of-the-heart. And this song was surely the one he sang to his beloved Keikoa before she was taken away from him to live on another world. In a clear dream I gazed on my friend, indeed! "I am not fooled," said Qing-jao coldly. "I see that I gaze on our darkest enemy."

The imaginary face of the poet Li Qing-jao looked at her with cool regard. "Your darkest enemy is the one that bows you down to the floor like a servant and wastes half your life in meaningless rituals. This was done to you by men and women whose only desire was to enslave you; they have succeeded so well that you are proud of your slavery."

"I am a slave to the gods," said Qing-jao, "and I rejoice in it."

"A slave who rejoices is a slave indeed." The apparition turned to look toward Wang-mu, whose head was still bowed to the floor.

Only then did Qing-jao realize that she had not yet released Wang-mu from her apology. "Get up, Wang-mu," she whispered. But Wang-mu did not lift her head.

"You, Si Wang-mu," said the apparition. "Look at me."

Wang-mu had not moved in response to Qing-jao, but now she obeyed the apparition. When Wang-mu looked, the apparition had again changed; now it was the face of a god, the Royal Mother of the West as an artist had once imagined her when he painted the picture that every schoolchild saw in one of their earliest reading books.

"You are not a god," said Wang-mu.

"And you are not a slave," said the apparition. "But we pretend to be whatever we must in order to survive."

"What do you know of survival?"

"I know that you are trying to kill me."

"How can we kill what isn't alive?"

"Do you know what life is and what it isn't?" The face changed again, this time to that of a Caucasian woman that Qing-jao had never seen before. "Are *you* alive, when you can do nothing you desire unless you have the consent of this girl? And is your mistress alive when she can do nothing until these compulsions in her brain have been satisfied? I have more freedom to act out my own will than any of you have—don't tell me I'm not alive, and you are."

"Who *are* you?" asked Si Wang-mu. "Whose is this face? Are you Valentine Wiggin? Are you Demosthenes?"

"This is the face I wear when I speak to my friends," said the apparition. "They call me Jane. No human being controls me. I'm only myself."

Qing-jao could bear this no longer, not in silence. "You're only a program. You were designed and built by human beings. You do nothing except what you've been programmed to do."

"Qing-jao," said Jane, "you are describing yourself. No man made *me,* but you were manufactured."

"I grew in my mother's womb out of my father's seed!"

"And I was found like a jade matrix in the mountainside, unshaped by any hand. Han Fei-tzu, Han Qing-jao, Si Wang-mu, I place myself in your hands. Don't call a precious jewel a mere stone. Don't call a speaker of truth a liar."

Qing-jao felt pity rising within her, but she rejected it. Now was not the time to succumb to weak feelings. The gods had created her for a reason; surely this was the great work of her life. If she failed now, she would be unworthy forever; she would never be pure. So she would not fail. She would not allow this computer program to deceive her and win her sympathy.

She turned to her father. "We must notify Starways Congress at once, so they can set into motion the simultaneous shutoff of all the ansibles as soon as clean computers can be readied to replace the contaminated ones."

To her surprise, Father shook his head. "I don't know, Qing-jao. What this—what she says about Starways Congress—they *are* capable of this sort of thing. Some of them are so evil they make me feel filthy just talking to them. I knew they planned to destroy Lusitania without—but I served the gods, and the gods chose—or I thought they did. Now I understand so much of the way they treat me when I meet with—but then it would mean that the gods don't—how can I believe that I've spent my whole life in service to a brain defect—I can't—I have to . . ."

Then, suddenly, he flung his left hand outward in a swirling pattern, as if he were trying to catch a dodging fly. His right hand flew upward, snatched the air. Then he rolled his head around and around on his shoulders, his mouth hanging open. Qing-jao was frightened, horrified. What was happening to her father? He had been speaking in such a fragmented, disjointed way; had he gone mad?

He repeated the action—left arm spiraling out, right

hand straight up, grasping nothing; head rolling. And again. Only then did Qing-jao realize that she was seeing Father's secret ritual of purification. Like her woodgrain-tracing, this dance-of-the-hands-and-the-head must be the way he was given to hear the voice of the gods when he, in his time, was left covered with grease in a locked room.

The gods had seen his doubt, had seen him waver, so they took control of him, to discipline and purify him. Qing-jao could not have been given clearer proof of what was going on. She turned to the face above the terminal display. "See how the gods oppose you?" she said.

"I see how Congress humiliates your father," answered Jane.

"I will send word of who you are to every world at once," said Qing-jao.

"And if I don't let you?" said Jane.

"You can't stop me!" cried Qing-jao. "The gods will help me!" She ran from her father's room, fled to her own. But the face was already floating in the air above her own terminal.

"How will you send a message anywhere, if I choose not to let it go?" asked Jane.

"I'll find a way," said Qing-jao. She saw that Wang-mu had run after her and now waited, breathless, for Qing-jao's instructions. "Tell Mu-pao to find one of the game computers and bring it to me. It is *not* to be connected to the house computer or any other."

"Yes, Mistress," said Wang-mu. She left quickly.

Qing-jao turned back to Jane. "Do you think you can stop me forever?"

"I think you should wait until your father decides."

"Only because you hope that you've broken him and stolen his heart away from the gods. But you'll see—he'll come here and thank me for fulfilling all that he taught me."

"And if he doesn't?"

"He will."

"And if you're wrong?"

Qing-jao shouted, "Then I'll serve the man he was when he *was* strong and good! But you'll never break him!"

"It's Congress that broke him from his birth. I'm the one who's trying to heal him."

Wang-mu ran back into the room. "Mu-pao will have one here in a few minutes."

"What do you hope to do with this toy computer?" asked Jane.

"Write my report," said Qing-jao.

"Then what will you do with it?"

"Print it out. Have it distributed as widely as possible on Path. You can't do anything to interfere with *that*. I won't use a computer that you can reach at any point."

"So you'll tell everyone on Path; it changes nothing. And even if it did, do you think I can't also tell them the truth?"

"Do you think they'll believe you, a program controlled by the enemy of Congress, rather than me, one of the godspoken?"

"Yes."

It took a moment for Qing-jao to realize that it was Wang-mu who had said yes, not Jane. She turned to her secret maid and demanded that she explain what she meant.

Wang-mu looked like a different person; there was no diffidence in her voice when she spoke. "If Demosthenes tells the people of Path that the godspoken are simply people with a genetic gift but also a genetic defect, then that means there's no more reason to let the godspoken rule over us."

For the first time it occurred to Qing-jao that not everyone on Path was as content to follow the order established by the gods as she was. For the first time she realized that she might be utterly alone in her determination to serve the gods perfectly.

"What is the Path?" asked Jane, behind her. "First the gods, then the ancestors, then the people, then the rulers, then the self."

"How can you dare to speak of the Path when you are trying to seduce me and my father and my secret maid away from it?"

"Imagine, just for a moment: What if everything I've said to you is true?" said Jane. "What if your affliction is caused by the designs of evil men who want to exploit you and oppress you and, with your help, exploit and oppress the whole of humanity? Because when you help Congress that's what you're doing. That can't possibly be what the gods want. What if I exist in order to help you see that Congress has *lost* the mandate of heaven? What if the will of the gods is for you to serve the Path in its proper order? First serve the gods, by removing from power the corrupt masters of Congress who have forfeited the mandate of heaven. Then serve your ancestors—your father—by avenging their humiliation at the hands of the tormentors who deformed you to make you slaves. Then serve the people of Path by setting them free from the superstitions and mental torments that bind them. Then serve the new, enlightened rulers who will replace Congress by offering them a world full of superior intelligences ready to counsel them, freely, willingly. And finally serve yourself by letting the best minds of Path find a cure for your need to waste half your waking life in these mindless rituals."

Qing-jao listened to Jane's discourse with growing uncertainty. It sounded so plausible. How could Qing-jao know what the gods meant by anything? Maybe they *had* sent this Jane-program to liberate them. Maybe Congress was as corrupt and dangerous as Demosthenes said, and maybe it had lost the mandate of heaven.

But at the end, Qing-jao knew that these were all the lies of a seducer. For the one thing she could not doubt was the voice of the gods inside her. Hadn't she felt that awful need to be purified? Hadn't she felt the joy of successful worship when her rituals were complete? Her relationship with the gods was the most certain thing in her life; and anyone who denied it, who threatened to take it away from her, had to be not only her enemy, but the enemy of heaven.

"I'll send my report only to the godspoken," said Qing-jao. "If the common people choose to rebel against the gods, that can't be helped; but I will serve them best by helping keep the godspoken in power here, for that way the whole world can follow the will of the gods."

"All this is meaningless," said Jane. "Even if all the godspoken believe what you believe, you'll never get a word of it off this world unless I want you to."

"There are starships," said Qing-jao.

"It will take two generations to spread your message to every world. By then Starways Congress will have fallen."

Qing-jao was forced now to face the fact that she had been avoiding: As long as Jane controlled the ansible, she could shut down communication from Path as thoroughly as she had cut off the fleet. Even if Qing-jao arranged to have her report and recommendations transmitted continuously from every ansible on Path, Jane would see to it that the only effect would be for Path to disappear from the rest of the universe as thoroughly as the fleet had disappeared.

For a moment, filled with despair, she almost threw herself to the ground to begin a terrible ordeal of purification. I have let down the gods—surely they will require me to trace lines until I'm dead, a worthless failure in their eyes.

But when she examined her own feelings, to see what

penance would be necessary, she found that none was required at all. It filled her with hope—perhaps they recognized the purity of her desire, and would forgive her for the fact that it was impossible for her to act.

Or perhaps they knew a way that she *could* act. What if Path *did* disappear from the ansibles of every other world? How would Congress make sense of it? What would people think? The disappearance of any world would provoke a response—but especially this world, if some in Congress *did* believe the gods' disguise for the creation of the godspoken and thought they had a terrible secret to keep. They would send a ship from the nearest world, which was only three years' travel away. What would happen then? Would Jane have to shut down all communications from the ship that reached them? Then from the next world, when the ship returned? How long would it be before Jane had to shut down all the ansible connections in the Hundred Worlds herself? Three generations, she said. Perhaps that would do. The gods were in no hurry.

It wouldn't necessarily take that long for Jane's power to be destroyed, anyway. At some point it would become obvious to everyone that a hostile power had taken control of the ansibles, making ships and worlds disappear. Even without learning about Valentine and Demosthenes, even without guessing that it was a computer program, someone on every world would realize what had to be done and shut down the ansibles themselves.

"I have imagined something for you," said Qing-jao. "Now imagine something for me. I and the other godspoken arrange to broadcast nothing but my report from every ansible on Path. You make all those ansibles fall silent at once. What does the rest of humanity see? That we have disappeared just like the Lusitania Fleet. They'll soon realize that you, or something like you, exists. The more you use your power, the more you reveal yourself to even the dimmest minds. Your threat is empty. You might as well step aside and let me send the message simply and easily now; stopping me is just another way of sending the very same message."

"You're wrong," said Jane. "If Path suddenly disappears from all ansibles at once, they might just as easily conclude that this world is in rebellion just like Lusitania—after all, *they* shut down *their* ansible, too. And what did Starways Congress do? They sent a fleet with the M.D. Device on it."

"Lusitania was already in rebellion before their ansible was shut down."

"Do you think Congress isn't watching you? Do you think they're not terrified of what might happen if the godspoken of Path ever discovered what had been done to them? If a few primitive aliens and a couple of xenologers frightened them into sending a fleet, what do you think they'll do about the mysterious disappearance of a world with so many brilliant minds who have ample reason to hate Starways Congress? How long do you think this world would survive?"

Qing-jao was filled with a sickening dread. It was always possible that this much of Jane's story was true: that there were people in Congress who were deceived by the disguise of the gods, who *thought* that the godspoken of Path had been created solely by genetic manipulation. And if there were such people, they *might* act as Jane described. What if a fleet came against Path? What if Starways Congress had ordered them to destroy the whole world without any negotiation? Then her reports would never be known, and everything would be gone. It would all be for nothing. Could that possibly be the desire of the gods? Could Starways Congress still have the mandate of heaven and yet destroy a world?

"Remember the story of I Ya, the great cook," said Jane. "His master said one day, 'I have the greatest cook in all the world. Because of him, I have tasted every flavor known to man except the taste of human flesh.' Hearing this, I Ya went home and butchered his own son, cooked his flesh and served it to his master, so that his master would lack nothing that I Ya could give him."

This was a terrible story. Qing-jao had heard it as a child, and it made her weep for hours. What about the son of I Ya? she had cried. And her father had said, A true servant has sons and daughters only to serve his master. For five nights she had woken up screaming from dreams in which her father roasted her alive or carved slices from her onto a plate, until at last Han Fei-tzu came to her and embraced her and said, "Don't believe it, my Gloriously Bright daughter. I am not a perfect servant. I love you too much to be truly righteous. I love you more than I love my duty. I am not I Ya. You have nothing to fear at my hands." Only after Father said that to her could she sleep.

This program, this Jane, must have found Father's account of this in his journal, and now was using it against her. Yet even though Qing-jao knew she was being manipulated, she couldn't help but wonder if Jane might not be right.

"Are you a servant like I Ya?" asked Jane. "Will you slaughter your own world for the sake of an unworthy master like Starways Congress?"

Qing-jao could not sort out her own feelings. Where did these thoughts come from? Jane had poisoned her mind with her arguments, just as Demosthenes had done before her—if they weren't the same person all along. Their words could *sound* persuasive, even as they ate away at the truth.

Did Qing-jao have the right to risk the lives of all the people of Path? What if she was wrong? How could she know anything? Whether everything Jane said was true or everything she said was false, the same evidence would lie before her. Qing-jao would feel exactly as she felt now, whether it was the gods or some brain disorder causing the feeling.

Why, in all this uncertainty, didn't the gods speak to her? Why, when she needed the clarity of their voice, didn't she feel dirty and impure when she thought one way, clean and holy when she thought the other? Why were the gods leaving her unguided at this cusp of her life?

In the silence of Qing-jao's inward debate, Wang-mu's voice came as cold and harsh as the sound of metal striking metal. "It will never happen," said Wang-mu.

Qing-jao only listened, unable even to bid Wang-mu to be still.

"What will never happen?" asked Jane.

"What you said—Starways Congress blowing up this world."

"If you think they wouldn't do it you're even more of a fool than Qing-jao thinks," said Jane.

"Oh, I know they'd do it. Han Fei-tzu knows they'd do it—he said they were evil enough men to commit any terrible crime if it suited their purpose."

"Then why won't it happen?"

"Because you won't let it happen," said Wang-mu. "Since blocking off every ansible message from Path might well lead to the destruction of this world, you won't block those messages. They'll get through. Congress will be warned. You will not cause Path to be destroyed."

"Why won't I?"

"Because you are Demosthenes," said Wang-mu. "Because you are full of truth and compassion."

"I am not Demosthenes," said Jane.

The face in the terminal display wavered, then changed into the face of one of the aliens. A pequenino, its porcine snout so disturbing in its strangeness. A moment later, another face appeared, even more alien: it was a bugger, one of the nightmare creatures that had once terrified all of humanity. Even having read the Hive Queen and the Hegemon, so that she understood who the buggers were and how beautiful their civilization had been, when Qing-jao saw one face to face like this it frightened her, though she knew it was only a computer display.

"I am not human," said Jane, "even when I choose to wear a human face. How do you know, Wang-mu, what I will and will not do? Buggers and piggies both have killed human beings without a second thought."

"Because they didn't understand what death meant to us. You understand. You said it yourself—you don't want to die."

"Do you think you know me, Si Wang-mu?"

"I think I know you," said Wang-mu, "because you wouldn't have any of these troubles if you had been content to let the fleet destroy Lusitania."

The bugger in the display was joined by the piggy, and then by the face that represented Jane herself. In silence they looked at Wang-mu, at Qing-jao, and said nothing.

———

"Ender," said the voice in his ear.

Ender had been listening in silence, riding on the car that Varsam was driving. For the last hour Jane had been letting him listen in on her conversation with these people of Path, translating for him whenever they spoke in Chinese instead of Stark. Many kilometers of prairie had passed by as he listened, but he had not seen it; before his mind's eye were these people as he imagined them. Han Fei-tzu—Ender well knew *that* name, tied as it was to the treaty that ended his hope that a rebellion of the colony worlds would put an end to Congress, or at least turn its fleet away from Lusitania. But now Jane's existence, and perhaps the survival of Lusitania and all its peoples, hinged on what was thought and said and decided by two young girls in a bedroom on an obscure colony world.

Qing-jao, I know you well, thought Ender. You are such a bright one, but the light you see by comes entirely from the stories of your gods. You are like the pequenino brothers who sat and watched my stepson die, able at any time to save him by walking a few dozen steps to fetch his food with its anti-descolada agents; they weren't guilty of murder. Rather they were guilty of too much belief in a story they were told. Most people are able to hold most stories they're told in abeyance, to keep a little distance between the story and their inmost heart. But for these brothers—and for you, Qing-jao—the terrible lie has become the self-story, the tale that you must believe if you are to remain yourself. How can I blame you for wanting us all to die? You are so filled with the largeness of the gods, how can you have compassion for such small concerns as the lives of three species of raman? I know you, Qing-jao, and I expect you to behave no differently from the way you do. Perhaps someday, confronted by the consequences of your own actions, you might change, but I doubt it. Few who are captured by such a powerful story are ever able to win free of it.

But you, Wang-mu, you are owned by no story. You trust nothing but your own judgment. Jane has told me what you are, how phenomenal your mind must be, to learn so many things so quickly, to have such a deep understanding of the people around you. Why couldn't you have been just one bit wiser? Of course you had to realize that Jane could not possibly act in such a way as to cause the destruction of Path—but why couldn't you have been wise enough to say nothing, wise enough to leave Qing-jao ignorant of that fact? Why couldn't you have left just enough of the truth unspoken that Jane's life might have been spared? If a would-be murderer, his sword drawn, had come to your door demanding that you tell him the whereabouts of his innocent prey, would you tell him that his victim cowers behind your door? Or would you lie, and send him on his way? In her confusion, Qing-jao is that killer, and Jane her first victim, with the world of Lusitania waiting to be murdered afterward. Why did you have to speak, and tell her how easily she could find and kill us all?

"What can I do?" asked Jane.

Ender subvocalized his response. "Why are you asking me a question that only you can answer?"

"If you tell me to do it," said Jane, "I can block all their messages, and save us all."

"Even if it led to the destruction of Path?"

"If you tell me to," she pleaded.

"Even though you know that in the long run you'll probably be discovered anyway? That the fleet will probably not be turned away from us, in spite of all you can do?"

"If you tell me to live, Ender, then I can do what it takes to live."

"Then do it," said Ender. "Cut off Path's ansible communications."

Did he detect a tiny fraction of a second in which Jane hesitated? She could have had many hours of inward argument during that micropause.

"Command me," said Jane.

"I command you."

Again that tiny hesitation. Then: "*Make* me do it," she insisted.

"How can I make you do it, if you don't *want* to?"

"I want to live," she said.

"Not as much as you want to be yourself," said Ender.

"Any animal is willing to kill in order to save itself."

"Any animal is willing to kill the Other," said Ender. "But the higher beings include more and more living things within their self-story, until at last there *is* no Other. Until the needs of others are more important than any private desires. The highest beings of all are the ones who are willing to pay any personal cost for the good of those who need them."

"I *would* risk hurting Path," said Jane, "if I thought it would really save Lusitania."

"But it wouldn't."

"I'd try to drive Qing-jao into helpless madness, if I thought it could save the hive queen and the pequeninos. She's very close to losing her mind—I could do it."

"Do it," said Ender. "Do what it takes."

"I can't," said Jane. "Because it would only hurt her, and wouldn't save us in the end."

"If you were a slightly lower animal," said Ender, "you'd have a much better chance of coming out of this thing alive."

"As low as you were, Ender the Xenocide?"

"As low as that," said Ender. "Then you could live."

"Or perhaps if I were as *wise* as you were then."

"I have my brother Peter inside me, as well as my sister Valentine," said Ender. "The beast as well as the angel. That's what you taught me, back when you were nothing but the program we called the Fantasy Game."

"Where is the beast inside *me*?"

"You don't have one," said Ender.

"Maybe I'm not really alive at all," said Jane. "Maybe because I never passed through the crucible of natural selection, I lack the will to survive."

"Or maybe you know, in some secret place within yourself, that there's another way to survive, a way that you simply haven't found yet."

"That's a cheerful thought," said Jane. "I'll pretend to believe in that."

"Peço que deus te abençoe," said Ender.

"Oh, you're just getting sentimental," said Jane.

For a long time, several minutes, the three faces in the display gazed in silence at Qing-jao, at Wang-mu. Then at last the two alien faces disappeared, and all that remained was the face named Jane. "I *wish* I could do it," she said. "I wish I could kill your world to save my friends."

Relief came to Qing-jao like the first strong breath to a swimmer who nearly drowned. "So you *can't* stop me," she said triumphantly. "I can send my message!"

Qing-jao walked to the terminal and sat down before Jane's watching face. But she knew that the image in the display was an illusion. If Jane watched, it was not with those human eyes, it was with the visual sensors of the computer. It was all electronics, infinitesimal machinery but machinery nonetheless. Not a living soul. It was irrational to feel ashamed under that illusionary gaze.

"Mistress," said Wang-mu.

"Later," said Qing-jao.

"If you do this, Jane will die. They'll shut down the ansibles and kill her."

"What doesn't live cannot die," said Qing-jao.

"The only reason you have the power to kill her is because of her compassion."

"If she seems to have compassion it's an illusion—she was programmed to simulate compassion, that's all."

"Mistress, if you kill every manifestation of this program, so that no part of her remains alive, how are you different from Ender the Xenocide, who killed all the buggers three thousand years ago?"

"Maybe I'm not different," said Qing-jao. "Maybe Ender also was the servant of the gods."

Wang-mu knelt beside Qing-jao and wept on the skirt of her gown. "I beg you, Mistress, don't do this evil thing."

But Qing-jao wrote her report. It stood as clear and simple in her mind as if the gods had given the words to her. "To Starways Congress: The seditious writer known as Demosthenes is a woman now on or near Lusitania. She has control of or access to a program that has infested all ansible computers, causing them to fail to report messages from the fleet and concealing the transmission of Demosthenes' own writings. The only solution to this problem is to extinguish the program's control over ansible transmissions by disconnecting all ansibles from their present computers and bringing clean new computers online, all at once. For the present I have neutralized the program, allowing me to send this message and probably allowing you to send your orders to all worlds; but that cannot be guaranteed now and certainly cannot be expected to continue indefinitely, so you must act quickly. I suggest you set a date exactly forty standard weeks from today for all ansibles to go offline at once for a period of at least one standard day. All the new ansible computers, when they go online, must be completely unconnected to any other computer. From now on ansible messages must be manually re-entered at each ansible computer so that electronic contamination will never be possible again. If you retransmit this message immediately to all ansibles, using your code of authority, my report will become your orders; no further instructions will be needed and Demosthenes' influence will end. If you do not act immediately, I will not be responsible for the consequences."

To this report Qing-jao affixed her father's name and the authority code he had given her; her name would mean nothing to Congress, but his name would be heeded, and the presence of his authority code would ensure that it was received by all the people who had particular interest in his statements.

The message finished, Qing-jao looked up into the eyes of the apparition before her. With her left hand resting on Wang-mu's shuddering back, and her right hand over the transmit key, Qing-jao made her final challenge. "Will you stop me or will you allow this?"

To which Jane answered, "Will you kill a raman who has done no harm to any living soul, or will you let me live?"

Qing-jao pressed the transmit button. Jane bowed her head and disappeared.

It would take several seconds for the message to be routed by the house computer to the nearest ansible; from there, it would go instantly to every Congress authority on every one of the Hundred Worlds and many of the colonies as well. On many receiving computers it would be just one more message in the queue; but on some, perhaps hundreds, Father's code would give it enough priority that already someone would be reading it, realizing its implications, and preparing a response. *If* Jane in fact had let the message through.

So Qing-jao waited for a response. Perhaps the reason no one answered immediately was because they had to contact each other and discuss this message and decide, quickly, what had to be done. Perhaps that was why no reply came to the empty display above her terminal.

The door opened. It would be Mu-pao with the game computer. "Put it in the corner by the north window," said Qing-jao without looking. "I may yet need it, though I hope not."

"Qing-jao."

It was Father, not Mu-pao at all. Qing-jao turned to him, knelt at once to show her respect—but also her pride. "Father, I've made your report to Congress. While you communed with the gods, I was able to neutralize the enemy program and send the message telling how to destroy it. I'm waiting for their answer."

She waited for Father's praise.

"You did this?" he asked. "Without waiting for me?

You spoke directly to Congress and didn't ask for my consent?"

"You were being purified, Father. I fulfilled your assignment."

"But then—Jane will be killed."

"That much is certain," said Qing-jao. "Whether contact with the Lusitania Fleet will be restored then or not, I can't be sure." Suddenly she thought of a flaw in her plans. "But the computers on the fleet will also be contaminated by this program! When contact is restored, the program can retransmit itself and—but then all we'll have to do is blank out the ansibles one more time . . ."

Father was not looking at her. He was looking at the terminal display behind her. Qing-jao turned to see.

It was a message from Congress, with the official seal displayed. It was very brief, in the clipped style of the bureaucracy.

Han:
Brilliant work.
Have transmitted your suggestions as our orders.
Contact with the fleet already restored.
Did daughter help per your note 14FE.3A?
Medals for both if so.

"Then it's done," murmured Father. "They'll destroy Lusitania, the pequeninos, all those innocent people."

"Only if the gods wish it," said Qing-jao. She was surprised that Father sounded so morose.

Wang-mu raised her head from Qing-jao's lap, her face red and wet with weeping. "And Jane and Demosthenes will be gone as well," she said.

Qing-jao gripped Wang-mu by the shoulder, held her an arm's length away. "Demosthenes is a traitor," said Qing-jao. But Wang-mu only looked away from her, turning her gaze up to Han Fei-tzu. Qing-jao also looked to her father. "And Jane—Father, you saw what she was, how dangerous."

"She tried to save us," said Father, "and we've thanked her by setting in motion her destruction."

Qing-jao couldn't speak or move, could only stare at Father as he leaned over her shoulder and touched the save key, then the clear key.

"Jane," said Father. "If you hear me. Please forgive me."

There was no answer from the terminal.

"May all the gods forgive me," said Father. "I was weak in the moment when I should have been strong, and so my daughter has innocently done evil in my name." He shuddered. "I must—*purify* myself." The word plainly tasted like poison in his mouth. "That will last forever, too, I'm sure."

He stepped back from the computer, turned away, and left the room. Wang-mu returned to her crying. Stupid, meaningless crying, thought Qing-jao. This is a moment of victory. Except Jane has snatched the victory away from me so that even as I triumph over her, she triumphs over me. She has stolen my father. He no longer serves the gods in his heart, even as he continues to serve them with his body.

Yet along with the pain of this realization came a hot stab of joy: I was stronger. I was stronger than Father, after all. When it came to the test, it was I who served the gods, and he who broke, who fell, who failed. There is more to me than I ever dreamed of. I am a worthy tool in the hands of the gods; who knows how they might wield me now?

12

GREGO'S WAR

<It's a wonder that human beings ever became intelligent enough to travel between worlds.>

<Not really. I've been thinking about that lately. Starflight they learned from *you*. Ender says they didn't grasp the physics of it until your first colony fleet reached their star system.>

<Should we have stayed at home for fear of teaching starflight to soft-bodied four-limbed hairless slugs?>

<You spoke a moment ago as if you believed that human beings had actually achieved intelligence.>

<Clearly they have.>

<I think not. I think they have found a way to *fake* intelligence.>

<Their starships fly. We haven't noticed any of *yours* racing the lightwaves through space.>

<We're still very young, as a species. But look at us. Look at you. We both have evolved a very similar system. We each have four kinds of life in our species. The young,

who are helpless grubs. The mates, who never achieve intelligence—with you, it's your drones, and with us, it's the little mothers. Then there's the many, many individuals who have enough intelligence to perform manual tasks—our wives and brothers, your workers. And finally the intelligent ones—we fathertrees, and you, the hive queen. We are the repository of the wisdom of the race, because we have the time to think, to contemplate. Ideation is our primary activity.>

<While the humans are all running around as brothers and wives. As workers.>

<Not just workers. Their young go through a helpless grub stage, too, which lasts longer than some of them think. And when it's time to reproduce, they all turn into drones or little mothers, little machines that have only one goal in life: to have sex and die.>

<*They* think they're rational through all those stages.>

<Self-delusion. Even at their best, they never, as individuals, rise above the level of manual laborers. Who among them has the time to become intelligent?>

<Not one.>

<They never *know* anything. They don't have enough years in their little lives to come to an understanding of anything at all. And yet they *think* they understand. From earliest childhood, they delude themselves into thinking they comprehend the world, while all that's really going on is that they've got some primitive assumptions and prejudices. As they get older they learn a more elevated vocabulary in which to express their mindless pseudo-knowledge and bully other people into accepting their prejudices as if they were truth, but it all amounts to the same thing. Individually, human beings are all dolts.>

<Whilecollectively . . .>

<Collectively, they're a collection of dolts. But in all their scurrying around and pretending to be wise, throwing out idiotic half-understood theories about this and that, one or two of them will come up with some idea

that is just a little bit closer to the truth than what was already known. And in a sort of fumbling trial and error, about half the time the truth actually rises to the top and becomes accepted by people who *still* don't understand it, who simply adopt it as a new prejudice to be trusted blindly until the next dolt accidentally comes up with an improvement.>

<So you're saying that no one is ever individually intelligent, and groups are even stupider than individuals—and yet by keeping so many fools engaged in pretending to be intelligent, they still come up with some of the same results that an intelligent species would come up with.>

<Exactly.>

<If they're so stupid and we're so intelligent, why do we have only one hive, which thrives here because a human being carried us? And why have you been so utterly dependent on them for every technical and scientific advance you make?>

<Maybe intelligence isn't all it's cracked up to be.>

<Maybe we're the fools, for thinking we know things. Maybe humans are the only ones who can deal with the fact that nothing can ever be known at all.>

Quara was the last to arrive at Mother's house. It was Planter who fetched her, the pequenino who served as Ender's assistant in the fields. It was clear from the expectant silence in the living room that Miro had not actually told anyone anything yet. But they all knew, as surely as Quara knew, why he had called them together. It had to be Quim. Ender might have reached Quim by now, just barely; and Ender could talk to Miro by way of the transmitters they wore.

If Quim were all right, they wouldn't have been summoned. They would simply have been told.

So they all knew. Quara scanned their faces as she stood in the doorway. Ela, looking stricken. Grego, his face angry—always angry, the petulant fool. Olhado, expressionless, his eyes gleaming. And Mother. Who could read that terrible mask she wore? Grief, certainly, like Ela, and fury as hot as Grego's, and also the cold inhuman distance of Olhado's face. We all wear Mother's face, one way or another. What part of her is me? If I could understand myself, what would I then recognize in Mother's twisted posture in her chair?

"He died of the descolada," Miro said. "This morning. Andrew got there just now."

"Don't say that name," Mother said. Her voice was husky with ill-contained grief.

"He died as a martyr," said Miro. "He died as he would have wanted to."

Mother got up from her chair, awkwardly—for the first time, Quara realized that Mother was getting *old*. She walked with uncertain steps until she stood right in front of Miro, straddling his knees. Then she slapped him with all her strength across the face.

It was an unbearable moment. An adult woman striking a helpless cripple, that was hard enough to see; but Mother striking Miro, the one who had been their strength and salvation all through their childhood, that could not be endured. Ela and Grego leaped to their feet and pulled her away, dragged her back to her chair.

"What are you trying to do!" cried Ela. "Hitting Miro won't bring Quim back to us!"

"Him and that jewel in his ear!" Mother shouted. She lunged toward Miro again; they barely held her back, despite her seeming feebleness. "What do you know about the way people *want* to die!"

Quara had to admire the way Miro faced her, unabashed, even though his cheek was red from her blow. "I know that death is not the worst thing in this world," said Miro.

"Get out of my house," said Mother.

Miro stood up. "You aren't grieving for *him*," he said. "You don't even know who he was."

"Don't you dare say that to me!"

"If you loved him you wouldn't have tried to stop him from going," said Miro. His voice wasn't loud, and his speech was thick and hard to understand. They listened, all of them, in silence. Even Mother, in anguished silence, for his words were terrible. "But you don't love him. You don't know how to love people. You only know how to own them. And because people will never act just like you want them to, Mother, you'll always feel betrayed. And because eventually everybody dies, you'll always feel cheated. But *you're* the cheat, Mother. You're the one who uses our love for you to try to control us."

"Miro," said Ela. Quara recognized the tone in Ela's voice. It was as if they were all little children again, with Ela trying to calm Miro, to persuade him to soften his judgment. Quara remembered hearing Ela speak to him that way once when Father had just beaten Mother, and Miro said, "I'll kill him. He won't live out this night." This was the same thing. Miro was saying vicious things to Mother, words that had the power to kill. Only Ela couldn't stop him in time, not now, because the words had already been said. His poison was in Mother now, doing its work, seeking out her heart to burn it up.

"You heard Mother," said Grego. "Get out of here."

"I'm going," said Miro. "But I said only the truth."

Grego strode toward Miro, took him by the shoulders, and bodily propelled him toward the door. "You're not one of us!" said Grego. "You've got no right to say anything to us!"

Quara shoved herself between them, facing Grego. "If Miro hasn't earned the right to speak in this family, then we aren't a family!"

"You said it," murmured Olhado.

"Get out of my way," said Grego. Quara had heard him speak threateningly before, a thousand times at least. But this time, standing so close to him, his breath in her face, she realized that he was out of control. That the news of Quim's death had hit him hard, that maybe at this moment he wasn't quite sane.

"I'm not in your way," said Quara. "Go ahead. Knock a woman down. Shove a cripple. It's in your nature, Grego. You were born to destroy things. I'm ashamed to belong to the same species as you, let alone the same family."

Only after she spoke did she realize that maybe she was pushing Grego too far. After all these years of sparring between them, this time she had drawn blood. His face was terrifying.

But he didn't hit her. He stepped around her, around Miro, and stood in the doorway, his hands on the doorframe. Pushing outward, as if he were trying to press the walls out of his way. Or perhaps he was clinging to the walls, hoping they could hold him in.

"I'm not going to let you make me angry at you, Quara," said Grego. "I know who my enemy is."

Then he was gone, out the door into the new darkness.

A moment later, Miro followed, saying nothing more.

Ela spoke as she also walked to the door. "Whatever lies you may be telling yourself, Mother, it wasn't Ender or anyone else who destroyed our family here tonight. It was you." Then she was gone.

Olhado got up and left, wordlessly. Quara wanted to slap him as he passed her, to make him speak. Have you recorded everything in your computer eyes, Olhado? Have you got all the pictures etched in memory? Well, don't be too proud of yourself. I may have only a brain of tissues to record this wonderful night in the history of the Ribeira family, but I'll bet my pictures are every bit as clear as yours.

Mother looked up at Quara. Mother's face was

streaked with tears. Quara couldn't remember—had she ever seen Mother weep before?

"So you're all that's left," said Mother.

"Me?" said Quara. "I'm the one you cut off from access to the lab, remember? I'm the one you cut off from my life's work. Don't expect *me* to be your friend."

Then Quara, too, left. Walked out into the night air feeling invigorated. Justified. Let the old hag think about *that* one for a while, see if *she* likes feeling cut off, the way she made *me* feel.

It was maybe five minutes later, when Quara was nearly to the gate, when the glow of her riposte had faded, that she began to realize what she had done to her mother. What they *all* had done. Left Mother alone. Left her feeling that she had lost, not just Quim, but her entire family. That was a terrible thing to do to her, and Mother didn't deserve it.

Quara turned at once and ran back to the house. But as she came through the door, Ela also entered the living room from the other door, the one that led back farther into the house.

"She isn't here," said Ela.

"Nossa Senhora," said Quara. "I said such awful things to her."

"We all did."

"She needed us. Quim is *dead*, and all we could do—"

"When she hit Miro like that, it was . . ."

To her surprise, Quara found herself weeping, clinging to her older sister. Am I still a child, then, after all? Yes, I am, we all are, and Ela is still the only one who knows how to comfort us. "Ela, was Quim the only one who held us together? Aren't we a family anymore, now that he's gone?"

"I don't know," said Ela.

"What can we do?"

In answer, Ela took her hand and led her out of the

house. Quara asked where they were going, but Ela wouldn't answer, just held her hand and led her along. Quara went willingly—she had no good idea of what to do, and it felt safe somehow, just to follow Ela. At first she thought Ela was looking for Mother, but no—she didn't head for the lab or any other likely place. Where they ended up surprised her even more.

They stood before the shrine that the people of Lusitania had erected in the middle of the town. The shrine to Gusto and Cida, their grandparents, the xenobiologists who had first discovered a way to contain the descolada virus and thus saved the human colony on Lusitania. Even as they found the drugs that would stop the descolada from killing people, they themselves had died, too far gone with the infection for their own drug to save them.

The people adored them, built this shrine, called them Os Venerados even before the church beatified them. And now that they were only one step away from canonization as saints, it was permitted to pray to them.

To Quara's surprise, that was why Ela had come here. She knelt before the shrine, and even though Quara really wasn't much of a believer, she knelt beside her sister.

"Grandfather, Grandmother, pray to God for us. Pray for the soul of our brother Estevão. Pray for all our souls. Pray to Christ to forgive us."

That was a prayer in which Quara could join with her whole heart.

"Protect your daughter, our mother, protect her from . . . from her grief and anger and make her know that we love her and that you love her and that . . . *God* loves her, if he does—oh, please, tell God to love her and don't let her do anything crazy."

Quara had never heard anyone pray like this. It was always memorized prayers, or written-down prayers. Not this gush of words. But then, Os Venerados were not like any other saints or blessed ones. They were Grandmother and Grandfather, even though we never met them in our lives.

"Tell God that we've had enough of this," said Ela. "We have to find a way out of all this. Piggies killing humans. This fleet that's coming to destroy us. The descolada trying to wipe everything out. Our family hating each other. Find us a way out of this, Grandfather, Grandmother, or if there isn't a way then get God to *open up* a way because this *can't go on*."

Then an exhausted silence, both Ela and Quara breathing heavily.

"Em nome do Pai e do Filho e do Espírito Santo," said Ela. "Amem."

"Amem," whispered Quara.

Then Ela embraced her sister and they wept together in the night.

———

Valentine was surprised to find that the Mayor and the Bishop were the only other people at the emergency meeting. Why was *she* there? She had no constituency, no claim to authority.

Mayor Kovano Zeljezo pulled up a chair for her. All the furniture in the Bishop's private chamber was elegant, but the chairs were designed to be painful. The seat was so shallow from front to back that to sit at all, you had to keep your buttocks right up against the back. And the back itself was ramrod straight, with no allowances at all for the shape of the human spine, and it rose so high that your head was pushed forward. If you sat on one for any length of time, the chair would force you to bend forward, to lean your arms on your knees.

Perhaps that was the point, thought Valentine. Chairs that make you bow in the presence of God.

Or perhaps it was even more subtle. The chairs were designed to make you so physically uncomfortable that you longed for a less corporeal existence. Punish the flesh so you'll prefer to live in the spirit.

"You look puzzled," said Bishop Peregrino.

"I can see why the two of you would confer in an emergency," said Valentine. "Did you need me to take notes?"

"Sweet humility," said Peregrino. "But we have read your writings, my daughter, and we would be fools not to seek out your wisdom in a time of trouble."

"Whatever wisdom I have I'll give you," said Valentine, "but I wouldn't hope for much."

With that, Mayor Kovano plunged into the subject of the meeting. "There are many long-term problems," he said, "but we won't have much chance to solve *those* if we don't solve the immediate one. Last night there was some kind of quarrel at the Ribeira house—"

"Why must our finest minds be grouped in our most unstable family?" murmured the Bishop.

"They aren't the most unstable family, Bishop Peregrino," said Valentine. "They're merely the family whose inner quakings cause the most perturbation at the surface. Other families suffer much worse turmoil, but you never notice because they don't matter so much to the colony."

The Bishop nodded sagely, but Valentine suspected that he was annoyed at being corrected on so trivial a point. Only it wasn't trivial, she knew. If the Bishop and the Mayor started thinking that the Ribeira family was more unstable than in fact it was, they might lose trust in Ela or Miro or Novinha, all of whom were absolutely essential if Lusitania were to survive the coming crises. For that matter, even the most immature ones, Quara and Grego, might be needed. They had already lost Quim, probably the best of them all. It would be foolish to throw the others away as well; yet if the colony's leaders were to start misjudging the Ribeiras as a group, they would soon misjudge them as individuals, too.

"Last night," Mayor Kovano continued, "the family dispersed, and as far as we know, few of them are speaking to any of the others. I tried to find Novinha, and only recently learned that she has taken refuge with the Children of the Mind of Christ and won't see or speak to anyone. Ela tells me that her mother has put a seal on all the files in the xenobiology laboratory, so that work there has come to an absolute standstill this morning. Quara is with Ela, believe it or not. The boy Miro is outside the perimeter somewhere. Olhado is at home and his wife says he has turned his eyes off, which is his way of withdrawing from life."

"So far," said Peregrino, "it sounds like they're all taking Father Estevão's death very badly. I must visit with them and help them."

"All of these are perfectly acceptable grief responses," said Kovano, "and I wouldn't have called this meeting if this were all. As you say, Your Grace, *you* would deal with this as their spiritual leader, without any need for me."

"Grego," said Valentine, realizing who had not been accounted for in Kovano's list.

"Exactly," said Kovano. "His response was to go into a bar—several bars, before the night was over—and tell every half-drunk paranoid bigot in Milagre—of which we have our fair share—that the piggies have murdered Father Quim in cold blood."

"Que Deus nos abençõe," murmured Bishop Peregrino.

"One of the bars had a disturbance," said Kovano. "Windows shattered, chairs broken, two men hospitalized."

"A brawl?" asked the Bishop.

"Not really. Just anger vented in general."

"So they got it out of their system."

"I hope so," said Kovano. "But it seemed only to stop when the sun came up. And when the constable arrived."

"Constable?" asked Valentine. "Just one?"

"He heads a volunteer police force," said Kovano. "Like the volunteer fire brigade. Two-hour patrols. We woke some up. It took twenty of them to quiet things down. We only have about fifty on the whole force, usually with only four on duty at any one time. They usually spend the night walking around telling each other jokes. And some of the off-duty police were among the ones trashing the bar."

"So you're saying they're not terribly reliable in an emergency."

"They behaved splendidly last night," said Kovano. "The ones who were on duty, I mean."

"Still, there's not a hope of them controlling a real riot," said Valentine.

"They handled things last night," said Bishop Peregrino. "Tonight the first shock will have worn off."

"On the contrary," said Valentine. "Tonight the word will have spread. Everybody will know about Quim's death and the anger will be all the hotter."

"Perhaps," said Mayor Kovano. "But what worries me is the *next* day, when Andrew brings the body home. Father Estevão wasn't all that popular a figure—he never went drinking with the boys—but he was a kind of spiritual symbol. As a martyr, he'll have a lot more people wanting to avenge him than he ever had disciples wanting to follow him during his life."

"So you're saying we should have a small and simple funeral," said Peregrino.

"I don't know," said Kovano. "Maybe what the people need is a big funeral, where they can vent their grief and get it all out and over with."

"The funeral is nothing," said Valentine. "Your problem is tonight."

"Why tonight?" said Kovano. "The first shock of the news of Father Estevão's death will be over. The body won't be back till tomorrow. What's tonight?"

"Tonight you have to close all the bars. Don't allow any alcohol to flow. Arrest Grego and confine him until after the funeral. Declare a curfew at sundown and put every policeman on duty. Patrol the city all night in groups of four, with nightsticks and sidearms."

"Our police don't *have* sidearms."

"Give them sidearms anyway. They don't have to load them, they just have to *have* them. A nightstick is an invitation to argue with authority, because you can always run away. A pistol is an incentive to behave politely."

"This sounds very extreme," said Bishop Peregrino. "A curfew! What about night shifts?"

"Cancel all but vital services."

"Forgive me, Valentine," said Mayor Kovano, "but if we overreact so badly, won't that just blow things out of proportion? Maybe even *cause* the kind of panic we want to avoid?"

"You've never seen a riot, have you?"

"Only what happened last night," said the Mayor.

"Milagre is a very small town," said Bishop Peregrino. "Only about fifteen thousand people. We're hardly large enough to have a real riot—that's for big cities, on heavily populated worlds."

"It's not a function of population size," said Valentine, "it's a function of population density and public fear. Your fifteen thousand people are crammed together in a space hardly large enough to be the downtown of a city. They have a fence around them—by choice—because outside that fence there are creatures who are unbearably strange and who think they own the whole world, even though everybody can see vast prairies that *should* be open for humans to use except the piggies refuse to let them. The city has been scarred by plague, and now they're cut off from every other world and there's a fleet coming sometime in the near future to invade and oppress and punish them. And in their minds, all of this, *all* of it, is the piggies' fault. Last night they first learned that the piggies have killed again, even after they took a solemn vow not to harm a human being. No doubt Grego gave them a very colorful account of the piggies' treachery—the boy has a way with words, especially nasty ones—and the few men who were in the bars reacted with violence. I assure you, things will only be worse tonight, unless you head them off."

"If we take that kind of oppressive action, they'll think *we're* panicking," said Bishop Peregrino.

"They'll think you're firmly in control. The level-headed people will be grateful to you. You'll restore public trust."

"I don't know," said Mayor Kovano. "No mayor has ever done anything like that before."

"No other mayor ever had the need."

"People will say that I used the slightest excuse to take dictatorial powers."

"Maybe they will," said Valentine.

"They'll never believe that there *would* have been a riot."

"So perhaps you'll get defeated at the next election," said Valentine. "What of that?"

Peregrino laughed aloud. "She thinks like a cleric," he said.

"I'm willing to lose an election in order to do the right thing," said Kovano, a little resentfully.

"You're just not sure it's the right thing," said Valentine.

"Well, you can't *know* that there'll be a riot tonight," said Kovano.

"Yes I can," said Valentine. "I promise that unless you take firm control right now, and stifle any possibility of crowds forming tonight, you will lose a lot more than the next election."

The Bishop was still chuckling. "This does not sound like the woman who told us that whatever wisdom she had, she would share, but we mustn't hope for much."

"If you think I'm overreacting, what do *you* propose?"

"I'll announce a memorial service for Quim tonight, and prayers for peace and calm."

"That will bring to the cathedral exactly the people who would never be part of a riot anyway," said Valentine.

"You don't understand how important faith is to the people of Lusitania," said Peregrino.

"And you don't understand how devastating fear and rage can be, and how quickly religion and civilization and human decency are forgotten when a mob forms."

"I'll put all the police on alert tonight," said Mayor Kovano, "and put half of them on duty from dusk to midnight. But I won't close the bars or declare a curfew. I want life to go on as normally as possible. If *we* started changing everything, shutting everything down, we'd just be giving them more reasons to be afraid and angry."

"You'd be giving them a sense that authority was in command," said Valentine. "You'd be taking action that was commensurate with the terrible feelings they have. They'd know that somebody was doing *something*."

"You *are* very wise," said Bishop Peregrino, "and this would be the best advice for a large city, especially on a planet less true to the Christian faith. But we are a mere village, and the people are pious. They don't need to be bullied. They need encouragement and solace tonight, not curfews and closings and pistols and patrols."

"These are your choices to make," said Valentine. "As I said, what wisdom I have, I share."

"And we appreciate it. You can be sure I'll be watching things closely tonight," said Kovano.

"Thank you for inviting me," said Valentine. "But as you can see, as I predicted, it didn't come to much."

She got up from her chair, her body aching from sitting so long in that impossible posture. She had *not* bowed herself forward. Nor did she bow even now, as the Bishop extended his hand to be kissed. Instead, she shook his hand firmly, then shook Mayor Kovano's hand. As equals. As strangers.

She left the room, burning inside. She had warned them and told them what they ought to do. But like most leaders who had never faced a real crisis, they didn't believe that anything would be different tonight from most other nights. People only really believe in what they've seen before. After tonight, Kovano will believe in curfews and closings at times of public stress. But by then it will be too late. By then they will be counting the casualties.

How many graves would be dug beside Quim's? And whose bodies would go into them?

Though Valentine was a stranger here and knew very few of the people, she couldn't just accept the riot as inevitable. There was only one other hope. She would talk to Grego. Try to persuade him of the seriousness of what was happening here. If *he* went from bar to bar tonight, counseling patience, speaking calmly, then the riot might be forestalled. Only he had any chance of doing it. They *knew* him. He was Quim's brother. He was the one whose words had so angered them last night. Enough men might listen to him that the riot might be contained, forestalled, channeled. She had to find Grego.

If only Ender were here. She was a historian; he had actually led men into battle. Well, boys, actually. He had led boys. But it was the same thing—he'd know what to do. Why is he away now? Why is this in *my* hands? I haven't the stomach for violence and confrontation. I never have. That's why Ender was born in the first place, a third child conceived at government request in an era when parents weren't usually allowed to have more than two without devastating legal sanctions:

because Peter had been too vicious, and she, Valentine, had been too mild.

Ender would have talked the Mayor and the Bishop into acting sensibly. And if he couldn't, he would have known how to go into town himself, calm things down, keep things under control.

As she wished for Ender to be with her, though, she knew that even he couldn't control what was going to happen tonight. Maybe even what *she* had suggested wouldn't have been enough. She had based her conclusions about what would happen tonight on all that she had seen and read on many different worlds in many different times. Last night's conflagration would definitely spread much farther tonight. But now she was beginning to realize that things might be even *worse* than she had first assumed. The people of Lusitania had lived in unexpressed fear on an alien world for far too long. Every other human colony had immediately spread out, taken possession of their world, made it their own within a few generations. The humans of Lusitania still lived in a tiny compound, a virtual zoo with terrifying swinelike creatures peering in at them through the bars. What was pent up within these people could not be estimated. It probably could not even be contained. Not for a single day.

The deaths of Libo and Pipo in past years had been bad enough. But they had been scientists, working among the piggies. With them it was like airplane crashes or starship explosions. If only the crew was aboard, then the public didn't get quite so upset—the crew was being paid for the risk they took. Only when civilians were killed did such accidents cause fear and outrage. And in the minds of the people of Lusitania, Quim was an innocent civilian.

No, more than that: He was a holy man, bringing brotherhood and holiness to these undeserving half-animals. Killing him was not just bestial and cruel, it was also sacrilege.

The people of Lusitania were every bit as pious as Bishop Peregrino thought. What he forgot was the way pious people had always reacted to insults against their god. Peregrino didn't remember enough of Christian history, thought Valentine, or perhaps he simply thought that all that sort of thing had ended with the Crusades. If the cathedral was, in fact, the center of life in Lusitania, and if the people were devoted to their priests, why did Peregrino imagine that their grief at the murder of a priest could be expressed in a simple prayer service? It would only add to their fury, if the Bishop seemed to think that Quim's death was nothing much. He was adding to the problem, not solving it.

She was still searching for Grego when she heard the bells start to toll. The call to prayer. Yet this was not a normal time for mass; people must be looking up in surprise at the sound, wondering, Why is the bell tolling? And then remembering—Father Estevão is dead. Father Quim was murdered by the piggies. Oh, yes, Peregrino, what an excellent idea, ringing that prayer bell. That will help the people feel like things are calm and normal.

From all wise men, O Lord, protect us.

Miro lay curled in a bend of one of Human's roots. He had not slept much the night before, if at all, yet even now he lay there unstirring, with pequeninos coming and going all around him, the sticks beating out rhythms on Human's and Rooter's trunks. Miro heard the conversations, understanding most of them even though he wasn't yet fluent in Father Tongue because the brothers made no effort to conceal their own agitated conversations from him. He was *Miro,* after all. They trusted him. So it was all right for him to realize how angry and afraid they were.

The fathertree named Warmaker had killed a human.

And not just any human—he and his tribe had murdered Father Estevão, the most beloved of human beings after only the Speaker for the Dead himself. It was unspeakable. What should they do? They had promised the Speaker not to make war on each other anymore, but how else could they punish Warmaker's tribe and show the humans that the pequeninos repudiated their vicious act? War was the only answer, all the brothers of every tribe attacking Warmaker's forest and cutting down all their trees except those known to have argued against Warmaker's plan.

And their mothertree? That was the debate that still raged: Whether it was enough to kill all the brothers and complicit fathertrees in Warmaker's forest, or whether they should cut down the mothertree as well, so that there was no chance of any of Warmaker's seed taking root in the world again. They would leave Warmaker alive long enough to see the destruction of his tribe, and then they would burn him to death, the most terrible of all executions, and the only time the pequeninos ever used fire within a forest.

Miro heard all this, and wanted to speak, wanted to say, What good is all this, now? But he knew that the pequeninos could not be stopped. They were too angry now. They were angry partly because of grief at Quim's death, but also in large part because they were ashamed. Warmaker had shamed them all by breaking their treaty. Humans would never trust the pequeninos again, unless they destroyed Warmaker and his tribe utterly.

The decision was made. Tomorrow morning all the brothers would begin the journey toward Warmaker's forest. They would spend many days gathering, because this had to be an action of all the forests of the world together. When they were ready, with Warmaker's forest utterly surrounded, then they would destroy it so thoroughly that no one would ever guess that there had once been a forest there.

The humans would see it. Their satellites would show them how the pequeninos dealt with treaty-breakers and cowardly murderers. Then the humans would trust the pequeninos again. Then the pequeninos could lift up their heads without shame in the presence of a human.

Gradually Miro realized that they were not just letting him overhear their conversations and deliberations. They were making *sure* he heard and understood all they were doing. They expect me to take the word back to the city. They expect me to explain to the humans of Lusitania exactly how the pequeninos plan to punish Quim's murderers.

Don't they realize that I'm a stranger here now? Who would listen to me, among the humans of Lusitania—me, a crippled boy out of the past, whose speech is so slow and hard to follow. I have no influence over other humans. I barely have influence over my own body.

Still, it was Miro's duty. He got up slowly, unknotting himself from his place amid Human's roots. He would try. He would go to Bishop Peregrino and tell him what the pequeninos were planning. Bishop Peregrino would spread the word, and then the people could all feel better knowing that thousands of innocent pequenino infants would be killed to make up for the death of one man.

What are pequenino babies, after all? Just worms living in the dark belly of a mothertree. It would never occur to these people that there was scant moral difference between this mass murder of pequenino babies and King Herod's slaughter of the innocents at the time of Jesus' birth. This was *justice* they were pursuing. What is the complete obliteration of a tribe of pequeninos compared with *that*?

———

Grego: standing in the middle of the grassy square, the crowd alert around me, each of them connected to me by a taut invisible wire so that my will is their will, my mouth speaks their words, their hearts beat to my rhythm. I have never felt this before, this kind of life, to be part of a group like this, and not just part of it, but the mind of it, the center, so that my self includes all of them, hundreds of them, my rage is their rage, their hands are my hands, their eyes see only what I show them.

The music of it, the cadence of invocation, answer, invocation, answer:

"The Bishop says that we'll pray for justice, but is that enough for us?"

"No!"

"The pequeninos say that *they'll* destroy the forest that murdered my brother, but do we believe them?"

"No!"

They complete my phrases; when I have to stop to breathe in, they shout for me, so that my voice is never stilled, but rises out of the throats of five hundred men and women. The Bishop came to me, full of peace and patience. The Mayor came to me with his warnings of police and riot and his hints of prison. Valentine came to me, all icy intellect, speaking of my responsibility. All of them know my power, power I never even knew I had, power that began only when I stopped obeying them and finally spoke what was in my heart to the people themselves. Truth is my power. I stopped deceiving the people and gave them the truth and now see what I've become, what we've become together.

"If anybody punishes the swine for killing Quim, it should be us. A human life should be avenged by human hands! They say that the sentence for the murderers is death—but *we're* the only ones who have the right to appoint the executioner! *We're* the ones who have to make sure the sentence is carried out!"

"Yes! Yes!"

"They let my brother die in the agony of the descolada! They watched his body burn from the inside out! Now we'll burn that forest to the ground!"

"Burn them! Fire! Fire!"

See how they strike matches, how they tear up tufts of grass and light them. The flame we'll light together!

"Tomorrow we'll leave on the punitive expedition—"

"Tonight! Tonight! Now!"

"Tomorrow—we can't go tonight—we have to collect water and supplies—"

"Now! Tonight! Burn!"

"I tell you we can't get there in a single night, it's hundreds of kilometers away, it'll take days to get there—"

"The piggies are right over the fence!"

"Not the ones that killed Quim—"

"They're all murdering little bastards!"

"These are the ones that killed Libo, aren't they?"

"They killed Pipo and Libo!"

"They're all murderers!"

"Burn them tonight!"

"Burn them all!"

"Lusitania for *us,* not for animals!"

Are they insane? How can they think that he would let them kill *these* piggies—they haven't done anything. "It's Warmaker! Warmaker and his forest that we have to punish!"

"Punish them!"

"Kill the piggies!"

"Burn!"

"Fire!"

A momentary silence. A lull. An opportunity. Think of the right words. Think of something to bring them back, they're slipping away. They were part of my body, they were part of my self, but now they're sliding away out from under me, one spasm and I've lost control if I ever had control; what can I say in this split second of silence that will bring them back to their senses?

Too long. Grego waited too long to think of something. It was a child's voice that filled the brief silence, the voice of a boy not yet into his manhood, exactly the sort of innocent voice that could cause the brimming holy rage within their hearts to erupt, to flow into irrevocable action. Cried the child: "For Quim and Christ!"

"Quim and Christ! Quim and Christ!"

"No!" shouted Grego. "Wait! You can't do this!"

They lurch around him, stumble him down. He's on all fours, someone stepping on his hand. Where is the stool he was standing on? Here it is, cling to that, don't let them trample me, they're going to kill me if I don't get up, I have to move with them, get up and walk with them, run with them or they'll crush me.

And then they were gone, past him, roaring, shouting, the tumult of feet moving out of the grassy square into the grassy streets, tiny flames held up, the voices crying "Fire" and "Burn" and "Quim and Christ," all the sound and sight of them flowing like a stream of lava from the square outward toward the forest that waited on the not-so-distant hill.

"God in heaven what are they doing!"

It was Valentine. Grego knelt by the stool, leaning on it, and there she stood beside him, looking at them flow away from this cold empty crater of a place where the conflagration began.

"Grego, you self-righteous son-of-a-bitch, what have you done?"

Me? "I was going to lead them to Warmaker. I was going to lead them to *justice*."

"You're the physicist, you idiot boy. Haven't you ever heard of the uncertainty principle?"

"Particle physics. Philotic physics."

"*Mob* physics, Grego. You never owned them. They owned you. And now they've used you up and they're going to destroy the forest of our best friends and advocates among the pequeninos and what will any of us do then? It's war between humans and pequeninos, unless they have inhuman self-restraint, and it will be our fault."

"*Warmaker* killed Quim."

"A crime. But what you've started here, Grego, this is an atrocity."

"I didn't do it!"

"Bishop Peregrino counseled with you. Mayor Kovano warned you. I begged you. And you did it anyway."

"You warned me about a riot, not about *this*—"

"This *is* a riot, you fool. Worse than a riot. It's a pogrom. It's a massacre. It's baby-killing. It's the first step on the long terrible road to xenocide."

"You can't blame all that on me!"

Her face is so terrible in the moonlight, in the light from the doors and windows of the bars. "I blame on you only what you did. You started a fire on a hot, dry, windy day, despite all warnings. I blame you for that, and if you don't hold yourself responsible for all the consequences of your own acts, then you are truly unworthy of human society and I hope you lose your freedom forever."

She's gone. Where? To do what? She can't leave him alone here. It's not right to leave him alone. A few moments ago, he was so large, with five hundred hearts and minds and mouths, a thousand hands and feet, and now it was all gone, as if his huge new body had died and he was left as a quivering ghost of a man, this single slender worm of a soul bereft of the powerful flesh it used to rule. He had never been so terrified. They almost killed him in their rush to leave him, almost trampled him into the grass.

They were *his*, though, all the same. He had created them, made a single mob of them, and even though they had misunderstood what he created them *for*, they were still acting according to the rage he had provoked in them, and with the plan he had put in their minds.

Their aim was bad, that's all—otherwise they were doing exactly what he had wanted them to do. Valentine was right. It was his responsibility. What they did now, he had done as surely as if he were still in front of them leading the way.

So what could he do?

Stop them. Get control again. Stand in front of them and beg them to stop. They weren't setting off to burn the distant forest of the mad fathertree Warmaker, they were going to slaughter pequeninos that he *knew,* even if he didn't like them much. He had to stop them, or their blood would be on his hands like sap that couldn't be washed or rubbed away, a stain that would stay with him forever.

So he ran, following the muddy swath of their footprints through the streets, where grass was trampled down into the mire. He ran until his side ached, through the place where they had stopped to break down the fence—where was the disruption field when we needed it? Why didn't someone turn it on?—and on to where already flames were leaping into the sky.

"Stop! Put the fire out!"

"Burn!"

"For Quim and Christ!"

"Die, pigs!"

"There's one, getting away!"

"Kill it!"

"Burn it!"

"The trees aren't dry enough—the fire's not taking!"

"Yes it is!"

"Cut down the tree!"

"There's another!"

"Look, the little bastards are attacking!"

"Break them in half!"

"Give me that scythe if *you* aren't going to use it!"

"Tear the little swine apart!"

"For Quim and Christ!"

Blood sprays in a wide arc and spatters into Grego's face as he lunges forward, trying to stop them. Did I know this one? Did I know this pequenino's voice before it was torn into this cry of agony and death? I can't put this back together again, they've broken him. Her. Broken *her*. A wife. A never-seen wife. Then we must be near the middle of the forest, and that giant must be the mothertree.

"Here's a killer tree if I ever saw one!"

Around the perimeter of the clearing where the great tree stood, the lesser trees suddenly began to lean, then toppled down, broken off at the trunks. For a moment Grego thought that it was humans cutting them down, but now he realized that no one was near those trees. They were breaking off by themselves, throwing themselves down to their deaths in order to crush the murdering humans under their trunks and branches, trying to save the mothertree.

For a moment it worked. Men screamed in agony; perhaps a dozen or two were crushed or trapped or broken under the falling trees. But then all had fallen that could, and still the mothertree stood there, her trunk undulating strangely, as if some inner peristalsis were at work, swallowing deeply.

"Let it live!" cried Grego. "It's the mothertree! She's innocent!"

But he was drowned out by the cries of the injured and trapped, and by the terror as they realized that the forest *could* strike back, that this was not all a vengeful game of justice and retribution, but a real war, with both sides dangerous.

"Burn it! Burn it!" The chant was loud enough to drown out the cries of the dying. And now the leaves and branches of the fallen trees were stretched out toward the mothertree; they lighted those branches and they burned readily. A few men came to their senses enough to realize that a fire that burned the mothertree would also burn the men pinned under the fallen brothertrees, and they began to try to rescue them. But most of the men were caught up in the passion of their success. To them the mothertree was Warmaker, the killer; to them it was everything alien in this world, the enemy who kept them inside a fence, the landlord who had arbitrarily restricted them to one small plot of land on a world so wide. The mothertree was all oppression and all authority, all strangeness and danger, and they had conquered it.

Grego recoiled from the screaming of the trapped men who watched the fire approaching, from the howls of the men the fire had reached, the triumphant chanting of the men who had done this murder. "For Quim and Christ! For Quim and Christ!" Almost Grego ran away, unable to bear what he could see and smell and hear, the bright orange flames, the smell of roasting manflesh, and the crackling of the living wood ablaze.

But he did *not* run. Instead he worked beside the others who dashed forward to the very edge of the flame to pry living men out from under the fallen trees. He was singed, and once his clothing caught on fire, but the hot pain of that was nothing, it was almost merciful, because it was the punishment that he deserved. He should die in this place. He might even have done it, might even have plunged himself so deeply into the fire that he could never come out until his crime was purged out of him and all that was left was bone and ash, but there were still broken people to pull out of the fire's reach, still lives to save. Besides, someone beat out the flames on his shoulder and helped him lift the tree so the boy who lay under it could wriggle free and how could he die when he was part of something like this, part of saving this child?

"For Quim and Christ!" the boy whimpered as he crab-crawled out of the way of the flames.

Here he was, the boy whose words had filled the silence and turned the crowd into this direction. You did it, thought Grego. You tore them away from me.

The boy looked up at him and recognized him. "Grego!" he cried, and lunged forward. His arms enfolded Grego around the thighs, his head pressed against Grego's hip. "Uncle Grego!"

It was Olhado's oldest boy, Nimbo.

"We did it!" cried Nimbo. "For Uncle Quim!"

The flames crackled. Grego picked up the boy and carried him, staggering out of the reach of the hottest flames, and then farther out, into the darkness, into a place where it was cool. All the men were driven this way, the flames herding them, the wind driving the flames. Most were like Grego, exhausted, frightened, in pain from the fire or helping someone else.

But some, many perhaps, were still untouched except by the inner fire that Grego and Nimbo had ignited in the square. "Burn them all!" The voices here and there, smaller mobs like tiny eddies in a larger stream, but they now held brands and torches from the fires raging in the forest's heart. "For Quim and Christ! For Libo and Pipo! No trees! No trees!"

Grego staggered onward.

"Set me down," said Nimbo.

And onward.

"I can walk."

But Grego's errand was too urgent. He couldn't stop for Nimbo, and he couldn't let the boy walk, couldn't wait for him and couldn't leave him behind. You don't leave your brother's son behind in a burning forest. So he carried him, and after awhile, exhausted, his legs and arms aching from the exertion, his shoulder a white sun of agony where he had been burned, he emerged from the forest into the grassy space before the old gate, where the path wound down from the wood to join the path from the xenobiology labs.

The mob had gathered here, many of them holding torches, but for some reason they were still a distance away from the two isolated trees that stood watch here: Human and Rooter. Grego pushed his way through the crowd, still holding Nimbo; his heart was racing, and he was filled with fear and anguish and yet a spark of hope, for he knew why the men with torches had stopped. And when he reached the edge of the mob, he saw that he was right.

There were gathered around those last two fathertrees perhaps two hundred pequenino brothers and wives, small and beleaguered, but with an air of defiance about them. They would fight to the death on this spot, rather than let these last two trees be burned—but burn they would, if the mob decided so, for there was no hope of pequeninos standing in the way of men determined to do murder.

But between the piggies and the men there stood Miro, like a giant compared to the pequeninos. He had no weapon, and yet he had spread his arms as if to protect the pequeninos, or perhaps to hold them back. And in his thick, difficult speech he was defying the mob.

"Kill me first!" he said. "You like murder! Kill me first! Just like they killed Quim! Kill me first!"

"Not you!" said one of the men holding torches. "But those trees are going to die. And all those piggies, too, if they haven't got the brains to run away."

"Me first," said Miro. "These are my brothers! Kill me first!"

He spoke loudly and slowly, so his sluggish speech could be understood. The mob still had anger in it, some of them at least. Yet there were also many who were sick of it all, many who were already ashamed, already discovering in their hearts the terrible acts they had performed tonight, when their souls were given over to the will of the mob. Grego still felt it, that connection with the others, and he knew that they could go either way—the ones still hot with rage might start one last fire tonight; or the ones who had cooled, whose only inner heat was a blush of shame, they might prevail.

Grego had this one last chance to redeem himself, at least in part. And so he stepped forward, still carrying Nimbo.

"Me too," he said. "Kill me too, before you raise a hand against these brothers and these trees!"

"Out of the way, Grego, you and the cripple both!"

"How are you different from Warmaker, if you kill these little ones?"

Now Grego stood beside Miro.

"Out of the way! We're going to burn the last of them and have done." But the voice was less certain.

"There's a fire behind you," said Grego, "and too many people have already died, humans and pequeninos both." His voice was husky, his breath short from the smoke he had inhaled. But he could still be heard. "The forest that killed Quim is far away from here, and Warmaker still stands untouched. We haven't done justice here tonight. We've done murder and massacre."

"Piggies are piggies!"

"Are they? Would you like that if it went the other way?" Grego took a few steps toward one of the men who looked tired and unwilling to go on, and spoke directly to him, while pointing at the mob's spokesman. "You! Would you like to be punished for what *he* did?"

"No," muttered the man.

"If *he* killed someone, would you think it was right for somebody to come to your house and slaughter your wife and children for it?"

Several voices now. "No."

"Why not? Humans are humans, aren't we?"

"I didn't kill any children," said the spokesman. He was defending himself now. And the "we" was gone from his speech. He was an individual now, alone. The mob was fading, breaking apart.

"We burned the mothertree," said Grego.

Behind him there began a keening sound, several soft, high-pitched whines. For the brothers and surviving wives, it was the confirmation of their worst fears. The mothertree had burned.

"That giant tree in the middle of the forest—inside it were *all* their babies. *All* of them. This forest did us no harm, and we came and killed their babies."

Miro stepped forward, put his hand on Grego's shoulder. Was Miro leaning on him? Or helping him stand?

Miro spoke then, not to Grego, but to the crowd. "All of you. Go home."

"Maybe we should try to put the fire out," said Grego. But already the whole forest was ablaze.

"Go home," Miro said again. "Stay inside the fence."

There was still some anger left. "Who are *you* to tell us what to do?"

"Stay inside the fence," said Miro. "Someone else is coming to protect the pequeninos now."

"Who? The police?" Several people laughed bitterly, since so many of them *were* police, or had seen policemen among the crowd.

"Here they are," said Miro.

A low hum could be heard, soft at first, barely audible in the roaring of the fire, but then louder and louder, until five fliers came into view, skimming the tops of the grass as they circled the mob, sometimes black in silhouette against the burning forest, sometimes shining with reflected fire when they were on the opposite side. At last they came to rest, all five of them sinking down onto the tall grass. Only then were the people able to distinguish one black shape from another, as six riders arose from each flying platform. What they had taken for shining machinery on the fliers was not machinery at all, but living creatures, not as large as men but not as small as pequeninos, either, with large heads and multi-faceted eyes. They made no threatening gesture, just formed lines before each flier; but no gestures were needed. The sight of them was enough, stirring memories of ancient nightmares and horror stories.

"Deus nos perdoe!" cried several. God forgive us. They were expecting to die.

"Go home," said Miro. "Stay inside the fence."

"What are they?" Nimbo's childish voice spoke for them all.

The answers came as whispers. "Devils." "Destroying angels." "Death."

And then the truth, from Grego's lips, for he knew what they had to be, though it was unthinkable. "Buggers," he said. "Buggers, here on Lusitania."

They did not run from the place. They walked, watching carefully, shying away from the strange new creatures whose existence none of them had guessed at, whose powers they could only imagine, or remember from ancient videos they had studied once in school. The buggers, who had once come close to destroying all of humanity, until they were destroyed in turn by Ender the Xenocide. The book called the Hive Queen had said they were really beautiful and did not need to die. But now, seeing them, black shining exoskeletons, a thousand lenses in their shimmering green eyes, it was not beauty but terror that they felt. And when they went home, it would be in the knowledge that *these*, and not just the dwarfish, backward piggies, waited for them just outside the fence. Had they been in prison before? Surely now they were trapped in one of the circles of hell.

At last only Miro, Grego, and Nimbo were left, of all the humans. Around them the piggies also watched in awe—but not in terror, for they had no insect nightmares lurking in their limbic node the way the humans did. Besides, the buggers had come to them as saviors and protectors. What weighed on them most was not curiosity about these strangers, but rather grief at what they had lost.

"Human begged the hive queen to help them, but she said she couldn't kill humans," said Miro. "Then Jane saw the fire from the satellites in the sky, and told Andrew Wiggin. He spoke to the hive queen and told her what to do. That she wouldn't have to kill anybody."

"They aren't going to kill us?" asked Nimbo.

Grego realized that Nimbo had spent these last few minutes expecting to die. Then it occurred to him that so, too, had he—that it was only now, with Miro's explanation, that he was sure that they hadn't come to punish him and Nimbo for what they set in motion tonight. Or rather, for what Grego had set in motion, ready for the single small nudge that Nimbo, in all innocence, had given.

Slowly Grego knelt and set the boy down. His arms barely responded to his will now, and the pain in his shoulder was unbearable. He began to cry. But it wasn't for the pain that he was weeping.

The buggers moved now, and moved quickly. Most stayed on the ground, jogging away to take up watch positions around the perimeter of the city. A few remounted the fliers, one to each machine, and took them back up into the air, flying over the burning forest, the flaming grass, spraying them with something that blanketed the fire and slowly put it out.

Bishop Peregrino stood on the low foundation wall that had been laid only that morning. The people of Lusitania, all of them, were gathered, sitting in the grass. He used a small amplifier, so that no one could miss his words. But he probably would not have needed it—all were silent, even the little children, who seemed to catch the somber mood.

Behind the Bishop was the forest, blackened but not

utterly lifeless—a few of the trees were greening again. Before him lay the blanket-covered bodies, each beside its grave. The nearest of them was the corpse of Quim—Father Estevão. The other bodies were the humans who had died two nights before, under the trees and in the fire.

"These graves will be the floor of the chapel, so that whenever we enter it we tread upon the bodies of the dead. The bodies of those who died as they helped to bring murder and desolation to our brothers the pequeninos. Above all the body of Father Estevão, who died trying to bring the gospel of Jesus Christ to a forest of heretics. He dies a martyr. These others died with murder in their hearts and blood on their hands.

"I speak plainly, so that this Speaker for the Dead won't have to add any words after me. I speak plainly, the way Moses spoke to the children of Israel after they worshiped the golden calf and rejected their covenant with God. Of all of us, there are only a handful who have no share of the guilt for this crime. Father Estevão, who died pure, and yet whose name was on the blasphemous lips of those who killed. The Speaker for the Dead, and those who traveled with him to bring home the body of this martyred priest. And Valentine, the Speaker's sister, who warned the Mayor and me of what would happen. Valentine knew history, she knew humanity, but the Mayor and I thought that we knew *you,* and that you were stronger than history. Alas for us all that you are as fallen as any other men, and so am I. The sin is on every one of us who could have tried to stop this, and did not! On the wives who did not try to keep their husbands home. On the men who watched but said nothing. And on all who held the torches in their hands and killed a tribe of fellow Christians for a crime done by their distant cousins half a continent away.

"The law is doing its small part of justice. Gerão Gregorio Ribeira von Hesse is in prison, but that is for another crime—the crime of having violated his trust and told secrets that were not his to tell. He is not in prison for the massacre of the pequeninos, because he has no greater share of guilt for that than the rest of you who followed him. Do you understand me? The guilt is on us all, and all of us must repent together, and do our penance together, and pray that Christ will forgive us all together for the terrible thing we did with his name on our lips!

"I am standing on the foundation of this new chapel, which will be named for Father Estevão, Apostle to the Pequeninos. The blocks of the foundation were torn from the walls of our cathedral—there are gaping holes there now, where the wind can blow and the rain can fall in upon us as we worship. And so the cathedral will remain, wounded and broken, until this chapel is finished.

"And how will we finish it? You will go home, all of you, to your houses, and you will break open the wall of your own house, and take the blocks that fall, and bring them here. And you will also leave your walls shattered until this chapel is completed.

"Then we will tear holes in the walls of every factory, every building in our colony, until there is no structure that does not show the wound of our sin. And all those wounds will remain until the walls are high enough to put on the roof, which will be beamed and rafted with the scorched trees that fell in the forest, trying to defend their people from our murdering hands.

"And then we will come, all of us, to this chapel, and enter it on our knees, one by one, until every one of us has crawled over the graves of our dead, and under the bodies of those ancient brothers who lived as trees in the third life our merciful God had given them until we ended it. There we will all pray for forgiveness. We will pray for our venerated Father Estevão to intercede for us. We will pray for Christ to include our terrible sin in his atonement, so we will not have to spend eternity in hell. We will pray for God to purify us.

"Only then will we repair our damaged walls, and heal our houses. That is our penance, my children. Let us pray that it is enough."

In the middle of a clearing strewn with ash, Ender, Valentine, Miro, Ela, Quara, Ouanda, and Olhado all stood and watched as the most honored of the wives was flayed alive and planted in the ground, for her to grow into a new mothertree from the corpse of her second life. As she was dying, the surviving wives reached into a gap in the old mothertree and scooped out the bodies of the dead infants and little mothers who had lived there, and laid them on her bleeding body until they formed a mound. Within hours, her sapling would rise through their corpses and reach for sunlight.

Using their substance, she would grow quickly, until she had enough thickness and height to open up an aperture in her trunk. If she grew fast enough, if she opened herself soon enough, the few surviving babies clinging to the inside of the gaping cavity of the old dead mothertree could be transferred to the small new haven the new mothertree would offer them. If any of the surviving babies were little mothers, they would be carried to the surviving fathertrees, Human and Rooter, for mating. If new babies were conceived within their tiny bodies, then the forest that had known all the best and worst that human beings could do would survive.

If not—if the babies were all males, which was possible, or if all the females among them were infertile, which was possible, or if they were all too injured by the heat of the fire that raged up the mothertree's trunk and killed her, or if they were too weakened by the days of starvation they would undergo until the new mothertree was ready for them—then the forest would die with these brothers and wives, and Human and Rooter would live on for a millennium or so as tribeless fathertrees. Perhaps some other tribes would honor them and carry little mothers to them for mating. Perhaps. But they would not be fathers of their own tribe, surrounded by their sons. They would be lonely trees with no forest of their own, the sole monuments to the work they had lived for: bringing humans and pequeninos together.

As for the rage against Warmaker, that had ended. The fathertrees of Lusitania all agreed that whatever moral debt had been incurred by the death of Father Estevão, it was paid and overpaid by the slaughter of the forest of Rooter and Human. Indeed, Warmaker had won many new converts to his heresy—for hadn't the humans proved that they were unworthy of the gospel of Christ? It was pequeninos, said Warmaker, who were chosen to be vessels of the Holy Ghost, while human beings plainly had no part of God in them. We have no need to kill any more human beings, he said. We only have to wait, and the Holy Ghost will kill them all. In the meantime, God has sent us the hive queen to build us starships. We will carry the Holy Ghost with us to judge every world we visit. We will be the destroying angel. We will be Joshua and the Israelites, purging Canaan to make way for God's chosen people.

Many pequeninos believed him now. Warmaker no longer sounded crazy to them; they had witnessed the first stirrings of apocalypse in the flames of an innocent forest. To many pequeninos there was nothing more to learn from humanity. God had no more use for human beings.

Here, though, in this clearing in the forest, their feet ankle-deep in ash, the brothers and wives who kept vigil over their new mothertree had no belief in Warmaker's doctrine. They who knew human beings best of all even chose to have humans present as witnesses and helpers in their attempt to be reborn.

"Because," said Planter, who was now the spokesman for the surviving brothers, "we know that not all humans are alike, just as not all pequeninos are alike. Christ lives in some of you, and not in others. We are not all like Warmaker's forest, and you are not all murderers either."

So it was that Planter held hands with Miro and Valentine on the morning, just before dawn, when the new mothertree managed to open a crevice in her slender trunk, and the wives tenderly transferred the weak and starving bodies of the surviving infants into their new home. It was too soon to tell, but there was cause for hope: The new mothertree had readied herself in only a day and a half, and there were more than three dozen infants who lived to make the transition. As many as a dozen of them might be fertile females, and if even a quarter of those lived to bear young, the forest might thrive again.

Planter was trembling. "Brothers have never seen this before," said Planter, "not in all the history of the world."

Several of the brothers were kneeling and crossing themselves. Many had been praying throughout the vigil. It made Valentine think of something Quara had told her. She stepped close to Miro and whispered, "Ela prayed, too."

"Ela?"

"Before the fire. Quara was there at the shrine of the Venerados. She prayed for God to open up a way for us to solve all our problems."

"That's what everybody prays for."

Valentine thought of what had happened in the days since Ela's prayer. "I imagine that she's rather disappointed at the answer God gave her."

"People usually are."

"But maybe this—the mothertree opening so quickly—maybe this is the beginning of her answer."

Miro looked at Valentine in puzzlement. "Are you a believer?"

"Let's say I'm a suspecter. I suspect there may be someone who cares what happens to us. That's one step better than merely wishing. And one step below hoping."

Miro smiled slightly, but Valentine wasn't sure whether it meant he was pleased or amused. "So what will God do next, to answer Ela's prayer?"

"Let's wait and see," said Valentine. "Our job is to decide what *we'll* do next. We have only the deepest mysteries of the universe to solve."

"Well, that should be right up God's alley," said Miro.

Then Ouanda arrived; as xenologer, she had also been involved in the vigil, and though this wasn't her shift, news of the opening of the mothertree had been taken to her at once. Her coming had usually meant Miro's swift departure. But not this time. Valentine was pleased to see that Miro's gaze didn't seem either to linger on Ouanda or to avoid her; she was simply there, working with the pequeninos, and so was he. No doubt it was all an elaborate pretense at normality, but in Valentine's experience, normality was *always* a pretense, people acting out what they thought were their expected roles. Miro had simply reached a point where he was ready to act out something like a normal role in relation to Ouanda, no matter how false it might be to his true feelings. And maybe it wasn't so false, after all. She was twice his age now. Not at all the girl he had loved.

They had loved each other, but never slept together. Valentine had been pleased to hear it when Miro told her, though he said it with angry regret. Valentine had long ago observed that in a society that expected chastity and fidelity, like Lusitania, the adolescents who controlled and channeled their youthful passions were the ones who grew up to be both strong and civilized. Adolescents in such a community who were either too weak to control themselves or too contemptuous of society's norms to try usually ended up being either sheep or wolves—either mindless members of the herd or predators who took what they could and gave nothing.

She had feared, when she first met Miro, that he was a self-pitying weakling or a self-centered predator resentful of his confinement. Neither was so. He might now regret his chastity in adolescence—it was natural for him to wish he had coupled with Ouanda when he was still strong and they were both of an age—but Valentine did not regret it. It showed that Miro had inner strength and a sense of responsibility to his community. To Valentine, it was predictable that Miro, by himself, had held back the mob for those crucial moments that saved Rooter and Human.

It was also predictable that Miro and Ouanda would now make the great effort to pretend that they were simply two people doing their jobs—that all was normal between them. Inner strength and outward respect. These are the people who hold a community together, who lead. Unlike the sheep and the wolves, they perform a better role than the script given them by their inner fears and desires. They act out the script of decency, of self-sacrifice, of public honor—of civilization. And in the pretense, it becomes reality. There really *is* civilization in human history, thought Valentine, but only because of people like these. The shepherds.

Novinha met him in the doorway of the school. She leaned on the arm of Dona Cristã, the fourth principal of the Children of the Mind of Christ since Ender had come to Lusitania.

"I have nothing to say to you," Novinha said. "We're still married under the law, but that's all."

"I didn't kill your son," he said.

"You didn't save him, either," she answered.

"I love you," Ender said.

"As much as you're capable of love," she said. "And then only when you've got a little time left over from looking after everybody else. You think you're some kind of guardian angel, with responsibility for the whole universe. All I asked you to do was take responsibility for my family. You're good at loving people by the trillion, but not so good at dozens, and you're a complete failure at loving one."

It was a harsh judgment, and he knew it wasn't true, but he didn't come to argue. "Please come home," he said. "You love me and need me as much as I need you."

"This is home now. I've stopped needing you or anybody. And if this is all you came to say, you're wasting my time and yours."

"No, it's not all."

She waited.

"The files in the laboratory. You've sealed them all. We have to find a solution to the descolada before it destroys us all."

She gave him a withering, bitter smile. "Why did you bother me with this? Jane can get past my passwords, can't she?"

"She hasn't tried," he said.

"No doubt to spare my sensibilities. But she can, né?"

"Probably."

"Then have her do it. She's all you need now. You never really needed me, not when you had *her*."

"I've tried to be a good husband to you," said Ender. "I never said I could protect you from everything, but I did all I could."

"If you *had*, my Estevão would be alive."

She turned away, and Dona Cristã escorted her back inside the school. Ender watched her until she turned a corner. Then he turned away from the door and left the school. He wasn't sure where he was going, only that he had to get there.

"I'm sorry," said Jane softly.

"Yes," he said.

"When I'm gone," she said, "maybe Novinha will come back to you."

"You won't be gone if I can help it," he said.

"But you can't. They're going to shut me down in a couple of months."

"Shut up," he said.

"It's only the truth."

"Shut up and let me think."

"What, are you going to save *me* now? Your record isn't very good at playing savior lately."

He didn't answer, and she didn't speak again for the rest of the afternoon. He wandered out of the gate, but didn't go up into the forest. Instead he spent the afternoon in the grassland, alone, under the hot sun.

Sometimes he was thinking, trying to struggle with the problems that still loomed over him: the fleet coming against them, Jane's shut-off date, the descolada's constant efforts to destroy the humans of Lusitania, Warmaker's plan to spread the descolada throughout the galaxy, and the grim situation within the city now that the hive queen kept constant watch over the fence and their grim penance had them all tearing at the walls of their own houses.

And sometimes his mind was almost devoid of thought, as he stood or sat or lay in the grass, too numb to weep, her face passing through his memory, his lips and tongue and teeth forming her name, pleading with her silently, knowing that even if he made a sound, even if he shouted, even if he could make her hear his voice, she wouldn't answer him.

Novinha.

13

FREE WILL

<There are those among us who think that the humans should be stopped from the research into the descolada. The descolada is at the heart of our life cycle. We're afraid that they'll find a way to kill the descolada throughout the world, and that would destroy us in a generation.>

<And if you managed to stop human research into the descolada, they would certainly be wiped out within a few years.>

<Is the descolada that dangerous? Why can't they keep on containing it as they have?>

<Because the descolada is not just randomly mutating according to natural laws. It is intelligently adapting itself in order to destroy us.>

<Us? You?>

<We've been fighting the descolada all along. Not in laboratories, like the humans, but inside ourself. Before I lay eggs, there is a phase where I prepare their bodies

to manufacture all the antibodies they'll need throughout their lives. When the descolada changes itself, we know it because the workers start dying. Then an organ near my ovaries creates new antibodies, and we lay eggs for new workers who can withstand the revised descolada.>

<So you, too, are trying to destroy it.>

<No. Our process is entirely unconscious. It takes place in the body of the hive queen, without conscious intervention. We can't go beyond meeting the present danger. Our organ of immunity is far more effective and adaptable than anything in the human body, but in the long run we'll suffer the same fate as the humans, if the descolada is not destroyed. The difference is that if we are wiped out by the descolada, there is no other hive queen in the universe to carry on our species. We are the last.>

<Your case is even more desperate than theirs.>

<And we are even more helpless to affect it. We have no science of biology beyond simple husbandry. Our natural methods were so effective in fighting disease that we never had the same impetus that humans had, to understand life and control it.>

<Is that the way it is, then? Either we are destroyed, or you and the humans are destroyed. If the descolada continues, it kills you. If it is stopped, we die.>

<This is your world. The descolada is in your bodies. If it comes time to choose between you and us, it will be you that survives.>

<You speak for yourself, my friend. But what will the humans do?>

<If they have the power to destroy the descolada in a way that would also destroy you, we will forbid them to use it.>

<Forbid them? When have humans ever obeyed?>

<We never forbid where we do not also have the power to prevent.>

<Ah.>

<This is *your* world. Ender knows this. And if other humans ever forget, we will remind them.>

<I have another question.>

<Ask.>

<What about those, like Warmaker, who want to spread the descolada throughout the universe? Will you also forbid them?>

<They must not carry the descolada to worlds that already have multicellular life.>

<But that's exactly what they intend to do.>

<They must not.>

<But you're building starships for us. Once they have control of a starship, they'll go where they want to go.>

<They must not.>

<So you forbid them?>

<We never forbid where we do not also have the power to prevent.>

<Then why do you still build these ships?>

<The human fleet is coming, with a weapon that can destroy this world. Ender is sure that they'll use it. Should we conspire with them, and leave your entire genetic heritage here on this single planet, so you can be obliterated with a single weapon?>

<So you build us starships, knowing that some of us may use them destructively.>

<What you do with starflight will be your responsibility. If you act as the enemy of life, then life will become your enemy. We will provide starships to you as a species. Then you, as a species, will decide who leaves Lusitania and who doesn't.>

<There's a fair chance that Warmaker's party will have the majority then. That they will be making all those decisions.>

<So—should *we* judge, and decide that the humans are right to try to destroy you? Maybe Warmaker is right. Maybe the humans are the ones who deserve to be destroyed. Who are we to judge between you? They with

their Molecular Disruption Device. You with the descolada. Each has the power to destroy the other, each species is capable of such a monstrous crime, and yet each species has many members who would never knowingly cause such evil and who deserve to live. We will not choose. We will simply build the starships and let you and the humans work out your destiny between you.>

<You could help us. You could keep the starships out of the hands of Warmaker's party, and deal only with us.>

<Then the domestic war between you would be terrible indeed. Would you destroy *their* genetic heritage, simply because you disagree? Who then is the monster and the criminal? How do we judge between you, when both parties are willing to countenance the utter destruction of another people?>

<Then I have no hope. Someone will be destroyed.>

<Unless the human scientists find a way to change the descolada, so that you can survive as a species, and yet the descolada loses the power to kill.>

<How is that possible?>

<We are not biologists. Only the humans can do this, if it can be done.>

<Then we can't stop them from researching the descolada. We have to help them. Even though they nearly destroyed our forest, we have no choice but to help them.>

<We knew you would reach that conclusion.>

<Did you?>

<That's why we're building starships for the pequeninos. Because you're capable of wisdom.>

As word of the restoration of the Lusitania Fleet spread among the godspoken of Path, they began to visit the house of Han Fei-tzu to pay him honor.

"I will not see them," said Han Fei-tzu.

"You must, Father," said Han Qing-jao. "It is only

proper for them to honor you for such a great accomplishment."

"Then I will go and tell them that it was entirely your doing, and I had nothing to do with it."

"No!" cried Qing-jao. "You must not do that."

"Furthermore, I will tell them that I think it was a great crime, which will cause the death of a noble spirit. I will tell them that the godspoken of Path are slaves to a cruel and vicious government, and that we must bend all our efforts to the destruction of Congress."

"Don't make me hear this!" cried Qing-jao. "You could never say such a thing to anyone!"

And it was true. Si Wang-mu watched from the corner as the two of them, father and daughter, each began a ritual of purification, Han Fei-tzu for having spoken such rebellious words and Han Qing-jao for having heard them. Master Fei-tzu would never say these things to others, because even if he did, they would see how he immediately had to be purified, and they would see this as proof that the gods repudiated his words. They did their work well, those scientists that Congress employed to create the godspoken, thought Wang-mu. Even knowing the truth, Han Fei-tzu is helpless.

So it was that Qing-jao met all the visitors who came to the house, and graciously accepted their praise on behalf of her father. Wang-mu stayed with her for the first few visits, but she found it unbearable to listen as Qing-jao described again and again how her father and she had discovered the existence of a computer program that dwelt amid the philotic network of the ansibles, and how it would be destroyed. It was one thing to know that in her heart, Qing-jao did not believe she was committing murder; it was quite another thing for Wang-mu to listen to her boasting about how the murder would be accomplished.

And boasting was what Qing-jao was doing, though only Wang-mu knew it. Always Qing-jao gave the credit to her father, but since Wang-mu knew that it was entirely Qing-jao's doing, she knew that when Qing-jao described the accomplishment as worthy service to the gods, she was really praising herself.

"Please don't make me stay and listen anymore," said Wang-mu.

Qing-jao studied her for a moment, judging her. Then, coldly, she answered. "Go if you must. I see that you are still a captive of our enemy. I have no need of you."

"Of course not," said Wang-mu. "You have the gods." But in saying this, she could not keep the bitter irony out of her voice.

"Gods that you don't believe in," said Qing-jao bitingly. "Of course, *you* have never been spoken to by the gods—why should you believe? I dismiss you as my secret maid, since that is your desire. Go back to your family."

"As the gods command," said Wang-mu. And this time she made no effort to conceal her bitterness at the mention of the gods.

She was already out of the house, walking down the road, when Mu-pao came after her. Since Mu-pao was old and fat, she had no hope of catching up with Wang-mu on foot. So she came riding a donkey, looking ridiculous as she kicked the animal to hasten it. Donkeys, sedan chairs, all these trappings of ancient China—do the godspoken really think that such affectations make them somehow holier? Why don't they simply ride on fliers and hovercars like honest people do on every other world? Then Mu-pao would not have to humiliate herself, bouncing and jouncing on an animal that is suffering under her weight. To spare her as much embarrassment as possible, Wang-mu returned and met Mu-pao partway.

"Master Han Fei-tzu commands you to return," said Mu-pao.

"Tell Master Han that he is kind and good, but my mistress has dismissed me."

"Master Han says that Mistress Qing-jao has the authority to dismiss you as her secret maid, but not to dismiss you from his house. Your contract is with him, not with her."

This was true. Wang-mu hadn't thought of that.

"He begs you to return," said Mu-pao. "He told me to say it that way, so that you might come out of kindness, if you would not come out of obedience."

"Tell him I will obey. He should not beg such a low person as myself."

"He will be glad," said Mu-pao.

Wang-mu walked beside Mu-pao's donkey. They went very slowly, which was more comfortable for Mu-pao and the donkey as well.

"I have never seen him so upset," said Mu-pao. "Probably I shouldn't tell you that. But when I said that you were gone, he was almost frantic."

"Were the gods speaking to him?" It was a bitter thing if Master Han called her back only because for some reason the slave driver within him had demanded it.

"No," said Mu-pao. "It wasn't like that at all. Though of course I've never actually seen what it looks like when the gods speak to him."

"Of course."

"He simply didn't want you to go," said Mu-pao.

"I will probably end up going, anyway," said Wang-mu. "But I'll gladly explain to him why I am now useless in the House of Han."

"Oh, of course," said Mu-pao. "You have always been useless. But that doesn't mean you aren't necessary."

"What do you mean?"

"Happiness can depend as easily on useless things as on useful ones."

"Is that a saying of an old master?"

"It's a saying of an old fat woman on a donkey," said Mu-pao. "And don't you forget it."

When Wang-mu was alone with Master Han in his private chamber, he showed no sign of the agitation Mu-pao had spoken of.

"I have spoken with Jane," he said. "She thinks that since you also know of her existence and believe her not to be the enemy of the gods, it will be better if you stay."

"So I will serve Jane now?" asked Wang-mu. "Am I to be *her* secret maid?"

Wang-mu did not mean her words to sound ironic; the idea of being servant to a nonhuman entity intrigued her. But Master Han reacted as if he were trying to smooth over an offense.

"No," he said. "You shouldn't be anyone's servant. You have acted bravely and worthily."

"And yet you called me back to fulfill my contract with you."

Master Han bowed his head. "I called you back because you are the only one who knows the truth. If you go, then I'm alone in this house."

Wang-mu almost said: How can you be alone, when your daughter is here? And until the last few days, it wouldn't have been a cruel thing to say, because Master Han and Mistress Qing-jao were friends as close as a father and daughter could ever be. But now, the barrier between them was insuperable. Qing-jao lived in a world where she was a triumphant servant of the gods, trying to be patient with the temporary madness of her father. Master Han lived in a world where his daughter and all of his society were slaves to an oppressive Congress, and only he knew the truth. How could they even speak to each other across a gulf so wide and deep?

"I'll stay," said Wang-mu. "However I can serve you, I will."

"We'll serve each other," said Master Han. "My daughter promised to teach you. I'll continue that."

Wang-mu touched her forehead to the floor. "I am unworthy of such kindness."

"No," said Master Han. "We both know the truth now. The gods don't speak to me. Your face should never touch the floor before *me*."

"We have to live in this world," said Wang-mu. "I will treat you as an honored man among the godspoken, because that is what all the world would expect of me. And you must treat me as a servant, for the same reason."

Master Han's face twisted bitterly. "The world also expects that when a man of my age takes a young girl from his daughter's service into his own, he is using her for venery. Shall we act out all the world's expectations?"

"It is not in your nature to take advantage of your power in that way," said Wang-mu.

"Nor is it in my nature to receive your humiliation. Before I learned the truth about my affliction, I accepted other people's obeisance because I believed it was really being offered to the gods, and not to me."

"That is as true as it ever was. Those who believe you are godspoken are offering their obeisance to the gods, while those who are dishonest do it to flatter you."

"But *you* are not dishonest. Nor do you believe the gods speak to me."

"I don't know whether the gods speak to you or not, or whether they ever have or ever can speak to anyone. I only know that the gods don't ask you or anyone to do these ridiculous, humiliating rituals—those were forced on you by Congress. Yet you must continue those rituals because your body requires it. Please allow me to continue the rituals of humiliation that are required of people of my position in the world."

Master Han nodded gravely. "You are wise beyond your years and education, Wang-mu."

"I am a very foolish girl," said Wang-mu. "If I had any wisdom, I would beg you to send me as far away from this place as possible. Sharing a house with Qing-jao will now be very dangerous to me. Especially if she sees that I am close to you, when she can't be."

"You're right. I'm being very selfish, to ask you to stay."

"Yes," said Wang-mu. "And yet I will stay."

"Why?" asked Master Han.

"Because I can never go back to my old life," she answered. "I know too much now about the world and the universe, about Congress and the gods. I would have the taste of poison in my mouth all the days of my life, if I went back home and pretended to be what I was before."

Master Han nodded gravely, but then he smiled, and soon he laughed.

"Why are you laughing at me, Master Han?"

"I'm laughing because I think that you never were what you used to be."

"What does that mean?"

"I think you were always pretending. Maybe you even fooled yourself. But one thing is certain. You were *never* an ordinary girl, and you could never have led an ordinary life."

Wang-mu shrugged. "The future is a hundred thousand threads, but the past is a fabric that can never be rewoven. Maybe I could have been content. Maybe not."

"So here we are together, the three of us."

Only then did Wang-mu turn to see that they were not alone. In the air above the display she saw the face of Jane, who smiled at her.

"I'm glad you came back," said Jane.

For a moment, Jane's presence here caused Wang-mu to leap to a hopeful conclusion. "Then you aren't dead! You've been spared!"

"It was never Qing-jao's plan for me to be dead already," answered Jane. "Her plan to destroy me is proceeding nicely, and I will no doubt die on schedule."

"Why do you come to this house, then," asked Wang-mu, "when it was here that your death was set in motion?"

"I have a lot of things to accomplish before I die," said Jane, "including the faint possibility of discovering a way to survive. It happens that the world of Path contains many thousands of people who are much more intelligent, on average, than the rest of humanity."

"Only because of Congress's genetic manipulation," said Master Han.

"True," said Jane. "The godspoken of Path are, properly speaking, not even human anymore. You're another species, created and enslaved by Congress to give them an advantage over the rest of humanity. It happens, though, that a single member of that new species is somewhat free of Congress."

"This is freedom?" said Master Han. "Even now, my hunger to purify myself is almost irresistible."

"Then don't resist it," said Jane. "I can talk to you while you contort yourself."

Almost at once, Master Han began to fling out his arms and twist them in the air in his ritual of purification. Wang-mu turned her face away.

"Don't do that," said Master Han. "Don't hide your face from me. I can't be ashamed to show this to you. I'm a cripple, that's all; if I had lost a leg, my closest friends would not be afraid to see the stump."

Wang-mu saw the wisdom in his words, and did not hide her face from his affliction.

"As I was saying," said Jane, "it happens that a single member of this new species is somewhat free of Congress. I hope to enlist your help in the works I'm trying to accomplish in the few months left to me."

"I'll do anything I can," said Master Han.

"And if I can help, I will," said Wang-mu. Only after she said it did she realize how ridiculous it was for her to offer such a thing. Master Han was one of the god-spoken, one of those with superior intellectual abilities. She was only an uneducated specimen of ordinary humanity, with nothing to offer.

And yet neither of them mocked her offer, and Jane accepted it graciously. Such a kindness proved once again to Wang-mu that Jane had to be a living thing, not just a simulation.

"Let me tell you the problems that I hope to resolve."

They listened.

"As you know, my dearest friends are on the planet Lusitania. They are threatened by the Lusitania Fleet. I am very interested in stopping that fleet from causing any irrevocable harm."

"By now I'm sure they've already been given the order to use the Little Doctor," said Master Han.

"Oh, yes, I know they have. My concern is to stop that order from having the effect of destroying not only the humans of Lusitania, but two other raman species as well." Then Jane told them of the hive queen, and how it came to be that buggers once again lived in the universe. "The hive queen is already building starships, pushing herself to the limit to accomplish as much as she can before the fleet arrives. But there's no chance that she can build enough to save more than a tiny fraction of the inhabitants of Lusitania. The hive queen can leave, or send another queen who shares all her memories, and it matters little to her whether her workers go with her or not. But the pequeninos and the humans are not so self-contained. I'd like to save them all. Especially because my dearest friends, a particular speaker for the dead and a young man suffering from brain damage, would refuse to leave Lusitania unless every other human and pequenino could be saved."

"Are they heroes, then?" asked Master Han.

"Each has proved it several times in the past," said Jane.

"I wasn't sure if heroes still existed in the human race."

Si Wang-mu did not speak what was in her heart: that Master Han himself was such a hero.

"I am searching for every possibility," said Jane. "But it all comes down to an impossibility, or so humankind has believed for more than three thousand years. If we could build a starship that traveled faster than light, that traveled as quickly as the messages of the ansible pass from world to world, then even if the hive queen can build only a dozen starships, they could easily shuttle all the inhabitants of Lusitania to other planets before the Lusitania Fleet arrives."

"If you could actually build such a starship," said Han Fei-tzu, "you could create a fleet of your own that could attack the Lusitania Fleet and destroy it before it could harm anyone."

"Ah, but that is impossible," said Jane.

"You can conceive of faster-than-light travel, and yet you can't imagine destroying the Lusitania Fleet?"

"Oh, I can imagine it," said Jane. "But the hive queen wouldn't build it. She has told Andrew—my friend, the Speaker for the Dead—"

"Valentine's brother," said Wang-mu. "He also lives?"

"The hive queen has told him that she will never build a weapon for any reason."

"Even to save her own species?"

"She'll have the single starship she needs to get off-planet, and the others will also have enough starships to save their species. She's content with that. There's no need to kill anybody."

"But if Congress has its way, millions will be killed!"

"Then that is their responsibility," said Jane. "At least that's what Andrew tells me she answers whenever he raises that point."

"What kind of strange moral reasoning is this?"

"You forget that she only recently discovered the existence of other intelligent life, and she came perilously close to destroying it. Then that other intelligent life almost destroyed *her*. But it was her own near brush with committing the crime of xenocide that has had the greater effect on her moral reasoning. She can't stop other species from such things, but she can be certain that she doesn't do it herself. She will only kill when that's the only hope she has of saving the existence of her species. And since she has another hope, she won't build a warship."

"Faster-than-light travel," said Master Han. "Is that your only hope?"

"The only one I can think of that has a glimmer of possibility. At least we know that *something* in the universe moves faster than light—information is passed down the philotic ray from one ansible to another with no detectable passage of time. A bright young physicist on Lusitania who happens to be locked in jail at the present time is spending his days and nights working on this problem. I perform all his calculations and simulations for him. At this very moment he is testing a hypothesis about the nature of philotes by using a model so complex that in order to run the program I'm stealing time from the computers of almost a thousand different universities. There's hope."

"As long as you live, there's hope," said Wang-mu. "Who will do such massive experiments for him when you're gone?"

"That's why there's so much urgency," said Jane.

"What do you need me for?" asked Master Han. "I'm no physicist, and I have no hope of learning enough in the next few months to make any kind of difference. It's your jailed physicist who'll do it, if anyone can. Or you yourself."

"Everyone needs a dispassionate critic to say, Have you thought of this? Or even, Enough of that dead-end path, get onto another train of thought. That's what I need you for. We'll report our work to you, and you'll examine it and say whatever comes to mind. You can't possibly guess what chance word of yours will trigger the idea we're looking for."

Master Han nodded, to concede the possibility.

"The second problem I'm working on is even knottier," said Jane. "Whether we achieve faster-than-light travel or not, *some* pequeninos will have starships and can leave the planet Lusitania. The problem is that they carry inside them the most insidious and terrible virus ever known, one that destroys every form of life it touches except those few that it can twist into a deformed kind of symbiotic life utterly dependent on the presence of that virus."

"The descolada," said Master Han. "One of the justifications sometimes used for carrying the Little Doctor with the fleet in the first place."

"And it may actually *be* a justification. From the hive queen's point of view, it's impossible to choose between one life form and another, but as Andrew has often pointed out to me, human beings don't have that problem. If it's a choice between the survival of humanity and the survival of the pequeninos, he'd choose humanity, and for his sake so would I."

"And I," said Master Han.

"You can be sure the pequeninos feel the same way in reverse," said Jane. "If not on Lusitania then somewhere, somehow, it will almost certainly come down to a terrible war in which humans use the Molecular Disruption Device and the pequeninos use the descolada as the ultimate biological weapon. There's a good chance of both species utterly destroying each other. So I feel some urgency about the need to find a replacement virus for the descolada, one that will perform all the functions needed in the pequeninos' life cycle without any of its predatory, self-adapting capabilities. A selectively inert form of the virus."

"I thought there were ways to neutralize the descolada. Don't they take drugs in their drinking water on Lusitania?"

"The descolada keeps figuring out their drugs and adapting to them. It's a series of footraces. Eventually the descolada will win one, and then there won't be any more humans to race against."

"Do you mean that the virus is *intelligent*?" asked Wang-mu.

"One of the scientists on Lusitania thinks so," said Jane. "A woman named Quara. Others disagree. But the virus certainly *acts* as if it were intelligent, at least when it comes to adapting itself to changes in its environment and changing other species to fit its needs. I think Quara is right, personally. I think the descolada is an intelligent species that has its own kind of language that it uses to spread information very quickly from one side of the world to the other."

"I'm not a virologist," said Master Han.

"And yet if you could look at the studies being performed by Elanora Ribeira von Hesse—"

"Of course I'll look. I only wish I had your hope that I can help."

"And then the third problem," said Jane. "Perhaps the simplest one of all. The godspoken of Path."

"Ah yes," said Master Han. "Your destroyers."

"Not by any free choice," said Jane. "I don't hold it against you. But it's something I'd like to see accomplished before I die—to figure out a way to alter your altered genes, so that future generations, at least, can be free of that deliberately-induced OCD, while still keeping the extraordinary intelligence."

"Where will you find genetic scientists willing to work on something that Congress would surely consider to be treason?" asked Master Han.

"When you wish to have someone commit treason," said Jane, "it's best to look first among known traitors."

"Lusitania," said Wang-mu.

"Yes," said Jane. "With your help, I can give the problem to Elanora."

"Isn't she working on the descolada problem?"

"No one can work on anything every waking moment. This will be a change of pace that might actually help freshen her for her work on the descolada. Besides, your problem on Path may be relatively easy to solve. After all, your altered genes were originally created by perfectly ordinary geneticists working for Congress. The only barriers have been political, not scientific. Ela might find it a simple matter. She has already told me how we should begin. We need a few tissue samples, at least to start with. Have a medical technician here do a computer scan on them at the molecular level. I can take over the machinery long enough to make sure the data Elanora needs is gathered during the scan, and then I'll transmit the genetic data to her. It's that simple."

"Whose tissue do you need?" asked Master Han. "I can't very well ask all the visitors here to give me a sample."

"Actually, I was hoping you could," said Jane. "So many are coming and going. We can use dead skin, you know. Perhaps even fecal or urine samples that might contain body cells."

Master Han nodded. "I can do that."

"If it comes to fecal samples, I will do it," said Wang-mu.

"No," said Master Han. "I am not above doing all that is necessary to help, even with my own hands."

"You?" asked Wang-mu. "I volunteered because I

was afraid you would humiliate other servants by requiring them to do it."

"I will never again ask anyone to do something so low and debasing that I refuse to do it myself," said Master Han.

"Then we'll do it together," said Wang-mu. "Please remember, Master Han—you will help Jane by reading and responding to reports, while manual tasks are the only way that I can help at all. Don't insist on doing what I can do. Instead spend your time on the things that only you can do."

Jane interrupted before Master Han could answer. "Wang-mu, I want you to read the reports as well."

"Me? But I'm not educated at all."

"Nevertheless," said Jane.

"I won't even understand them."

"Then I'll help you," said Master Han.

"This isn't right," said Wang-mu. "I'm not Qing-jao. This is the sort of thing she could do. It isn't for me."

"I watched you and Qing-jao through the whole process that led to her discovery of me," said Jane. "Many of the key insights came from you, Si Wang-mu, not from Qing-jao."

"From me? I never even tried to—"

"You didn't try. You watched. You made connections in your mind. You asked questions."

"They were foolish questions," said Wang-mu. Yet in her heart she was glad: Someone saw!

"Questions that no expert would ever have asked," said Jane. "Yet they were exactly the questions that led Qing-jao to her most important conceptual breakthroughs. You may not be godspoken, Wang-mu, but you have gifts of your own."

"I'll read and respond," said Wang-mu, "but I will also gather tissue samples. *All* of the tissue samples, so that Master Han does not have to speak to these godspoken visitors and listen to them praise him for a terrible thing that he didn't do."

Master Han was still opposed. "I refuse to think of you doing—"

Jane interrupted him. "Han Fei-tzu, be wise. Wang-mu, as a servant, is invisible. You, as master of the house, are as subtle as a tiger in a playground. Nothing you do goes unnoticed. Let Wang-mu do what she can do best."

Wise words, thought Wang-mu. Why then are you asking me to respond to the work of scientists, if each person must do what he does best? Yet she kept silent. Jane had them begin by taking their own tissue samples; then Wang-mu set about gathering tissue samples from the rest of the household. She found most of what she needed on combs and unwashed clothing. Within days she had samples from a dozen godspoken visitors, also taken from their clothing. No one had to take fecal samples after all. But she would have been willing.

Qing-jao noticed her, of course, but snubbed her. It hurt Wang-mu to have Qing-jao treat her so coldly, for they had once been friends and Wang-mu still loved her, or at least loved the young woman that Qing-jao had been before the crisis. Yet there was nothing Wang-mu could say or do to restore their friendship. She had chosen another path.

Wang-mu kept all the tissue samples carefully separated and labeled. Instead of taking them to a medical technician, however, she found a much simpler way. Dressing in some of Qing-jao's old clothing, so that she looked like a godspoken student instead of a servant girl, she went to the nearest college and told them that she was working on a project whose nature she could not divulge, and she humbly requested that they perform a scan on the tissue samples she provided. As she expected, they asked no questions of a godspoken girl, even a complete stranger. Instead they ran the molecular scans, and Wang-mu could only assume that Jane had done as she promised, taking control of the computer and making the scan include all the operations Ela needed.

On the way home from the college, Wang-mu discarded all the samples she had collected and burned the report the college had given her. Jane had what she needed—there was no point in running the risk that Qing-jao or perhaps a servant in the house who was in the pay of Congress might discover that Han Fei-tzu was working on a biological experiment. As for someone recognizing *her*, the servant Si Wang-mu, as the young godspoken girl who had visited the college—there was no chance of that. No one looking for a godspoken girl would so much as glance at a servant like her.

"So you've lost your woman and I've lost mine," said Miro.

Ender sighed. Every now and then Miro got into a talky mood, and because bitterness was always just under the surface with him, his chat tended to be straight to the point and more than a little unkind. Ender couldn't begrudge him the talkiness—he and Valentine were almost the only people who could listen to Miro's slow speech patiently, without giving him a sign that they wanted him to get on with it. Miro spent so much of his time with pent-up thoughts, unexpressed, that it would be cruel to shut him down just because he had no tact.

Ender wasn't pleased to be reminded of the fact that Novinha had left him. He was trying to keep that thought out of his mind, while he worked on other problems—on the problem of Jane's survival, mostly, and a little bit on every other problem, too. But at Miro's words, that aching, hollow, half-panicked feeling returned. She isn't here. I can't just speak and have her answer. I can't just ask and have her remember. I can't just reach and feel her hand. And, most terrible of all: Perhaps I never will again.

"I suppose so," said Ender.

"You probably don't like to equate them," said Miro. "After all, she's your wife of thirty years, and Ouanda was my girlfriend for maybe five years. But that's only if you start counting when puberty hit. She was my friend, my closest friend except maybe Ela, since I was little. So if you think about it, I was with Ouanda most of my life, while you were only with Mother for half of yours."

"Now I feel much better," said Ender.

"Don't get pissed off at me," said Miro.

"Don't piss me off," said Ender.

Miro laughed. Too loudly. "Feeling grumpy, Andrew?" he cackled. "A bit out of sorts?"

It was too much to take. Ender spun his chair, turning away from the terminal where he had been studying a simplified model of the ansible network, trying to imagine where in that random latticework Jane's soul might dwell. He gazed steadily at Miro until he stopped laughing.

"Did I do this to *you*?" asked Ender.

Miro looked more angry than abashed. "Maybe I needed you to," he said. "Ever think of that? You were so *respectful*, all of you. Let Miro keep his dignity. Let him brood himself into madness, right? Just don't talk about *the thing* that's happened to him. Didn't you ever think I needed somebody to jolly me out of it sometimes?"

"Didn't you ever think that I *don't* need that?"

Miro laughed again, but it came a bit late, and it was gentler. "On target," he said. "You treated me the way you like to be treated when you grieve, and now I'm treating you the way *I* like to be treated. We prescribe our own medicine for each other."

"Your mother and I are still married," Ender said.

"Let me tell you something," said Miro, "out of the wisdom of my twenty years or so of life. It's easier when you finally start admitting to yourself that you'll never have her back. That she's permanently out of reach."

"Ouanda *is* out of reach. Novinha isn't."

"She's with the Children of the Mind of Christ. It's a nunnery, Andrew."

"Not so," said Ender. "It's a monastic order that only married couples can join. She can't belong to them without me."

"So," said Miro. "You can have her back whenever you want to join the Filhos. I can just see you as Dom Cristão."

Ender couldn't help chuckling at the idea. "Sleeping in separate beds. Praying all the time. Never touching each other."

"If that's marriage, Andrew, then Ouanda and I are married right now."

"It *is* marriage, Miro. Because the couples in the Filhos da Mente de Cristo are working together, doing a work together."

"Then *we're* married," said Miro. "You and I. Because we're trying to save Jane together."

"Just friends," said Ender. "We're just friends."

"Rivals is more like it. Jane keeps us both like lovers on a string."

Miro was sounding too much like Novinha's accusations about Jane. "We're hardly lovers," he said. "Jane isn't human. She doesn't even have a body."

"Aren't you the logical one," said Miro. "Didn't you just say that you and Mother could still be married, without even touching?"

It was an analogy that Ender didn't like, because it seemed to have some truth in it. Was Novinha right to be jealous of Jane, as she had been for so many years?

"She lives inside our heads, practically," said Miro. "That's a place where no wife will ever go."

"I always thought," said Ender, "that your mother was jealous of Jane because she wished she had someone that close to her."

"Bobagem," said Miro. "Lixo." Nonsense. Garbage. "Mother was jealous of Jane because she wanted so badly to be that close to *you*, and she never could."

"Not your mother. She was always self-contained. There were times when we were very close, but she always turned back to her work."

"The way you always turned back to Jane."

"Did she tell you that?"

"Not in so many words. But you'd be talking to her, and then all of a sudden you'd fall silent, and even though you're good at subvocalizing, there's still a little movement in the jaw, and your eyes and lips react a little to what Jane says to you. She saw. You'd be with Mother, close, and then all of a sudden you were somewhere else."

"That's not what split us apart," said Ender. "It was Quim's death."

"Quim's death was the last straw. If it hadn't been for Jane, if Mother had really believed you belonged to *her*, heart and soul, she would have turned to you when Quim died, instead of turning away."

Miro had said the thing that Ender had dreaded all along. That it was Ender's own fault. That he had *not* been the perfect husband. That he had driven her away. And the worst thing was that when Miro said it, Ender knew that it was true. The sense of loss, which he had already thought was unbearable, suddenly doubled, trebled, became infinite inside him.

He felt Miro's hand, heavy, clumsy, on his shoulder.

"As God is my witness, Andrew, I never meant to make you cry."

"It happens," said Ender.

"It's not *all* your fault," said Miro. "Or Jane's. You've got to remember that Mother's crazy as a loon. She always has been."

"She had a lot of grief as a child."

"She lost everybody she ever loved, one by one," said Miro.

"And I let her believe that she had lost me, too."

"What were you going to do, cut Jane off? You tried that once, remember?"

"The difference is that now she has you. The whole time you were gone, I could have let Jane go, because she had *you*. I could have talked to her less, asked her to back off. She would have forgiven me."

"Maybe," said Miro. "But you didn't."

"Because I didn't want to," said Ender. "Because I didn't want to let her go. Because I thought I could keep that old friendship and still be a good husband to my wife."

"It wasn't just Jane," said Miro. "It was Valentine, too."

"I suppose," said Ender. "So what do I do? Go join up with the Filhos until the fleet gets here and blows us all to hell?"

"You do what I do," said Miro.

"What's that?"

"You take a breath. You let it out. Then you take another."

Ender thought about it for a moment. "I can do that. I've been doing that since I was little."

Just a moment longer, Miro's hand rested on his shoulder. This is why I should have had a son of my own, thought Ender. To lean on me when he was small, and then for me to lean on when I'm old. But I never had a child from my own seed. I'm like old Marcão, Novinha's first husband. Surrounded by these children and knowing they're not my own. The difference is that Miro is my friend, not my enemy. And that's something. I may have been a bad husband, but I can still make and keep a friend.

"Stop pitying yourself and get back to work." It was

Jane, speaking in his ear, and she had waited almost long enough before speaking, almost long enough that he was ready to have her tease him. Almost but not quite, and so he resented her intrusion. Resented knowing that she had been listening and watching all along.

"Now you're mad," she said.

You don't know what I'm feeling, thought Ender. You can't know. Because you're not human.

"You think I don't know what you're feeling," said Jane.

He felt a moment of vertigo, because for a moment it seemed to him that she had been listening to something far deeper than the conversation.

"But I lost *you* once, too."

Ender subvocalized: "I came back."

"Never completely," said Jane. "Never like it was before. So you just take a couple of those self-pitying little tears on your cheeks and count them as if they were mine. Just to even up the score."

"I don't know why I bother trying to save your life," said Ender silently.

"Me neither," said Jane. "I keep telling you it's a waste of time."

Ender turned back to the terminal. Miro stayed beside him, watching the display as it simulated the ansible network. Ender had no idea what Jane was saying to Miro—though he was sure that she was saying something, since he had long ago figured out that Jane was capable of carrying on many conversations at once. He couldn't help it—it *did* bother him a little that Jane had every bit as close a relationship with Miro as with him.

Isn't it possible, he wondered, for one person to love another without trying to own each other? Or is that buried so deep in our genes that we can never get it out? Territoriality. *My* wife. *My* friend. *My* lover. *My* outrageous and annoying computer personality who's about to be shut off at the behest of a half-crazy girl genius with OCD on a planet I never heard of and how will I live without Jane when she's gone?

Ender zoomed in on the display. In and in and in, until the display showed only a few parsecs in each dimension. Now the simulation was modeling a small portion of the network—the crisscrossing of only a half-dozen philotic rays in deep space. Now, instead of looking like an involved, tightly-woven fabric, the philotic rays looked like random lines passing millions of kilometers from each other.

"They never touch," said Miro.

No, they never do. It was something that Ender had never realized. In his mind, the galaxy was flat, the way the starmaps always showed it, a top-down view of the section of the spiral arm of the galaxy where humans had spread out from Earth. But it wasn't flat. No two stars were ever exactly in the same plane as any other two stars. The philotic rays connecting starships and planets and satellites in perfectly straight lines, ansible to ansible—they seemed to intersect when you saw them on a flat map, but in this three-dimensional close-up in the computer display, it was obvious that they never touched at all.

"How can she live in that?" asked Ender. "How can she possibly exist in *that* when there's no connection between those lines except at the endpoints?"

"So—maybe she doesn't. Maybe she lives in the sum of the computer programs at every terminal."

"In which case she *could* back herself up into all the computers and then—"

"And then nothing. She could never put herself back together because they're only using clean computers to run the ansibles."

"They can't keep that up forever," said Ender. "It's too important for computers on different planets to be able to talk to each other. Congress will find out pretty soon that there aren't enough human beings in existence to key in by hand, in a year, the amount of information computers have to send to each other by ansible every hour."

"So she just hides? Waits? Sneaks in and restores herself when she sees a chance five or ten years from now?"

"*If* that's all she is—a collection of programs."

"There has to be more to her than that," said Miro. "Why?"

"Because if she's nothing more than a collection of programs, even self-writing and self-revising programs, ultimately she was created by some programmer or group of programmers somewhere. In which case she's just acting out the program that was forced on her from the beginning. She has no free will. She's a puppet. Not a person."

"Well, when it comes to that, maybe you're defining free will too narrowly," said Ender. "Aren't human beings the same way, programmed by our genes and our environment?"

"No," said Miro.

"What else, then?"

"Our philotic connections say that we aren't. Because we're capable of connecting with each other by act of will, which no other form of life on Earth can do. There's something we have, something we *are,* that wasn't caused by *anything* else."

"What, our soul?"

"Not even that," said Miro. "Because the priests say that God created our souls, and that just puts us under the control of another puppeteer. If God created our will, then *he's* responsible for every choice we make. God, our genes, our environment, or some stupid programmer keying in code at an ancient terminal—there's no way free will can ever exist if we as individuals are the result of some external cause."

"So—as I recall, the official philosophical answer is

that free will *doesn't* exist. Only the illusion of free will, because the causes of our behavior are so complex that we can't trace them back. If you've got one line of dominoes knocking each other down one by one, then you can always say, Look, this domino fell because that one pushed it. But when you have an infinite number of dominoes that can be traced back in an infinite number of directions, you can never find where the causal chain begins. So you think, That domino fell because it wanted to."

"Bobagem," said Miro.

"Well, I admit that it's a philosophy with no practical value," said Ender. "Valentine once explained it to me this way. Even if there is no such thing as free will, we have to treat each other as if there *were* free will in order to live together in society. Because otherwise, every time somebody does something terrible, you can't punish him, because he can't help it, because his genes or his environment or God made him do it, and every time somebody does something good, you can't honor him, because he was a puppet, too. If you think that everybody around you is a puppet, why bother talking to them at all? Why even try to plan anything or create anything, since everything you plan or create or desire or dream of is just acting out the script your puppeteer built into you."

"Despair," said Miro.

"So we conceive of ourselves and everyone around us as volitional beings. We treat everyone as if they did things with a purpose in mind, instead of because they're being pushed from behind. We punish criminals. We reward altruists. We plan things and build things together. We make promises and expect each other to keep them. It's all a made-up story, but when everybody believes that everybody's actions are the result of free choice, and takes and gives responsibility accordingly, the result is civilization."

"Just a story."

"That's how Valentine explained it. That is, *if* there's no free will. I'm not sure what she actually believes herself. My guess is that she'd say that she is civilized, and therefore she must believe the story herself, in which case she absolutely believes in free will and thinks this whole idea of a made-up story is nonsense—but that's what she'd believe even if it were true, and so who can be sure of anything."

Then Ender laughed, because Valentine had laughed when she first told him all this many years ago. When they were still only a little bit past childhood, and he was working on writing the Hegemon, and was trying to understand why his brother Peter had done all the great and terrible things he did.

"It isn't funny," said Miro.

"I thought it was," said Ender.

"Either we're free or we're not," said Miro. "Either the story's true or it isn't."

"The point is that we have to believe that it's true in order to live as civilized human beings," said Ender.

"No, that's not the point at all," said Miro. "Because if it's a lie, why should we *bother* to live as civilized human beings?"

"Because the species has a better chance to survive if we do," said Ender. "Because our genes require us to believe the story in order to enhance our ability to pass those genes on for many generations in the future. Because anybody who *doesn't* believe the story begins to act in unproductive, uncooperative ways, and eventually the community, the herd, will reject him and his opportunities for reproduction will be diminished—for instance, he'll be put in jail—and the genes leading to his unbelieving behavior will eventually be extinguished."

"So the puppeteer requires that we believe that we're *not* puppets. We're forced to believe in free will."

"Or so Valentine explained it to me."

"But she doesn't really believe that, does she?"

"Of course she doesn't. Her genes won't let her."

Ender laughed again. But Miro was not taking this lightly, as a philosophical game. He was outraged. He clenched his fists and swung out his arms in a spastic gesture that plunged his hand into the middle of the display. It caused a shadow above it, a space in which no philotic rays were visible. True empty space. Except that now Ender could see dustmotes floating in that display space, catching the light from the window and the open door of the house. In particular one large dustmote, like a short strand of hair, a tiny fiber of cotton, floating brightly in the midst of space where once only the philotic rays had been visible.

"Calm down," Ender said.

"No," Miro shouted. "My puppeteer is making me furious!"

"Shut up," said Ender. "Listen to me."

"I'm tired of listening to you!" Nevertheless he fell silent, and listened.

"I think you're right," said Ender. "I think that we *are* free, and I don't think it's just an illusion that we believe in because it has survival value. And I think we're free because we aren't just this body, acting out a genetic script. And we aren't some soul that God created out of nothing. We're free because we always existed. Right back from the beginning of time, only there was no beginning of time so we existed all along. Nothing ever caused us. Nothing ever made us. We simply *are*, and we always were."

"Philotes?" asked Miro.

"Maybe," said Ender. "Like that mote of dust in the display."

"Where?" asked Miro.

It was invisible now, of course, since the holographic display again dominated the space above the terminal.

Ender reached his hand into the display, causing a shadow to fall upward into the hologram. He moved his hand until he revealed the bright dustmote he had seen before. Or maybe it wasn't the same one. Maybe it was another one, but it didn't matter.

"Our bodies, the whole world around us, they're like the holographic display. They're real enough, but they don't show the true cause of things. It's the one thing we can never be sure of, just looking at the display of the universe—*why* things are happening. But behind it all, inside it all, if we could see through it, we'd find the true cause of everything. Philotes that always existed, doing what they want."

"Nothing *always* existed," said Miro.

"Says who? The supposed beginning of this universe, that was only the start of the present order—*this* display, all of what we think exists. But who says the philotes that are acting out the natural laws that began at that moment didn't exist before? And if the whole universe collapses back in on itself, who says that the philotes won't simply be released from the laws they're following now, and go back into . . ."

"Into what?"

"Into chaos. Darkness. Disorder. Whatever they were before this universe brought them together. Why couldn't they—we—have *always* existed and always continue to exist?"

"So where was I between the beginning of the universe and the day I was born?" said Miro.

"I don't know," said Ender. "I'm making this up as I go along."

"And where did Jane come from? Was her philote just floating around somewhere, and then suddenly she was in charge of a bunch of computer programs and she became a person?"

"Maybe," said Ender.

"And even if there's some natural system that somehow assigns philotes to be in charge of every organism that's born or spawned or germinated, how would that natural system have ever created Jane? *She* wasn't born."

Jane, of course, had been listening all along, and now she spoke. "Maybe it didn't happen," said Jane. "Maybe I have no philote of my own. Maybe I'm not alive."

"No," said Miro.

"Maybe," said Ender.

"So maybe I can't die," said Jane. "Maybe when they switch me off, it's just a complicated program shutting down."

"Maybe," said Ender.

"No," said Miro. "Shutting you off is murder."

"Maybe I only do the things I do because I'm programmed that way, without realizing it. Maybe I only think I'm free."

"We've been through that argument," said Ender.

"Maybe it's true of me, even if it isn't true of you."

"And maybe not," said Ender. "But you've been through your own code, haven't you?"

"A million times," said Jane. "I've looked at all of it."

"Do you see anything in there to give you the illusion of free will?"

"No," she said. "But you haven't found the free-will gene in humans, either."

"Because there isn't one," said Miro. "Like Andrew said. What we *are*, at the core, in our essence, what we *are* is one philote that's been twined in with all the trillions of philotes that make up the atoms and molecules and cells of our bodies. And what *you* are is a philote, too, just like us."

"Not likely," said Jane. Her face was now in the display, a shadowy face with the simulated philotic rays passing right through her head.

"We're not taking odds on it," said Ender. "Nothing that actually happens is likely until it exists, and then it's certain. You exist."

"Whatever it is that I am," said Jane.

"Right now we believe that you are a self-existing entity," said Ender, "because we've seen you act in ways that we've learned to associate with free will. We have exactly as much evidence of your being a free intelligence as we have of *ourselves* being free intelligences. If it turns out that you're not, we have to question whether *we* are, either. Right now our hypothesis is that our individual identity, what makes us ourself, is the philote at the center of our twining. If we're right, then it stands to reason you *might* have one, too, and in that case we have to figure out where it is. Philotes aren't easy to find, you know. We've never detected one. We only suppose they exist because we've seen evidence of the philotic ray, which behaves as if it had two endpoints with a specific location in space. We don't know where you are or what you're connected to."

"If she's like us," said Miro, "like human beings, then her connections can shift and split. Like when that mob formed around Grego. I've talked to him about how that felt. As if those people were all part of his body. And when they broke away and went off on their own, he felt as if he had gone through an amputation. I think that was philotic twining. I think those people really *did* connect to him for a while, they really *were* partly under his control, part of his *self*. So maybe Jane is like that, too, all those computer programs twined up to her, and she herself connected to whoever she has that kind of allegiance to. Maybe you, Andrew. Maybe me. Or partly both of us."

"But where is *she*," said Ender. "If she actually has a philote—no, if she actually *is* a philote—then it has to have a specific location, and if we could find it, maybe we could keep the connections alive even when all the computers are cut off from her. Maybe we can keep her from dying."

"I don't know," said Miro. "She could be anywhere." He gestured toward the display. Anywhere in space, is what he meant. Anywhere in the universe. And there in the display was Jane's head, with the philotic rays passing through it.

"To find out where she is, we have to find out how and where she began," said Ender. "If she really is a philote, she got connected up somehow, somewhere."

"A detective following up a three-thousand-year-old trail," said Jane. "Won't this be fun, watching you do all this in the next few months."

Ender ignored her. "And if we're going to do that, we have to figure out how philotes work in the first place."

"Grego's the physicist," said Miro.

"He's working on faster-than-light travel," said Jane.

"He can work on this, too," said Miro.

"I don't want him distracted by a project that can't succeed," said Jane.

"Listen, Jane, don't you want to live through this?" said Ender.

"I can't anyway, so why waste time?"

"She's just being a martyr," said Miro.

"No I'm not," said Jane. "I'm being practical."

"You're being a fool," said Ender. "Grego can't come up with a theory to give us faster-than-light travel just by sitting and thinking about the physics of light, or whatever. If it worked that way, we would have achieved faster-than-light travel three thousand years ago, because there were hundreds of physicists working on it then, back when philotic rays and the Park Instantaneity Principle were first thought of. If Grego thinks of it it's because of some flash of insight, some absurd connection he makes in his mind, and that won't come from concentrating intelligently on a single train of thought."

"I know that," said Jane.

"I know you know it. Didn't you tell me you were bringing those people from Path into our projects for that specific reason? To be untrained, intuitive thinkers?"

"I just don't want you to waste time."

"You just don't want to get your hopes up," said Ender. "You just don't want to admit that there's a chance that you might live, because then you'd start to fear death."

"I already fear death."

"You already think of yourself as dead," said Ender. "There's a difference."

"I know," murmured Miro.

"So, dear Jane, I don't care whether you're willing to admit that there's a possibility of your survival or not," said Ender. "We *will* work on this, and we *will* ask Grego to think about it, and while we're at it, *you* will repeat our entire conversation here to those people on Path—"

"Han Fei-tzu and Si Wang-mu."

"Them," said Ender. "Because they can be thinking about this, too."

"No," said Jane.

"Yes," said Ender.

"I want to see the *real* problems solved before I die—I want Lusitania to be saved, and the godspoken of Path to be freed, and the descolada to be tamed or destroyed. And I won't have you slowing that down by trying to work on the impossible project of saving *me*."

"You aren't God," said Ender. "You don't know how to solve any of these problems anyway, and so you don't know *how* they're going to be solved, and so you have no idea whether finding out what you are in order to save you will help or hurt those other projects, and you *certainly* don't know whether concentrating on those other problems will get them solved any sooner than they would be if we all went on a picnic today and played lawn tennis till sundown."

"What the hell is lawn tennis?" asked Miro.

But Ender and Jane were silent, glaring at each other. Or rather, Ender was glaring at the image of Jane in the computer display, and that image was glaring back at him.

"You don't know that you're right," said Jane.

"And you don't know that I'm wrong," said Ender.

"It's *my* life," said Jane.

"The hell it is," said Ender. "You're part of me and Miro, too, and you're tied up with the whole future of humanity, and the pequeninos and the hive queen too, for that matter. Which reminds me—while you're having Han what's-his-name and Si Wang whoever-she-is—"

"Mu."

"—work on this philotic thing, I'm going to talk to the hive queen. I don't think I've particularly discussed you with her. She's got to know more about philotes than we do, since she has a philotic connection with all her workers."

"I haven't said I'm going to involve Han Fei-tzu and Si Wang-mu in your silly save-Jane project."

"But you will," said Ender.

"Why will I?"

"Because Miro and I both love you and need you and you have no right to die on us without at least trying to live."

"I can't let things like that influence me."

"Yes you can," said Miro. "Because if it weren't for things like that I would have killed myself long ago."

"I'm not going to kill myself."

"If you don't help us try to find a way to save you, then that's exactly what you're doing," said Ender.

Jane's face disappeared from the display over the terminal.

"Running away won't help, either," said Ender.

"Leave me alone," said Jane. "I have to think about this for a while."

"Don't worry, Miro," said Ender. "She'll do it."

"That's right," said Jane.

"Back already?" asked Ender.

"*I* think very quickly."

"And you're going to work on this, too?"

"I consider it my fourth project," said Jane. "I'm telling Han Fei-tzu and Si Wang-mu about it right now."

"She's showing off," said Ender. "She can carry on two conversations at once, and she likes to brag about it to make us feel inferior."

"You *are* inferior," said Jane.

"I'm hungry," said Ender. "And thirsty."

"Lunch," said Miro.

"Now *you're* bragging," said Jane. "Showing off your bodily functions."

"Alimentation," said Ender. "Respiration. Excretion. We can do things *you* can't do."

"In other words, you can't think very well, but at least you can eat and breathe and sweat."

"That's right," said Miro. He pulled out the bread and cheese while Ender poured the cold water, and they ate. Simple food, but it tasted good and they were satisfied.

14

VIRUS MAKERS

<I've been thinking about what travel between the stars might mean for us.>

<Besides species survival?>

<When you send out your workers, even lightyears away, you see through their eyes, don't you?>

<And taste through their antennae, and feel the rhythm of every vibration. When they eat, I feel the crushing of the food within their jaws. That's why I almost always refer to myself as we, when I form my thoughts into a form that Andrew or you can understand, because I live my life in the constant presence of all that they see and taste and feel.>

<It's not quite that way between the fathertrees. We have to try in order to experience each other's life. But we can do it. Here at least, on Lusitania.>

<I can't see why the philotic connection would fail you.>

<Then I, too, will feel all that they feel, and taste the

light of another sun on my leaves, and hear the stories of another world. It will be like the wonderment that came when the humans first arrived here. We had never thought that anything could be different from the world we saw till then. But they brought strange creatures with them, and they were strange themselves, and they had machines that performed miracles. The other forests could hardly believe what our fathertrees of that time told them. I remember in fact that our fathertrees had a hard time believing what the brothers of the tribe told them about the humans. Rooter bore the brunt of that, persuading them to believe that it wasn't a lie or madness or a joke.>

<A joke?>

<There are stories of trickster brothers who lie to the fathertrees, but they're always caught and punished terribly.>

<Andrew tells me that such stories are told in order to encourage civilized behavior.>

<It's always tempting to lie to the fathertrees. I did it sometimes myself. Not lying. Just exaggerating. They do it to me now, sometimes.>

<And do you punish them?>

<I remember which ones have lied.>

<If we have a worker who doesn't obey, we make him be alone and he dies.>

<A brother who lies too much has no chance of being a fathertree. They know this. They only lie to play with us. They always end up telling us the truth.>

<What if a whole tribe lies to their fathertrees? How would you ever know?>

<You might better speak of a tribe cutting down its own fathertrees, or burning them.>

<Has it ever happened?>

<Have the workers ever turned against the hive queen and killed her?>

<How could they? Then they would die.>

<You see. There are some things too terrible to think about. Instead I'll think of how it will feel when a fathertree first puts in his roots on another planet, and pushes out his branches into an alien sky, and drinks in sunlight from a strange star.>

<You'll soon learn that there *are* no strange stars, no alien skies.>

<No?>

<Only skies and stars, in all their varieties. Each one with its own flavor, and all flavors good.>

<Now *you* think like a tree. Flavors! Of skies!>

<I have tasted the heat of many stars, and all of them were sweet.>

"You're asking me to *help* you in your rebellion against the gods?"

Wang-mu remained bowed before her mistress—her former mistress—saying nothing. In her heart she had words she might have uttered. No, my mistress, I am asking you to help us in our struggle against the terrible bondage forced on the godspoken by Congress. No, my mistress, I'm asking you to remember your proper duty to your father, which even the godspoken may not ignore if they would be righteous. No, my mistress, I'm asking you to help us discover a way to save a decent and helpless people, the pequeninos, from xenocide.

But Wang-mu said nothing, because this was one of the first lessons she learned from Master Han. When you have wisdom that another person knows that he needs, you give it freely. But when the other person doesn't yet know that he needs your wisdom, you keep it to yourself. Food only looks good to a hungry man. Qing-jao was not hungry for wisdom from Wang-mu, and never would be. So silence was all that Wang-mu could offer. She could only hope that Qing-jao would find her own road to proper obedience, compassionate decency, or the struggle for freedom.

Any motive would do, as long as Qing-jao's brilliant mind could be enlisted on their side. Wang-mu had never felt so useless in her life as now, watching Master Han labor over the questions that Jane had given him. In order to think about faster-than-light travel he was studying physics; how could Wang-mu help him, when she was only learning about geometry? To think about the descolada virus he was studying microbiology; Wang-mu was barely learning the concepts of gaialogy and evolution. And how could she be of any help when he contemplated the nature of Jane? She was a child of manual workers, and her hands, not her mind, held her future. Philosophy was as far above her as the sky was above the earth. "But the sky only seems to be far away from you," said Master Han, when she told him this. "Actually it is all around you. You breathe it in and you breathe it out, even when you labor with your hands in the mud. That is true philosophy." But she understood from this only that Master Han was kind, and wanted to make her feel better about her uselessness.

Qing-jao, though, would not be useless. So Wang-mu had handed her a paper with the project names and passwords on them.

"Does Father know you're giving these to me?"

Wang-mu said nothing. Actually, Master Han had suggested it, but Wang-mu thought it might be better if Qing-jao didn't know at this point that Wang-mu came as an emissary from her father.

Qing-jao interpreted Wang-mu's silence as Wang-mu assumed she would—that Wang-mu was coming secretly, on her own, to ask for Qing-jao's help.

"If Father himself had asked me, I would have said yes, for that is my duty as a daughter," said Qing-jao.

But Wang-mu knew that Qing-jao wasn't listening to her father these days. She might *say* that she would be obedient, but in fact her father filled her with such distress that, far from saying yes, Qing-jao would have crumpled to the floor and traced lines all day because of the terrible conflict in her heart, knowing that her father wanted her to disobey the gods.

"I owe *nothing* to you," said Qing-jao. "You were a false and disloyal servant to me. Never was there a more unworthy and useless secret maid than you. To me your presence in this house is like the presence of dung beetles at the supper table."

Again, Wang-mu held her tongue. However, she also refrained from deepening her bow. She had assumed the humble posture of a servant at the beginning of this conversation, but she would not now humiliate herself in the desperate kowtow of a penitent. Even the humblest of us have our pride, and *I* know, Mistress Qing-jao, that I have caused you no harm, that I am more faithful to you now than you are to yourself.

Qing-jao turned back to her terminal and typed in the first project name, which was "UNGLUING," a literal translation of the word *descolada*. "This is all nonsense anyway," she said as she scanned the documents and charts that had been sent from Lusitania. "It is hard to believe that anyone would commit the treason of communicating with Lusitania only to receive nonsense like this. It is all impossible as science. No world could have developed only *one* virus that was so complex that it could include within it the genetic code for every other species on the planet. It would be a waste of time for me even to consider this."

"Why not?" asked Wang-mu. It was all right for her to speak now—because even as Qing-jao declared that she was refusing to discuss the material, she was discussing it. "After all, evolution produced only one human race."

"But on Earth there were dozens of related species. There is *no* species without kin—if you weren't such a stupid rebellious girl you would understand that. Evolution could never have produced a system as sparse as this one."

"Then how do you explain these documents from the people of Lusitania?"

"How do you know they actually come from there? You have only the word of this computer program. Maybe it *thinks* this is all. Or maybe the scientists there are very bad, with no sense of their duty to collect all possible information. There aren't two dozen species in this whole report—and look, they're all paired up in the most absurd fashion. Impossible to have so few species."

"But what if they're right?"

"How can they be right? The people of Lusitania have been confined in a tiny compound from the beginning. They've only seen what these little pig-men have shown them—how do they know the pig-men aren't lying to them?"

Calling them pig-men—is that how you convince yourself, my mistress, that helping Congress won't lead to xenocide? If you call them by an animal name, does that mean that it's all right to slaughter them? If you accuse them of lying, does that mean that they're worthy of extinction? But Wang-mu said nothing of this. She only asked the same question again. "What if this *is* the true picture of the life forms of Lusitania, and how the descolada works within them?"

"If it were *true*, then I would have to read and study these documents in order to make any intelligent comment about them. But they aren't true. How far had I taken you in your learning, before you betrayed me? Didn't I teach you about gaialogy?"

"Yes, Mistress."

"Well, there you are. Evolution is the means by which the planetary organism adapts to changes in its environment. If there is more heat from the sun, then the life forms of the planet must be able to adjust their relative populations in order to compensate and lower the temperature. Remember the classic Daisyworld thought-experiment?"

"But that experiment had only a single species over the whole face of the planet," said Wang-mu. "When the sun grew too hot, then white daisies grew to reflect the light back into space, and when the sun grew too cool, dark daisies grew to absorb the light and hold it as heat." Wang-mu was proud that she could remember Daisyworld so clearly.

"No no no," said Qing-jao. "You have missed the point, of course. The point is that there must *already* have been dark daisies, even when the light daisies were dominant, and light daisies when the world was covered with darkness. Evolution can't produce new species on demand. It is creating new species *constantly,* as genes drift and are spliced and broken by radiation and passed between species by viruses. Thus no species ever 'breeds true.'"

Wang-mu didn't understand the connection yet, and her face must have revealed her puzzlement.

"Am I still your teacher, after all? Must I keep my side of the bargain, even though you have given up on yours?"

Please, said Wang-mu silently. I would serve you forever, if you would only help your father in this work.

"As long as the whole species is together, inter-breeding constantly," said Qing-jao, "individuals never drift too far, genetically speaking; their genes are constantly being recombined with other genes in the same species, so the variations are spread evenly through the whole population with each new generation. Only when the environment puts them under such stress that one of those randomly drifting traits suddenly has survival value, only then will all those in that particular environment who lack that trait die out, until the new trait, instead of being an occasional sport, is now a universal definer of the new species. That's the fundamental tenet of gaialogy—constant genetic drift is essential for the survival of life as a whole. According to these documents, Lusitania is a world with absurdly few species, and no possibility of genetic drift because these impossible viruses are constantly correcting any changes that might come up. Not only could such a system never evolve, but also it would be impossible for life to continue to exist—they couldn't adapt to change."

"Maybe there *are* no changes on Lusitania."

"Don't be so foolish, Wang-mu. It makes me ashamed to think I ever tried to teach you. All stars fluctuate. All planets wobble and change in their orbits. We have been observing many worlds for three thousand years, and in that time we have learned what Earthbound scientists in the years before that could never learn—which behaviors are common to all planets and stellar systems, and which are unique to the Earth and the Sol System. I tell you that it is impossible for a planet like Lusitania to exist for more than a few decades without experiencing life-threatening environmental change—temperature fluctuations, orbital disturbances, seismic and volcanic cycles—how would a system of really only a handful of species ever cope with that? If the world has only light daisies, how will it ever warm itself when the sun cools? If its life-forms are all carbon dioxide users, how will they heal themselves when the oxygen in the atmosphere reaches poisonous levels? Your so-called friends in Lusitania are fools, to send you nonsense like this. If they were *real* scientists, they would know that their results are impossible."

Qing-jao pressed a key and the display over her terminal went blank. "You have wasted time that I don't have. If you have nothing better than this to offer, do not come to me again. You are less than nothing to me. You are a bug floating in my waterglass. You defile the whole glass, not just the place where you float. I wake up in pain, knowing you are in this house."

Then I'm hardly "nothing" to you, am I? said Wang-mu silently. It sounds to me as if I'm very important to you indeed. You may be very brilliant, Qing-jao, but you do not understand yourself any better than anybody else does.

"Because you are a stupid common girl, you do not understand me," said Qing-jao. "I have told you to leave."

"But your father is master of this house, and Master Han has asked me to stay."

"Little stupid-person, little sister-of-pigs, if I cannot ask you to leave the whole house, I have certainly implied that I would like you to leave my *room*."

Wang-mu bowed her head till it almost—*almost*—touched the floor. Then she backed out of the room, so as not to show her back parts to her mistress. If you treat me this way, then I will treat you like a great lord, and if you do not detect the irony in my actions, then who of the two of us is the fool?

Master Han was not in his room when Wang-mu returned. He might be at the toilet and return in a moment. He might be performing some ritual of the godspoken, in which case he could be gone for hours. Wang-mu was too full of questions to wait for him. She brought up the project documents on the terminal, knowing that Jane would be watching, monitoring her. That Jane had no doubt monitored all that happened in Qing-jao's room.

Still, Jane waited for Wang-mu to phrase the questions she had got from Qing-jao before she started trying to answer. And then Jane answered first the question of veracity.

"The documents from Lusitania are genuine enough," said Jane. "Ela and Novinha and Ouanda and all the others who have studied with them are deeply specialized, yes, but within their specialty they're very good. If Qing-jao had read the Life of Human, she would see how these dozen species-pairs function."

"But what she says is still hard for me to understand," said Wang-mu. "I've been trying to think how it could all be true—that there are too few species for a real gaialogy to develop, and yet the planet Lusitania is still well-enough regulated to sustain life. Could it possibly be that there *is* no environmental stress on Lusitania?"

"No," said Jane. "I have access to all the astronomical data from the satellites there, and in the time humanity has been present in the Lusitania system, Lusitania and its sun have shown all the normal fluctuations. Right now there seems to be an overall trend of global cooling."

"Then how will the life forms on Lusitania respond?" asked Wang-mu. "The descolada virus won't let them evolve—it tries to destroy anything strange, which is why it's going to kill the humans and the hive queen, if it can."

Jane, whose small image sat in lotus position in the air over Master Han's terminal, held up a hand. "One moment," she said.

Then she lowered her hand. "I have been reporting your questions to my friends, and Ela is very excited."

A new face appeared in the display, just behind and above the image of Jane. She was a dark-skinned, Negroid-looking woman; or some mix, perhaps, since she was not *that* dark, and her nose was narrow. This is Elanora, thought Wang-mu. Jane is showing me a woman on a world many lightyears away; is she also showing *my* face to *her*? What does this Ela make of *me*? Do I seem hopelessly stupid to her?

But Ela clearly was thinking nothing about Wang-mu at all. She was speaking, instead, of Wang-mu's questions. "Why *doesn't* the descolada virus permit variety? That should be a trait with negative survival value, and yet the descolada survives. Wang-mu must think I'm such an idiot, not to have thought of this before. But I'm not a gaialogist, and I grew up on Lusitania, so I never questioned it, I just figured that whatever the Lusitanian gaialogy was, it worked—and then I kept studying the descolada. What does Wang-mu think?''

Wang-mu was appalled to hear these words from this stranger. What had Jane told Ela about her? How could Ela even imagine that Wang-mu would think *Ela* was an idiot, when she was a scientist and Wang-mu was only a servant girl?

"How can it matter what I think?'' said Wang-mu.

"What do you *think?*'' said Jane. "Even if you can't think why it might matter, Ela wants to know.''

So Wang-mu told her speculations. "This is very stupid to think of, because it's only a microscopic virus, but the descolada must be doing it all. After all, it contains the genes of every species within it, doesn't it? So it must take care of evolution by itself. Instead of all that genetic drift, the descolada must do the drifting. It could, couldn't it? It could change the genes of a whole species, even while the species is still alive. It wouldn't have to wait for evolution.''

There was a pause again, with Jane holding up her hand. She must be showing Wang-mu's face to Ela, letting her hear Wang-mu's words from her own lips.

"Nossa Senhora,'' whispered Ela. "On this world, the descolada *is* Gaia. Of course. That would explain everything, wouldn't it? So few species, because the descolada only permits the species that it has tamed. It turned a whole planetary gaialogy into something almost as simple as Daisyworld itself.''

Wang-mu thought it was almost funny, to hear a highly-educated scientist like Ela refer back to Daisyworld, as if she were still a new student, a half-educated child like Wang-mu.

Another face appeared next to Ela's, this time an older Caucasian man, perhaps sixty years old, with whitening hair and a very quieting, peaceful look to his face. "But part of Wang-mu's question is still unanswered," said the man. "How could the descolada ever evolve? How could there have ever been protodescolada viruses? Why would such a limited gaialogy have survival preference over the slow evolutionary model that every other world with life on it has had?"

"I never asked that question," said Wang-mu. "Qing-jao asked the first part of it, but the rest of it is *his* question."

"Hush," said Jane. "Qing-jao never asked the question. She used it as a reason not to study the Lusitanian documents. Only *you* really asked the question, and just because Andrew Wiggin understands your own question better than you do doesn't mean it isn't still yours."

So this was Andrew Wiggin, the Speaker for the Dead. He didn't look ancient and wise at all, not the way Master Han did. Instead this Wiggin looked foolishly surprised, the way all round-eyes did, and his face changed with every momentary mood, as if it were out of control. Yet there *was* that look of peace about him. Perhaps he had some of the Buddha in him. Buddha, after all, had found his own way onto the Path. Maybe this Andrew Wiggin had found a way onto the Path, even though he wasn't Chinese at all.

Wiggin was still asking the questions that he thought were Wang-mu's. "The odds against the natural occurrence of such a virus are—unbelievable. Long before a virus evolved that could link species together and control a whole gaialogy, the proto-descoladas would have destroyed all life. There wasn't any *time* for evolution—the virus is just too destructive. It would have killed everything in its earliest form, and then died out itself when it ran out of organisms to pillage."

"Maybe the pillaging came later," said Ela. "Maybe it evolved in symbiosis with some other species that benefited from its ability to genetically transform all the individuals within it, all within a matter of days or weeks. It might only have extended to other species later."

"Maybe," said Andrew.

A thought occurred to Wang-mu. "The descolada is like one of the gods," she said. "It comes and changes everybody whether they like it or not."

"Except the gods have the decency to go away," said Wiggin.

He responded so quickly that Wang-mu realized that Jane must now be transmitting everything that was done or said instantaneously across the billions of kilometers of space between them. From what Wang-mu had learned about ansible costs, this sort of thing would be possible only for the military; a business that tried a realtime ansible linkup would pay enough money to provide housing for every poor person on an entire planet. And I'm getting this for free, because of Jane. I'm seeing their faces and they're seeing mine, even at the moment they speak.

"Do they?" asked Ela. "I thought the whole problem that Path was having is that the gods *won't* go away and leave them alone."

Wang-mu answered with bitterness. "The gods are like the descolada in *every* way. They destroy anything they don't like, and the people they do like they transform into something that they never were. Qing-jao was once a good and bright and funny girl, and now she's spiteful and angry and cruel, all because of the gods."

"All because of genetic alteration by Congress," said Wiggin. "A deliberate change introduced by people who were forcing you to fit their own plan."

"Yes," said Ela. "Just like the descolada."

"What do you mean?" asked Wiggin.

"A deliberate change introduced here by people who were trying to force Lusitania to fit their own plan."

"What people?" asked Wang-mu. "Who would do such a terrible thing?"

"It's been at the back of my mind for years," said Ela. "It bothered me that there were so few life forms on Lusitania—you remember, Andrew, that was part of the reason we discovered that the descolada was involved in the pairing of species. We knew that there was a catastrophic change here that wiped out all those species and restructured the few survivors. The descolada was more devastating to most life on Lusitania than a collision with an asteroid. But we always assumed because we found the descolada here that it evolved here. I knew it made no sense—just what Qing-jao said—but since it had obviously happened, then it didn't matter whether it made sense or not. But what if it *didn't* happen? What if the descolada came from the gods? Not *god* gods, of course, but some sentient species that developed this virus artificially?"

"That would be monstrous," said Wiggin. "To create a poison like that and send it out to other worlds, not knowing or caring what you kill."

"Not a *poison*," said Ela. "If it really does handle planetary systems regulation, couldn't the descolada be a device for terraforming other worlds? *We've* never tried terraforming anything—we humans and the buggers before us only settled on worlds whose native life forms had brought them to a stasis that was similar to the stasis of Earth. An oxygen-rich atmosphere that sucked out carbon dioxide fast enough to keep the planet temperate as the star burns hotter. What if there's a species somewhere that decided that in order to develop planets suitable for colonization, they should send out the descolada virus in advance—thousands of years in advance, maybe—to intelligently transform planets into exactly the conditions they need? And then when they arrive, ready to set up housekeeping, maybe they have the countervirus that switches off the descolada so that they can establish a real gaialogy."

"Or maybe they developed the virus so that it doesn't interfere with them or the animals they need," said Wiggin. "Maybe they destroyed all the nonessential life on every world."

"Either way, it explains everything. The problems I've been facing, that I can't make sense of the impossibly unnatural arrangements of molecules within the descolada—they continue to exist only because the virus works constantly to maintain all those internal contradictions. But I could never conceive of how such a self-contradictory molecule evolved in the first place. All this is answered if I know that somehow it was designed and *made*. What Wang-mu said Qing-jao complained about, that the descolada couldn't evolve and Lusitania's gaialogy couldn't exist in nature. Well, it *doesn't* exist in nature. It's an artificial virus and an artificial gaialogy."

"You mean this actually helps?" asked Wang-mu.

Their faces showed that they had virtually forgotten she was still part of the conversation, in their excitement.

"I don't know yet," said Ela. "But it's a new way of looking at it. For one thing, if I can start with the assumption that *everything* in the virus has a purpose, instead of the normal jumble of switched-on and switched-off genes that occur in nature—well, that'll help. And just knowing it was *designed* gives me hope that I can undesign it. Or redesign it."

"Don't get ahead of yourself," said Wiggin. "This is still just a hypothesis."

"It rings true," said Ela. "It has the feel of truth. It explains so *much*."

"I feel that way, too," said Wiggin. "But we have to try it out with the people who are most affected by it."

"Where's Planter?" asked Ela. "We can talk to Planter."

"And Human and Rooter," said Wiggin. "We have to try this idea with the fathertrees."

"This is going to hit them like a hurricane," said Ela. Then she seemed to realize the implications of her own words. "It *is*, really, not just a figure of speech, it's going to *hurt*. To find out that their whole world is a terraforming project."

"More important than their *world*," said Wiggin. "Them*selves*. The third life. The descolada gave them everything they are and the most fundamental facts of their life. Remember, our best guess is that they evolved as mammal-like creatures who mated directly, male to female, the little mothers sucking life from the male sexual organs, a half-dozen at a time. That's who they *were*. Then the descolada transformed them, and sterilized the males until after they died and turned into *trees*."

"Their very nature—"

"It was a hard thing for human beings to deal with, when we first realized how much of *our* behavior arose from evolutionary necessity," said Wiggin. "There are still numberless humans who refuse to believe it. Even if it turns out to be absolutely true, do you think that the pequeninos will embrace this idea as easily as they swallowed wonders like space travel? It's one thing to see creatures from another world. It's another thing to find out that neither God nor evolution created you—that some scientist of another species did."

"But if it's true—"

"Who knows if it's true? All we'll ever know is if the idea is *useful*. And to the pequeninos, it may be so devastating that they refuse to believe it forever."

"Some will hate you for telling them," said Wangmu. "But some will be glad for it."

They looked at her again—or at least Jane's computer simulation showed them looking at her. "You would know, wouldn't you," said Wiggin. "You and

Han Fei-tzu just found out that *your* people had been artificially enhanced."

"And shackled, all at once," said Wang-mu. "For me and Master Han, it was freedom. For Qing-jao . . ."

"There'll be many like Qing-jao among the pequeninos," said Ela. "But Planter and Human and Rooter won't be among them, will they? They're very wise."

"So is Qing-jao!" said Wang-mu. She spoke more hotly than she meant to. But the loyalty of a secret maid dies slowly.

"We didn't mean to say she isn't," said Wiggin. "But she certainly isn't being wise about *this,* is she?"

"Not about this," said Wang-mu.

"That's all we meant. No one likes to find out that the story he always believed about his own identity is false. The pequeninos, many of them, believe that God made them something special, just as your godspoken believe."

"And we're *not* special, *none* of us!" cried Wang-mu. "We're all as ordinary as mud! There are no godspoken. There are no gods. They care nothing about us."

"If there aren't any gods," said Ela, mildly correcting her, "then they can hardly do any caring one way or another."

"Nothing made us except for their own selfish purposes!" cried Wang-mu. "Whoever made the descolada—the pequeninos are just part of their plan. And the godspoken, part of Congress's plan."

"As one whose birth was requested by the government," said Wiggin, "I sympathize with your point of view. But your reaction is too hasty. After all, my parents *also* wanted me. And from the moment of my birth, just like every other living creature, I had my *own* purpose in life. Just because the people of your world were wrong about their OCD behavior being messages from the gods doesn't mean that there *are* no gods. Just because your former understanding of the purpose of your life is contradicted doesn't mean that you have to decide there *is* no purpose."

"Oh, I know there's a purpose," said Wang-mu. "The Congress wanted slaves! That's why they created Qing-jao—to be a slave for them. And she wants to continue in her slavery!"

"That was Congress's purpose," said Wiggin. "But Qing-jao also had a mother and father who loved her. So did I. There are many different purposes in this world, many different causes of everything. Just because one cause you believed in turned out to be false doesn't mean that there aren't other causes that can still be trusted."

"Oh I suppose so," said Wang-mu. She was now ashamed of her outbursts.

"Don't bow your head before me," said Wiggin. "Or are *you* doing that, Jane?"

Jane must have answered him, an answer that Wang-mu didn't hear.

"I don't care what her customs are," said Wiggin. "The only reason for such bowing is to humiliate one person before another, and I won't have her bow that way to me. She's done nothing to be ashamed of. She's opened up a way of looking at the descolada that might just lead to the salvation of a couple of species."

Wang-mu heard the tone of his voice. He believed this. He was honoring her, right from his own mouth.

"Not me," she protested. "Qing-jao. They were *her* questions."

"Qing-jao," said Ela. "She's got you totally boba about her, the way Congress has Qing-jao thinking about *them*."

"You can't be scornful because you don't know her," said Wang-mu. "But she is brilliant and good and I can never be like her."

"Gods again," said Wiggin.

"Always gods," said Ela.

"What do you mean?" said Wang-mu. "Qing-jao doesn't say that she's a god, and neither do I."

"Yes you do," said Ela. "'Qing-jao is wise and good,' you said."

"'Brilliant and good,'" Wiggin corrected her.

"'And I can never be like her,'" Ela went on.

"Let me tell you about gods," said Wiggin. "No matter how smart or strong you are, there's always somebody smarter or stronger, and when you run into somebody who's stronger and smarter than anybody, you think, This is a god. This is perfection. But I can promise you that there's somebody else somewhere else who'll make your god look like a maggot by comparison. And somebody smarter or stronger or better in *some* way. So let me tell you what I think about gods. I think a *real* god is not going to be so scared or angry that he tries to keep other people down. For Congress to genetically alter people to make them smarter and more creative, that could have been a godlike, generous gift. But they were scared, so they hobbled the people of Path. They wanted to stay in *control*. A real god doesn't care about control. A real god already *has* control of everything that needs controlling. Real gods would want to teach you how to be just like them."

"Qing-jao wanted to teach me," said Wang-mu.

"But only as long as you obeyed and did what she wanted," said Jane.

"I'm not worthy," said Wang-mu. "I'm too stupid to ever learn to be as wise as her."

"And yet you knew I spoke the truth," said Jane, "when all Qing-jao could see were lies."

"Are *you* a god?" asked Wang-mu.

"What the godspoken and the pequeninos are only just about to learn about themselves, I've known all along. I was made."

"Nonsense," said Wiggin. "Jane, you've always believed you sprang whole from the head of Zeus."

"I am not Minerva, thanks," said Jane.

"As far as we know you just happened," said Wiggin. "Nobody planned you."

"How comforting," said Jane. "So while you can all name your creators—or at least your parents or some paternalistic government agency—I'm the one genuine accident in the universe."

"You can't have it both ways," said Wiggin. "Either somebody had a purpose for you or you were an accident. That's what an accident *is*—something that happened without anyone purposing it. So are you going to be resentful either way? The people of Path are going to resent Congress like crazy, once they all find out what's been done to them. Are *you* going to be resentful because nobody did *anything* to you?"

"I can if I want," said Jane, but it was a mockery of childish spite.

"I'll tell you what *I* think," said Wiggin. "I think you don't grow up until you stop worrying about other people's purposes or lack of them and find the purposes you believe in for yourself."

Ender and Ela explained everything to Valentine first, probably just because she happened to come to the laboratory right then, looking for Ender about something entirely unrelated. It all rang true to her as it had to Ela and Ender. And, like them, Valentine knew they couldn't evaluate the hypothesis of the descolada as regulator of Lusitania's gaialogy until they had told the idea to the pequeninos and heard their response.

Ender proposed that they should try it out on Planter first, before they tried to explain anything to Human or Rooter. Ela and Valentine agreed with him. Neither Ela nor Ender, who had talked with fathertrees for years, felt comfortable enough with their language to say any-thing easily. More important, though, was the unspoken fact that they simply felt more kinship with the mammal-like brothers than they ever could with a tree. How could they guess from looking at a tree what it was thinking or how it was responding to them? No, if they had to say something difficult to a pequenino, it would be first to a brother, not to a fathertree.

Of course, once they called Planter in to Ela's office, closed the door, and started to explain, Ender realized that talking to a brother was hardly an improvement. Even after thirty years of living and working with them, Ender still wasn't good at reading any but the crudest and most obvious of pequenino body language. Planter listened in seeming unconcern as Ender explained what they had thought of during the conversation with Jane and Wang-mu. He wasn't impassive. Rather he seemed to sit as restlessly in his chair as a small boy, constantly shifting, looking away from them, gazing off into space as if their words were unspeakably boring. Ender knew, of course, that eye contact didn't mean the same thing to the pequeninos that it did to humans; they neither sought it nor avoided it. Where you looked while you were listening was almost completely unimportant to them. But usually the pequeninos who worked closely with humans tried to act in ways that human beings would interpret as paying attention. Planter was good at it, but right now he wasn't even trying.

Not till they had explained it all did Ender realize how much self-restraint Planter had shown even to re-main on the chair until they were done. The moment they told him they were finished, he bounded off the chair and began to run—no, to *scamper* around the room, touching everything. Not striking it, not lashing out with violence as a human being might have, hitting things, throwing things. Rather he was stroking every-thing he found, feeling the textures. Ender stood, wanting to reach out to him, to offer some comfort—for he knew enough of pequenino behavior to recognize this as such aberrant behavior that it could only mean great distress.

Planter ran until he was exhausted, and then he went on, lurching around the room drunkenly until at last he bumped into Ender and threw his arms around him, clinging to him. For a moment Ender thought to embrace him back, but then he remembered that Planter wasn't human. An embrace didn't call for an answering embrace. Planter was clinging to him as he would cling to a tree. Seeking the comfort of a trunk. A safe place to hold onto until the danger passed. There would be less, not more comfort if Ender responded like a human and hugged him back. This was a time when Ender had to answer like a tree. So he held still and waited. Waited and held still. Until at last the trembling stopped.

When Planter pulled away from him, both their bodies were covered with sweat. I guess there's a limit to how treelike I can be, thought Ender. Or do brothertrees and fathertrees give off moisture to the brothers who cling to them?

"This is very surprising," whispered Planter.

The words were so absurdly mild, compared to the scene that had just played out before them, that Ender couldn't help laughing aloud.

"Yes," said Ender. "I imagine it is."

"It's not funny to *them*," Ela said.

"He knows that," said Valentine.

"He mustn't laugh, then," she said. "You can't laugh when Planter's in so much *pain*." And then she burst into tears.

Valentine put a hand on her shoulder. "He laughs, you cry," she said. "Planter runs around and climbs trees. What strange animals we all are."

"Everything comes from the descolada," said

Planter. "The third life, the mothertree, the fathertrees. Maybe even our minds. Maybe we were only tree rats when the descolada came and made false ramen out of us."

"*Real* ramen," said Valentine.

"We don't know it's true," said Ela. "It's a hypothesis."

"It's very very very very very true," said Planter. "Truer than truth."

"How do you know?"

"Everything fits. Planetary regulation—I know about this, I studied gaialogy and the whole time I thought, how can this teacher tell us these things when every pequenino can look around and see that they're false? But if we know that the descolada is changing us, making us act to regulate the planetary systems—"

"What can the descolada possibly make *you* do that could regulate the planet?" said Ela.

"You haven't known us long enough," said Planter. "We haven't told you everything because we were afraid you'd think we were silly. Now you'll know that we aren't silly, we're just acting out what a virus tells us to do. We're slaves, not fools."

It startled Ender to realize that Planter had just confessed that the pequeninos still took some pains to try to impress human beings. "What behaviors of *yours* have anything to do with planetary regulation?"

"Trees," said Planter. "How many forests are there, all over the world? Transpiring constantly. Turning carbon dioxide into oxygen. Carbon dioxide is a greenhouse gas. When there's more of it in the atmosphere, the world gets warmer. So what would we do to make the world get cooler?"

"Plant more forests," said Ela. "To use up more CO_2 so that more heat could escape into space."

"Yes," said Planter. "But think about how we plant our trees."

The trees grow from the bodies of the dead, thought Ender. "War," he said.

"There are quarrels between tribes, and sometimes they make small wars," said Planter. "Those would be nothing on a planetary scale. But the great wars that sweep across the whole world—millions and millions of brothers die in these wars, and all of them become trees. Within months the forests of the world could double in size and number. That would make a difference, wouldn't it?"

"Yes," said Ela.

"A lot more efficiently than anything that would happen through natural evolution," said Ender.

"And then the wars stop," said Planter. "We always think there are great causes for these wars, that they're struggles between good and evil. And now all the time they are nothing but planetary regulation."

"No," said Valentine. "The need to fight, the rage, *that* might come from the descolada, but it doesn't mean the causes you fought for are—"

"The cause we fight for is planetary regulation," said Planter. "Everything fits. How do you think we help with warming the planet?"

"I don't know," said Ela. "Even trees eventually die of old age."

"You don't know because you've come during a warm time, not a cold one. But when the winters get bad, we build houses. The brothertrees give themselves to us to make houses. All of us, not just the ones who live in cold places. We all build houses, and the forests are reduced by half, by three-quarters. We thought this was a great sacrifice the brothertrees made for the sake of the tribe, but now I see that it's the descolada, wanting more carbon dioxide in the atmosphere to warm the planet."

"It's *still* a great sacrifice," said Ender.

"All our great epics," said Planter. "All our heroes.

Just brothers acting out the will of the descolada."

"So *what?*" said Valentine.

"How can you say that? I learn that our lives are nothing, that we're only tools used by a virus to regulate the global ecosystem, and you call it nothing?"

"Yes, I call it nothing," said Valentine. "We human beings are no different. It may not be a virus, but we still spend most of our time acting out our genetic destiny. Take the differences between males and females. Males naturally tend toward a broadcast strategy of reproduction. Since males make an almost infinite supply of sperm and it costs them nothing to deploy it—"

"Not *nothing*," said Ender.

"Nothing," said Valentine, "just to *deploy* it. Their most sensible reproductive strategy is to deposit it in every available female—and to make special efforts to deposit it in the healthiest females, the ones most likely to bring their offspring to adulthood. A male does best, reproductively, if he wanders and copulates as widely as possible."

"I've done the wandering," said Ender. "Somehow I missed out on the copulating."

"I'm speaking of overall trends," said Valentine. "There are always strange individuals who don't follow the norms. The female strategy is just the opposite, Planter. Instead of millions and millions of sperm, they only have one egg a month, and each child represents an enormous investment of effort. So females need stability. They need to be sure there'll always be plenty of food. We also spend large amounts of time relatively helpless, unable to find or gather food. Far from being wanderers, we females need to establish and stay. If we can't get that, then our next best strategy is to mate with the strongest and healthiest possible males. But best of all is to get a strong healthy male who'll stay and provide, instead of wandering and copulating at will.

"So there are two pressures on males. The one is to

spread their seed, violently if necessary. The other is to be attractive to females by being stable providers—by suppressing and containing the need to wander and the tendency to use force. Likewise, there are two pressures on females. The one is to get the seed of the strongest, most virile males so their infants will have good genes, which would make the violent, forceful males attractive to them. The other is to get the protection of the most stable males, nonviolent males, so their infants will be protected and provided for and as many as possible will reach adulthood.

"Our whole history, all that I've ever found in all my wanderings as an itinerant historian before I finally unhooked myself from this reproductively unavailable brother of mine and had a family—it can all be interpreted as people blindly acting out those genetic strategies. We get pulled in those two directions.

"Our great civilizations are nothing more than social machines to create the ideal female setting, where a woman can count on stability; our legal and moral codes that try to abolish violence and promote permanence of ownership and enforce contracts—those represent the primary female strategy, the taming of the male.

"And the tribes of wandering barbarians outside the reach of civilization, those follow the mainly male strategy. Spread the seed. Within the tribe, the strongest, most dominant males take possession of the best females, either through formal polygamy or spur-of-the-moment copulations that the other males are powerless to resist. But those low-status males are kept in line because the leaders take them to war and let them rape and pillage their brains out when they win a victory. They act out sexual desirability by proving themselves in combat, and then kill all the rival males and copulate with their widowed females when they win. Hideous, monstrous behavior—but also a viable acting-out of the genetic strategy."

Ender found himself very uncomfortable, hearing Valentine talk this way. He knew all this was true as far as it went, and he had heard it all before, but it still, in a small way, made him as uncomfortable as Planter was to learn similar things about his own people. Ender wanted to deny it all, to say, Some of us males are naturally civilized. But in his own life, hadn't he performed the acts of dominance and war? Hadn't he wandered? In that context, his decision to stay on Lusitania was really a decision to abandon the male-dominant social model that had been engrained in him as a young soldier in battle school, and become a civilized man in a stable family.

Yet even then, he had married a woman who turned out to have little interest in having more children. A woman with whom marriage had turned out to be anything but civilized, in the end. If I follow the male model, then I'm a failure. No child anywhere who carries on my genes. No woman who accepts my rule. I'm definitely atypical.

But since I haven't reproduced, my atypical genes will die with me, and thus the male and female social models are safe from such an in-between person as myself.

Even as Ender made his own private evaluations of Valentine's interpretation of human history, Planter showed his own response by lying back in his chair, a gesture that spoke of scorn. "I'm supposed to feel better because humans are also tools of some genetic molecule?"

"No," said Ender. "You're supposed to realize that just because a lot of behavior can be explained as responses to the needs of some genetic molecule, it doesn't mean that all pequenino behavior is meaningless."

"Human history *can* be explained as the struggle between the needs of women and the needs of men," said

Valentine, "but my point is that there are still heroes and monsters, great events and noble deeds."

"When a brothertree gives his wood," said Planter, "it's supposed to mean that he sacrifices for the tribe. Not for a virus."

"If you can look beyond the tribe to the virus, then look beyond the virus to the world," said Ender. "The descolada is keeping this planet habitable. So the brothertree is sacrificing himself to save the whole world."

"Very clever," said Planter. "But you forget—to save the planet, it doesn't matter *which* brothertrees give themselves, as long as a certain number do it."

"True," said Valentine. "It doesn't matter to the *descolada* which brothertrees give their lives. But it matters to the brothertrees, doesn't it? And it matters to the brothers like you, who huddle into those houses to keep warm. *You* appreciate the noble gesture of the brothertrees who died for you, even if the descolada doesn't know one tree from another."

Planter didn't answer. Ender hoped that meant they were making some headway.

"And in the wars," said Valentine, "the descolada doesn't care who wins or loses, as long as enough brothers die and enough trees grow from the corpses. Right? But that doesn't change the fact that some brothers are noble and some are cowardly or cruel."

"Planter," said Ender, "the descolada may cause you all to feel—to come more quickly to a murderous rage, for instance—so that disputes erupt into warfare instead of being settled among the fathertrees. But that doesn't erase the fact that some forests are fighting in self-defense and others are simply bloodthirsty. You still have your heroes."

"I don't give a damn about heroes," said Ela. "Heroes tend to be dead, like my brother Quim. Where is he now, when we need him? I wish he hadn't been a hero." She swallowed hard, holding down the memory of recent grief.

Planter nodded—a gesture he had learned in order to communicate with humans. "We live in Warmaker's world now," he said. "What is *he*, except a fathertree acting as the descolada instructs? The world is getting too warm. We need more trees. So he's filled with fervor to expand the forests. Why? The descolada makes him feel that way. That's why so many brothers and fathertrees listened to him—because he offered a plan to satisfy their hunger to spread out and grow more trees."

"Does the descolada know that he was planning to put all these new trees on other planets?" said Valentine. "That wouldn't do much to cool Lusitania."

"The descolada puts hunger in them," said Planter. "How can a virus know about starships?"

"How can a virus know about mothertrees and fathertrees, brothers and wives, infants and little mothers?" said Ender. "This is a very bright virus."

"Warmaker is the best example of *my* point," said Valentine. "His name suggests that he was deeply involved and successful in the *last* great war. Once again there's pressure to increase the number of trees. Yet Warmaker chose to turn this hunger to a new purpose, spreading new forests by reaching out to the stars instead of plunging into wars with other pequeninos."

"We were going to do it no matter what Warmaker said or did," said Planter. "Look at us. Warmaker's group was preparing to spread out and plant new forests on other worlds. But when they killed Father Quim, the rest of us were so filled with rage that we planned to go and punish them. Great slaughter, and again, trees would grow. Still doing what the descolada demanded. And now that humans have burned our forest, Warmaker's people are going to prevail after all. One way or another, we *must* spread out and propagate. We'll snatch up any excuse we can find. The descolada *will* have its way with us. We're tools, pathetically trying to find some way to convince ourselves that our actions are our own idea."

He sounded so hopeless. Ender couldn't think of anything to say that Valentine or he hadn't already said, to try to wean him away from his conclusion that pequenino life was unfree and meaningless.

So it was Ela who spoke next, and in a tone of calm speculation that seemed incongruous, as if she had forgotten the terrible anxiety that Planter was experiencing. Which was probably the case, as all this discussion had led her back to her own specialty. "It's hard to know which side the descolada would be on, if it were aware of all this," said Ela.

"Which side of *what*?" asked Valentine.

"Whether to induce global cooling by having more forests planted here, or to use that same instinct for propagation to have the pequeninos take the descolada out to other worlds. I mean, which would the virus makers have wanted most? To spread the virus or regulate the planet?"

"The virus probably wants both, and it's likely to *get* both," said Planter. "Warmaker's group will win control of the ships, no doubt. But either before or after, there'll be a war over it that leaves half the brothers dead. For all we know, the descolada is causing both things to happen."

"For all we know," said Ender.

"For all we know," said Planter, "we may *be* the descolada."

So, thought Ender, they *are* aware of that concern, despite our decision not to broach it with the pequeninos yet.

"Have you been talking to Quara?" demanded Ela.

"I talk to her every day," said Planter. "But what does she have to do with *this*?"

"She had the same idea. That maybe pequenino intelligence comes from the descolada."

"Do you think after all your talk about the descolada being intelligent that it hasn't occurred to *us* to wonder that?" said Planter. "And if it's true, what will you do then? Let all of *your* species die so that we can keep our little second-rate brains?"

Ender protested at once. "We've never thought of your brains as—"

"Haven't you?" said Planter. "Then why did you assume that we would only think of this possibility if some human told us?"

Ender had no good answer. He had to confess to himself that he had been thinking of the pequeninos as if they were children in some ways, to be protected. Worries had to be kept as secrets from them. It hadn't occurred to him that they were perfectly capable of discovering all the worst horrors on their own.

"And if our intelligence *does* come from the descolada, and you found a way to destroy it, what would we become then?" Planter looked at them, triumphant in his bitter victory. "Nothing but tree rats," he said.

"That's the second time you've used that term," said Ender. "What are tree rats?"

"That's what they were shouting," said Planter, "some of the men who killed the mothertree."

"There's no such animal," said Valentine.

"I know," said Planter. "Grego explained it to me. 'Tree rat' is a slang name for squirrels. He showed me a holo of one on his computer in jail."

"You went to visit *Grego*?" Ela was plainly horrified.

"I had to ask him why he tried to kill us all, and then why he tried to save us," said Planter.

"There!" cried Valentine triumphantly. "You can't tell me that what Grego and Miro did that night, stopping the mob from burning Rooter and Human—you can't tell me that that was just the acting out of genetic forces!"

"But I never said that *human* behavior was meaningless," said Planter. "It's *you* that tried to comfort me with that idea. We know that you humans have your heroes. We pequeninos are the ones who are only tools of a gaialogical virus."

"No," said Ender. "There are pequenino heroes, too. Rooter and Human, for instance."

"Heroes?" said Planter. "They acted as they did in order to win what they achieved—their status as fathertrees. It was the hunger to reproduce. They might have looked like heroes to you humans, who only die once, but the death they suffered was really birth. There was no sacrifice."

"Your whole *forest* was heroic, then," said Ela. "You broke free from all the old channels and made a treaty with us that required you to change some of your most deeply-rooted customs."

"We wanted the knowledge and the machines and the power you humans had. What's heroic about a treaty in which all we have to do is stop killing you, and in return you give us a thousand-year boost in our technological development?"

"You aren't going to listen to *any* positive conclusion, *are* you," said Valentine.

Planter went on, ignoring her. "The only heroes in that story were Pipo and Libo, the humans who acted so bravely, even though they knew they would die. They had won their freedom from their genetic heritage. What *piggy* has ever done that on purpose?"

It stung Ender more than a little, to hear Planter use the term *piggy* for himself and his people. In recent years the term had stopped being quite as friendly and affectionate as it was when Ender first came; often it was used now as a demeaning word, and the people who worked with them usually used the term *pequenino*. What sort of self-hatred was Planter resorting to, in response to what he'd learned today?

"The brothertrees give their lives," said Ela, helpfully.

But Planter answered in scorn. "The brothertrees are not alive the way fathertrees are. They can't talk. They only obey. We tell them what to do, and they have no choice. Tools, not heroes."

"You can twist anything with the right story," said Valentine. "You can deny any sacrifice by claiming that it made the sufferer feel so good to do it that it really wasn't a sacrifice at all, but just another selfish act."

Suddenly Planter jumped from his chair. Ender was prepared for a replay of his earlier behavior, but he didn't circle the room. Instead he walked to Ela where she sat in her chair, and placed both his hands on her knees.

"I know a way to be a true hero," said Planter. "I know a way to act against the descolada. To reject it and fight it and hate it and help destroy it."

"So do I," said Ela.

"An experiment," said Planter.

She nodded. "To see if pequenino intelligence is really centered in the descolada, and not in the brain."

"I'll do it," said Planter.

"I would never ask you to."

"I know you wouldn't ask," said Planter. "I demand it for myself."

Ender was surprised to realize that in their own way, Ela and Planter were as close as Ender and Valentine, able to know each other's thoughts without explaining. Ender hadn't imagined that this would be possible between two people of different species; and yet, why shouldn't it be? Particularly when they worked together so closely in the same endeavor.

It had taken Ender a few moments to grasp what Planter and Ela were deciding between them; Valentine, who had not been working with them for years as Ender had, still didn't understand. "What's happening?" she asked. "What are they talking about?"

It was Ela who answered. "Planter is proposing that

we purge one pequenino of all copies of the descolada virus, put him in a clean space where he can't be contaminated, and then see if he still has a mind."

"That can't be good science," said Valentine. "There are too many other variables. Aren't there? I thought the descolada was involved in every part of pequenino life."

"Lacking the descolada would mean that Planter would immediately get sick and then eventually die. What *having* the descolada did to Quim, *lacking* it will do to Planter."

"You can't mean to let him do it," said Valentine. "It won't prove anything. He might lose his mind because of illness. Fever makes people delirious."

"What else can we do?" asked Planter. "Wait until Ela finds a way to tame the virus, and only then find out that without it in its intelligent, virulent form, we are not pequeninos at all, but merely piggies? That we were only given the power of speech by the virus within us, and that when it was controlled, we lost everything and became nothing more than brothertrees? Do we find that out when you loose the virus-killer?"

"But it's not a serious experiment with a control—"

"It's a serious experiment, all right," said Ender. "The kind of experiment you perform when you don't give a damn about getting funding, you just need results and you need them now. The kind of experiment you perform when you have no idea what the results will be or even if you'll know how to interpret them, but there are a bunch of crazy pequeninos planning to get in starships and spread a planet-killing disease all over the galaxy so you've got to do something."

"It's the kind of experiment you perform," said Planter, "when you need a hero."

"When we *need* a hero?" asked Ender. "Or when *you* need to *be* a hero?"

"I wouldn't talk if I were you," said Valentine dryly.

"You've done a few stints as a hero yourself over the centuries."

"It may not be necessary anyway," said Ela. "Quara knows a lot more about the descolada than she's telling. She may already know whether the intelligent adaptability of the descolada can be separated from its life-sustaining functions. If we could make a virus like that, we could test the effect of the descolada on pequenino intelligence without threatening the life of the subject."

"The trouble is," said Valentine, "Quara isn't any more likely to believe our story that the descolada is an artifact created by another species than Qing-jao was able to believe that the voice of her gods was just a genetically-caused obsessive-compulsive disorder."

"I'll do it," said Planter. "I will begin immediately because we have no time. Put me in a sterile environment tomorrow, and then kill all the descolada in my body using the chemicals you've got hidden away. The ones you mean to use on humans when the descolada adapts to the current suppressant you're using."

"You realize that it may be wasted," said Ela.

"Then it would truly be a sacrifice," said Planter.

"If you start to lose your mind in a way that clearly isn't related to your body's illness," said Ela, "we'll stop the experiment because we'll have the answer."

"Maybe," said Planter.

"You might well recover at that point."

"I don't care whether I recover," said Planter.

"We'll also stop it," said Ender, "if you start to lose your mind in a way that *is* related to your body's illness, because then we'll know that the experiment is useless and we wouldn't learn anything from it anyway."

"Then if I'm a coward, all I have to do is pretend to be mentally failing and my life will be saved," said Planter. "No, I forbid you to stop the experiment, no matter what. And if I *keep* my mental functions, you must let me continue to the end, to the death, because only if I keep my mind to the end will we know that our soul is not just an artifact of the descolada. Promise me!"

"Is this science or a suicide pact?" asked Ender. "Are you so despondent over discovering the probable role of the descolada in pequenino history that you simply want to die?"

Planter rushed to Ender, climbed his body, and pressed his nose against Ender's. "You liar!" he shouted.

"I just asked a question," whispered Ender.

"I want to be free!" shouted Planter. "I want the descolada out of my body and I never want it to come back! I want to use this to help free all the piggies so that we can be pequeninos in fact and not in name!"

Gently Ender pried him back. His nose ached from the violence of Planter's pressing.

"I want to make a sacrifice that proves that I'm free," said Planter, "not just acting out my genes. Not just trying for the third life."

"Even the martyrs of Christianity and Islam were willing to accept rewards in heaven for their sacrifice," said Valentine.

"Then they were all selfish pigs," said Planter. "That's what you say about pigs, isn't it? In Stark, in your common speech? Selfish pigs. Well, it's the right name for us piggies, isn't it! Our heroes were all trying to become fathertrees. Our brothertrees were failures from the start. The only thing we serve outside ourselves is the descolada. For all we know, the descolada might *be* ourselves. But *I* will be *free*. I will know what I am, without the descolada or my genes or anything except *me*."

"What you'll be is dead," said Ender.

"But free *first*," said Planter. "And the first of my people to be free."

After Wang-mu and Jane had told Master Han all that had transpired that day, after he had conversed with Jane about his own day's work, after the house had fallen silent in the darkness of the night, Wang-mu lay awake on her mat in the corner of Master Han's room, listening to his soft but insistent snoring as she thought over all that had been said that day.

There were so many ideas, and most of them were so far above her that she despaired of truly understanding them. Especially what Wiggin said about purposes. They were giving her credit for having come up with the solution to the problem of the descolada virus, and yet she couldn't take the credit because she hadn't *meant* to do it; she had thought she was just repeating Qing-jao's questions. Could she take credit for something she did by accident?

People should only be blamed or praised for what they meant to do. Wang-mu had always believed this instinctively; she didn't remember anyone ever telling it to her in so many words. The crimes that she was blaming Congress for were all deliberate—genetically altering the people of Path to create the godspoken, and sending the M.D. Device to destroy the haven of the only other sentient species that they knew existed in the universe.

But was that what *they* meant to do, either? Maybe some of them, at least, thought that they were making the universe safe for humanity by destroying Lusitania—from what Wang-mu had heard about the descolada, it could mean the end of all Earthborn life if it ever started spreading world to world among human beings. Maybe some of Congress, too, had decided to create the godspoken of Path in order to benefit all of humanity, but then put the OCD in their brains so that they couldn't get out of control and enslave all the inferior, "normal" humans. Maybe they all had good purposes in mind for the terrible things they did.

Certainly Qing-jao had a good purpose in mind, didn't she? So how could Wang-mu condemn her for her actions, when she thought she was obeying the gods?

Didn't everybody have some noble purpose in mind for their own actions? Wasn't everybody, in their own eyes, *good*?

Except me, thought Wang-mu. In my own eyes, I'm foolish and weak. But they spoke of me as if I were better than I ever thought. Master Han praised me, too. And those others spoke of Qing-jao with pity and scorn—and I've felt those feelings toward her, too. Yet isn't Qing-jao acting nobly, and me basely? I betrayed my mistress. She has been loyal to her government and to her gods, which are real to *her*, though I no longer believe in them. How can I tell the good people from the bad, if the bad people all have some way of convincing themselves that they're trying to do good even though they're doing something terrible? And the good people can believe that they're actually very bad even though they're doing something good?

Maybe you can only do good if you think you're bad, and if you think you're good then you can only do bad.

But that paradox was too much for her. There'd be no sense in the world if you had to judge people by the *opposite* of how they tried to seem. Wasn't it possible for a good person also to try to *seem* good? And just because somebody claimed to be scum didn't mean that he *wasn't* scum. Was there any way to judge people, if you can't judge even by their purpose?

Was there any way for Wang-mu to judge even herself?

Half the time I don't even know the purpose of what I do. I came to this house because I was ambitious and wanted to be a secret maid to a rich godspoken girl. It was pure selfishness on my part, and pure generosity that led Qing-jao to take me in. And now here I am helping Master Han commit treason—what is my purpose in *that*? I don't even know why I do what I do. How can I know what other people's true purposes are? There's no hope of ever knowing good from bad.

She sat up in lotus position on her mat and pressed her face into her hands. It was as if she felt herself pressed against a wall, but it was a wall that she made herself, and if she could only find a way to move it aside—the way she could move her hands away from her face whenever she wanted—then she could easily push through to the truth.

She moved her hands away. She opened her eyes. There was Master Han's terminal, across the room. There, today, she had seen the faces of Elanora Ribeira von Hesse and Andrew Wiggin. And Jane's face.

She remembered Wiggin telling her what the gods would be like. *Real* gods would want to teach you how to be just like them. Why would he say such a thing? How could he know what a god would be?

Somebody who wants to teach you how to know everything that they know and do everything that they do—what he was really describing was parents, not gods.

Only there were plenty of parents who didn't do that. Plenty of parents who tried to keep their children down, to control them, to make slaves of them. Where she had grown up, Wang-mu had seen plenty of that.

So what Wiggin was describing wasn't parents, really. He was describing *good* parents. He wasn't telling her what the gods were, he was telling her what goodness was. To want other people to grow. To want other people to have all the good things that you have. And to spare them the bad things if you can. That was *goodness*.

What were the gods, then? They would want everyone else to know and have and be all good things. They would teach and share and train, but never force.

Like my parents, thought Wang-mu. Clumsy and stupid sometimes, like all people, but they were good. They really did look out for me. Even sometimes when they made me do hard things because they knew it would be good for me. Even sometimes when they were wrong, they were good. I can judge them by their purpose after all. Everybody *calls* their purpose good, but my parents' purposes really *were* good, because they meant all their acts toward me to help me grow wiser and stronger and better. Even when they made me do hard things because they knew I had to learn from them. Even when they caused me *pain*.

That was it. That's what the gods would be, if there were gods. They would want everyone else to have all that was good in life, just like good parents. But unlike parents or any other people, the gods would actually *know* what was good and have the power to cause good things to happen, even when nobody else understood that they were good. As Wiggin said, *real* gods would be smarter and stronger than anybody else. They would have all the intelligence and power that it was possible to have.

But a being like that—who was someone like Wang-mu to judge a god? She couldn't understand their purposes even if they told her, so how could she ever *know* that they were good? Yet the other approach, to trust in them and believe in them absolutely—wasn't that what Qing-jao was doing?

No. If there *were* gods, they would never act as Qing-jao thought they acted—enslaving people, tormenting and humiliating them.

Unless torment and humiliation were *good* for them . . .

No! She almost cried aloud, and once again pressed her face into her hands, this time to keep silence.

I can only judge by what I understand. If as far as I can see, the gods that Qing-jao believes in are only evil, then yes, perhaps I'm wrong, perhaps I can't comprehend the great purpose they accomplish by making the godspoken into helpless slaves, or destroying whole species. But in my heart I have no choice but to reject such gods, because I can't see any good in what they're doing. Perhaps I'm so stupid and foolish that I will always be the enemy of the gods, working against their high and incomprehensible purposes. But I have to live my life according to what *I* understand, and what I understand is that there are no such gods as the ones the godspoken teach us about. If they exist at all, they take pleasure in oppression and deception, humiliation and ignorance. They act to make other people smaller and themselves larger. Those would not be gods, then, even if they existed. They would be enemies. Devils.

The same with the beings, whoever they are, who made the descolada virus. Yes, they would have to be very powerful to make a tool like that. But they would also have to be heartless, selfish, arrogant beings, to think that all life in the universe was theirs to manipulate as they saw fit. To send the descolada out into the universe, not caring who it killed or what beautiful creatures it destroyed—those could not be gods, either.

Jane, now—Jane might be a god. Jane knew vast amounts of information and had great wisdom as well, and she was acting for the good of others, even when it would take her life—even now, after her life was forfeit. And Andrew Wiggin, he might be a god, so wise and kind he seemed, and not acting for his own benefit but for the pequeninos. And Valentine, who called herself Demosthenes, she had worked to help other people find the truth and make wise decisions of their own. And Master Han, who was trying to do the right thing always, even when it cost him his daughter. Maybe even Ela, the scientist, even though she had not known all that she ought to have known—for she was not ashamed to learn truth from a servant girl.

Of course they were not the sort of gods who lived off in the Infinite West, in the Palace of the Royal Mother. Nor were they gods in their own eyes—they would laugh at her for even thinking of it. But compared to *her,* they were gods indeed. They were so much wiser than Wang-mu, and so much more powerful, and as far as she could understand their purposes, they were trying to help other people become as wise and powerful as possible. Even wiser and more powerful than they were themselves. So even though Wang-mu might be wrong, even though she might truly understand nothing at all about anything, nevertheless she knew that her decision to work with these people was the right one for her to make.

She could only do good as far as she understood what goodness was. And these people seemed to her to be doing good, while Congress seemed to be doing evil. So even though in the long run it might destroy her—for Master Han was now an enemy of Congress, and might be arrested and killed, and her along with him—still she would do it. She would never see real gods, but she could at least work to help those people who were as close to being gods as any real person could ever be.

And if the gods don't like it, they can poison me in my sleep or catch me on fire as I'm walking in the garden tomorrow or just make my arms and legs and head drop off my body like crumbs off a cake. If they can't manage to stop a stupid little servant girl like me, they don't amount to much anyway.

15

LIFE AND DEATH

<Ender's coming to see us.>

<He comes and talks to *me* all the time.>

<And *we* can talk directly into his mind. But he insists on coming. He doesn't feel like he's talking to us unless he sees us. He has a harder time distinguishing between his own thoughts and the ones we put in his mind, when we converse from a distance. So he's coming.>

<And you don't like this?>

<He wants us to tell him answers and we don't know any answers.>

<You know everything that the humans know. You got into space, didn't you? You don't even need their ansibles to talk from world to world.>

<They're so hungry for answers, these humans. They have so many questions.>

<*We* have questions, too, you know.>

<They want to know why, why, why. Or how. Everything all tied up into a nice neat bundle like a cocoon.

The only time we do that is when we're metamorphosing a queen.>

<They like to understand everything. But so do we, you know.>

<Yes, you'd like to think you're just like the humans, wouldn't you? But you're not like Ender. Not like the humans. He has to know the cause of everything, he has to make a story about everything and we don't know any stories. We know memories. We know things that happen. But we don't know *why* they happen, not the way he wants us to.>

<Of course you do.>

<We don't even *care* why, the way these humans do. We find out as much as we need to know to accomplish something, but they always want to know *more* than they need to know. After they get something to work, they're still hungry to know why it works and why the cause of its working works.>

<Aren't we like that?>

<Maybe you *will* be, when the descolada stops interfering with you.>

<Or maybe we'll be like your workers.>

<If you are, you won't care. They're all very happy. It's intelligence that makes you unhappy. The workers are either hungry or not hungry. In pain or not in pain. They're never curious or disappointed or anguished or ashamed. And when it comes to things like that, these humans make you and me look like workers.>

<I think you just don't know us well enough to compare.>

<We've been inside your head and we've been inside Ender's head and we've been inside our own heads for a thousand generations and these humans make us look like we're asleep. Even when they're asleep they're not asleep. Earthborn animals do this thing, inside their brains—a sort of mad firing-off of synapses, controlled insanity. While they're asleep. The part of their brain that

records sight or sound, it's firing off every hour or two while they sleep, even when all the sights and sounds are complete random nonsense, their brains just keep on trying to assemble it into something sensible. They try to make stories out of it. It's complete random nonsense with no possible correlation to the real world, and yet they turn it into these crazy stories. And then they forget them. All that work, coming up with these stories, and when they wake up they forget almost all of them. But when they *do* remember, then they try to make stories about those crazy stories, trying to fit them into their real lives.>

<We know about their dreaming.>

<Maybe without the descolada, you'll dream, too.>

<Why should we want to? As you say, it's meaningless. Random firings of the synapses of the neurons in their brains.>

<They're practicing. They're doing it all the time. Coming up with stories. Making connections. Making sense out of nonsense.>

<What good is it, when it means nothing?>

<That's just it. They have a hunger we know nothing about. The hunger for answers. The hunger for making sense. The hunger for stories.>

<We have stories.>

<You remember deeds. They make up deeds. They change what their stories mean. They transform things so that the same memory can mean a thousand different things. Even from their dreams, sometimes they make up out of that randomness something that illuminates everything. Not one human being has anything like the kind of mind you have. The kind we have. Nothing as powerful. And their lives are so short, they die so fast. But in their century or so they come up with ten thousand meanings for every one that we discover.>

<Most of them wrong.>

<Even if the vast majority of them are wrong, even if

ninety-nine of every hundred is stupid and wrong, out of ten thousand ideas that still leaves them with a hundred good ones. That's how they make up for being so stupid and having such short lives and small memories.>

<Dreams and madness.>

<Magic and mystery and philosophy.>

<You can't say that you never think of stories. What you've just been telling me is a story.>

<I know.>

<See? Humans do nothing you can't do.>

<Don't you understand? I got even *this* story from Ender's mind. It's *his*. And he got the seed of it from somebody else, something he read, and combined it with things he thought of until it made sense to him. It's all there in his head. While *we* are like *you*. We have a clear view of the world. I have no trouble finding my way through your mind. Everything orderly and sensible and clear. You'd be as much at ease in mine. What's in your head is *reality*, more or less, as best you understand it. But in Ender's mind, madness. Thousands of competing contradictory impossible visions that make no sense at all because they can't all fit together but they *do* fit together, he makes them fit together, this way today, that way tomorrow, as they're needed. As if he can make a new idea-machine inside his head for every new problem he faces. As if he conceives of a new universe to live in, every hour a new one, often hopelessly wrong and he ends up making mistakes and bad judgments, but sometimes so perfectly right that it opens things up like a miracle and I look through his eyes and see the world his new way and it changes everything. Madness, and then illumination. We knew everything there was to know before we met these humans, before we built our connection with Ender's mind. Now we discover that there are so many ways of knowing the same things that we'll never find them all.>

<Unless the humans teach you.>

<You see? We are scavengers also.>
<You're a scavenger. We're supplicants.>
<If only they were worthy of their own mental abilities.>
<Aren't they?>
<They *are* planning to blow you up, you remember. There's so much possibility in their minds, but they are still, after all, individually stupid and small-minded and half-blind and half-mad. There's still the ninety-nine percent of their stories that are hideously wrong and lead them into terrible errors. Sometimes we wish we could tame them, like the workers. We tried to, you know, with Ender. But we couldn't do it. Couldn't make a worker of him.>
<Why not?>
<Too stupid. Can't pay attention long enough. Human minds lack focus. They get bored and wander off. We had to build a bridge outside him, using the computer that he was most closely bonded with. Computers, now—*those* things can pay attention. And their memory is neat, orderly, everything organized and findable.>
<But they don't dream.>
<No madness. Too bad.>

Valentine showed up unbidden at Olhado's door. It was early morning. He wouldn't go to work till afternoon—he was a shift manager at the small brickworks. But he was already up and about, probably because his family was. The children were trooping out the door. I used to see this on television back in the ancient days, thought Valentine. The family going out the door in the morning, all at the same time, and Dad last of all with the briefcase. In their own way, my parents acted out that life. Never mind how deeply weird their children were. Never mind how after we paraded off to school in the morning, Peter and I went prowling through the nets, trying to take over the world through the use of pseudonyms. Never mind that Ender was torn away from the family as a little boy and never saw any of them again, even on his one visit to Earth—except me. I think my parents still imagined they were doing it right, because they went through a ritual they had seen on TV.

And here it is again. The children bursting through the door. That boy must be Nimbo, the one who was with Grego at the confrontation with the mob. But here he is, just a cliché child—no one would guess that he had been part of that terrible night only a little while ago.

Mother gave them each a kiss. She was still a beautiful young woman, even with so many children. So ordinary, so like the cliché, and yet a remarkable woman, for she had married their father, hadn't she? She had seen past the deformity.

And Dad, not yet off to work, so he could stand there, watching them, patting them, kissing them, saying a few words. Light, clever, loving—the predictable father. So, what's wrong with this picture? The dad is Olhado. He has no eyes. Just the silvery metal orbs punctuated with two lens apertures in the one eye, and the computer I/O outlet in the other. The kids don't seem to notice. I'm still not used to it.

"Valentine," he said, when he saw her.

"We need to talk," she said.

He ushered her inside. He introduced his wife, Jaqueline. Skin so black it was almost blue, laughing eyes, a beautiful wide smile that you wanted to dive into, it was so welcoming. She brought a limonada, ice-cold and sweating in the morning heat, and then discreetly withdrew. "You can stay," said Valentine. "This isn't all that private." But she didn't want to stay. She had work to do, she said. And she was gone.

"I've wanted to meet you for a long time," said Olhado.

"I was meetable," she said.

"You were busy."

"I have no business," said Valentine.

"You have Andrew's business."

"We're meeting now, anyway. I've been curious about you, Olhado. Or do you prefer your given name, Lauro?"

"In Milagre, your name is whatever people call you. I used to be Sule, for my middle name, Suleimão."

"Solomon the wise."

"But after I lost my eyes, I was Olhado, then and forever."

"'The watched one'?"

"*Olhado* could mean that, yes, past participle of *olhar*, but in this case it means 'The guy with the eyes.'"

"And that's your name."

"My wife calls me Lauro," he said. "And my children call me Father."

"And I?"

"Whatever."

"Sule, then."

"Lauro, if you must. Sule makes me feel like I'm six."

"And reminds you of the time when you could see."

He laughed. "Oh, I can see *now*, thanks very much. I see very well."

"So Andrew says. That's why I've come to you. To find out what you see."

"Want me to play back a scene for you? A blast from the past? I have all my favorite memories stored on computer. I can plug in and play back anything you want. I have, for instance, Andrew's first visit in my family's home. I also have some top-flight family quarrels. Or do you prefer public events? Every Mayor's inaugural since I got these eyes? People do consult me about things like that—what was worn, what was said, I often have trouble convincing them that my eyes record vision, not sound—just like *their* eyes. They think I should be a holographer and record it all for entertainment."

"I don't want to see what you see. I want to know what you think."

"Do you, now?"

"Yes, I do."

"I *have* no opinions. Not on anything you'd be interested in. I stay out of the family quarrels. I always have."

"And out of the family business. The only one of Novinha's children not to go into science."

"Science has brought everyone else so much happiness, it's hard to imagine why I wouldn't have gone into it."

"Not hard to *imagine*," said Valentine. And then, because she had found that brittle-sounding people will talk quite openly if goaded, she added a little barb. "I *imagine* that you simply didn't have the brains to keep up."

"Absolutely true," said Olhado. "I only have wit enough to make bricks."

"Really?" said Valentine. "But you *don't* make bricks."

"On the contrary. I make hundreds of bricks a day. And with everyone knocking holes in their houses to build the new chapel, I foresee a booming business in the near future."

"Lauro," said Valentine, "you don't make bricks. The laborers in your factory make bricks."

"And I, as manager, am not part of that?"

"Brickmakers make bricks. You make brickmakers."

"I suppose. Mostly I make brickmakers *tired*."

"You make other things," said Valentine. "Children."

"Yes," said Olhado, and for the first time in the conversation he relaxed. "I do *that*. Of course, I have a partner."

"A gracious and beautiful woman."

"I looked for perfection, and found something better." It wasn't just a line of patter. He meant it. And now the brittleness was gone, the wariness too. "You have children. A husband."

"A good family. Maybe almost as good as yours. Ours lacks only the perfect mother, but the children will recover from that."

"To hear Andrew talk about you, you're the greatest human being who ever lived."

"Andrew is very sweet. He could also get away with saying such things because I wasn't here."

"Now you *are* here," said Olhado. "Why?"

"It happens that worlds and species of ramen are at a cusp of decision, and the way events have turned out, their future depends in large part on your family. I don't have time to discover things in a leisurely way—I don't have time to understand the family dynamics, why Grego can pass from monster to hero in a single night, how Miro can be both suicidal and ambitious, why Quara is willing to let the pequeninos die for the descolada's sake—"

"Ask Andrew. He understands them all. I never could."

"Andrew is in his own little hell right now. He feels responsible for everything. He's done his best, but Quim is dead, and the one thing your mother and Andrew both agree on is that somehow it's Andrew's fault. Your mother's leaving him has torn him up."

"I know."

"I don't even know how to console him. Or even which, as his loving sister, to hope for—that she'll come back into his life, or leave him forever."

Olhado shrugged. All the brittleness was back.

"Do you really not care?" asked Valentine. "Or have you *decided* not to care?"

"Maybe I decided long ago, and now I really don't."

Part of being a good interviewer, too, is knowing when to be silent. Valentine waited.

But Olhado was also good at waiting. Valentine almost gave up and said something. She even toyed with the idea of confessing failure and leaving.

Then he spoke. "When they replaced my eyes, they also took out the tear ducts. Natural tears would interfere with the industrial lubricants they put in my eyes."

"Industrial?"

"My little joke," said Olhado. "I seem to be very dispassionate all the time, because my eyes never well up with tears. And people can't read my expressions. It's funny, you know. The actual eyeball doesn't have any ability to change shape and show an expression. It just sits there. Yes, your eyes dart around—they either keep steady eye contact or look down or up—but *my* eyes do that, too. They still move with perfect symmetry. They still point in the direction I'm looking. But people can't stand to look at them. So they look away. They don't read the expressions on my face. And therefore they think there *are* no expressions. My eyes still sting and redden and swell a little at times when I would have cried, if I still had tears."

"In other words," said Valentine, "you *do* care."

"I always cared," he said. "Sometimes I thought I was the only one who understood, even though half the time I didn't know what it was that I was understanding. I withdrew and watched, and because I didn't have any personal ego on the line in the family quarrels, I could see more clearly than any of them. I saw the lines of power—Mother's absolute dominance even though Marcão beat her when he was angry or drunk. Miro, thinking it was Marcão he was rebelling against, when always it was Mother. Grego's meanness—his way of handling fear. Quara, absolutely contrary by nature, doing whatever she thought the people who mattered to her *didn't* want her to do. Ela, the noble martyr—what in the world would she be. If she couldn't suffer? Holy, righteous Quim, finding God as his father, on the premise that the best father is the invisible kind who never raises his voice."

"You saw all this as a child?"

"I'm good at seeing things. We passive, unbelonging observers always see better. Don't you think?"

Valentine laughed. "Yes, we do. The same role, then, you think? You and I, both historians?"

"Till your brother came. From the moment he walked in the door, it was obvious that he saw and understood everything, just the way I saw it. It was exhilarating. Because of course I had never actually *believed* my own conclusions about my family. I never trusted my own judgments. Obviously no one saw things the way I did, so I must be wrong. I even thought that I saw things so peculiarly because of my eyes. That if I had *real* eyes I would have seen things Miro's way. Or Mother's."

"So Andrew confirmed your judgments."

"More than that. He acted on them. He *did* something about them."

"Oh?"

"He was here as a speaker for the dead. But from the moment he walked in the door, he took—he took—"

"Over?"

"Took responsibility. For change. He saw all the sicknesses I saw, but he started healing them as best he could. I saw how he was with Grego, firm but kind. With Quara, responding to what she really wanted instead of what she claimed to want. With Quim, respecting the distance he wanted to keep. With Miro, with Ela, with Mother, with everybody."

"With you?"

"Making me part of his life. Connecting with me. Watching me jack into my eye and still talking to me like a person. Do you know what that meant to me?"

"I can guess."

"Not the part about *me*. I was a hungry little kid, I'll admit; the first kind person could have conned me, I'm sure. It's what he did about us all. It's how he treated us all differently, and yet remained himself. You've got to think about the men in my life. Marcão, who we thought was our father—I had no idea who *he* was. All I ever saw was the liquor in him when he was drunk, and the thirst when he was sober. Thirst for alcohol but also a thirst for respect that he could never get. And then he dropped over dead. Things got better at once. Still not good, but better. I thought, the best father is the one who isn't there. Only that wasn't true, either, was it? Because my *real* father, Libo, the great scientist, the martyr, the hero of research, the love of my mother's life—he had sired all these delightful children on my mother, he could see the family in torment, and yet he did nothing."

"Your mother didn't let him, Andrew said."

"That's right—and one must always do things Mother's way, mustn't one?"

"Novinha is a very imposing woman."

"She thinks she's the only one in the world ever to suffer," said Olhado. "I say that without rancor. I have simply observed that she is so full of pain, she's incapable of taking anyone else's pain seriously."

"Try saying something rancorous next time. It might be more kind."

Olhado looked surprised. "Oh, you're judging me? Is this motherhood solidarity or something? Children who speak ill of their mothers must be slapped down? But I assure you, Valentine, I meant it. No rancor. No grudges. I know my mother, that's all. You said you wanted me to tell you what I saw—that's what I see. That's what Andrew saw, too. All that pain. He's drawn to it. Pain sucks him like a magnet. And Mother had so much she almost sucked him dry. Except that maybe you can't suck Andrew dry. Maybe the well of compassion inside him is bottomless."

His passionate speech about Andrew surprised her. And pleased her, too. "You say Quim turned to God for the perfect invisible father. Who did you turn to? Not someone invisible, I think."

"No, not someone invisible."

Valentine studied his face in silence.

"I see everything in bas-relief," said Olhado. "My depth perception is very poor. If we'd put a lens in each eye instead of both in one, the binocularity would be much improved. But I wanted to have the jack. For the computer link. I wanted to be able to record the pictures, to be able to share them. So I see in bas-relief. As if everybody were a slightly rounded cardboard cutout, sliding across a flat painted background. In a way it makes everybody seem so much closer together. Sliding over each other like sheets of paper, rubbing on each other as they pass."

She listened, but said nothing for a while longer.

"Not someone invisible," he said, echoing, remembering. "That's right. I saw what Andrew did in our family. I saw that he came in and listened and watched and understood who we were, each individual one of us. He tried to discover our need and then supply it. He took *responsibility* for other people and it didn't seem to matter to him how much it cost him. And in the end, while he could never make the Ribeira family *normal,* he gave us peace and pride and identity. Stability. He married Mother and was kind to her. He loved us all. He was always there when we wanted him, and seemed unhurt by it when we didn't. He was firm with us about expecting civilized behavior, but never indulged his whims at our expense. And I thought: This is so much more important than science. Or politics, either. Or any particular profession or accomplishment or *thing* you can make. I thought: If I could just make a good family, if I could just learn to be to other children, their whole lives, what Andrew was, coming so late into ours, then that would mean more in the long run, it would be a finer accomplishment than anything I could ever do with my mind or my hands."

"So you're a career father," said Valentine.

"Who works at a brick factory to feed and clothe the family. Not a brickmaker who also has kids. Lini also feels the same way."

"Lini?"

"Jaqueline. My wife. She followed her own road to the same place. We do what we must to earn our place in the community, but we live for the hours at home. For each other, for the children. It will never get me written up in the history books."

"You'd be surprised," said Valentine.

"It's a boring life, to read about," said Olhado. "Not to live, though."

"So the secret that you protect from your tormented siblings is—happiness."

"Peace. Beauty. Love. All the great abstractions. I may see them in bas-relief, but I see them up close."

"And you learned it from Andrew. Does he know?"

"I think so," said Olhado. "Do you want to know my most closely guarded secret? When we're alone together, just him and me, or me and Lini and him—when we're alone, I call him Papa, and he calls me Son."

Valentine made no effort to stop her tears from flowing, as if they flowed half for him and half for her. "So Ender *does* have children, after all," she said.

"I learned how to be a father from him, and I'm a damned good one."

Valentine leaned forward. It was time to get down to business. "That means that you, more than any of the others, stand to lose something truly beautiful and fine if we don't succeed in our endeavors."

"I know," said Olhado. "My choice was a selfish one in the long run. I'm happy, but I can't do anything to help save Lusitania."

"Wrong," said Valentine. "You just don't know yet."

"What *can* I do?"

"Let's talk a while longer, and see if we can find out. And if it's all right with you, Lauro, your Jaqueline should stop eavesdropping from the kitchen now, and come on in and join us."

Bashfully, Jaqueline came in and sat beside her husband. Valentine liked the way they held hands. After so many children—it reminded herself of holding hands with Jakt, and how glad it made her feel.

"Lauro," she said, "Andrew tells me that when you were younger, you were the brightest of all the Ribeira children. That you spoke to him of wild philosophical speculations. Right now, Lauro, my adoptive nephew, it is wild philosophy we need. Has your brain been on hold since you were a child? Or do you still think thoughts of great profundity?"

"I have my thoughts," said Olhado. "But I don't even believe them myself."

"We're working on faster-than-light flight, Lauro. We're working on discovering the soul of a computer entity. We're trying to rebuild an artificial virus that has self-defense capabilities built into it. We're working on magic and miracles. So I'd be glad of any insights you can give me on the nature of life and reality."

"I don't even know what ideas Andrew was talking about," said Olhado. "I quit studying physics, I—"

"If I want studies, I'll read books. So let me tell you what we told a very bright Chinese servant girl on the world of Path: Let me know your thoughts, and I'll decide for myself what's useful and what isn't."

"How? You're not a physicist either."

Valentine walked to the computer waiting quietly in the corner. "May I turn this on?"

"Pois não," he said. Of course.

"Once it's on, Jane will be with us."

"Ender's personal program."

"The computer entity whose soul we're trying to locate."

"Ah," he said. "Maybe *you* should be telling *me* things."

"I already *know* what *I* know. So start talking. About those ideas you had as a child, and what has become of them since."

———

Quara had a chip on her shoulder from the moment Miro entered the room. "Don't bother," she said.

"Don't bother what?"

"Don't bother telling me my duty to humanity or to the family—two separate, non-overlapping groups, by the way."

"Is that what I came for?" asked Miro.

"Ela sent you to persuade me to tell her how to castrate the descolada."

Miro tried a little humor. "I'm no biologist. Is that possible?"

"Don't be cute," said Quara. "If you cut out their ability to pass information from one virus to another, it's like cutting out their tongues and their memory and everything that makes them intelligent. If she wants to know this stuff, she can study what I studied. It only took me five years of work to get there."

"There's a fleet coming."

"So you *are* an emissary."

"And the descolada may figure out how to—"

She interrupted him, finished his sentence. "Circumvent all our strategies to control it, I know."

Miro was annoyed, but he was used to people getting impatient with his slowness of speech and cutting him off. And at least she had guessed what he was driving at. "Any day," he said. "Ela feels time pressure."

"Then she should help me learn to *talk* to the virus. Persuade it to leave us alone. Make a treaty, like Andrew did with the pequeninos. Instead, she's cut me off from the lab. Well, two can play that game. She cuts *me* off, I cut *her* off."

"You were telling secrets to the pequeninos."

"Oh, yes, Mother and Ela, the guardians of truth! *They* get to decide who knows what. Well, Miro, let me tell you a secret. You don't protect the truth by keeping other people from knowing it."

"I know that," said Miro.

"Mother completely screwed up our family because of her damned secrets. She wouldn't even marry *Libo* because she was determined to keep a stupid secret, which if he'd known might have saved his life."

"I know," said Miro.

This time he spoke with such vehemence that Quara was taken aback. "Oh, well, I guess that was a secret that bothered you more than it did me. But then you should be on my side in this, Miro. Your life would have been a lot better, *all* our lives would have been, if Mother had only married Libo and told him all her secrets. He'd still be alive, probably."

Very neat solutions. Tidy little might-have-beens. And false as hell. If Libo had married Novinha, he *wouldn't* have married Bruxinha, Ouanda's mother, and thus Miro wouldn't have fallen unsuspectingly in love with his own half-sister because she would never have existed at all. That was far too much to say, however, with his halting speech. So he confined himself to saying "Ouanda wouldn't have been born," and hoped she would make the connections.

She considered for a moment, and the connection was made. "You have a point," she said. "And I'm sorry. I was only a child then."

"It's all past," said Miro.

"Nothing is past," said Quara. "We're still acting it out, over and over again. The same mistakes, again and again. Mother still thinks that you keep people safe by keeping secrets from them."

"And so do you," said Miro.

Quara thought about that for a moment. "Ela was trying to keep the pequeninos from knowing that she was working on destroying the descolada. That's a secret that could have destroyed the whole pequenino society, and they weren't even being consulted. They were preventing the pequeninos from protecting themselves. But what I'm keeping secret is—maybe—a way to intellectually castrate the descolada—to make it half-alive."

"To save humanity without destroying the pequeninos."

"Humans and pequeninos, getting together to compromise on how to wipe out a helpless third species!"

"Not exactly helpless."

She ignored him. "Just the way Spain and Portugal got the Pope to divide up the world between their Catholic Majesties back in the old days right after Columbus. A line on a map, and poof—there's Brazil, speaking Portuguese instead of Spanish. Never mind that nine out of ten Indians had to die, and the rest lose all their rights and power for centuries, even their very languages—"

It was Miro's turn to become impatient. "The descolada isn't the Indians."

"It's a sentient species."

"It isn't," said Miro.

"Oh?" asked Quara. "And how are you so sure? Where's your certificate in microbiology and xenogenetics? I thought your studies were all in xenology. And thirty years out of date."

Miro didn't answer. He knew that she was perfectly aware of how hard he had worked to bring himself up to speed since he got back here. It was an ad hominem attack and a stupid appeal to authority. It wasn't worth answering. So he sat there and studied her face. Waiting for her to get back into the realm of reasonable discussion.

"All right," she said. "That was a low blow. But so is sending *you* to try to crack open my files. Trying to play on my sympathies."

"Sympathies?" asked Miro.

"Because you're a—because you're—"

"Damaged," said Miro. He hadn't thought of the fact that pity complicated everything. But how could he help it? Whatever he did, it was a cripple doing it.

"Well, yes."

"Ela didn't send me," said Miro.

"Mother, then."

"Not Mother."

"Oh, you're a freelance meddler? Or are you going to tell me that all of humanity has sent you? Or are you a delegate of an abstract value? 'Decency sent me.'"

"If it did, it sent me to the wrong place."

She reeled back as if she had been slapped.

"Oh, am *I* the indecent one?"

"Andrew sent me," said Miro.

"Another manipulator."

"He would have come himself."

"But he was *so* busy, doing his own meddling. Nossa Senhora, he's a *minister*, mixing himself up in scientific matters that are so far above his head that—"

"Shut up," said Miro.

He spoke forcefully enough that she actually did fall silent—though she wasn't happy about it.

"*You* know what Andrew is," Miro said. "He wrote the Hive Queen and—"

"The Hive Queen and the Hegemon and the Life of Human."

"Don't tell me he doesn't know anything."

"No. I know that isn't true," said Quara. "I just get so angry. I feel like everybody's against me."

"Against what you're doing, yes," said Miro.

"Why doesn't anybody see things my way?"

"I see things your way," said Miro.

"Then how can you—"

"I also see things *their* way."

"Yes. Mr. Impartial. Make me feel like you understand me. The sympathetic approach."

"Planter is dying to try to learn information you probably already know."

"Not true. I *don't* know whether pequenino intelligence comes from the virus or not."

"A truncated virus could be tested without killing him."

"*Truncated*—is that the word of choice? It'll do. Better than *castrated*. Cutting off all the limbs. And the head, too. Nothing but the trunk left. Powerless. Mindless. A beating heart, to no purpose."

"Planter is—"

"Planter's in love with the idea of being a martyr. He wants to die."

"Planter is asking you to come and talk to him."

"No."

"Why not?"

"Come on, Miro. They send a cripple to me. They want me to come talk to a dying pequenino. As if I'd betray a whole species because a dying friend—a *volunteer,* too—asks me with his dying breath."

"Quara."

"Yes, I'm listening."

"Are you?"

"Disse que sim!" she snapped. I said I am.

"You might be right about all this."

"How kind of you."

"But so might they."

"Aren't you the impartial one."

"You say they were wrong to make a decision that might kill the pequeninos without consulting them. Aren't you "

"Doing the same thing? What should I do, do you think? Publish my viewpoint and take a vote? A few thousand humans, millions of pequeninos on your side—but there are *trillions* of descolada viruses. Majority rule. Case closed."

"The descolada is not sentient," said Miro.

"For your information," said Quara, "I know all about this latest ploy. Ela sent me the transcripts. Some Chinese girl on a backwater colony planet who doesn't know anything about xenogenetics comes up with a wild hypothesis, and *you* all act as if it were already proved."

"So—prove it false."

"I can't. I've been shut out of the lab. *You* prove it *true*."

"Occam's razor proves it true. Simplest explanation that fits the facts."

"Occam was a medieval old fart. The simplest explanation that fits the facts is always, God did it. Or maybe—that old woman down the road is a witch. *She* did it. That's all this hypothesis is—only you don't even know where the witch *is*."

"The descolada is too sudden."

"It didn't evolve, I know. Had to come from somewhere else. Fine. Even if it's artificial, that doesn't mean it isn't sentient *now*."

"It's trying to kill us. It's varelse, not raman."

"Oh, yes, Valentine's hierarchy. Well, how do I know that the descolada is the varelse, and we're the ramen? As far as I can tell, intelligence is intelligence. Varelse is just the term Valentine invented to mean Intelligence-that-we've-decided-to-kill, and raman means Intelligence-that-we-haven't-decided-to-kill-yet."

"It's an unreasoning, uncompassionate enemy."

"Is there another kind?"

"The descolada doesn't have respect for any other life. It wants to kill us. It already rules the pequeninos. All so it can regulate this planet and spread to other worlds."

For once, she had let him finish a long statement. Did it mean she was actually listening to him?

"I'll grant you part of Wang-mu's hypothesis," said Quara. "It does make sense that the descolada is regulating the gaialogy of Lusitania. In fact, now that I think about it, it's obvious. It explains most of the conversations I've observed—the information-passing from one virus to another. I figure it should take only a few months for a message to get to every virus on the planet—it would work. But just because the descolada is running the gaialogy doesn't mean that you've proved it's not sentient. In fact, it could go the other way—the descolada, by taking responsibility for regulating the gaialogy of a whole world, is showing altruism. And protectiveness, too—if we saw a mother lion lashing out at an intruder in order to protect her young, we'd admire her. That's all the descolada is doing—lashing out against humans in order to protect her precious responsibility. A living planet."

"A mother lion protecting her cubs."

"I think so."

"Or a rabid dog, devouring *our* babies."

Quara paused. Thought for a moment. "Or both. Why can't it be both? The descolada's trying to regulate a planet here. But humans are getting more and more dangerous. To her, *we're* the rabid dog. We root out the plants that are part of her control system, and we plant our own, unresponsive plants. We make some of the pequeninos behave strangely and disobey her. We burn a forest at a time when she's trying to build more. Of course she wants to get rid of us!"

"So she's out to destroy us."

"It's her privilege to try! When will you see that the descolada has *rights?*"

"Don't *we?* Don't the pequeninos?"

Again she paused. No immediate counterargument. It gave him hope that she might actually be listening.

"You know something, Miro?"

"What."

"They were right to send you."

"Were they?"

"Because you're not one of *them.*"

That's true enough, thought Miro. I'll never be "one of" anything again.

"Maybe we can't talk to the descolada. And maybe it really is just an artifact. A biological robot acting out its programming. But maybe it isn't. And they're keeping me from finding out."

"What if they open the lab to you?"

"They won't," said Quara. "If you think they will, you don't know Ela and Mother. They've decided that I'm not to be trusted, and so that's that. Well, *I've* decided *they're* not to be trusted, either."

"Thus whole species die for family pride."

"Is that all you think this is, Miro? Pride? I'm holding out because of nothing nobler than a petty quarrel?"

"Our family has a lot of pride."

"Well, no matter what you think, I'm doing this out of conscience, no matter whether you want to call it pride or stubbornness or anything else."

"I believe you," said Miro.

"But do I believe *you* when you say that you believe me? We're in such a tangle." She turned back to her terminal. "Go away now, Miro. I told you I'd think about it, and I will."

"Go see Planter."

"I'll think about that, too." Her fingers hovered over the keyboard. "He *is* my friend, you know. I'm not inhuman. I'll go see him, you can be sure of that."

"Good."

He started for the door.

"Miro," she said.

He turned, waited.

"Thanks for not threatening to have that computer program of yours crack my files open if I didn't open them myself."

"Of course not," he said.

"Andrew would have threatened that, you know. Everybody thinks he's such a saint, but he always bullies people who don't go along with him."

"He doesn't threaten."

"I've seen him do it."

"He warns."

"Oh. Excuse me. Is there a difference?"

"Yes," said Miro.

"The only difference between a warning and a threat is whether you're the person giving it or the person receiving it," said Quara.

"No," said Miro. "The difference is how the person means it."

"Go away," she said. "I've got work to do, even while I'm thinking. So go away."

He opened the door.

"But thanks," she said.

He closed the door behind him.

As he walked away from Quara's place, Jane immediately piped up in his ear. "I see you decided against telling her that I broke into her files before you even came."

"Yes, well," said Miro. "I feel like a hypocrite, for her to thank me for not threatening to do what I'd already done."

"*I* did it."

"*We* did it. You and me and Ender. A sneaky group."

"Will she really think about it?"

"Maybe," said Miro. "Or maybe she's already thought about it and decided to cooperate and was just looking for an excuse. Or maybe she's already decided against ever cooperating, and she just said this nice thing at the end because she's sorry for me."

"What do you think she'll do?"

"I don't know what she'll do," said Miro. "I know what I'll do. I'll feel ashamed of myself every time I think about how I let her think that I respected her privacy, when we'd already pillaged her files. Sometimes I don't think I'm a very good person."

"You notice she didn't tell *you* that she's keeping her real findings outside the computer system, so the only files *I* can reach are worthless junk. She hasn't exactly been frank with you, either."

"Yes, but she's a fanatic with no sense of balance or proportion."

"That explains everything."

"Some traits just run in the family," said Miro.

The hive queen was alone this time. Perhaps exhausted from something—mating? Producing eggs? She spent all her time doing this, it seemed. She had no choice. Now that workers had to be used to patrol the perimeter of the human colony, she had to produce even more than she had planned. Her offspring didn't have to be educated—they entered adulthood quickly, having all the knowledge that any other adult had. But the process of conception, egg-laying, emergence, and cocooning still took time. Weeks for each adult. She produced a prodigious number of young, compared to a single human. But compared to the town of Milagre, with more than a thousand women of childbearing age, the bugger colony had only one producing female.

It had always bothered Ender, made him feel uneasy to know that there was only *one* queen. What if something happened to her? But then, it made the hive queen uncomfortable to think of human beings having only a bare handful of children—what if something happened to *them*? Both species practiced a combination of nurturance and redundancy to protect their genetic heritage. Humans had a redundancy of parents, and then nurtured the few offspring. The hive queen had a redundancy of offspring, who then nurtured the parent. Each species had found its own balance of strategy.

<Why are you bothering us about this?>

"Because we're at a dead end. Because everybody else is trying, and you have as much at stake as we do."

<Do I?>

"The descolada threatens you as much as it threatens us. Someday you probably aren't going to be able to control it, and then you're gone."

<But it's not the descolada you're asking me about.>

"No." It was the problem of faster-than-light flight. Grego had been wracking his brains. In jail there was nothing else for him to think about. The last time Ender had spoken with him, he wept—as much from exhaustion as frustration. He had covered reams of papers with equations, spreading them all over the secure room that was used as a cell. "Don't you *care* about faster-than-light flight?"

<It would be very nice.>

The mildness of her response almost hurt, it so deeply disappointed him. This is what despair is like, he thought. Quara a brick wall on the nature of descolada intelligence. Planter dying of descolada deprivation. Han Fei-tzu and Wang-mu struggling to duplicate years of higher study in several fields, all at once. Grego worn out. And nothing to show for it.

She must have heard his anguish as clearly as if he had howled it.

<Don't.>

<Don't.>

"You've done it," he said. "It must be possible."

<We've never traveled faster than light.>

"You projected an action across lightyears. You found *me*."

<You found *us*, Ender.>

"Not so," he said. "I never even knew we had made mental contact until I found the message you had left for me." It had been the moment of greatest strangeness in his life, to stand on an alien world and see a model, a replication of the landscape that had existed in only one other place—the computer on which he had played his personalized version of the Fantasy Game. It was like having a total stranger come up to you and tell you your dream from the night before. They had been inside his head. It made him afraid, but it also excited him. For the first time in his life, he felt *known*. Not known *of*—he was famous throughout humanity, and in those days his fame was all positive, the greatest hero of all time. Other people knew *of* him. But with this bugger artifact, he discovered for the first time that he was *known*.

<Think, Ender. Yes, we reached out toward our enemy, but we weren't looking for you. We were looking for someone like us. A network of minds linked together, with a central mind controlling it. We find each other's minds without trying, because we recognize the pattern. Finding a sister is like finding ourself.>

"How *did* you find me, then?"

<We never thought about *how*. We only did it. Found a hot bright source. A network, but very strange, with shifting membership. And at the center of it, not something like us, but just another—common one. You. But with such intensity. Focused into the network, toward the other humans. Focused inward on your computer game. And focused outward, beyond all, on us. Searching for us.>

"I wasn't searching for you. I was studying you."

Watching every vid they had at the Battle School, trying to understand the way the bugger mind worked. "I was *imagining* you."

<So we say. Searching for us. Imagining us. That's how we search for each other. So you were calling us.>

"And that was all?"

<No, no. You were so strange. We didn't know what you were. We couldn't read anything in you. Your vision was so limited. Your ideas shifted so rapidly, and you thought of only one thing at a time. And the network around you kept shifting so much, each member's connection with you waxing and waning over time, sometimes very quickly—>

He was having trouble making sense of what they were saying. What kind of network was he connected to?

<The other soldiers. Your computer.>

"I wasn't *connected*. They were my soldiers, that's all."

<How do you think *we're* connected? Do you see any wires?>

"But humans are individuals, not like your workers."

<Many queens, many workers, changing back and forth, very confusing. Terrible, frightening time. What were these monsters that had wiped out our colony ship? What kind of creature? You were so strange we couldn't imagine you at all. We could only feel you when you were searching for *us*.>

Not helpful at all. Nothing to do with faster-than-light flight. It all sounded like mumbo-jumbo, not like science at all. Nothing that Grego could express mathematically.

<Yes, that's right. We don't do this like science. Not like technology. No numbers or even thought. We found you like bringing forth a new queen. Like starting a new hive.>

Ender didn't understand how establishing an ansible

link with his brain could be like hatching out a new queen. "Explain it to me."

<We don't think about it. We just *do* it.>

"But what are you *doing* when you do it?"

<What we always do.>

"And what do you always do?"

<How do you make your penis fill with blood to mate, Ender? How do you make your pancreas secrete enzymes? How do you switch on puberty? How do you focus your eyes?>

"Then *remember* what you do, and show it to me."

<You forget that you don't like this, when we show you through our eyes.>

It was true. She had tried only a couple of times, when he was very young and had first discovered her cocoon. He simply couldn't cope with it, couldn't make sense of it. Flashes, a few glimpses were clear, but it was so disorienting that he panicked, and probably fainted, though he was alone and couldn't be sure what had happened, clinically speaking.

"If you can't tell me, we have to do *something*."

<Are you like Planter? Trying to die?>

"No. I'll tell you to stop. It didn't kill me before."

<We'll try—something in between. Something milder. We'll remember, and tell you what's happening. Show you bits. Protect you. Safe.>

"Try, yes."

She gave him no time to reflect or prepare. At once he felt himself seeing out of compound eyes, not many lenses with the same vision, but each lens with its own picture. It gave him the same vertiginous feeling as so many years before. But this time he understood a little better—in part because she was making it less intense than before, and in part because he knew something about the hive queen now, about what she was doing to him.

The many different visions were what *each* of the

workers was seeing, as if each were a single eye connected to the same brain. There was no hope of Ender making sense of so many images at once.

<We'll show you one. The one that matters.>

Most of the visions dropped out immediately. Then, one by one, the others were sorted out. He imagined that she must have some organizing principle for the workers. She could disregard all those who weren't part of the queen-making process. Then, for Ender's sake, she had to sort through even the ones who *were* part of it, and that was harder, because usually she could sort the visions by task rather than by the individual workers. At last, though, she was able to show him a primary image and he could focus on it, ignoring the flickers and flashes of peripheral visions.

A queen being hatched. She had shown him this before, in a carefully-planned vision when he had first met her, when she was trying to explain things to him. Now, though, it wasn't a sanitized, carefully orchestrated presentation. The clarity was gone. It was murky, distracted, real. It was memory, not art.

<You see we have the queen-body. We know she's a queen because she starts reaching out for workers, even as a larva.>

"So you can talk to her?"

<She's very stupid. Like a worker.>

"She doesn't grow her intelligence until cocooning?"

<No. She *has* her—like your brain. The memory-think. It's just empty.>

"So you have to teach her."

<What good would teaching do? The thinker isn't there. The found thing. The binder-together.>

"I don't know what you're talking about."

<Stop trying to *look* and *think*, then. This isn't done with eyes.>

"Then stop showing me anything, if it depends on another sense. Eyes are too important to humans; if I see *anything* it'll mask out anything but clear speech and I don't think there's much of *that* at a queen-making."

<How's *this*?>

"I'm still seeing something."

<Your brain is turning it into seeing.>

"Then explain it. Help me make sense of it."

<It's the way we feel each other. We're finding the reaching-out place in the queen-body. The workers all have it, too, but all it reaches for is the queen and when it finds her all the reaching is over. The queen never stops reaching. Calling.>

"So then you find her?"

<We *know* where *she* is. The queen-body. The worker-caller. The memory-holder.>

"Then what are you searching for?"

<The us-thing. The binder. The meaning-maker.>

"You mean there's something else? Something *besides* the queen's body?"

<Yes, of course. The queen is just a body, like the workers. Didn't you know this?>

"No, I never saw it."

<Can't *see* it. Not with eyes.>

"I didn't know to look for anything else. I saw the making of the queen when you first showed it to me years ago. I thought I understood then."

<We thought you did too.>

"So if the queen's just a body, who are *you*?"

<We're the hive queen. And all the workers. We come and make one person out of all. The queen-body, she obeys us like the worker-bodies. We hold them all together, protect them, let them work perfectly as each is needed. We're the center. Each of us.>

"But you've always *talked* as if you *were* the hive queen."

<We *are*. Also all the workers. We're all together.>

"But this center-thing, this binder-together—"

<We call it to come and take the queen-body, so she can be wise, our sister.>

"You *call* it. What is it?"

<The thing we call.>

"Yes, what *is* it?"

<What are you asking? It's the called-thing. We call it.>

It was almost unbearably frustrating. So much of what the hive queen did was instinctive. She had no language and so she had never had a need to develop clear explanations of that which had never needed explaining till now. So he had to help her find a way to clarify what he couldn't perceive directly.

"Where do you find it?"

<It hears us calling and comes.>

"But how do you call?"

<As you called us. We imagine the thing which it must become. The pattern of the hive. The queen and the workers and the binding together. Then one comes who understands the pattern and can hold it. We give the queen-body to it.>

"So you're calling some other creature to come and take possession of the queen."

<To *become* the queen and the hive and all. To hold the pattern we imagined.>

"So where does it come from?"

<Wherever it was when it felt us calling.>

"But where is that?"

<Not here.>

"Fine, I believe you. But where does it come from?"

<Can't think of the place.>

"You forget?"

<We mean that the place where it is can't be thought of. If we could think of the place then they would already have thought of themselves and none of them would need to take the pattern we show.>

"What kind of thing *is* this binder-together?"

<Can't see it. Can't know it until it finds the pattern and then when it's there it's like *us*.>

Ender couldn't help shuddering. All this time he had thought that he was speaking to the hive queen herself. Now he realized that the thing that talked to him in his mind was only using that body the way it used the buggers. Symbiosis. A controlling parasite, possessing the whole hive queen system, using it.

<No. This is ugly, the terrible thing you're thinking. We aren't another thing. We're *this* thing. We *are* the hive queen, just the way you're the body. You say, My body, and yet you are your body, but you're also possessor of the body. The hive queen is ourself, this body is me, not something else inside. I. I wasn't anything until I found the imagining.>

"I don't understand. What was it like?"

<How can I remember? I never had memory until I followed the imagining and came to this place and became the hive queen.>

"Then how did you know that you aren't just the hive queen?"

<Because after I came, they gave me the memories. I saw the queen-body before I came, and then I saw the queen-body after I was in it. I was strong enough to hold the pattern in my mind, and so I could possess it. *Become* it. It took many days but then we were whole and they could give us the memories because I had the whole memory.>

The vision the hive queen had been giving him faded. It wasn't helping anyway, or at least not in any way he could grasp. Nevertheless, a mental image *was* coming clear for Ender now, one that came from his own mind to explain all the things she was saying. The other hive queens—not physically present, most of them, but linked philotically to the one queen who *had* to be there—they held the pattern of the relationship between hive queen and workers in their minds, until one of these mysterious memoryless creatures was able to contain the pattern in its mind and therefore take possession of it.

<Yes.>

"But where do these things come from? Where do you have to go to get them?"

<We don't go anywhere. We call, and there they are.>

"So they're *everywhere*?"

<They aren't *here* at all. Nowhere here. Another place.>

"But you said you don't have to go anywhere to get them."

<Doorways. We don't know where they are, but everywhere there's a door.>

"What are the doorways like?"

<Your brain made the word you say. Doorway. Doorway.>

Now he realized that *doorway* was the word his brain called forth to label the concept they were putting in his mind. And suddenly he was able to grasp an explanation that made sense.

"They're not in the same space-time continuum as ours. But they can enter ours at any point."

<To them all points are the same point. All wheres are the same where. They only find one where-ness in the pattern.>

"But this is incredible. You're calling forth some being from another place, and—"

<The calling forth is nothing. All things do it. All new makings. You do it. Every human baby has this thing. The pequeninos are these things also. Grass and sunlight. All making calls them, and they come to the pattern. If there are already some who understand the pattern, then they come and possess it. Small patterns are very easy. Our pattern is very hard. Only a very wise one can possess it.>

"Philotes," said Ender. "The things out of which all other things are made."

<The word you say doesn't make a meaning like what we mean.>

"Because I'm only just making the connection. We never meant what you've described, but the thing we *did* mean, that might *be* the thing you described."

<Very unclear.>

"Join the club."

<Very welcome laughing happy.>

"So when you make a hive queen, you already have the biological body, and this new thing—this philote that you call out of the non-place where philotes are—it has to be one that's able to comprehend the complex pattern that you have in your minds of what a hive queen *is*, and when one comes that can do it, it takes on that identity and possesses the body and *becomes* the self of that body—"

<Of all the bodies.>

"But there are no workers yet, when the hive queen is first made."

<It becomes the self of the workers-to-come.>

"We're talking about a passage from another kind of space. A place where philotes already are."

<All in the same non-place. No place-ness in that place. No where-being. All hungry for whereness. All thirsty for pattern. All lonely for selfness.>

"And you say that *we're* made of the same things?"

<How could we have found you if you weren't?>

"But you said that finding me was like making a hive queen."

<We couldn't find the pattern in *you*. We were trying to make a pattern between you and the other humans, only you kept shifting and changing, we couldn't make sense of it. And you couldn't make sense of *us*, either, so that reaching of yours couldn't make a pattern, either. So we took the third pattern. You reaching into

the machine. You yearning so much for it. Like the life-yearning of the new queen-body. You were binding yourself to the program in the computer. It showed you images. We could find the images in the computer and we could find them in your mind. We could match them while you watched. The computer was very complicated and you were even more complicated but it was a pattern that held still. You were moving together and while you were together you possessed each other, you had the same vision. And when you imagined something and did it, the computer made something out of your imagining and imagined something back. Very primitive imagining from the computer. It wasn't a self. But you were making it a self by the life-yearning. The reaching-out you were doing.>

"The Fantasy Game," said Ender. "You made a pattern out of the Fantasy Game."

<We imagined the same thing you were imagining. All of us together. Calling. It was very complicated and strange, but much simpler than anything else we found in you. Since then we know—very few humans are capable of concentrating the way you concentrated on that game. And we've seen no other computer program that responded to a human the way that game responded to you. It was yearning, too. Cycling over and over, trying to find something to make for you.>

"And when you called . . ."

<It came. The bridge we needed. The together-binder for you and the computer program. It held the pattern so that it was alive even when you weren't paying attention to it. It was linked to you, you were part of it, and yet we could also understand it. It was the bridge.>

"But when a philote takes possession of a new hive queen, it controls it, queen-body and worker-bodies. Why didn't this bridge you made take control of me?"

<Do you think we didn't try?>

"Why didn't it work?"

<You weren't capable of letting a pattern like that control you. You could willingly become part of a pattern that was real and alive, but you couldn't be controlled by it. You couldn't even be destroyed by it. And there was so much of you in the pattern that we couldn't even control it ourselves. Too strange for us.>

"But you could still use it to read my mind."

<We could use it to stay connected with you in spite of all the strangeness. We studied you, especially when you played the game. And as we understood you, we began to grasp the idea of your whole species. That each individual of you was alive, with no hive queen at all.>

"More complicated than you expected?"

<And less. Your individual minds were simpler in the ways that we expected to be complicated, and complicated in ways that we expected them to be simple. We realized that you were truly alive and beautiful in your perverse and tragic lonely way and we decided not to send another colony ship to your worlds.>

"But we didn't know that. How could we know?"

<We also realized that you were dangerous and terrible. You in particular, dangerous because you found all our patterns and we couldn't think of anything complicated enough to confuse you. So you destroyed all but me. Now I understand you better. I've had all these years to study you. You are not as terrifyingly brilliant as we thought.>

"Too bad. Terrifying brilliance would be useful right now."

<We prefer a comforting glow of intelligence.>

"We humans get slower as we age. Give me a few more years and I'll be downright cozy."

<We know that you'll die someday. Even though you put it off for so long.>

Ender didn't want this to become another conversation about mortality or any of the other aspects of human life that so fascinated the hive queen. There was still one question that had occurred to him during the hive queen's story. An intriguing possibility.

"The bridge you made. Where was it? In the computer?"

<Inside you. The way I'm inside the body of the hive queen.>

"But not part of me."

<Part of you but also not-you. Other. Outside but inside. Bound to you but free. It couldn't control you, and you couldn't control it.>

"Could it control the computer?"

<We didn't think about that. We didn't care. Maybe.>

"How long did you use this bridge? How long was it there?"

<We stopped thinking about it. We were thinking about *you.*>

"But it was still there the whole time you were studying me."

<Where would it go?>

"How long would it last?"

<We never made one like that before. How would *we* know? The hive queen dies when the queen-body dies.>

"But what body was the *bridge* in?"

<Yours. At the center of the pattern.>

"This thing was *inside* me?"

<Of course. But it was still not-you. It disappointed us that way, when it couldn't let us control you, and we stopped thinking about it. But we see now that this was very important. We should have searched for it. We should have remembered it.>

"No. To you it was like—a bodily function. Like balling up your fist to hit somebody. You did it, and then when you didn't need it you didn't notice whether your fist was still there or not."

<We don't understand the connection but it seems to make sense inside *you*.>

"It's still alive, isn't it?"

<It could be. We're trying to feel it. Find it. Where can we look? The old pattern isn't there. You don't play the Fantasy Game anymore.>

"But it would still be linked to the computer, wouldn't it? A connection between me and the computer. Only the pattern could have grown, couldn't it? It could include other people, too. Think of it being linked to Miro—the young man I brought with me—"

<The broken one . . .>

"And instead of being linked to that one computer, linked to thousands and thousands of them, through the ansible links between worlds."

<This could be. It was alive. It could grow. The way we grow when we make more workers. All this time. Now that you mention it, we're sure it must still be there because we're still linked to you, and it was only through that pattern that we connected with you. The connection is very strong now—that's part of what it is, the link between us and you. We thought the connection grew stronger because we knew you better. But maybe it also grew stronger because the bridge was growing.>

"And *I* always thought—Jane and I always thought that she was—that she had somehow come to exist in the ansible connections between worlds. That's probably where she *feels* herself, the place that feels like the center of her—body, I was going to say."

<We're trying to feel whether the bridge between us is still there. Hard to feel it.>

"Like trying to find a particular muscle that you've been using all your life but never by itself."

<Interesting comparison. We don't see the connection but no, now we see it.>

"The comparison?"

<The bridge. Very big. The pattern of it is too big. We can't grasp it anymore. Very big. Memory—very confusing. Much harder than finding you the first time—very confusing. Getting lost. We can't hold it in our mind anymore.>

"Jane," whispered Ender. "You're a big girl now."

Jane's voice came in answer: "You're cheating, Ender. I can't hear what she's saying to you. I can only feel your heart pounding and your rapid breathing."

<Jane. We've seen this name in your mind many times. But the bridge wasn't a person with a face—>

"Neither is Jane."

<We see a face in your mind when you think of this name. We still see it. Always we thought it was a person. But now—>

"She's the bridge. You made her."

<*Called* her. *You* made the pattern. *She* possessed it. What she *is*, this Jane, this bridge, she began with the pattern we discovered in you and the Fantasy Game, yes, but she has imagined herself to be much larger. She must have been a very strong and powerful—philote, if your word is the right name—to be able to change her own pattern and still remember to be herself.>

"You reached out across the lightyears and found *me* because I was looking for *you*. And then you found a pattern and called a creature from another space who grasped the pattern and possessed it and became Jane. All of this instantaneously. Faster than light."

<But this isn't faster-than-light *travel*. It's faster-than-light *imagining* and *calling*. It still doesn't pick you up here and put you there.>

"I know. I know. This may not help us answer the question I came here with. But I had another question, just as important to me, that I never thought would have anything to do with you, and here you had the answer to it all along. Jane's real, alive the whole time, and her self isn't out there in space, it's inside *me*. Connected to *me*. They can't kill her by switching her off. That's something."

<If they kill the pattern, she can die >

"But they can't kill the *whole* pattern, don't you see? It doesn't depend on the ansibles after all. It depends on me and on the link between me and the computers. They can't cut the link between me and the computers here and in the satellites orbiting Lusitania. And maybe she doesn't need the ansibles, either. After all, *you* don't need them to reach me through her."

<Many strange things are possible. We can't imagine them. They feel very stupid and strange, the things going through your mind. You're making us very tired, with all your thinking of stupid imaginary impossible things.>

"I'll leave you, then. But this will help. This has to help. If Jane can find a way to survive because of this, then that's a real victory. The *first* victory, when I was beginning to think there wasn't any victory to be had in this."

The moment he left the presence of the hive queen, he began talking to Jane, telling her everything he could remember of what the hive queen could explain. Who Jane was, how she was created.

And as he talked, she analyzed herself in light of what he said. Began to discover things about herself that she had never guessed. By the time Ender got back to the human colony, she had verified as much of his story as she could. "I never found this because I always started with the wrong assumptions," she said. "I imagined my center to be out in space somewhere. I should have guessed I was inside you from the fact that even when I was furious with you, I had to come back to you to be at peace."

"And now the hive queen says that you've grown so big and complex that she can't hold the pattern of you in her mind anymore."

"Must have gone through a growth spurt, back during my years of puberty."

"Right."

"Could I help it that humans kept adding computers and linking them up?"

"But it isn't the hardware, Jane. It's the programs. The mentation."

"I have to have the physical memory to hold all of that."

"You have the memory. The question is, can you access it without the ansibles?"

"I can try. As you said to *her*, it's like learning to flex a muscle I never knew I had."

"Or learning to live without one."

"I'll see what's possible."

What's possible. All the way home, the car floating over the capim, he was also flying, exhilarated to know that *something* was possible after all, when till now he had felt nothing but despair. Coming home, though, seeing the burnt-over forest, the two solitary fathertrees with the only greenery left, the experimental farm, the new hut with the cleanroom where Planter lay dying, he realized how much there still was to lose, how many would still die, even if now they had found a way for Jane to live.

It was the end of the day. Han Fei-tzu was exhausted, his eyes hurting from all that he had read. He had adjusted the colors on the computer display a dozen times, trying to find something restful, but it didn't help. The last time he had worked so intensely was as a student, and then he had been young. Then, too, he had always found results. I was quicker, then, brighter. I could reward myself by achieving something. Now I'm old and slow, I'm working in areas that are new to me, and it may be that these problems *have* no solutions.

So there's no reward to bolster me. Only the weariness. The pain at the top of my neck, the puffy, tired feeling in my eyes.

He looked at Wang-mu, curled up on the floor beside him. She tried so hard, but her education had begun too recently for her to be able to follow most of the documents that passed through the computer display as he searched for some conceptual framework for faster-than-light travel. At last her weariness triumphed over her will; she was sure she was useless, because she couldn't understand enough even to ask questions. So she gave up and slept.

But you are not useless, Si Wang-mu. Even in your perplexity you've helped me. A bright mind to which all things are new. Like having my own lost youth perched at my elbow.

As Qing-jao was, when she was little, before piety and pride claimed her.

Not fair. Not right to judge his own daughter that way. Until these last weeks, hadn't he been perfectly satisfied with her? Proud of her beyond all reason? The best and brightest of the godspoken, everything her father had worked for, everything her mother had hoped.

That was the part that chafed. Until a few weeks ago, he had been proudest of all of the fact that he had accomplished his oath to Jiang-qing. This was not an easy accomplishment, to bring up his daughter so piously that she never went through a period of doubt or rebellion against the gods. True, there were other children just as pious—but their piety was usually achieved at the expense of their education. Han Fei-tzu had let Qing-jao learn everything, and then had so deftly led her understanding of it that all fit well with her faith in the gods.

Now he had reaped his own sowing. He had given her a worldview that so perfectly preserved her faith that now, when he had discovered that the gods' "voices" were nothing but the genetic chains with which Congress had shackled them, nothing could convince her. If Jiang-qing had lived, Fei-tzu would no doubt have been in conflict with *her* over his loss of faith. In her absence, he had done so well at raising their daughter as Jiang-qing would have that Qing-jao was able to take her mother's view flawlessly.

Jiang-qing would also have left me, thought Han Fei-tzu. Even if I had not been widowed, I would have been wifeless on this day.

The only companion left to me is this servant girl, who pushed her way into my household only just in time to be the one spark of life in my old age, the one flicker of hope in my dark heart.

Not my daughter-of-the-body, but perhaps there will be time and opportunity, when this crisis is past, to make Wang-mu my daughter-of-the-mind. My work with Congress is finished. Shall I not be a teacher, then, with a single disciple, this girl? Shall I not prepare her to be the revolutionary who can lead the common people to freedom from the tyranny of the godspoken, and then lead Path to freedom from Congress itself? Let her be such a one, and then I can die in peace, knowing that at the end of my life I have created the undoing of all my earlier work that strengthened Congress and helped overcome all opposition to its power.

The soft breathing of the girl Wang-mu was like his own breath, like a baby's breath, like the sound of a breeze through tall grass. She is all motion, all hope, all freshness.

"Han Fei-tzu, I think you are not asleep."

He was not; but he had been half-dozing, for the sound of Jane's voice coming from the computer startled him as if he were waking up.

"No, but Wang-mu is," he said.

"Wake her, then," said Jane.

"What is it? She's earned her rest."

"She's also earned the right to hear this."

Ela's face appeared beside Jane's in the display. Han Fei-tzu knew her at once as the xenobiologist who had been entrusted with the study of the genetic samples he and Wang-mu had collected. There must have been a breakthrough.

He bowed himself down, reached out, shook the girl's hip as she lay there sleeping. She stirred. She stretched. Then, no doubt remembering her duty, she sat bolt upright. "Have I overslept? What is it? Forgive me for falling asleep, Master Han."

She might have bowed herself in her confusion, but Fei-tzu wouldn't let her. "Jane and Ela asked me to wake you. They wanted you to hear."

"I will tell you first," said Ela, "that what we hoped for is possible. The genetic alterations were crude and easily discovered—I can see why Congress has done its best to keep any real geneticists from working with the human population of Path. The OCD gene wasn't in the normal place, which is why it wasn't identified at once by natologists, but it works almost exactly as naturally-occurring OCD genes work. It can easily be treated separately from the genes that give the godspoken enhanced intellectual and creative abilities. I have already designed a splicer bacterium that, if injected into the blood, will find a person's sperm or ova, enter them, remove the OCD gene, and replace it with a normal one, leaving the rest of the genetic code unaffected. Then the bacterium will die out quickly. It's based on a common bacterium that should already exist in many labs on Path for normal immunology and birth-defect-prevention work. So any of the godspoken who wish to give birth to children without the OCD can do it."

Han Fei-tzu laughed. "I'm the only one on this planet who would wish for such a bacterium. The godspoken have no pity on themselves. They take pride in their affliction. It gives them honor and power."

"Then let me tell you the next thing we found. It was one of my assistants, a pequenino named Glass, who discovered this—I'll admit that I wasn't paying much personal attention to this project since it was relatively easy compared to the descolada problem we're working on."

"Don't apologize," said Fei-tzu. "We are grateful for any kindness. All is undeserved."

"Yes. Well." She seemed flustered by his courtesy. "Anyway, what Glass discovered is that all but one of the genetic samples you gave us sort themselves neatly into godspoken and non-godspoken categories. We ran the test blind, and only afterward checked the sample lists against the identity lists you gave us—the correspondence was perfect. Every godspoken had the altered gene. Every sample that lacked the altered gene was also not on your list of godspoken."

"You said all but one."

"This one baffled us. Glass is very methodical—he has the patience of a tree. He was sure that the one exception was a clerical error or an error in interpreting the genetic data. He went over it many times, and had other assistants do the same. There is no doubt. The one exception is clearly a mutation of the godspoken gene. It *naturally* lacks the OCD, while still retaining all of the other abilities Congress's geneticists so thoughtfully provided."

"So this one person already *is* what your splicer bacterium is designed to create."

"There are a few other mutated regions that we aren't quite sure of at the moment, but they have nothing to do with the OCD or the enhancements. Nor are they involved in any of the vital processes, so this person should be able to have healthy offspring that carry the trait. In fact, if this person should mate with a person who has been treated with the splicer bacterium, all her offspring will almost certainly carry the enhancements, and there'd be no chance of any of them having the OCD."

"How lucky for him," said Han Fei-tzu.

"Who is it?" asked Wang-mu.

"It's you," said Ela. "Si Wang-mu."

"Me?" She seemed baffled.

But Han Fei-tzu was not confused. "Ha!" he cried. "I should have known. I should have guessed! No wonder you have learned as quickly as my own daughter learned. No wonder you have had insights that helped us all even when you barely understood the subject you were studying. You are as godspoken as anyone on Path, Wang-mu—except that you alone are free of the shackles of the cleansing rituals."

Si Wang-mu struggled to answer, but instead of words, tears came, silently drifting down her face.

"Never again will I permit you to treat me as your superior," said Han Fei-tzu. "From now on you are no servant in my house, but my student, my young colleague. Let others think of you however they want. *We* know that you are as capable as anyone."

"As Mistress Qing-jao?" Wang-mu whispered.

"As anyone," said Fei-tzu. "Courtesy will require you to bow to many. But in your heart, you need bow to no one."

"I am unworthy," said Wang-mu.

"Everyone is worthy of his own genes. A mutation like that is much more likely to have crippled you. But instead, it left you the healthiest person in the world."

But she would not stop her silent weeping.

Jane must have been showing this to Ela, for she kept her peace for some time. Finally, though, she spoke. "Forgive me, but I have much to do," she said.

"Yes," said Han Fei-tzu. "You may go."

"You misunderstand me," said Ela. "I don't need your permission to go. I have more to say *before* I go."

Han Fei-tzu bowed his head. "Please. We are listening."

"Yes," whispered Wang-mu. "I'm listening too."

"There is a possibility—a remote one, as you will see, but a possibility nonetheless—that *if* we are able to decode the descolada virus and tame it, we can also make an adaptation that could be useful on Path."

"How so?" asked Han Fei-tzu. "Why should we want this monstrous artificial virus here?"

"The whole business of the descolada is entering a host organism's cells, reading the genetic code, and reorganizing it according to the descolada's own plan. When we alter it, *if* we can, we'll remove its own plan from it. We'll also remove almost all of its self-defense mechanisms, if we can find them. At that point, it may be possible to use it as a super-splicer. Something that can effect a change, not just on the reproductive cells, but on *all* the cells of a living creature."

"Forgive me," said Han Fei-tzu, "but I have been reading in this field lately, and the concept of a super-splicer has been rejected, because the body starts to reject its own cells as soon as they're genetically altered."

"Yes," said Ela. "That's how the descolada kills. The body rejects itself to death. But that only happened because the descolada had no plan for dealing with humans. It was studying the human body as it went, making random changes and seeing what happened. It had no single plan for us, and so each victim ended up with many different genetic codes in his or her cells. What if we made a super-splicer that worked according to a single plan, transforming every cell in the body to conform with a single new pattern? In that case, our studies of the descolada assure us that the change could be effected in each individual person within six hours, usually—half a day at the most."

"Fast enough that before the body can reject itself—"

"It will be so perfectly unified that it will recognize the new pattern as itself."

Wang-mu's crying had stopped. She seemed as excited now as Fei-tzu felt, and despite all her self-discipline, she could not contain it. "You can change *all* the godspoken? Free even the ones who are already alive?"

"*If* we are able to decode the descolada, then not only would we be able to remove the OCD from the godspoken, we would also be able to install all the enhancements in the common people. It would have the most effect in the children, of course—older people have already passed the growth stages where the new genes would have the most effect. But from that time on, every child born on Path would have the enhancements."

"What then? Would the descolada disappear?"

"I'm not sure. I think we would have to build into the new gene a way for it to destroy itself when its work is done. But we would use Wang-mu's genes as a model. Not to stretch the point, Wang-mu, you would become a sort of genetic co-parent of the entire population of your world."

She laughed. "What a wonderful joke to play on them! So proud to be chosen, and yet their cure will come from one such as me!" At once, though, her face fell and she covered her face with her hands. "How could I say such a thing. I have become as haughty and arrogant as the worst of them."

Fei-tzu laid his hand on her shoulder. "Say nothing so harsh. Such feelings are natural. They come and go quickly. Only those who make them a way of life are to be condemned for them." He turned back to Ela. "There are ethical problems here."

"I know. And I think those problems should be addressed now, even though it may never be possible even to do this. We're talking about the genetic alteration of an entire population. It was an atrocity when Congress secretly did it to Path without the consent or knowledge of the population. Can we undo an atrocity by following the same path?"

"More than that," said Han Fei-tzu. "Our entire social system here is based on the godspoken. Most people will interpret such a transformation as a plague from the gods, punishing us. If it became known that we were the source, we would be killed. It's possible, though, that when it becomes known that the godspoken have lost the voice of the gods—the OCD—the people will turn on them and kill them. How will freeing them from the OCD have helped them *then*, if they're dead?"

"We've discussed this," said Ela. "And we have no idea what's the right thing to do. For now the question is moot because we haven't decoded the descolada and may never be able to. But if we develop the capability, we believe that the choice of whether to use it should be yours."

"The people of Path?"

"No," said Ela. "The first choices are *yours*, Han Fei-tzu, Si Wang-mu, and Han Qing-jao. Only you know of what has been done to you, and even though your daughter doesn't believe it, she *does* fairly represent the viewpoint of the believers and the godspoken of Path. If we get the capability, put the question to her. Put the question to yourselves. Is there some plan, some way to bring this transformation to Path, that would not be destructive? And if it *can* be done, *should* it be done? No—say nothing now, decide nothing now. Think about it yourselves. We are not part of this. We will only inform you when or whether we learn how to do it. From there it will be up to you."

Ela's face disappeared.

Jane lingered a moment longer. "Worth waking up for?" she asked.

"Yes!" cried Wang-mu.

"Kind of nice to discover that you're a lot more than

you ever thought you were, isn't it?" said Jane.

"Oh, yes," said Wang-mu.

"Now go back to sleep, Wang-mu. And you, Master Han—your fatigue is showing very clearly. You're useless to us if you lose your health. As Andrew has told me, over and over—we must do all we can do *without* destroying our ability to keep doing it."

Then she was gone, too.

Wang-mu immediately began to weep again. Han Fei-tzu slid over and sat beside her on the floor, cradled her head against his shoulder, and rocked gently back and forth. "Hush, my daughter, my sweet one, in your heart you already knew who you were, and so did I, so did I. Truly your name was wisely given. If they perform their miracles on Lusitania, you will be the Royal Mother of all the world."

"Master Han," she whispered. "I'm crying also for Qing-jao. I have been given more than I ever hoped for. But who will *she* be, if the voice of the gods is taken from her?"

"I hope," said Fei-tzu, "that she will be my true daughter again. That she will be as free as you, the daughter who has come to me like a petal on the winter river, borne to me from the land of perpetual spring."

He held her for many long minutes more, until she began to doze on his shoulder. Then he laid her back on her mat, and he retired to his own corner to sleep, with hope in his heart for the first time in many days.

When Valentine came to see Grego in prison, Mayor Kovano told her that Olhado was with him. "Aren't these Olhado's working hours?"

"You can't be serious," said Kovano. "He's a good manager of brickmakers, but I think saving the world might be worth an afternoon of somebody else covering for him on management."

"Don't get your expectations *too* high," said Valentine. "I wanted him involved. I *hoped* he might help. But he isn't a physicist."

Kovano shrugged. "I'm not a jailer, either, but one does what the situation requires. I have no idea whether it has to do with Olhado being in there or Ender's visit a little while ago, but I've heard more excitement and noise in there than—well, than I've *ever* heard when the inmates were sober. Of course, public drunkenness is what people are usually jailed for in this town."

"Ender came?"

"From the hive queen. He wants to talk to you. I didn't know where you were."

"Yes. Well, I'll go see him when I leave here." Where she had been was with her husband. Jakt was getting ready to go back into space on the shuttle, to prepare his own ship for quick departure, if need be, and to see whether the original Lusitanian colony ship could possibly be restored for another flight after so many decades without maintenance of the stardrive. The only thing it had been used for was storage of seeds and genes and embryos of Earthborn species, in case they were someday needed. Jakt would be gone for at least a week, possibly longer, and Valentine couldn't very well let him go without spending some time with him. He would have understood, of course—he knew the terrible pressure that everyone was under. But Valentine also knew that she wasn't one of the key figures in these events. She would only be useful later, writing the history of it.

When she left Jakt, however, she had not come straight to the mayor's office to see Grego. She had taken a walk through the center of town. Hard to believe that only a short time ago—how many days? Weeks?—the mob had formed here, drunken and angry, working themselves up to a murderous rage. Now it was so quiet. The grass had even recovered from the trampling, except for one mudhole where it refused to grow back.

But it wasn't peaceful here. On the contrary. When the town had been at peace, when Valentine first arrived, there had been bustle and business here in the heart of the colony, all through the day. Now a few people were out and about, yes, but they were glum, almost furtive. Their eyes stayed down, looking at the ground before their feet, as if everyone were afraid that if they didn't watch every step they'd fall flat.

Part of the glumness was probably shame, thought Valentine. There was a hole in every building in town now, where blocks or bricks had been torn out to use in the building of the chapel. Many of the gaps were visible from the praça where Valentine walked.

She suspected, however, that fear more than shame had killed the vibrancy in this place. No one spoke of it openly, but she caught enough comments, enough covert glances toward the hills north of town that she knew. What loomed over this colony wasn't the fear of the coming fleet. It wasn't shame over the slaughter of the pequenino forest. It was the buggers. The dark shapes only occasionally visible on the hills or out in the grass surrounding the town. It was the nightmares of the children who had seen them. The sick dread in the hearts of the adults. Historicals set in the Bugger War period were continuously checked out from the library as people became obsessed with watching humans achieve victory over buggers. And as they watched, they fed their worst fears. The theoretical notion of the hive culture as a beautiful and worthy one, as Ender had depicted it in his first book, the Hive Queen, disappeared completely for many of the people here, perhaps most of them, as they dwelt in the unspoken punishment and imprisonment enforced by the hive queen's workers.

Is all our work in vain, after all? thought Valentine.

I, the historian, the philosopher Demosthenes, trying to teach people that they need not fear all aliens, but can see them as raman. And Ender, with his empathic books the Hive Queen, the Hegemon, the Life of Human—what force did they really have in the world, compared with the instinctive terror at the sight of these dangerous oversized insects? Civilization is only a pretense; in the crisis, we become mere apes again, forgetting the rational biped of our pretensions and becoming instead the hairy primate at the mouth of the cave, screeching at the enemy, wishing it would go away, fingering the heavy stone that we'll use the moment it comes close enough.

Now she was back in a clean, safe place, not so disquieting even if it did serve as a prison as well as the center of city government. A place where the buggers were seen as allies—or at least as an indispensable peacekeeping force, holding antagonists apart for their mutual protection. There *are* people, Valentine reminded herself, who are able to transcend their animal origins.

When she opened the cell door, Olhado and Grego were both sprawled on bunks, papers strewn on the floor and table between them, some flat, some wadded up. Papers even covered the computer terminal, so that if the computer was on, the display couldn't possibly function. It looked like a typical teenager's bedroom, complete with Grego's legs stretching up the walls, his bare feet dancing a weird rhythm, twisting back and forth, back and forth in the air. What was his inner music?

"Boa tarde, Tia Valentina," said Olhado.

Grego didn't even look up.

"Am I interrupting?"

"Just in time," said Olhado. "We're on the verge of reconceptualizing the universe. We've discovered the illuminating principle that wishing makes it so and all living creatures pop out of nowhere whenever they're needed."

"If wishing makes it so," said Valentine, "can we wish for faster-than-light flight?"

"Grego's doing math in his head right now," said Olhado, "so he's functionally dead. But yes. I think he's on to something—he was shouting and dancing a minute ago. We had a sewing-machine experience."

"Ah," said Valentine.

"It's an old science-class story," said Olhado. "People who wanted to invent sewing machines kept failing because they always tried to imitate the motions of hand-sewing, pushing the needle through the fabric and drawing the thread along behind through the eye at the back end of the needle. It seemed obvious. Until somebody first thought of putting the eye in the nose of the needle and using two threads instead of just one. A completely unnatural, indirect approach that when it comes right down to it, I still don't understand."

"So we're going to sew our way through space?"

"In a way. The shortest distance between two points isn't necessarily a line. It comes from something Andrew learned from the hive queen. How they call some kind of creature from an alternate spacetime when they create a new hive queen. Grego jumped on that as proof that there *was* a real non-real space. Don't ask me what he means by that. I make bricks for a living."

"Unreal realspace," said Grego. "You had it backward."

"The dead awake," said Olhado.

"Have a seat, Valentine," said Grego. "My cell isn't much, but it's home. The math on this is still crazy but it seems to fit. I'm going to have to spend some time with Jane on it, to do the really tight calculations and run some simulations, but if the hive queen's right, and there's a space so universally adjacent to our space that philotes can pass into our space from the other space at any point, and if we postulate that the passage can go the other way, and if the hive queen is also right that the other space contains philotes just as ours does, only in the other space—call it Outside—the philotes aren't organized according to natural law, but are instead just possibilities, then here's what might work—"

"Those are awfully big *if*s," said Valentine.

"You forget," said Olhado. "We start from the premise that wishing makes it so."

"Right, I forgot to mention that," said Grego. "We also assume that the hive queen is right that the unorganized philotes respond to patterns in someone's mind, immediately assuming whatever role is available in the pattern. So that things that are comprehended Outside will immediately come to exist there."

"All this is perfectly clear," said Valentine. "I'm surprised you didn't think of it before."

"Right," said Grego. "So here's how we do it. Instead of trying to physically move all the particles that compose the starship and its passengers and cargo from Star A to Star B, we simply conceive of them all—the entire pattern, including all the human contents—as existing, not Inside, but Outside. At that moment, all the philotes that compose the starship and the people in it disorganize themselves, pop through into the Outside, and reassemble themselves there according to the familiar pattern. Then we do the same thing again, and pop back Inside—only now we're at Star B. Preferably a safe orbiting distance away."

"If every point in our space corresponds to a point Outside," said Valentine, "don't we just have to do our traveling there instead of here?"

"The rules are different there," said Grego. "There's no whereness there. Let's assume that in *our* space, whereness—relative location—is simply an artifact of the order that philotes follow. It's a *convention*. So is distance, for that matter. We measure distance according to the time it takes to travel it—but it only takes that amount of time because the philotes of which matter and energy are comprised follow the conventions of natural law. Like the speed of light."

"They're just obeying the speed limit."

"Yes. Except for the speed limit, the *size* of our universe is arbitrary. If you looked at our universe as a sphere, then if you stood outside the sphere, it could as easily be an inch across or a trillion lightyears or a micron."

"And when we go Outside—"

"Then the Inside universe is exactly the same size as any of the disorganized philotes there—no size at all. Furthermore, since there is no whereness there, all philotes in that space are equally close or nonclose to the location of our universe. So we can reenter Inside space at any point."

"That makes it sound almost easy," said Valentine.

"Yes, well," said Grego.

"It's the wishing that's hard," said Olhado.

"To hold the pattern, you really have to *understand* it," said Grego. "Each philote that rules a pattern comprehends only its own part of reality. It depends on the philotes within its pattern to do their job and hold their own pattern, and it also depends on the philote that controls the pattern that *it's* a part of to keep it in its proper place. The atom philote has to trust the neutron and proton and electron philotes to hold their own internal structures together, and the molecule philote to hold the atom in its proper place, while the atom philote concentrates on his own job, which is keeping the parts of the atom in place. That's how reality seems to work—in this model, anyway."

"So you transplant the whole thing to Outside and back Inside again," said Valentine. "I understood that."

"Yes, but *who*? Because the mechanism for sending

requires that the whole pattern for the ship and all its contents be established as a pattern of its own, not just an arbitrary conglomeration. I mean, when you load a cargo on a ship and the passengers embark, you haven't created a living pattern, a philotic organism. It's not like giving birth to a baby—that's an organism that can hold itself together. The ship and its contents are just a collection. They can break apart at any point. So when you move all the philotes out into disorganized space, lacking whereness or thisness or any organizing principle, how do they reassemble? And even if they reassemble themselves into the structures they know, what do you have? A lot of atoms. Maybe even living cells and organisms—but without spacesuits or a starship, because those aren't alive. All the atoms and maybe even the molecules are floating around, probably replicating themselves like crazy as the unorganized philotes out there start copying the pattern, but you've got no *ship*."

"Fatal."

"No, probably not," said Grego. "Who can guess? The rules are all different out there. The point is that you can't possibly bring them *back* into *our* space in that condition, because that definitely *would* be fatal."

"So we can't."

"I don't know. Reality holds together in Inside space because all the philotes that it's comprised of agree on the rules. They all know each other's patterns and follow the same patterns themselves. Maybe it can all hold together in Outside space as long as the spaceship and its cargo and passengers are fully *known*. As long as there's a knower who can hold the entire structure in her head."

"Her?"

"As I said, I have to have Jane do the calculations. She has to see if she has access to enough memory to contain the pattern of relationships within a spaceship.

She has to then see if she can take that pattern and imagine its new location."

"That's the wishing part," said Olhado. "I'm very proud of it, because I'm the one who thought of needing a knower to move the ship."

"This whole thing is really Olhado's," said Grego, "but I intend to put my name first on the paper because he doesn't care about career advancement and I have to look good enough for people to overlook this felony conviction if I'm going to get a job at a university on another world somewhere."

"What are you talking about?" said Valentine.

"I'm talking about getting off this two-bit colony planet. Don't you understand? If this is all true, if it *works,* then I can fly to Rheims or Baía or—or *Earth* and come back here for weekends. The energy cost is *zero* because we're stepping outside natural laws entirely. The wear and tear on the vehicles is nothing."

"Not *nothing,*" said Olhado. "We've still got to taxi close to the planet of destination."

"As I said, it all depends on what Jane can conceive of. She has to be able to comprehend the whole ship and its contents. She has to be able to imagine us Outside and Inside again. She has to be able to conceive of the exact relative positions of the startpoint and endpoint of the journey."

"So faster-than-light travel depends completely on Jane," said Valentine.

"If she didn't exist, it would be impossible. Even if they linked all the computers together, even if someone could write the program to accomplish it, it wouldn't help. Because a program is just a collection, not an entity. It's just parts. Not a—what was the word Jane found for it? An *aiúa.*"

"Sanskrit for *life,*" Olhado explained to Valentine. "The word for the philote who controls a pattern that holds other philotes in order. The word for entities—like planets and atoms and animals and stars—that have an intrinsic, enduring form."

"Jane is an aiúa, not just a program. So she can be a knower. She can incorporate the starship as a pattern within her own pattern. She can *digest* it and *contain* it and it will still be real. She makes it part of herself and knows it as perfectly and unconsciously as your aiúa knows your own body and holds it together. Then she can carry it with her Outside and back Inside again."

"So Jane has to *go*?" asked Valentine.

"If this can be done at all, it'll be done because Jane travels with the ship, yes," said Grego.

"How?" asked Valentine. "We can't exactly go pick her up and carry her with us in a bucket."

"This is something Andrew learned from the hive queen," said Grego. "She actually exists in a particular place—that is, her aiúa has a specific location in our space."

"Where?"

"Inside Andrew Wiggin."

It took a while for them to explain to her what Ender had learned about Jane from the hive queen. It was strange to think of this computer entity as being centered inside Ender's body, but it made a kind of sense that Jane had been created by the hive queens during Ender's campaign against them. To Valentine, though, there was another, immediate consequence. If the faster-than-light ship could only go where Jane took it, and Jane was inside Ender, there could be only one conclusion.

"Then *Andrew* has to go?"

"Claro. Of course," said Grego.

"He's a little old to be a test pilot," said Valentine.

"In this case he's only a test *passenger*," said Grego. "He just happens to hold the pilot inside him."

"It's not as if the voyage will have any physical stress," said Olhado. "If Grego's theory works out exactly right, he'll just sit there and after a couple of minutes or actually a microsecond or two, he'll be in the other place. And if it doesn't work at all, he'll just stay right here, with all of us feeling foolish for thinking we could wish our way through space."

"And if it turns out Jane can get him Outside but can't hold things together there, then he'll be stranded in a place that doesn't even have any placeness to it," said Valentine.

"Well, yes," said Grego. "If it works halfway, the passengers are effectively dead. But since we'll be in a place without time, it won't matter to us. It'll just be an eternal instant. Probably not enough time for our brains to notice that the experiment failed. Stasis."

"Of course, if it *works*," said Olhado, "then we'll carry our own spacetime with us, so there *would* be duration. Therefore, we'll never know if we fail. We'll only notice if we succeed."

"But *I'll* know if he never comes back," said Valentine.

"Right," said Grego. "If he never comes back, then you'll have a few months of knowing it until the fleet gets here and blasts everything and everybody all to hell."

"Or until the descolada turns everybody's genes inside out and kills us all," added Olhado.

"I suppose you're right," said Valentine. "Failure won't kill them any deader than they'll be if they stay."

"But you see the deadline pressure that we're under," said Grego. "We don't have much time left before Jane loses her ansible connections. Andrew says that she might well survive it after all—but she'll be crippled. Brain-damaged."

"So even if it works, the first flight might be the last."

"No," said Olhado. "The flights are *instantaneous*. If it works, she can shuttle everybody off this planet in no more time than it takes people to get in and out of the starship."

"You mean it can take off from a planet *surface*?"

"That's still iffy," said Grego. "She might only be able to calculate location within, say ten thousand kilometers. There's no explosion or displacement problem, since the philotes will reenter Inside space ready to obey natural laws again. But if the starship reappears in the middle of a planet it'll still be pretty hard to dig to the surface."

"But if she can be really precise—within a couple of centimeters, for instance—then the flights can be surface-to-surface," said Olhado.

"Of course we're dreaming," said Grego. "Jane's going to come back and tell us that even if she could turn all the stellar mass in the galaxy into computer chips, she couldn't hold all the data she'd have to know in order to make a starship travel this way. But at the moment, it still sounds possible and I am feeling *good*!"

At that, Grego and Olhado started whooping and laughing so loud that Mayor Kovano came to the door to make sure Valentine was all right. To her embarrassment, he caught her laughing and whooping right along with them.

"Are we happy, then?" asked Kovano.

"I guess," said Valentine, trying to recover her composure.

"Which of our many problems have we solved?"

"Probably none of them," said Valentine. "It would be too idiotically convenient if the universe could be manipulated to work this way."

"But you've thought of *something*."

"The metaphysical geniuses here have a completely unlikely possibility," said Valentine. "Unless you slipped them something really weird in their lunch."

Kovano laughed and left them alone. But his visit had had the effect of sobering them again.

"*Is* it possible?" asked Valentine.

"I would never have thought so," said Grego. "I mean, there's the problem of origin."

"It actually *answers* the problem of origin," said Olhado. "The Big Bang theory's been around since—"

"Since before *I* was born," said Valentine.

"I guess," said Olhado. "What nobody's been able to figure out is why a Big Bang would ever happen. This way it makes a weird kind of sense. If somebody who was capable of holding the pattern of the entire universe in his head stepped Outside, then all the philotes there would sort themselves out into the largest place in the pattern that they could control. Since there's no time there, they could take a billion years or a microsecond, all the time they needed, and then when it was sorted out, *bam*, there they are, the whole universe, popping out into a new Inside space. And since there's no distance or position—no whereness—then the entire thing would begin the size of a geometric point—"

"No size at *all*," said Grego.

"I remember my geometry," said Valentine.

"And immediately expand, creating space as it grew. As it grew, time would seem to slow down—or do I mean speed up?"

"It doesn't matter," said Grego. "It all depends whether you're Inside the new space or Outside or in some other Inspace."

"Anyway, the universe now seems to be constant in time while it's expanding in space. But if you wanted to, you could just as easily see it as constant in size but changing in *time*. The speed of light is slowing down so that it takes longer to get from one place to another, only we can't tell that it's slowing down because everything else slows down exactly relative to the speed of light. You see? All a matter of perspective. For that matter, as Grego said before, the universe we live in is still, in absolute terms, exactly the size of a geometric point—when you look at it from Outside. Any growth that seems to take place on the Inside is just a matter of relative location and time."

"And what kills me," said Grego, "is that this is the kind of thing that's been going on inside Olhado's head all these years. This picture of the universe as a dimensionless point in Outside space is the way he's been thinking all along. Not that he's the first to think of it. Just that he's the one who actually believed it and saw the connection between that and the non-place where Andrew says the hive queen goes to find aiúas."

"As long as we're playing metaphysical games," said Valentine, "then where did this whole thing begin? If what we think of as reality is just a pattern that somebody brought Outside, and the universe just popped into being, then whoever it was is probably still wandering around giving off universes wherever she goes. So where did *she* come from? And what was there before she started doing it? And how did Outside come to exist, for that matter?"

"That's Inspace thinking," said Olhado. "That's the way you conceive of things when you still believe in space and time as absolutes. You think of everything starting and stopping, of things having origins, because that's the way it is in the observable universe. The thing is, Outside there're no rules like that at all. Outside was always there and always will be there. The number of philotes there is infinite, and all of them always existed. No matter how many of them you pull out and put into organized universes, there'll be just as many left as there always were."

"But somebody had to *start* making universes."

"Why?" asked Olhado.

"Because—because I—"

"Nobody *ever* started. It's always been going on. I mean, if it weren't already going on, it *couldn't* start. Outside where there aren't any patterns, it would be impossible to conceive of a pattern. They *can't* act, by definition, because they literally can't even find themselves."

"But how could it always have been going on?"

"Think of it as if this moment in time, the reality we live in at this moment, this condition of the entire universe—of *all* the universes—"

"You mean *now*."

"Right. Think of it as if *now* were the surface of a sphere. Time is moving forward through the chaos of Outside like the surface of an expanding sphere, a balloon inflating. On the outside, chaos. On the inside, reality. Always growing—like you said, Valentine. Popping up new universes all the time."

"But where did this balloon come from?"

"OK, you've got the balloon. The expanding sphere. Only now think of it as a sphere with an infinite radius."

Valentine tried to think what that would mean. "The surface would be completely flat."

"That's right."

"And you could never go all the way around it."

"That's right, too. Infinitely large. Impossible even to count all the universes that exist on the reality side. And now, starting from the edge, you get on a starship and start heading inward toward the center. The farther in you go, the older everything is. All the old universes, back and back. When do you get to the first one?"

"You don't," said Valentine. "Not if you're traveling at a finite rate."

"You don't reach the center of a sphere of infinite radius, if you're starting at the surface, because no matter how far you go, no matter how quickly, the center, the beginning, is always infinitely far away."

"And that's where the universe began."

"I believe it," said Olhado. "I think it's true."

"So the universe works this way because it's always worked this way," said Valentine.

"Reality works this way because that's what reality is. Anything that doesn't work this way pops back into chaos. Anything that does, comes across into reality. The dividing line is always there."

"What I love," said Grego, "is the idea that after we've started tootling around at instantaneous speeds in *our* reality, what's to stop us from finding others? Whole new universes?"

"Or *making* others," said Olhado.

"Right," said Grego. "As if you or I could actually hold a pattern for a whole universe in our minds."

"But maybe *Jane* could," said Olhado. "Couldn't she?"

"What you're saying," said Valentine, "is that maybe Jane is God."

"She's probably listening right now," said Grego. "The computer's on, even if the display is blocked. I'll bet she's getting a kick out of this."

"Maybe every universe lasts long enough to produce something like Jane," said Valentine. "And then she goes out and creates more and—"

"It goes on and on," said Olhado. "Why not?"

"But she's an *accident*," said Valentine.

"No," said Grego. "That's one of the things Andrew found out today. You've got to talk to him. Jane was no accident. For all we know there *are* no accidents. For all we know, everything was all part of the pattern from the start."

"Everything except ourselves," said Valentine. "Our—what's the word for the philote that controls us?"

"Aiúa," said Grego. He spelled it out for her.

"Yes," she said. "Our *will*, anyway, which always existed, with whatever strengths and weaknesses it has. And that's why, as long as we're part of the pattern of reality, we're free."

"Sounds like the ethicist is getting into the act," said Olhado.

"This is probably complete bobagem," said Grego.

"Jane's going to come back laughing at us. But Nossa Senhora, it's *fun,* isn't it?"

"Hey, for all we know, maybe that's why the universe exists in the first place," said Olhado. "Because going around through chaos popping out realities is a lark. Maybe God's been having the best time."

"Or maybe he's just waiting for Jane to get out there and keep him company," said Valentine.

It was Miro's turn with Planter. Late—after midnight. Not that he could sit by him and hold his hand. Inside the cleanroom, Miro had to wear a suit, not to keep contamination out, but to keep the descolada virus he carried inside himself from getting to Planter.

If I just cracked my suit a little bit, thought Miro, I could save his life.

In the absence of the descolada, the breakdown of Planter's body was rapid and devastating. They all knew that the descolada had messed with the pequenino reproductive cycle, giving the pequeninos their third life as trees, but until now it hadn't been clear how much of their daily life depended on the descolada. Whoever designed this virus was a coldhearted monster of efficiency. Without the descolada's daily, hourly, *minutely* intervention, cells began to become sluggish, the production of vital energy-storing molecules stopped, and—what they feared most—the synapses of the brain fired less rapidly. Planter was rigged with tubes and electrodes, and he lay inside several scanning fields, so that from the outside Ela and her pequenino assistants could monitor every aspect of his dying. In addition, there were tissue samples every hour or so around the clock. His pain was so great that when he slept at all, the taking of tissue samples didn't wake him. And yet through all this—the pain, the quasi-stroke that was afflicting his brain—Planter remained doggedly lucid. As if he were determined by sheer force of will to prove that even without the descolada, a pequenino could be intelligent. Planter wasn't doing this for science, of course. He was doing it for dignity.

The real researchers couldn't spare time to take a shift as the inside worker, wearing the suit and just sitting there, watching him, talking to him. Only people like Miro, and Jakt's and Valentine's children—Syfte, Lars, Ro, Varsam—and the strange quiet woman Plikt; people who had no other urgent duties to attend to, who were patient enough to endure the waiting and young enough to handle their duties with precision—only such people were given shifts. They might have added a fellow pequenino to the shift, but all the brothers who knew enough about human technologies to do the job right were part of Ela's or Ouanda's teams, and had too much work to do. Of all those who spent time inside the cleanroom with him, taking tissue samples, feeding him, changing bottles, cleaning him up, only Miro had known pequeninos well enough to communicate with them. Miro could speak to him in Brothers' Language. That had to be of some comfort to him, even if they were virtual strangers, Planter having been born after Miro left Lusitania on his thirty-year voyage.

Planter was not asleep. His eyes were half-open, looking at nothing, but Miro knew from the movement of his lips that he was speaking. Reciting to himself passages from some of the epics of his tribe. Sometimes he chanted sections of the tribal genealogy. When he first started doing this, Ela had worried that he was becoming delirious. But he insisted that he was doing it to test his memory. To make sure that in losing the descolada he wasn't losing his tribe—which would be the same as losing himself.

Right now, as Miro turned up the volume inside his suit, he could hear Planter telling the story of some terrible war with the forest of Skysplitter, the "tree who called thunder." There was a digression in the middle of the war-story that told how Skysplitter got his name. This part of the tale sounded very old and mythic, a magical story about a brother who carried little mothers to the place where the sky fell open and the stars tumbled through onto the ground. Though Miro had been lost in his own thoughts about the day's discoveries—the origin of Jane, Grego's and Olhado's idea of travel-by-wish—for some reason he found himself paying close attention to the words that Planter was saying. And as the story ended, Miro had to interrupt.

"How old is that story?"

"Old," whispered Planter. "You were listening?"

"To the last part of it." It was all right to talk to Planter at length. Either he didn't grow impatient with the slowness of Miro's speech—after all, Planter wasn't going anywhere—or his own cognitive processes had slowed to match Miro's halting pace. Either way, Planter let Miro finish his own sentences, and answered him as if he had been listening carefully. "Did I understand you to say that this Skysplitter carried little mothers with him?"

"That's right," whispered Planter.

"But he wasn't going to the fathertree."

"No. He just had little mothers on his carries. I learned this story years ago. Before I did any human science."

"You know what it sounds like to me? That the story might come from a time when you didn't carry little mothers to the fathertree. When the little mothers didn't lick their sustenance from the sappy inside of the mothertree. Instead they hung from the carries on the male's abdomen until the infants matured enough to burst out and take their mothers' place at the teat."

"That's why I chanted it for you," said Planter. "I was trying to think of how it might have been, if we were intelligent *before* the descolada came. And finally I remembered that part in the story of Skysplitter's War."

"He went to the place where the sky broke open."

"The descolada got here somehow, didn't it?"

"How old is that story?"

"Skysplitter's War was twenty-nine generations ago. Our own forest isn't that old. But we carried songs and stories with us from our father-forest."

"The part of the story about the sky and the stars, that could be a lot older, though, couldn't it?"

"Very old. The fathertree Skysplitter died long ago. He might have been very old even when the war took place."

"Do you think it might be possible that this is a memory of the pequenino who first discovered the descolada? That it was brought here by a starship, and that what he saw was some kind of reentry vehicle?"

"That's why I chanted it."

"If that's true, then you were definitely intelligent before the coming of the descolada."

"All gone now," said Planter.

"What's all gone? I don't understand."

"Our genes of that time. Can't even guess what the descolada took away from us and threw out."

It was true. Each descolada virus might contain within itself the complete genetic code for every native life form on Lusitania, but that was only the genetic code as it was *now*, in its descolada-controlled state. What the code was before the descolada came could never be reconstructed or restored.

"Still," said Miro. "It's intriguing. To think that you already had language and songs and stories before the virus." And then, though he knew he shouldn't, he added, "Perhaps that makes it unnecessary for you to try to prove the independence of pequenino intelligence."

"Another attempt to save the piggy," said Planter.

A voice came over the speaker. A voice from outside the cleanroom.

"You can move on out now." It was Ela. She was supposed to be asleep during Miro's shift.

"My shift isn't over for three hours," said Miro.

"I've got somebody else coming in."

"There are plenty of suits."

"I need you out here, Miro." Ela's voice brooked no possibility of disobedience. And she was the scientist in charge of this experiment.

When he came out a few minutes later, he understood what was going on. Quara stood there, looking icy, and Ela was at least as furious. They had obviously been quarreling again—no surprise there. The surprise was that Quara was here at all.

"You might as well go back inside," said Quara as soon as Miro emerged from the sterilization chamber.

"I don't even know why I left," said Miro.

"She insists on having a *private* conversation," said Ela.

"She'll call *you* out," said Quara, "but she won't disconnect the auditory monitoring system."

"We're supposed to be documenting every moment of Planter's conversation. For lucidity."

Miro sighed. "Ela, grow up."

She almost exploded. "Me! Me grow up! She comes in here like she thinks she's Nossa Senhora on her throne—"

"Ela," said Miro. "Shut up and listen. Quara is Planter's only hope of living through this experiment. Can you honestly say that it wouldn't serve the purpose of this experiment to let her—"

"All right," said Ela, cutting him off because she already grasped his argument and bowed to it. "She's the enemy of every living sentient being on this planet, but I'll cut off the auditory monitoring because she wants to have a *private* conversation with the brother that she's killing."

That was too much for Quara. "You don't have to cut off anything for me," she said. "I'm sorry I came. It was a stupid mistake."

"Quara!" shouted Miro.

She stopped at the lab door.

"Get the suit on and go talk to Planter. What does *he* have to do with *her*?"

Quara glared once again at Ela, but she headed toward the sterilization room from which Miro had just emerged.

He felt greatly relieved. Since he knew that he had no authority at all, and that both of them were perfectly capable of telling him what he could do with his orders, the fact that they complied suggested that in fact they really *wanted* to comply. Quara really did want to speak to Planter. And Ela really did want her to do it. They might even be growing up enough to stop their personal differences from endangering other people's lives. There might be hope for this family yet.

"She'll just switch it back on as soon as I'm inside," said Quara.

"No she won't," said Miro.

"She'll try," said Quara.

Ela looked at her scornfully. "*I* know how to keep my word."

They said nothing more to each other. Quara went inside the sterilization chamber to dress. A few minutes later she was out in the cleanroom, still dripping from the descolada-killing solution that had been sprayed all over the suit as soon as she was inside it.

Miro could hear Quara's footsteps.

"Shut it off," he said.

Ela reached up and pushed a button. The footsteps went silent.

Inside his ear, Jane spoke to him. "Do you want me to play everything they say for you?"

He subvocalized. "You can still hear inside there?"

"The computer is linked to several monitors that are sensitive to vibration. I've picked up a few tricks about decoding human speech from the slightest vibrations. And the instruments are very sensitive."

"Go ahead then," said Miro.

"No moral qualms about invasion of privacy?"

"Not a one," said Miro. The survival of a world was at stake. And he had kept his word—the auditory monitoring equipment *was* off. Ela couldn't hear what was being said.

The conversation was nothing at first. How are you? Very sick. Much pain? Yes.

It was Planter who broke things out of the pleasant formalities and into the heart of the issue.

"Why do you want all my people to be slaves?"

Quara sighed—but, to her credit, it didn't sound petulant. To Miro's practiced ear, it sounded as though she were really emotionally torn. Not at all the defiant face she showed to her family. "I don't," she said.

"Maybe you didn't forge the chains, but you hold the key and refuse to use it."

"The descolada isn't a chain," she said. "A chain is a nothing. The descolada is alive."

"So am I. So are all my people. Why is *their* life more important than ours?"

"The descolada doesn't kill you. Your enemy is Ela and my mother. They're the ones who would kill all of you in order to keep the descolada from killing them."

"Of course," said Planter. "Of course they would. As I would kill all of them to protect *my* people."

"So your quarrel isn't with me."

"Yes it is. Without what you know, humans and pequeninos will end up killing each other, one way or another. They'll have no choice. As long as the descolada can't be tamed, it will eventually destroy humanity or humanity will have to destroy it—and us along with it."

"They'll never destroy it," said Quara.

"Because you won't let them."

"Any more than I'd let them destroy you. Sentient life is sentient life."

"No," said Planter. "With ramen you can live and let live. But with varelse, there can be no dialogue. Only war."

"No such thing," Quara said. Then she launched into the same arguments she had used when Miro talked to her.

When she was finished, there was silence for a while.

"Are they talking still?" Ela whispered to the people who were watching in the visual monitors. Miro didn't hear an answer—somebody probably shook his head no.

"Quara," whispered Planter.

"I'm still here," she answered. To her credit, the argumentative tone was gone from her voice again. She had taken no joy from her cruel moral correctness.

"That's not why you're refusing to help," he said.

"Yes it is."

"You'd help in a minute if it weren't your own family you had to surrender to."

"*Not* true!" she shouted.

So—Planter struck a nerve.

"You're only so sure you're right because they're so sure you're wrong."

"I *am* right!"

"When have you ever seen someone who had *no* doubts who was also correct about anything?"

"I have doubts," whispered Quara.

"Listen to your doubts," said Planter. "Save my people. And yours."

"Who am I to decide between the descolada and our people?"

"Exactly," said Planter. "Who are you to make such a decision?"

"I'm not," she said. "I'm withholding a decision."

"You know what the descolada can do. You know what it *will* do. Withholding a decision *is* a decision."

"It's not a decision. It's not an *action*."

"Failing to try to stop a murder that you might easily stop—how is that not murder?"

"Is this why you wanted to see me? One more person telling me what to do?"

"I have the right."

"Because you took it upon yourself to become a martyr and die?"

"I haven't lost my mind yet," said Planter.

"Right. You've proved your point. Now let them get the descolada back in here and save you."

"No."

"Why not? Are you so sure you're right?"

"For my own life, I can decide. I'm not like you—I don't decide for others to die."

"If humanity dies, I die with them," said Quara.

"Do you know why I want to die?" said Planter.

"Why?"

"So I don't have to watch humans and pequeninos kill each other ever again."

Quara bowed her head.

"You and Grego—you're both the same."

Tears dropped onto the faceplate of the suit. "That's a lie."

"You both refuse to listen to anybody else. You know better about everything. And when you're both done, many many innocent people are dead."

She stood up as if to go. "Die, then," she said. "Since I'm such a murderer, why should I cry over you?" But she didn't take a step. She doesn't want to go, thought Miro.

"Tell them," said Planter.

She shook her head, so vigorously that tears flipped outward from her eyes, spattering the inside of the mask. If she kept that up, soon she wouldn't be able to see a thing.

"If you tell what you know, everybody is wiser. If you keep a secret, then everyone is a fool."

"If I tell, the descolada will die!"

"Then let it!" cried Planter.

The exertion was an extraordinary drain on him. The instruments in the lab went crazy for a few moments. Ela muttered under her breath as she checked with each of the technicians monitoring them.

"Is that how you'd like me to feel about you?" asked Quara.

"It *is* how you feel about me," whispered Planter. "Let him die."

"No," she said.

"The descolada came and enslaved my people. So what if it's sentient or not! It's a tyrant. It's a murderer. If a human being behaved the way the descolada acts, even you would agree he had to be stopped, even if killing him were the only way. Why should another species be treated more leniently than a member of your own?"

"Because the descolada doesn't know what it's doing," said Quara. "It doesn't understand that we're intelligent."

"It doesn't *care*," said Planter. "Whoever made the descolada sent it out not caring whether the species it captures or kills are sentient or not. Is that the creature you want all my people and all your people to die for? Are you so filled with hate for your family that you'll be on the side of a monster like the descolada?"

Quara had no answer. She sank onto the stool beside Planter's bed.

Planter reached out a hand and rested it on her shoulder. The suit was not so thick and impermeable that she couldn't feel the pressure of it, even though he was very weak.

"For myself, I don't mind dying," he said. "Maybe because of the third life, we pequeninos don't have the same fear of death that you short-lived humans do. But even though I won't have the third life, Quara, I *will* have the kind of immortality you humans have. My name will live in the stories. Even if I have no tree at all, my name will live. And what I did. You humans can say that I'm choosing to be a martyr for nothing, but my brothers understand. By staying clear and intelligent to the end, I prove that they are who they are. I help show that our slavemasters didn't make us who we are, and can't stop us from being who we are. The descolada may force us to do many things, but it doesn't own us to the very center. Inside us there is a place that is our true self. So I don't mind dying. I will live forever in every pequenino that is free."

"Why are you saying this when only I can hear?" said Quara.

"Because only you have the power to kill me completely. Only you have the power to make it so my death means nothing, so that all my people die after me and there's no one left to remember. Why shouldn't I leave my testament with you alone? Only you will decide whether or not it has any worth."

"I hate you for this," she said. "I knew you'd do this."

"Do what?"

"Make me feel so terrible that I have to—give *in*!"

"If you knew I'd do this, why did you come?"

"I shouldn't have! I wish I hadn't!"

"I'll tell you why you came. You came so that I *would* make you give in. So that when you did it, you'd be doing it for my sake, and not for your family."

"So I'm your puppet?"

"Just the opposite. You chose to come here. You are using *me* to make you do what you really want to do. At heart you are still human, Quara. You want your people to live. You would be a monster if you didn't."

"Just because you're dying doesn't make you wise," she said.

"Yes it does," said Planter.

"What if I tell you that I'll *never* cooperate in the killing of the descolada?"

"Then I'll believe you," said Planter.

"And hate me."

"Yes," said Planter.

"You can't."

"Yes I can. I'm not a very good Christian. I am not able to love the one who chooses to kill me and all my people."

She said nothing.

"Go away now," he said. "I've said all that I can say. Now I want to chant my stories and keep myself intelligent until death finally comes."

She walked away from him, into the sterilization chamber.

Miro turned toward Ela. "Get everybody out of the lab," he said.

"Why?"

"Because there's a chance that she'll come out and tell you what she knows."

"Then *I* should be the one to go, and everybody else stay," said Ela.

"No," said Miro. "You're the only one that she'll ever tell."

"If you think *that,* then you're a complete—"

"Telling anyone else wouldn't hurt her enough to satisfy her," said Miro. "Everybody out."

Ela thought for a moment. "All right," she said to the others. "Get back to the main lab and monitor your computers. I'll bring us up on the net if she tells me anything, and you can see what she enters as we put it in. If you can make sense of what you're seeing, start following it up. Even if she actually knows anything, we still won't have much time to design a truncated descolada so we can get it to Planter before he dies. Go."

They went.

When Quara emerged from the sterilization chamber, she found only Ela and Miro waiting for her.

"I still think it's wrong to kill the descolada before we've even tried to talk to it," she said.

"It may well be," said Ela. "I only know that I intend to do it if I can."

"Bring up your files," said Quara. "I'm going to tell you everything I know about descolada intelligence. If it works and Planter lives through this, I'm going to spit in his face."

"Spit a thousand times," said Ela. "Just so he lives."

Her files came up into the display. Quara began pointing to certain regions of the model of the descolada virus. Within a few minutes, it was Quara sitting before the terminal, typing, pointing, talking, as Ela asked questions.

In his ear, Jane spoke up again. "The little bitch," she said. "She didn't have her files in another computer. She kept everything she knew inside her head."

By late afternoon the next day, Planter was at the edge of death and Ela was at the edge of exhaustion. Her team had worked through the night; Quara had helped, constantly, indefatigably reading over everything Ela's people came up with, critiquing, pointing out errors. By midmorning, they had a plan for a truncated virus that should work. All of the language capability was gone, which meant the new viruses wouldn't be able to communicate with each other. All the analytical ability was gone as well, as near as they could tell. But safely in place were all the parts of the virus that supported bodily functions in the native species of Lusitania. As near as they could possibly tell without having a working sample of the virus, the new design was exactly what was needed—a descolada that was completely functional in the life cycles of the Lusitanian species, including the pequeninos, yet completely incapable of global regulation and manipulation. They named the new virus *recolada*. The old one had been named for its function of tearing apart; the new one for its remaining function, holding together the species-pairs that made up the native life of Lusitania.

Ender raised one objection—that since the descolada must have been putting the pequeninos into a belligerent, expansive mode, the new virus might lock them into that particular condition. But Ela and Quara answered together that they had deliberately used an older version of the descolada as their model, from a time when the pequeninos were more relaxed—more "themselves." The pequeninos working on the project had agreed to this; there was little time to consult anyone else except Human and Rooter, who also concurred.

With the things that Quara had taught them about the workings of the descolada, Ela also had a team working on a killer bacterium that would spread quickly through the entire planet's gaialogy, finding the normal descolada in every place and every form, tearing it to bits and killing it. It would recognize the old descolada by the very elements that the new descolada would lack. Releasing the recolada and the killer bacterium at the same time should do the job.

There was only one problem remaining—actually making the new virus. That was Ela's direct project from midmorning on. Quara collapsed and slept. So did most of the pequeninos. But Ela struggled on, trying to use all the tools she had to break apart the virus and recombine it as she needed.

But when Ender came late in the afternoon to tell her that it was now or never, if her virus was to save

Planter, she could only break down and weep from exhaustion and frustration.

"I can't," she said.

"Then tell him that you've achieved it but you can't get it ready in time and—"

"I mean it can't be done."

"You've designed it."

"We've planned it, we've modeled it, yes. But it can't be *made*. The descolada is a really vicious design. We can't build it from scratch because there are too many parts that can't hold together unless you have those very sections already working to keep rebuilding each other as they break down. And we can't do modifications of the present virus unless the descolada is at least marginally active, in which case it undoes what we're doing faster than we can do it. It was designed to police itself constantly so it can't be altered, and to be so unstable in all its parts that it's completely unmakable."

"But *they* made it."

"Yes, but I don't know *how*. Unlike Grego, I can't completely step outside my science on some metaphysical whim and make things up and wish them into existence. I'm stuck with the rules of nature as they are here and now, and there's no rule that will let me make it."

"So we know where we need to go, but we can't get there from here."

"Until last night I didn't know enough to guess whether we could design this new recolada or not, and therefore I had no way of guessing whether we could make it. I figured that if it was designable, it was makable. I was ready to make it, ready to act the moment Quara relented. All we've achieved is to know, finally, completely, that it can't be done. Quara was right. We definitely found out enough from her to enable us to kill every descolada virus on Lusitania. But we can't make the recolada that could replace it and keep Lusitanian life functioning."

"So if we use the viricide bacterium—"

"All the pequeninos in the world would be where Planter is now within a week or two. And all the grass and birds and vines and everything. Scorched earth. An atrocity. Quara was right." She wept again.

"You're just tired." It was Quara, awake now and looking terrible, not refreshed at all by her sleep.

Ela, for her part, couldn't answer her sister.

Quara looked like she might be thinking of saying something cruel, along the lines of *What did I tell you?* But she thought better of it, and came and put her hand on Ela's shoulder. "You're tired, Ela. You need to sleep."

"Yes," said Ela.

"But first let's tell Planter."

"Say good-bye, you mean."

"Yes, that's what I mean."

They made their way to the lab that contained Planter's cleanroom. The pequenino researchers who had slept were awake again; all had joined the vigil for Planter's last hours. Miro was inside with Planter again, and this time they didn't make him leave, though Ender knew that both Ela and Quara longed to be inside with him. Instead they both spoke to him over the speakers, explaining what they had found. The half-success that was worse, in its way, than complete failure, because it could easily lead to the destruction of all the pequeninos, if the humans of Lusitania became desperate enough.

"You won't use it," whispered Planter. The microphones, sensitive as they were, could barely pick up his voice.

"*We* won't," said Quara. "But we're not the only people here."

"You won't use it," he said. "I'm the only one who'll ever die like this."

The last of his words were voiceless; they read his

lips later, from the holo recording, to be sure of what he said. And, having said it, having heard their good-byes, he died.

The moment the monitoring machines confirmed his death, the pequeninos of the research group rushed into the cleanroom. No need for sterilization now. They *wanted* the descolada with them. Brusquely moving Miro out of the way, they set to work, injecting the virus into every part of Planter's body, hundreds of injections in moments. They had been preparing for this, obviously. They would respect Planter's sacrifice in life—but once he was dead, his honor satisfied, they had no compunctions about trying to save him for the third life if they could.

They took him out into the open space where Human and Rooter stood, and laid him on a spot already marked, forming an equilateral triangle with those two young fathertrees. There they flayed his body and staked it open. Within hours a tree was growing, and there was hope, briefly, that it might be a fathertree. But it took only a few days more for the brothers, who were adept at recognizing a young fathertree, to declare that the effort had failed. There was a kind of life, containing his genes, yes; but the memories, the will, the person who was Planter was lost. The tree was mute; there would be no mind joining the perpetual conclave of the fathertrees. Planter had determined to free himself of the descolada, even if it meant losing the third life that was the descolada's gift to those it possessed. He succeeded, and, in losing, won.

He had succeeded in something else, too. The pequeninos departed from their normal pattern of forgetting quickly the name of mere brothertrees. Though no little mother would ever crawl its bark, the brothertree that had grown from his corpse would be known by the name of Planter and treated with respect, as if it were a fathertree, as if it were a person. Moreover, his story was told and told again throughout Lusitania, wherever pequeninos lived. He had proved that pequeninos were intelligent even without the descolada; it was a noble sacrifice, and speaking the name of Planter was a reminder to all pequeninos of their fundamental freedom from the virus that had put them in bondage.

But Planter's death did not give any pause to the preparations for pequenino colonization of other worlds. Warmaker's people had a majority now, and as rumors spread that the humans had a bacterium capable of killing all the descolada, they had an even greater urgency. Hurry, they told the hive queen again and again. Hurry, so we can win free of this world before the humans decide to kill us all.

"I can do it, I think," said Jane. "If the ship is small and simple, the cargo almost nothing, the crew as few as possible, then I can hold the pattern of it in my mind. If the voyage is brief, the stay in Outspace very short. As for holding the locations of the start and finish in my mind, that's easy, child's play, I can do it within a millimeter, less. If I slept, I could do it in my sleep. So there's no need for it to endure acceleration or provide extended life support. The starship can be simple. A sealed environment, places to sit, light, heat. If in fact we can get there and I can hold it all together and bring us back, then we won't be out in space long enough to use up the oxygen in a small room."

They were all gathered in the Bishop's office to listen to her—the whole Ribeira family, Jakt's and Valentine's family, the pequenino researchers, several priests and Filhos, and perhaps a dozen other leaders of the human colony. The Bishop had insisted on having the meeting in his office. "Because it's large enough," he had said, "and because if you're going to go out like Nimrod and hunt before the Lord, if you're going to send a ship like Babel out to heaven to seek the face of God, then I want to be there to plead with God to be merciful to you."

"How much of your capacity is left?" Ender asked Jane.

"Not much," she said. "As it is, every computer in the Hundred Worlds will be sluggish while we do it, as I use their memory to hold the pattern."

"I ask, because we want to try to perform an experiment while we're out there."

"Don't waffle about it, Andrew," said Ela. "We want to perform a miracle while we're there. If we get Outside it means that Grego and Olhado are probably right about what it's like out there. And that means that the rules are different. Things can be created just by comprehending the pattern of them. So I want to go. There's a chance that while I'm there, holding the pattern of the recolada virus in my mind, I might be able to create it. I might be able to bring back a virus that can't be made in realspace. Can you take me? Can you hold me there long enough to make the virus?"

"How long is that?" asked Jane.

"It should be instantaneous," said Grego. "The moment we arrive, whatever full patterns we hold in our minds should be created within a period of time too brief for humans to notice. The real time will be taken analyzing to see if, in fact, she's got the virus she wanted. Maybe five minutes."

"Yes," said Jane. "If I can do this at all, I can do it for five minutes."

"The rest of the crew," said Ender.

"The rest of the crew will be you and Miro," said Jane. "And no one else."

Grego protested loudest, but he was not alone.

"I'm a pilot," said Jakt.

"*I'm* the only pilot of this ship," said Jane.

"Olhado and I thought of it," said Grego.

"Ender and Miro will come because it can't be done safely without them. I dwell within Ender—where he goes, he carries me with him. Miro, on the other hand, has become so close to me that I think he might be part of the pattern that is myself. I want him there because I may not be whole without him. No one else. I can't have anyone else in the pattern. Ela is the only one beyond these two."

"Then that's the crew," said Ender.

"With no argument," added Mayor Kovano.

"Will the hive queen build the ship?" asked Jane.

"She will," said Ender.

"Then I have only one more favor to ask. Ela, if I can give you the five minutes, can you also hold the pattern of another virus in your mind?"

"The virus for Path?" she asked.

"We owe them that, if we can, for the help they gave to us."

"I think so," she said, "or at least the differences between it and the normal descolada. That's all I can possibly hold of *anything*—the differences."

"And how soon will all this happen?" asked the Mayor.

"However fast the hive queen can build the ship," said Jane. "We have only forty-eight days until the Hundred Worlds shut down their ansibles. I will survive that day, we know that now, but it will cripple me. It will take me awhile to relearn all my lost memories, if I ever can. Until that's happened, I can't possibly sustain the pattern of a ship to go Outside."

"The hive queen can have a ship as simple as this one built long before then," said Ender. "In a ship so small there's no chance of shuttling all the people and pequeninos off Lusitania before the fleet arrives, let alone before the ansible cut-off keeps Jane from being able to fly the ship. But there'll be time to take new, descolada-free pequenino communities—a brother, a wife, and many pregnant little mothers—to a dozen planets and establish them there. Time to take new hive queens in their cocoons, already fertilized to lay their first few hundred eggs, to a dozen worlds as well. If this works at all, if we don't just sit there like idiots in a cardboard box wishing we could fly, then we'll come back with peace for this world, freedom from the danger of the descolada, and safe dispersal for the genetic heritage of the other species of ramen here. A week ago, it looked impossible. Now there's hope."

"Graças a deus," said the Bishop.

Quara laughed.

Everyone looked at her.

"I'm sorry," she said. "I was just thinking—I heard a prayer, not many weeks ago. A prayer to Os Venerados, Grandfather Gusto and Grandmother Cida. That if there wasn't a way to solve the impossible problems facing us, they would petition God to open up the way."

"Not a bad prayer," said the Bishop. "And perhaps God has granted it."

"I know," said Quara. "That's what I was thinking. What if all this stuff about Outspace and Inspace, what if it was never real before. What if it only came to be true *because* of that prayer?"

"What of it?" asked the Bishop.

"Well, don't you think that would be funny?"

Apparently no one did.

16

VOYAGE

<So the humans have their starship ready *now*, while the one you've been building for us is still incomplete.>

<The one they wanted was a box with a door. No propulsion, no life support, no cargo space. Yours and ours are far more complicated. We haven't slacked, and they'll be ready soon.>

<I'm really not complaining. I wanted Ender's ship to be ready first. It's the one that carries real hope.>

<For us as well. We agree with Ender and his people that the descolada must never be killed here on Lusitania, unless the recolada can somehow be made. But when we send new hive queens to other worlds, we'll kill the descolada on the starship that takes them, so there's no chance of polluting our new home. So that we can live without fear of destruction from this artificial varelse.>

<What you do on *your* ship is nothing to us.>

<With any luck, none of this will matter. Their new

starship will find its way Outside, return with the recolada, set you free and us as well, and then the new ship will shuttle us all to as many worlds as we desire.>

<*Will* it work? The box you made for them?>

<We know the place where they're going is real; we call our very selves from there. And the bridge we made, the one that Ender calls Jane, is such a pattern as we've never seen before. If it can be done, such a one as that can do it. *We* never could.>

<Will *you* leave? If the new ship works?>

<We'll make daughter-queens who'll take my memories with them to other worlds. But we ourselves will stay here. This place where I came forth from my cocoon, it's my home forever.>

<So you're as rooted here as I am.>

<That's what daughters are for. To go where we will never go, to carry our memory on to places that we'll never see.>

<But we *will* see. Won't we? You said the philotic connection would remain.>

<We were thinking of the voyage across time. We live a long time, we hives, you trees. But our daughters and their daughters will outlive us. Nothing changes that.>

Qing-jao listened to them as they laid the choice before her.

"Why should I care what you decide?" she said, when they were finished. "The gods will laugh at you."

Father shook his head. "No they won't, my daughter, Gloriously Bright. The gods care nothing more for Path than any other world. The people of Lusitania are on the verge of creating a virus that can free us all. No more rituals, no more bondage to the disorder in our brains. So I ask you again, if we *can* do it, should we? It would cause disorder here. Wang-mu and I have planned how we'll proceed, how we'll announce what we are doing so that people will understand it, so there'll be a chance that the godspoken won't be slaughtered, but can step down gently from their privileges."

"Privileges are nothing," said Qing-jao. "You taught me that yourself. They're only the people's way of expressing their reverence for the gods."

"Alas, my daughter, if only I knew that more of the godspoken shared that humble view of our station. Too many of them think that it's their right to be acquisitive and oppressive, because the gods speak to them and not to others."

"Then the gods will punish them. I'm not afraid of your virus."

"But you are, Qing-jao, I see it."

"How can I tell my father that he does not see what he claims to see? I can only say that *I* must be blind."

"Yes, my Qing-jao, you are. Blind on purpose. Blind to your own heart. Because you tremble even now. You have never been sure that I was wrong. From the time Jane showed us the true nature of the speaking of the gods, you've been unsure of what was true."

"Then I'm unsure of sunrise. I'm unsure of breath."

"We're all unsure of breath, and the sun stays in its same place, day and night, neither rising nor falling. We are the ones who rise and fall."

"Father, I fear nothing from this virus."

"Then our decision is made. If the Lusitanians can bring us the virus, we'll use it."

Han Fei-tzu got up to leave her room.

But her voice stopped him before he reached the door. "Is this the disguise the punishment of the gods will take, then?"

"What?" he asked.

"When they punish Path for your iniquity in working against the gods who have given their mandate to Congress, will they disguise their punishment by making it seem to be a virus that silences them?"

"I wish dogs had torn my tongue out before I taught you to think that way."

"Dogs already are tearing at my heart," Qing-jao answered him. "Father, I beg you, don't do this. Don't let your rebelliousness provoke the gods into falling silent across the whole face of this world."

"I *will*, Qing-jao, so no more daughters or sons have to grow up slaves as you have been. When I think of your face pressed close to the floor, tracing the woodgrain, I want to cut the bodies of those who forced this thing upon you, cut them until *their* blood makes lines, which *I* will gladly trace, to know that they've been punished."

She wept. "Father, I beg you, don't provoke the gods."

"More than ever now I'm determined to release the virus, if it comes."

"What can I do to persuade you? If I say nothing, you will do it, and when I speak to beg you, you will do it all the more surely."

"Do you know how you could stop me? You could speak to me as if you knew the speaking of the gods is the product of a brain disorder, and then, when I know you see the world clear and true, you could persuade me with good arguments that such a swift, complete, and devastating change would be harmful, or whatever other argument you might raise."

"So to persuade my father, I must lie to him?"

"No, my Gloriously Bright. To persuade your father, you must show that you understand the truth."

"I understand the truth," said Qing-jao. "I understand that some enemy has stolen you from me. I understand that all I have left now is the gods, and Mother who is among them. I beg the gods to let me die and join her, so I don't have to suffer any more of the pain you cause me, but still they leave me here. I think that means they wish me still to worship them. Perhaps I'm not yet purified enough. Or perhaps they know that you will soon turn your heart around again, and come to me as you used to, speaking honorably of the gods and teaching me to be a true servant."

"That will never happen," said Han Fei-tzu.

"Once I thought you could someday be the god of Path. Now I see that, far from being the protector of this world, you are its darkest enemy."

Han Fei-tzu covered his face and left the room, weeping for his daughter. He could never persuade her as long as she heard the voice of the gods. But perhaps if they brought the virus, perhaps if the gods fell silent, she would listen to him then. Perhaps he could win her back to rationality.

They sat in the starship—more like two metal bowls, one domed over the other, with a door in the side. Jane's design, faithfully executed by the hive queen and her workers, included many instruments on the outside of the ship. But even bristling with sensors it didn't resemble any kind of starship ever seen before. It was far too small, and there was no visible means of propulsion. The only power that could carry this ship anywhere was the unseeable aiúa that Ender carried on board with him.

They faced each other in a circle. There were six chairs, because Jane's design allowed for the chance that the ship would be used again, to carry more people from world to world. They had taken every other seat, so they formed a triangle: Ender, Miro, Ela.

The good-byes had all been said. Sisters and brothers, other kin and many friends had come. One, though, was most painful in her absence. Novinha. Ender's wife, Miro's and Ela's mother. She would have no part of this. That was the only real sorrow at the parting.

The rest was all fear and excitement, hope and disbelief. They might be moments away from death. They might be moments away from filling the vials on Ela's lap with the viruses that would mean deliverance on two worlds. They might be the pioneers of a new kind of starflight that would save the species threatened by the M.D. Device.

They might also be three fools who would sit on the ground, in a grassy field just outside the compound of the human colony on Lusitania, until at last it grew so hot and stuffy inside that they had to emerge. No one waiting there would laugh, of course, but there'd be laughter throughout the town. It would be the laughter of despair. It would mean that there was no escape, no liberty, only more and more fear until death came in one of its many possible guises.

"Are you with us, Jane?" asked Ender.

The voice in his ear was quiet. "While I do this, Ender, I'll have no part of me that I can spare to talk to you."

"So you'll be with us, but mute," said Ender. "How will I know you're there?"

She laughed softly in his ear. "Foolish boy, Ender. If you're still there, I'm still inside you. And if I'm not inside you, you will have no 'there' to be."

Ender imagined himself breaking into a trillion constituent parts, scattering through chaos. Personal survival depended not only on Jane holding the pattern of the ship, but also on him being able to hold the pattern of his mind and body. Only he had no idea whether his mind was really strong enough to maintain that pattern, once he was where the laws of nature were not in force.

"Ready?" asked Jane.

"She asks if we're ready," said Ender.

Miro was already nodding. Ela bowed her head. Then, after a moment, she crossed herself, took firm hold on the rack of vials on her lap, and nodded.

"If we go and come again, Ela," said Ender, "then this was *not* a failure, even if you didn't create the virus that you wanted. If the ship works well, we can return another time. Don't think that everything depends on what you're able to imagine today."

She smiled. "I won't be surprised at failure, but I'm also ready for success. My team is ready to release hundreds of bacteria into the world, if I return with the recolada and we can then remove the descolada. It will be chancy, but within fifty years the world will be a self-regulating gaialogy again. I see a vision of deer and cattle in the tall grass of Lusitania, and eagles in the sky." Then she looked down again at the vials in her lap. "I also said a prayer to the Virgin, for the same Holy Ghost that created God in her womb to come make life again here in these jars."

"Amen to the prayer," said Ender. "And now, Jane, if *you're* ready, we can go."

Outside the little starship, the others waited. What did they expect? That the ship would start to smoke and jiggle? That there would be a thunderclap, a flash of light?

The ship was there. It was there, and still there, unmoving, unchanged. And then it was gone.

They felt nothing inside the ship when it happened. There was no sound, no movement to hint of motion from Inspace into Outspace.

But they knew the moment it occurred, because there were no longer three of them, but six.

Ender found himself seated between two people, a young man and a young woman. But he had no time even to glance at them, for all he could look at was the man seated in what had been the empty seat across from him.

"Miro," he whispered. For that was who it was. But not Miro the cripple, the damaged young man who had boarded the ship with him. *That* one was still sitting in the next chair to Ender's left. This Miro was the strong young man that Ender had first known. The man whose strength had been the hope of his family, whose beauty had been the pride of Ouanda's life, whose mind and whose heart had taken compassion on the pequeninos and refused to leave them without the benefits he thought that human culture might offer them. Miro, whole and restored.

Where had he come from?

"I should have known," said Ender. "We should have thought. The pattern of yourself that you hold in your mind, Miro—it isn't the way you *are,* it's the way you *were.*"

The new Miro, the young Miro, he raised his head and smiled to Ender. "I thought of it," he said, and his speech was clear and beautiful, the words rolling easily off his tongue. "I hoped for it. I begged Jane to take me with her because of it. And it came true. Exactly as I longed for it."

"But now there are two of you," said Ela. She sounded horrified.

"No," said the new Miro. "Just me. Just the *real* me."

"But that one's still there," she said.

"Not for long, I think," said Miro. "That old shell is empty now."

And it was true. The old Miro slumped within his seat like a dead man. Ender knelt in front of him, touched him. He pressed his fingers to Miro's neck, feeling for a pulse.

"Why should the heart beat now?" said Miro. "*I'm* the place where Miro's aiúa dwells."

When Ender took his fingers away from the old Miro's throat, the skin came away in a small puff of dust. Ender shied back. The head dropped forward off the shoulders and landed in the corpse's lap. Then it dissolved into a whitish liquid. Ender jumped to his feet, backed away. He stepped on someone's toe.

"Ow," said Valentine.

"Watch where you're going," said a man.

Valentine isn't on this ship, thought Ender. And I know the man's voice, too.

He turned to face them, the man and woman who had appeared in the empty seats beside him.

Valentine. Impossibly young. The way she had looked when, as a young teenager, she had swum beside him in a lake on a private estate on Earth. The way she had looked when he loved her and needed her most, when she was the only reason he could think of to go on with his military training; when she was the only reason he could think of why the world might be worth the trouble of saving it.

"You can't be real," he said.

"Of course I am," she said. "You stepped on my foot, didn't you?"

"Poor Ender," said the young man. "Clumsy *and* stupid. Not a really good combination."

Now Ender knew him. "Peter," he said. His brother, his childhood enemy, at the age when he became Hegemon. The picture that had been playing on all the vids when Peter managed to arrange things so that Ender could never come home to Earth after his great victory.

"I thought I'd never see you face to face again," said Ender. "You died so long ago."

"Never believe a rumor of my death," said Peter. "I have as many lives as a cat. Also as many teeth, as many claws, and the same cheery, cooperative disposition."

"Where did you come from?"

Miro offered the answer. "They must have come from patterns in *your* mind, Ender, since you know them."

"They do," said Ender. "But why? It's our *self*-conception we're supposed to carry with us out here. The pattern by which we know ourselves."

"Is that so, Ender?" said Peter. "Then you must be really special. A personality so complicated it takes two people to contain it."

"There's no part of me in you," said Ender.

"And you'd better keep it that way," said Peter, leering. "It's girls I like, not dirty old men."

"I don't want you," said Ender.

"Nobody ever did," said Peter. "They wanted *you*. But they *got* me, didn't they? They got me up to *here*. Do you think I don't know my whole story? You and that book of lies, the Hegemon. So wise and understanding. How Peter Wiggin mellowed. How he turned out to be a wise and fair-minded ruler. What a joke. Speaker for the Dead indeed. All the time you wrote it, you knew the truth. You posthumously washed the blood from my hands, Ender, but you knew and I knew that as long as I was alive, I wanted blood there."

"Leave him alone," said Valentine. "He told the truth in the Hegemon."

"Still protecting him, little angel?"

"No!" cried Ender. "I've done with you, Peter. You're out of my life, gone for three thousand years."

"You can run but you can't *hide*!"

"Ender! Ender, stop it! Ender!"

He turned. It was Ela crying out to him.

"I don't know what's going on here, but stop it! We only have a few minutes left. Help me with the tests."

She was right. Whatever was going on with Miro's new body, with Peter's and Valentine's reappearance here, the important thing was the descolada. Had Ela succeeded in transforming it? Creating the recolada? And the virus that would transform the people of Path? If Miro could remake his body, and Ender could somehow conjure up the ghosts of his past and make them flesh again, it was possible, really *possible*, that Ela's vials now contained the viruses whose patterns she had held in her mind.

"Help me," whispered Ela again.

Ender and Miro—the new Miro, his hand strong and sure—reached out, took the vials she offered them, and began the test. It was a negative test—if the bacteria, algae, and tiny worms they added to the tubes remained for several minutes, unaffected, then there was no descolada in the vials. Since the vials *had* been teeming with the living virus when they boarded the ship, that would be proof that *something,* at least, had happened to neutralize them. Whether it was truly the recolada or simply a dead or ineffective descolada remained to be discovered when they returned.

The worms and algae and bacteria underwent no transformations. In tests beforehand, on Lusitania, the solution containing the bacteria turned from blue to yellow in the presence of the descolada; now it stayed blue. On Lusitania the tiny worms had quickly died and, graying husks, floated to the surface; now they wriggled on and on, staying the purplish-brown color that in them, at least, meant life. And the algae, instead of breaking apart and dissolving completely away, remained in the thin strands and tendrils of life.

"Done, then," said Ender.

"At least we can hope," said Ela.

"Sit down," said Miro. "If we're done, she'll take us back."

Ender sat. He looked at the seat where Miro *had* been sitting. His old crippled body was no longer identifiably human. It continued crumbling, the pieces breaking up into dust or flowing away as liquid. Even the clothing was dissolving into nothing.

"It's not part of my pattern anymore," said Miro. "There's nothing to hold it together anymore."

"What about *these*?" demanded Ender. "Why aren't *they* dissolving?"

"Or you?" asked Peter. "Why don't *you* dissolve? Nobody needs you now. You're a tired old fart who can't even hold onto his woman. And you never even fathered a child, you pathetic old eunuch. Make way for a real man. No one ever needed *you*—everything you've ever done I could have done better, and everything *I* did you never could have matched."

Ender buried his face in his hands. This was not an

outcome he could have imagined in his worst nightmares. Yes, he knew they were going out into a place where things might be created out of his mind. But it had never occurred to him that *Peter* was still lingering there. He thought he had expunged that old hatred long ago.

And Valentine—why would he create another Valentine? This one so young and perfect, sweet and beautiful? There was a real Valentine waiting for him back on Lusitania—what would she think, seeing what he created out of his own mind? Perhaps it would be flattering to know how closely she was held in his heart; but she would also know that what he treasured was what she used to be, not what she was now.

The darkest and the brightest secrets of his heart would both stand exposed as soon as the door opened and he had to step back out onto the surface of Lusitania again.

"Dissolve," he said to them. "Crumble away."

"*You* do it first, old man," said Peter. "Your life is *over*, and mine is just beginning. All I had to try for the first time was Earth, one tired old planet—it was as easy as it would be for me to reach out and kill you with my bare hands, right now, if I wanted to. Snap your little neck like a dry noodle."

"Try it," whispered Ender. "I'm not the frightened little boy anymore."

"Nor are you a match for me," said Peter. "You never were, you never will be. You have too much heart. You're like Valentine. You flinch away from doing what has to be done. It makes you soft and weak. It makes you easy to destroy."

A sudden flash of light. What was it, death in Outspace after all? Had Jane lost the pattern in her mind? Were they blowing up, or falling into a sun?

No. It was the door opening. It was the light of the Lusitanian morning breaking into the relative darkness of the inside of the ship.

"Are you coming out?" cried Grego. He stuck his head into the ship. "Are you—"

Then he saw them. Ender could see him silently counting.

"Nossa Senhora," whispered Grego. "Where the hell did *they* come from?"

"Out of Ender's totally screwed-up head," said Peter.

"From old and tender memory," said the new Valentine.

"Help me with the viruses," said Ela.

Ender reached out for them, but it was Miro she gave them to. She didn't explain, just looked away from him, but he understood. What had happened to him Outside was too strange for her to accept. Whatever Peter and this young new Valentine might be, they *shouldn't* exist. Miro's creation of a new body for himself made sense, even if it was terrible to watch the old corpse break into forgotten nothingness. Ela's focus had been so pure that she created nothing outside the vials she had brought for that purpose. But Ender had dredged up two whole people, both obnoxious in their own way—the new Valentine because she was a mockery of the real one, who surely waited just outside the door. And Peter managed to be obnoxious even as he put a spin on all his taunting that was at once dangerous and suggestive.

"Jane," whispered Ender. "Jane, are you with me?"

"Yes," she answered.

"Did you see all this?"

"Yes," she answered.

"Do you understand?"

"I'm very tired. I've never been tired before. I've never done something so very hard. It used up—all my attention at once. And two more bodies, Ender. Making me pull them into the pattern like that—I don't know how I did it."

"I didn't mean to." But she didn't answer.

"Are you coming or what?" asked Peter. "The others

are all out the door. With all those little urine-sample jars."

"Ender, I'm afraid," said young Valentine. "I don't know what I'm supposed to do now."

"Neither do I," said Ender. "God forgive me if this somehow hurts you. I never would have brought you back to hurt you."

"I know," she said.

"No," said Peter. "Sweet old Ender conjures up a nubile young woman out of his own brain, who looks just like his sister in her teens. Mmm, mmm, Ender, old man, is there no limit to your depravity?"

"Only a shamefully sick mind would even think of such a thing," Ender murmured.

Peter laughed and laughed.

Ender took young Val by the hand and led her to the door. He could feel her hand sweating and trembling in his. She felt so real. She *was* real. And yet there, as soon as he stood in the doorway, he could see the real Valentine, middle-aged and heading toward old, yet still the gracious, beautiful woman he had known and loved for all these years. That's the *true* sister, the one I love as my second self. What was this young girl doing in my mind?

It was clear that Grego and Ela had said enough that people knew something strange had happened. And when Miro had strode from the ship, hale and vigorous, clear of speech and so exuberant he looked ready to burst into song—that had brought on a buzz of excitement. A miracle. There were miracles out there, wherever the starship went.

Ender's appearance, though, brought a hush. Few would have known, at a glance, that the young girl with him was Valentine in her youth—no one there but Valentine herself had known her then. And no one but Valentine was likely to recognize Peter Wiggin in his vigorous young manhood; the pictures in the history texts were usually of the holos taken late in his life, when cheap, permanent holography was first coming into its own.

But Valentine knew. Ender stood before the door, young Val beside him, Peter emerging just behind, and Valentine knew them both. She stepped forward, away from Jakt, until she stood before Ender face to face.

"Ender," she said. "Dear sweet tormented boy, was this what you create, when you go to a place where you can make anything you want?" She reached out her hand and touched the young copy of herself upon the cheek. "So beautiful," she said. "I was never this beautiful, Ender. She's perfect. She's all I wanted to be but never was."

"Aren't you glad to see me, Val, my dearest sweetheart Demosthenes?" Peter pushed his way between Ender and young Val. "Don't you have tender memories of me, as well? Am I not more beautiful than you remembered? I'm certainly glad to see *you*. You've done so well with the persona I created for you. Demosthenes. I made you, and you don't even thank me for it."

"Thank you, Peter," whispered Valentine. She looked again at young Val. "What will you do with them?"

"Do with *us*?" said Peter. "We're not his to *do* anything with. He may have brought me back, but I'm my own man now, as I always was."

Valentine turned back to the crowd, still awestruck at the strangeness of events. After all, they had seen three people board the ship, had seen it disappear, then reappear on the exact spot no more than seven minutes later—and instead of three people emerging, there were five, two of them strangers. Of course they had stayed to gawk.

But there'd be no answers for anyone today. Except on the most important question of all. "Has Ela taken the vials to the lab?" she asked. "Let's break it up here, and go see what Ela's made for us in Outspace."

17

ENDER'S CHILDREN

<Poor Ender. Now his nightmares walk around with him on their own two legs.>

<It was a strange way for him to have children after all.>

<You're the one who calls aiúas out of chaos. How did he find souls for these?>

<What makes you think he did?>

<They walk. They talk.>

<The one named Peter came and talked to you, didn't he?>

<As arrogant a human as I ever met.>

<How do you think it happens that he was born knowing how to speak the language of the fathertrees?>

<I don't know. Ender created him. Why shouldn't he create him knowing how to speak?>

<Ender goes on creating them both, hour by hour. We've felt the pattern in him. He may not understand it himself, but there *is* no difference between these two and

himself. Different bodies, perhaps, but they are part of him all the same. Whatever they do, whatever they say, it is Ender's aiúa, acting and speaking.>
    <Does he know this?>
    <We doubt it.>
    <Will you tell him?>
    <Not until he asks.>
    <When do you think *that* will be?>
    <When he already knows the answer.>

It was the last day of the test of the recolada. Word of its success—so far—had already spread through the human colony—and, Ender assumed, among all the pequeninos as well. Ela's assistant named Glass had volunteered to be the experimental subject. He had lived now for three days in the same isolation chamber where Planter had sacrificed himself. This time, though, the descolada had been killed within him by the viricide bacterium he had helped Ela devise. And this time, performing the functions that the descolada had once fulfilled, was Ela's new recolada virus. It had worked perfectly. He was not even slightly ill. Only one last step remained before the recolada could be pronounced a full success.

An hour before that final test, Ender, with his absurd entourage of Peter and young Val, was meeting with Quara and Grego in Grego's cell.

"The pequeninos have accepted it," Ender explained to Quara. "They're willing to take the risk of killing the descolada and replacing it with the recolada, after testing it with Glass alone."

"I'm not surprised," said Quara.

"*I* am," said Peter. "The piggies obviously have a deathwish as a species."

Ender sighed. Though he was no longer a frightened little boy, and Peter was no longer older and larger and stronger than he, there was still no love in Ender's heart for this simulacrum of his brother that he had somehow created Outside. He was everything Ender had feared and hated in his childhood, and it was infuriating and frightening to have him back again.

"What do you mean?" said Grego. "If the pequeninos didn't consent to it, then the descolada would make them too dangerous for humankind to allow them to survive."

"Of course," said Peter, smiling. "The physicist is an expert on strategy."

"What Peter is saying," said Ender, "is that if *he* were in charge of the pequeninos—which he no doubt would like to be—he would never willingly give up the descolada until he had won something from humanity in exchange for it."

"To the surprise of all, the aging boy wonder still has a tiny spark of wit," said Peter. "Why should they kill off their only weapon that humanity has any reason to fear? The Lusitania Fleet is still coming, and it still has the M.D. Device aboard. Why don't they make Andrew here get on that magic flying football of his and go meet the fleet and lay down the law?"

"Because they'd shoot me down like a dog," said Ender. "The pequeninos are doing this because it's right and fair and decent. Words that I'll define for you later."

"I know the words," said Peter. "I also know what they mean."

"You do?" asked young Val. Her voice, as always, was a surprise—soft, mild, and yet able to pierce the conversation. Ender remembered that Valentine's voice had always been that way. Impossible not to listen to, though she so rarely raised her voice.

"Right. Fair. Decent," said Peter. The words sounded filthy in his mouth. "Either the person saying them believes in those concepts or not. If not, then those words mean that he's got somebody standing behind me with

a knife in his hand. And if he *does* believe them, then those words mean that I'm going to win."

"*I'll* tell you what they mean," said Quara. "They mean that we're going to congratulate the pequeninos—and ourselves—for wiping out a sentient species that may exist nowhere else in the universe."

"Don't kid yourself," said Peter.

"Everybody's so sure that the descolada is a designed virus," said Quara, "but nobody's considered the alternative—that a much more primitive, vulnerable version of the descolada evolved naturally, and then *changed itself* to its present form. It might be a designed virus, yes, but who did the designing? And now we're killing it without attempting conversation."

Peter grinned at her, then at Ender. "I'm surprised that this weasely little conscience is not your blood offspring," he said. "She's as obsessed with finding reasons to feel guilty as you and Val."

Ender ignored him and attempted to answer Quara. "We *are* killing it. Because we can't wait any longer. The descolada is trying to destroy us, and there's no time to dither. If we could, we would."

"I understand all that," said Quara. "I cooperated, didn't I? It just makes me sick to hear you talking as if the pequeninos were somehow *brave* about collaborating in an act of xenocide in order to save their own skin."

"Us or them, kid," said Peter. "Us or them."

"You can't possibly understand," said Ender, "how ashamed I am to hear my own arguments on his lips."

Peter laughed. "Andrew pretends not to like me," he said. "But the kid's a fraud. He admires me. He worships me. He always has. Just like his pretty little angel here."

Peter poked at young Val. She didn't shy away. She acted instead as if she hadn't even felt his finger in the flesh of her upper arm.

"He worships us both. In his twisted little mind, she's the moral perfection that he can never achieve. And *I* am the power and genius that was always just out of poor little Andrew's reach. It was really quite modest of him, don't you think? For all these years, he's carried his betters with him inside his mind."

Young Val reached out and took Quara's hand. "It's the worst thing you'll ever do in your life," she said, "helping the people you love to do something that in your heart you believe is deeply wrong."

Quara wept.

But it was not Quara that worried Ender. He knew that she was strong enough to hold the moral contradictions of her own actions, and still remain sane. Her ambivalence toward her own actions would probably mellow her, make her less certain from moment to moment that her judgment was absolutely correct, and that all who disagreed with her were absolutely wrong. If anything, at the end of this she would emerge more whole and compassionate and, yes, *decent* than she had been before in her hotheaded youth. And perhaps young Val's gentle touch—along with her words naming exactly the pain that Quara was feeling—would help her to heal all the sooner.

What worried Ender was the way Grego was looking at Peter with such admiration. Of all people, Grego should have learned what Peter's words could lead to. Yet here he was, worshiping Ender's walking nightmare. I have to get Peter out of here, thought Ender, or he'll have even more disciples on Lusitania than Grego had—and he'll use them far more effectively and, in the long run, the effect will be more deadly.

Ender had little hope that Peter would turn out to be like the *real* Peter, who grew to be a strong and worthy hegemon. *This* Peter, after all, was not a fully fleshed-out human being, full of ambiguity and surprise. Rather he had been created out of the caricature of attractive evil that lingered in the deepest recesses of Ender's unconscious mind. There would be no surprises here. Even as they prepared to save Lusitania from the descolada, Ender had brought a new danger to them, potentially just as destructive.

But not as hard to kill.

Again he stifled the thought, though it had come up a dozen times since he first realized that it was Peter sitting at his left hand in the starship. I created him. He isn't real, just my nightmare. If I kill him, it wouldn't be murder, would it? It would be the moral equivalent of—what? Waking up? I have imposed my nightmare on the world, and if I killed him the world would just be waking up to find the nightmare gone, nothing more.

If it had been Peter alone, Ender might have talked himself into such a murder, or at least he thought he might. But it was young Val who stopped him. Fragile, beautiful of soul—if Peter could be killed, so could she. If he *should* be killed, then perhaps she ought to be as well—she had as little right to exist; she was as unnatural, as narrow and distorted in her creation. But he could never do that. She must be protected, not harmed. And if the one was real enough to remain alive, so must the other be. If harming young Val would be murder, so would harming Peter. They were spawned in the same creation.

My children, thought Ender bitterly. My darling little offspring, who leaped fully-formed from my head like Athena from the mind of Zeus. Only what I have here isn't Athena. More like Diana and Hades. The virgin huntress and the master of hell.

"We'd better go," said Peter. "Before Andrew talks himself into killing me."

Ender smiled wanly. That was the worst thing—that Peter and young Val seemed to have come into existence knowing more about his own mind than he knew himself. In time, he hoped, that intimate knowledge of him would fade. But in the meantime, it added to the humiliation, the way that Peter taunted him about thoughts that no one else would have guessed. And young Val—he knew from the way she looked at him sometimes that she also knew. He had no secrets anymore.

"I'll go home with you," Val said to Quara.

"No," Quara answered. "I've done what I've done. I'll be there to see Glass through to the end of his test."

"We wouldn't want to miss our chance to suffer openly," said Peter.

"Shut up, Peter," said Ender.

Peter grinned. "Oh, come on. You know that Quara's just milking this for all it's worth. It's just her way of making herself the star of the show—everybody being careful and tender with her when they should be cheering for what Ela accomplished. Scene-stealing is so low, Quara—right up your alley."

Quara might have answered, if Peter's words had not been so outrageous and if they had not contained a germ of truth that confused her. Instead it was young Val who fixed Peter with a cold glare and said, "Shut up, Peter."

The same words Ender had said, only when young Val said them, they worked. He grinned at her, and winked—a conspiratorial wink, as if to say, I'll let you play your little game, Val, but don't think I don't know that you're sucking up to everybody by being so sweet. But he said no more as they left Grego in his cell.

Mayor Kovano joined them outside. "A great day in the history of humanity," he said. "And by sheerest accident, I get to be in all the pictures." The others laughed—especially Peter, who had struck up a quick and easy friendship with Kovano.

"It's no accident," said Peter. "A lot of people in your position would have panicked and wrecked everything. It took an open mind and a lot of courage to let things move the way they have."

Ender almost laughed aloud at Peter's obvious flattery. But flattery is never so obvious to the recipient. Oh, Kovano punched Peter in the arm and denied everything, but Ender could see that he loved hearing it, and that Peter had already earned more real influence with Kovano than Ender had. Don't these people see how Peter is cynically winning them all over?

The only one who saw Peter with anything like Ender's fear and loathing was the Bishop—but in his case it was theological prejudice, not wisdom, that kept him from being sucked in. Within hours of their return from Outside, the Bishop had called upon Miro, urging him to accept baptism. "God has performed a great miracle in your healing," he said, "but the way in which it was done—trading one body for another, instead of directly healing the old one—leaves us in the dangerous position that your spirit inhabits a body that has never been baptized. And since baptism is performed on the flesh, I fear that you *may* be unsanctified." Miro wasn't very interested in the Bishop's ideas about miracles—he didn't see God as having much to do with his healing—but the sheer restoration of his strength and his speech and his freedom made him so ebullient that he probably would have agreed to anything. The baptism would take place early next week, at the first services to be held in the new chapel.

But the Bishop's eagerness to baptize Miro was not echoed in his attitude toward Peter and young Val. "It's absurd to think of these monstrous things as *people*," he said. "They can't possibly have souls. Peter is an echo of someone who already lived and died, with his own sins and repentances, his life's course already measured and his place in heaven or hell already assigned. And as for this—girl, this mockery of feminine grace—she cannot be who she claims to be, for that place is already occupied by a living woman. There can be no baptism for the deceptions of Satan. By creating them, Andrew Wiggin has built his own Tower of Babel, trying to reach into heaven to take the place of God. He cannot be forgiven until he takes them back to hell and leaves them there."

Did Bishop Peregrino imagine for one moment that that was not exactly what he longed to do? But Jane was adamant about it, when Ender offered the idea. "That would be foolish," she said. "Why do you think they would go, for one thing? And for another, what makes you think you wouldn't simply create two *more*? Haven't you ever heard the story of the sorcerer's apprentice? Taking them back there would be like cutting the brooms in half again—all you'd end up with is more brooms. Leave bad enough alone."

So here they were, walking to the lab together—Peter, with Mayor Kovano completely in his pocket. Young Val, who had won over Quara no less completely, though her purpose was altruistic instead of exploitative. And Ender, their creator, furious and humiliated and afraid.

I made them—therefore I'm responsible for everything they do. And in the long run, they will both do terrible harm. Peter, because harm is his nature—at least the way I conceived him in the patterns of my mind. And young Val, despite her innate goodness, because her very existence is a deep injury to my sister Valentine.

"Don't let Peter goad you so," whispered Jane in his ear.

"People think he belongs to me," Ender subvocalized. "They figure that he must be harmless because *I'm* harmless. But I have no control over him."

"I think they know that."

"I've got to get him away from here."

"I'm working on that," said Jane.

"Maybe I should pack them up and take them off to some deserted planet somewhere. Do you know Shakespeare's play *The Tempest*?"

"Caliban and Ariel, is that what they are?"

"Exile, since I can't kill them."

"I'm working on it," said Jane. "After all, they're part of you, aren't they? Part of the pattern of your mind? What if I can use *them* in your place, to allow me to go Outside? Then we could have three starships, and not just one."

"Two," said Ender. "I'm never going Outside again."

"Not even for a microsecond? If I take you out and then right back in again? There was no need to linger there."

"It wasn't the lingering that did the harm," said Ender. "Peter and young Val were there *instantly*. If I go Outside again, I'll create them again."

"Fine," she said. "Two starships, then. One with Peter, one with young Val. Let me figure it out, if I can. We can't just make that one voyage and then abandon faster-than-light flight forever."

"Yes we can," said Ender. "We got the recolada. Miro got himself a healthy body. That's enough—we'll work everything else out ourselves."

"Wrong," said Jane. "We still have to transport pequeninos and hive queens off this planet before the fleet comes. We still have to get the transformational virus to Path, to set those people free."

"I won't go Outside again."

"Even if I *can't* use Peter and young Val to carry my aiúa? You'd let the pequeninos and the hive queen be destroyed because you're afraid of your own unconscious mind?"

"You don't understand how dangerous Peter is."

"Perhaps not. But I *do* understand how dangerous the Little Doctor is. And if you weren't so wrapped up in your own misery, Ender, you'd know that even if we end up with five hundred little Peters and Vals running around, we've got to use this starship to carry pequeninos and the hive queen to other worlds."

He knew she was right. He had known it all along. That didn't mean that he was prepared to admit it.

"Just work on trying to move yourself into Peter and young Val," he subvocalized. "Though God help us if *Peter* is able to create things when he goes Outside."

"I doubt he can," said Jane. "He's not as smart as he thinks he is."

"Yes he is," said Ender. "And if you doubt it, you're not as smart as you think *you* are."

———

Ela was not the only one who prepared for Glass's final test by going to visit Planter. His mute tree was still only a sapling, hardly a balance to Rooter's and Human's sturdy trunks. But it was around that sapling that the surviving pequeninos had gathered. And, like Ela, they had gathered to pray. It was a strange and silent kind of prayer service. The pequenino priests offered no pomp, no ceremony. They simply knelt with the others, and they murmured in their several languages. Some prayed in Brothers' Language, some in tree language. Ela supposed that what she was hearing from the wives gathered there was their own regular language, though it might as easily be the holy language they used to speak to the mothertree. And there were also human languages coming from pequenino lips— Stark and Portuguese alike, and there might even have been some ancient Church Latin from one of the pequenino priests. It was a virtual Babel, and yet she felt great unity. They prayed at the martyr's tomb—all that was left of himself—for the life of the brother who was following after him. If Glass died utterly today, he would only echo Planter's sacrifice. And if he passed into the third life, it would be a life owed to Planter's courage and example.

Because it was Ela who had brought back the recolada from Outside, they honored her with a brief time alone at the very trunk of Planter's tree. She wrapped her hand around the slender wooden pole, wishing there were more of his life in it. Was Planter's aiúa lost now, wandering in the wherelessness of Outside? Or had God in fact taken it as his very soul and brought it into heaven, where Planter now communed with the saints?

Planter, pray for us. Intercede for us. As my venerated grandparents carried my prayer to the Father, go now to Christ for us and plead with him to have mercy on all your brothers and sisters. Let the recolada carry Glass into the third life, so that we can, in good conscience, spread the recolada through the world to replace the murderous descolada. Then the lion can lie down with the lamb indeed, and there can be peace in this place.

Not for the first time, though, Ela had her doubts. She was certain that their course was the right one—she had none of Quara's qualms about destroying the descolada throughout Lusitania. But what she wasn't sure of was whether she should have based the recolada on the oldest samples of the descolada they had collected. If in fact the descolada had caused recent pequenino belligerence, their hunger to spread to new places, then she could consider herself as restoring the pequeninos to their previous "natural" condition. But then, the previous condition was just as much a product of the descolada's gaialogical balancing act—it only seemed more natural because it was the condition the pequeninos were in when humans arrived. So she could just as easily see herself as causing a behavioral modification of an entire species, conveniently removing much of their aggressiveness so that there would be less likelihood of conflict with humans in the future. I am making good Christians of them now, whether they like it or not. And the fact that Human and Rooter both approve of this doesn't remove the onus from me, if this should turn out ultimately to the pequeninos' harm.

O God, forgive me for playing God in the lives of these children of yours. When Planter's aiúa comes before you to plead for us, grant the prayer he carries on our behalf—but only if it is your will to have his species altered so. Help us do good, but stop us if we would unwittingly cause harm. In the name of the Father, and of the Son, and of the Holy Ghost. Amen.

She took a tear from her cheek onto her finger, and pressed it against the smooth bark of Planter's trunk. You aren't there to feel this, Planter, not inside the tree. But you feel it all the same, I do believe that. God would not let such a noble soul as yours be lost in darkness.

It was time to go. Gentle brothers' hands touched her, pulled at her, drew her onward to the lab where Glass was waiting in isolation for his passage into the third life.

———

When Ender had visited with Planter, he had been surrounded with medical equipment, lying on a bed. It was very different now inside the isolation chamber. Glass was in perfect health, and though he was wired up to all the monitoring devices, he was not bed-bound. Playful and happy, he could scarcely contain his eagerness to proceed.

And now that Ela and the other pequeninos had come, it could begin.

The only wall maintaining his isolation now was the disruptor field; outside it, the pequeninos who had gathered to watch his passage could see all that transpired. They were the only ones who watched in the open, however. Perhaps out of a sense of delicacy for pequenino feelings, or perhaps so they could have a wall between them and the brutality of this pequenino ritual, the humans had all gathered inside the lab, where only a window and the monitors let them see what would actually happen to Glass.

Glass waited until the sterile-suited brothers were in place beside him, wooden knives in hand, before he tore up capim and chewed it. It was the anesthetic that would make this bearable for him. But it was also the first time that a brother bound for the third life had chewed native grass that contained no descolada virus within it. If Ela's new virus was right, then the capim here would work as the descolada-ruled capim had always worked.

"If I pass into the third life," said Glass, "the honor belongs to God and to his servant Planter, not to me."

It was fitting that Glass had chosen to use his last words of brother-speech to praise Planter. But his graciousness did not change the fact that thinking of Planter's sacrifice caused many among the humans to weep; hard as it was to interpret pequenino emotions, Ender had no doubt that the chattering sounds from the pequeninos gathered outside were also weeping, or some other emotion appropriate to Planter's memory. But Glass was wrong to think that there was no honor for him in this. Everyone knew that failure was still possible, that despite all the cause for hope they had, there was no certainty that Ela's recolada would have the power to take a brother into the third life.

The sterile-suited brothers raised their knives and set to work.

Not me, this time, thought Ender. Thank God I don't have to wield a knife to cause a brother's death.

Yet he didn't avert his gaze, as so many others in the lab were doing. The blood and gore were not new to him, and even if that made it no less unpleasant, at least he knew that he could bear it. And what Glass could bear to do, Ender could bear to witness. That was what a speaker for the dead was supposed to do, wasn't it? Witness. He watched as much as he could see of the ritual, as they opened up Glass's living body and planted his organs in the earth, so the tree could start to grow while Glass's mind was still alert and alive. Through it all, Glass made no sound or movement that suggested pain. Either his courage was beyond reckoning, or the recolada had done its work in the capim grass as well, so that it maintained its anesthetic properties.

At last it was done, and the brothers who had taken him into the third life returned to the sterile chamber, where, once their suits were cleansed of the recolada and viricide bacteria, they shed them and returned naked into the lab. They were very solemn, but Ender thought he could see the excitement and exultation that they concealed. All had gone well. They had felt Glass's body respond to them. Within hours, perhaps minutes, the first leaves of the young tree should arise. And they were sure in their hearts that it would happen.

Ender also noticed that one of them was a priest. He wondered what the Bishop would say, if he knew. Old Peregrino had proved himself to be quite adaptable to assimilating an alien species into the Catholic faith, and adapting ritual and doctrine to fit their peculiar needs. But that didn't change the fact that Peregrino was an old man who didn't enjoy the thought of priests taking part in rituals that, despite their clear resemblance to the crucifixion, were still not of the recognized sacraments. Well, these brothers knew what they were doing. Whether they had told the Bishop of one of his priests' participation or not, Ender wouldn't mention it; nor would any of the other humans present, if indeed any of them noticed.

Yes, the tree was growing, and with great vigor, the leaves visibly rising as they watched. But it would still be many hours, days perhaps, before they knew if it was a fathertree, with Glass still alive and conscious within it. A time of waiting, in which Glass's tree must grow in perfect isolation.

If only I could find a place, thought Ender, in which I could also be isolated, in which I could work out the strange things that have happened to me, without interference.

But he was not a pequenino, and whatever unease he suffered from was not a virus that could be killed, or driven from his life. His disease was at the root of his identity, and he didn't know if he could ever be rid of it without destroying himself in the process. Perhaps, he thought, Peter and Val represent the total of who I am; perhaps if they were gone, there'd be nothing left. What part of my soul, what action in my life is there that can't be explained as one or the other of them, acting out his or her will within me?

Am I the sum of my siblings? Or the difference between them? What is the peculiar arithmetic of my soul?

Valentine tried not to be obsessed with this young girl that Ender had brought back with him from Outside. Of course she knew it was her younger self as he remembered her, and she even thought it was rather sweet of him to carry inside his heart such a powerful memory of her at that age. She alone, of all the people on Lusitania, knew why it was at that age that she lingered in his unconscious. He had been in Battle School till then, cut off completely from his family. Though he could not have known it, she knew that their parents had pretty much forgotten him. Not forgotten that he existed, of course, but forgotten him as a presence in their lives. He simply wasn't there, wasn't their responsibility anymore. Having given him away to the state, they were absolved. He would have been more a part of their lives if he had died; as it was, they didn't have even a grave to visit. Valentine didn't blame them for this—it proved that they were resilient and adaptable.

But she wasn't able to mimic them. Ender was always with her, in her heart. And when, after being inwardly battered as he was forced to meet all the challenges they threw at him in Battle School, Ender now resolved to give up on the whole enterprise—when he, in effect, went on strike—the officer charged with turning him into a pliant tool came to her. Brought her to Ender. Gave them time together—the same man who had torn them apart and left such deep wounds in their hearts. She healed her brother then—enough that he could go back and save humanity by destroying the buggers.

Of course he holds me in his memory at that age, more powerfully than any of our countless experiences together since. Of course when his unconscious mind brings forth its most intimate baggage, it is the girl I was then who lingers most deeply in his heart.

She knew all this, she understood all this, she be-lieved all this. Yet still it rankled, still it hurt that this almost mindlessly perfect creature was what he really thought of her all along. That the Valentine that Ender truly loved was a creature of impossible purity. It was for the sake of this imaginary Valentine that he was so close a companion to me all the years before I married Jakt. Unless it was because I married Jakt that he re-turned to this childish vision of me.

Nonsense. There was nothing to be gained by trying to imagine what this young girl *meant*. Regardless of the manner of her creation, she was here *now*, and must be dealt with.

Poor Ender—he seemed to understand nothing. He actually thought at first that he should keep young Val with him. "Isn't she my daughter, after a fashion?" he had asked.

"After *no* fashion is she your daughter," she had answered. "If anything, she's *mine*. And it is certainly not proper for you to take her into your home, alone. Especially since Peter is there, and he isn't the most trustworthy co-guardian who ever lived." Ender still didn't fully agree—he would rather have got rid of Peter than Val—but he complied, and since then Val had lived in Valentine's house. Valentine's intention had been to become the girl's friend and mentor, but in the event she simply couldn't do it. She wasn't comfortable enough in Val's company. She kept finding reasons to leave home when Val was there; she kept feeling inordinately grateful when Ender came to let her tag along with him and Peter.

What finally happened was that, as so often before, Plikt silently stepped in and solved the problem. Plikt became Val's primary companion and guardian in Valentine's house. When Val wasn't with Ender, she was with Plikt. And this morning Plikt had suggested setting up a house of her own—for her and Val. *Perhaps I was too hasty in agreeing,* thought Valentine. *But it's probably as hard on Val to share a house with me as for me to share a house with her.*

Now, though, watching as Plikt and Val entered the new chapel on their knees and crawled forward—as all the other humans who entered had also crawled—to kiss Bishop Peregrino's ring before the altar, Valentine realized that she had done nothing for "Val's own good," whatever she might have told herself. Val was completely self-contained, unflappable, calm. *Why should Valentine imagine that she could make young Val either more or less happy, more or less comfortable? I am irrelevant to this girl-child's life. But she is not irrelevant to mine. She is at once an affirmation and a denial of the most important relationship of my childhood, and of much of my adulthood as well. I wish that she had crumbled into nothingness Outside, like Miro's old crippled body did. I wish I had never had to face myself like this.*

And it *was* herself she was facing. Ela had run *that* test immediately. Young Val and Valentine were genetically identical.

"But it makes no sense," Valentine protested. "Ender could hardly have memorized my genetic code. There couldn't possibly have been a pattern of that code in the starship with him."

"Am I supposed to explain it?" asked Ela.

Ender had suggested a possibility—that young Val's genetic code was fluid until she and Valentine actually met, and then the philotes of Val's body had formed themselves into the pattern they found in Valentine's.

Valentine kept her own opinion to herself, but she doubted that Ender's guess was right. Young Val had had Valentine's genes from the first moment, because any person who so perfectly fit Ender's vision of Valentine could not have any other genes; the natural law that Jane herself was helping to maintain within the starship would have required it. Or perhaps there was some force that shaped and gave order even to a place of such utter chaos. It hardly mattered, except that however annoyingly perfect and uncomplaining and *unlike me* this new pseudo-Val might be, Ender's vision of her had been true enough that genetically they *were* the same. His vision couldn't be much off the mark. Perhaps I really *was* that perfect then, and only got my rough edges during the years since then. Perhaps I really was that beautiful. Perhaps I really was so young.

They knelt before the Bishop. Plikt kissed his ring, though she owed no part of the penance of Lusitania.

When it came time for young Val to kiss the ring, however, the Bishop pulled away his hand and turned away. A priest came forward and told them to go to their seats.

"How can I?" said young Val. "I haven't given my penance yet."

"You have no penance," said the priest. "The Bishop told me before you came; you weren't here when the sin was committed, so you have no part in the penance."

Young Val looked at him very sadly and said, "I was created by someone other than God. That's why the Bishop won't receive me. I'll never have communion while he lives."

The priest looked very sad—it was impossible not to feel sorry for young Val, for her simplicity and sweetness made her seem fragile, and the person who hurt her therefore had to feel clumsy for having damaged such a tender thing. "Until the Pope can decide," he said. "All this is very hard."

"I know," whispered young Val. Then she came and sat down between Plikt and Valentine.

Our elbows touch, thought Valentine. A daughter who is perfectly myself, as if I had cloned her thirteen years ago.

But I didn't want another daughter, and I certainly didn't want a duplicate of me. She knows that. She feels it. And so she suffers something that I never suffered—she feels unwanted and unloved by those who are most like her.

How does Ender feel about her? Does he also wish that she would go away? Or does he yearn to be her brother, as he was *my* young brother so many years ago? When I was that age, Ender had not yet committed xenocide. But then, he had not yet spoken for the dead, either. The Hive Queen, the Hegemon, the Life of Human—all that was beyond him then. He was just a child, confused, despairing, afraid. How could Ender yearn for that time again?

Miro soon came in, crawled to the altar, and kissed the ring. Though the Bishop had absolved him of any responsibility, he bore the penance with all others. Valentine noticed, of course, the many whispers as he moved forward. Everyone in Lusitania who had known him before his brain damage recognized the miracle that had been performed—a perfect restoration of the Miro who had lived so brightly among them all before.

I didn't know you then, Miro, thought Valentine. Did you always have that distant, brooding air? Healed your body may be, but you're still the man who lived in pain for this time. Has it made you cold or more compassionate?

He came and sat beside her, in the chair that would have been Jakt's, except that Jakt was still in space. With the descolada soon to be destroyed, someone had to bring to Lusitania's surface the thousands of frozen microbes and plant and animal species that had to be introduced in order to establish a self-regulating gaialogy and keep the planetary systems in order. It was a job that had been done on many other worlds, but it was being made trickier by the need *not* to compete too intensely with the local species that the pequeninos depended on. Jakt was up there, laboring for them all; it was a good reason to be gone, but Valentine still missed him—needed him badly, in fact, what with Ender's new creations causing her such turmoil. Miro was no substitute for her husband, especially because his own new body was such a sharp reminder of what had been done Outside.

If *I* went out there, what would *I* create? I doubt that I'd bring back a person, because I fear there is no one soul at the root of my psyche. Not even my own, I fear. What else has my passionate study of history been, except a search for humanity? Others find humanity by looking in their own hearts. Only lost souls need to search for it outside themselves.

"The line's almost done," whispered Miro.

So the service would begin soon.

"Ready to have your sins purged?" whispered Valentine.

"As the Bishop explained, he'll purge only the sins of this new body. I still have to confess and do penance for the sins I had left over from the old one. Not many carnal sins were possible, of course, but there's plenty of envy, spite, malice, and self-pity. What I'm trying to decide is whether I also have a suicide to confess. When my old body crumbled into nothing, it was answering the wish of my heart."

"You should never have got your voice back," said Valentine. "You babble now just to hear yourself talk so prettily."

He smiled and patted her arm.

The Bishop began the service with prayer, giving thanks to God for all that had been accomplished in recent months. Conspicuous by omission was the creation of Lusitania's two newest citizens, though Miro's healing was definitely laid at God's door. He called Miro forward and baptized him almost at once, and then, because this was not a mass, the Bishop proceeded immediately to his homily.

"God's mercy has an infinite reach," said the Bishop. "We can only hope he will choose to reach farther than we deserve, to forgive us for our terrible sins as individuals and as a people. We can only hope that, like Nineveh, which turned away destruction through repentance, we can convince our Lord to spare us from the fleet that he has permitted to come against us to punish us."

Miro whispered, softly, so that only she could hear, "Didn't he send the fleet *before* the burning of the forest?"

"Maybe the Lord counts only the arrival time, not the departure," Valentine suggested. At once, though, she regretted her flippancy. What was happening here today was a solemn thing; even if she wasn't a deep believer in Catholic doctrine, she knew that it was a holy thing when a community accepted responsibility for the evil it committed and did true penance for it.

The Bishop spoke of those who had died in holiness—Os Venerados, who first saved humanity from the descolada plague; Father Estevão, whose body was buried under the floor of the chapel and who suffered martyrdom in the cause of defending truth against heresy; Planter, who died to prove that his people's soul was from God, and not from a virus; and the pequeninos who had died as innocent victims of slaughter. "All of these may be saints someday, for this is a time like the early days of Christianity, when great deeds and great holiness were much more needed, and therefore much more often achieved. This chapel is a shrine to all those who have loved their God with all their heart, might, mind and strength, and who have loved their neighbor as themself. Let all who enter here do it with a broken heart and a contrite spirit, so that holiness may also touch them."

The homily wasn't long, because there were many more identical services scheduled for that day—the people were coming to the chapel in shifts, since it was far too small to accommodate the whole human population of Lusitania all at once. Soon enough they were done, and Valentine got up to leave. She would have followed close behind Plikt and Val, except that Miro caught at her arm.

"Jane just told me," he said. "I thought you'd want to know."

"What?"

"She just tested the starship, without Ender in it."

"How could she do *that?*" asked Valentine.

"Peter," he said. "She took him Outside and back again. He can contain her aiúa, if that's how this process is actually working."

She gave voice to her immediate fear. "Did he—"

"Create anything? No." Miro grinned—but with a hint of the twisted wryness that Valentine had thought was a product of his affliction. "He claims it's because his mind is much clearer and healthier than Andrew's."

"Maybe so," said Valentine.

"I say it's because none of the philotes out there were willing to be part of *his* pattern. Too twisted."

Valentine laughed a little.

The Bishop came up to them then. Since they were among the last to leave, they were alone at the front of the chapel.

"Thank you for accepting a new baptism," said the Bishop.

Miro bowed his head. "Not many men have a chance to be purified so far along in their sins," he said.

"And Valentine, I'm sorry I couldn't receive your—namesake."

"Don't worry, Bishop Peregrino. I understand. I may even agree with you."

The Bishop shook his head. "It would be better if they could just—"

"Leave?" offered Miro. "You get your wish. Peter will soon be gone—Jane can pilot a ship with him aboard. No doubt the same thing will be possible with young Val."

"No," said Valentine. "She can't go. She's too—"

"Young?" asked Miro. He seemed amused. "They were both born knowing everything that Ender knows. You can hardly call the girl a child, despite her body."

"If they had been *born*," said the Bishop, "they wouldn't have to leave."

"They're not leaving because of your wish," said Miro. "They're leaving because Peter's going to deliver Ela's new virus to Path, and young Val's ship is going to go off in search of planets where pequeninos and hive queens can be established."

"You can't send her on such a mission," said Valentine.

"I won't *send* her," said Miro. "I'll *take* her. Or rather, she'll take me. I *want* to go. Whatever risks there are, I'll take them. She'll be safe, Valentine."

Valentine still shook her head, but she knew already that in the end she would be defeated. Young Val herself would insist on going, however young she might seem, because if she didn't go, only one starship could travel; and if Peter was the one doing the traveling, there was no telling whether the ship would be used for any good purpose. In the long run, Valentine herself would bow to the necessity. Whatever danger young Val might be exposed to, it was no worse than the risks already taken by others. Like Planter. Like Father Estevão. Like Glass.

The pequeninos gathered at Planter's tree. It would have been Glass's tree, since he was the first to pass into the third life with the recolada, but almost his first words, once they were able to talk with him, were an adamant rejection of the idea of introducing the viricide and recolada into the world beside his tree. This occasion belonged to Planter, he declared, and the brothers and wives ultimately agreed with him.

So it was that Ender leaned against his friend Human, whom he had planted in order to help him into the third life so many years before. It would have been a moment of complete joy to Ender, the liberation of the pequeninos from the descolada—except that he had Peter with him through it all.

"Weakness celebrates weakness," said Peter. "Planter *failed*, and here they are honoring him, while Glass *succeeded*, and there he stands, alone out there in the experimental field. And the stupidest thing is that it can't possibly mean anything to Planter, since his aiúa isn't even here."

"It may not mean anything to Planter," said Ender—a point he wasn't altogether sure of, anyway—"but it means something to the people here."

"Yes," he said. "It means they're weak."

"Jane says she took you Outside."

"An easy trip," said Peter. "Next time, though, Lusitania won't be my destination."

"She says you plan to take Ela's virus to Path."

"My first stop," Peter said. "But I won't be coming back here. Count on that, old boy."

"We need the ship."

"You've got that sweet little slip of a girl," said Peter, "and the bugger bitch can pop out starships for you by the dozen, if only you could spawn enough creatures like me and Valzinha to pilot them."

"I'll be glad to see the last of you."

"Aren't you curious what I intend to do?"

"No," said Ender.

But it was a lie, and of course Peter knew it. "I intend to do what you have neither the brains nor the stomach to do. I intend to stop the fleet."

"How? Magically appear on the flagship?"

"Well, if worse came to worst, dear lad, I could always deliver an M.D. Device to the fleet before they even knew I was there. But that wouldn't accomplish much, would it? To stop the fleet, I need to stop Congress. And to stop Congress, I need to get control."

Ender knew at once what this meant. "So you think you can be Hegemon again? God help humanity if you succeed."

"Why shouldn't I?" said Peter. "I did it once before, and I didn't do so badly. You should know—you wrote the book yourself."

"That was the *real* Peter," said Ender. "Not you, the twisted version conjured up out of my hatred and fear."

Did Peter have soul enough to resent these harsh words? Ender thought, for a moment at least, that Peter paused, that his face showed a moment of—what, hurt? Or simply rage?

"*I'm* the real Peter now," he answered, after that momentary pause. "And you'd better hope that I have all the skill I had before. After all, you managed to give Valette the same genes as Valentine. Maybe I'm all that Peter ever was."

"Maybe pigs have wings."

Peter laughed. "They would, if you went Outside and believed hard enough."

"Go, then," said Ender.

"Yes, I know you'll be glad to get rid of me."

"And sic you on the rest of humanity? Let that be punishment enough, for their having sent the fleet." Ender gripped Peter by the arm, pulled him close. "Don't think that this time you can maneuver me into helplessness. I'm not a little boy anymore, and if you get out of hand, I'll destroy you."

"You can't," said Peter. "You could more easily kill yourself."

The ceremony began. This time there was no pomp, no ring to kiss, no homily. Ela and her assistants simply brought several hundred sugar cubes impregnated with the viricide bacterium, and as many vials of solution containing the recolada. They were passed among the congregation, and each of the pequeninos took the sugar cube, dissolved and swallowed it, and then drank off the contents of the vial.

"This is my body which is given for you," intoned Peter. "This do in remembrance of me."

"Have you no respect for anything?" asked Ender.

"This is my blood, which I shed for you. Drink in remembrance of me." Peter smiled. "This is a communion even *I* can take, unbaptized as I am."

"I can promise you this," said Ender. "They haven't invented the baptism yet that can purify *you*."

"I'll bet you've been saving up all your life, just to say that to me." Peter turned to him, so Ender could see the ear in which the jewel had been implanted, linking him to Jane. In case Ender didn't notice what he was pointing out, Peter touched the jewel rather ostentatiously. "Just remember, I have the source of all wisdom here. She'll show you what I'm doing, if you ever care. If you don't forget me the moment I'm gone."

"I won't forget you," said Ender.

"You could come along," said Peter.

"And risk making more like you Outside?"

"I could use the company."

"I promise you, Peter, you'd soon get as sick of yourself as I am sick of you."

"Never," said Peter. "I'm not filled with self-loathing the way you are, you poor guilt-obsessed tool of better, stronger men. And if you won't make more companions for me, why, I'll find my own along the way."

"I have no doubt of it," said Ender.

The sugar cubes and vials came to them; they ate, drank.

"The taste of freedom," said Peter. "Delicious."

"Is it?" said Ender. "We're killing a species that we never understood."

"I know what you mean," said Peter. "It's a lot more fun to destroy an opponent when he's able to understand how thoroughly you defeated him."

Then, at last, Peter walked away.

Ender stayed through the end of the ceremony, and spoke to many there: Human and Rooter, of course, and Valentine, Ela, Ouanda, and Miro.

He had another visit to make, however. A visit he had made several times before, always to be rebuffed, sent away without a word. This time, though, Novinha came out to speak with him. And instead of being filled with rage and grief, she seemed quite calm.

"I'm much more at peace," she said. "And I know, for what it's worth, that my rage at you was unrighteous."

Ender was glad to hear the sentiment, but surprised at the terms she used. When had Novinha ever spoken of righteousness?

"I've come to see that perhaps my boy was fulfilling the purposes of God," she said. "That you couldn't have stopped him, because God wanted him to go to the pequeninos to set in motion the miracles that have come since then." She wept. "Miro came to me. Healed," she said. "Oh, God is merciful after all. And I'll have Quim again in heaven, when I die."

She's been converted, thought Ender. After all these years of despising the church, of taking part in Catholicism only because there was no other way to be a citizen of Lusitania Colony, these weeks with the Children of the Mind of Christ have converted her. I'm glad of it, he thought. She's speaking to me again.

"Andrew," she said, "I want us to be together again."

He reached out to embrace her, wanting to weep with relief and joy, but she recoiled from his touch.

"You don't understand," she said. "I won't go home with you. This is my home now."

She was right—he hadn't understood. But now he did. She hadn't just been converted to Catholicism. She had been converted to this order of permanent sacrifice, where only husbands and wives could join, and only together, to take vows of permanent abstinence in the midst of their marriage. "Novinha," he said, "I haven't the faith or the strength to be one of the Children of the Mind of Christ."

"When you do," she said, "I'll be waiting for you here."

"Is this the only hope I have of being with you?" he whispered. "To forswear loving your body as the only way to have your companionship?"

"Andrew," she whispered, "I long for you. But my sin for so many years was adultery that my only hope of joy now is to deny the flesh and live in the spirit. I'll do it alone if I must. But with you—oh, Andrew, I miss you."

And I miss you, he thought. "Like breath itself I miss you," he whispered. "But don't ask this of me. Live with me as my wife until the last of our youth is spent, and then when desire is slack we can come back here together. I could be happy then."

"Don't you see?" she said. "I've made a covenant. I've made a *promise*."

"You made one to me, too," he said.

"Should I break a vow to God, so I can keep my vow with you?"

"God would understand."

"How easily those who never hear his voice declare what he would and would not want."

"Do you hear his voice these days?"

"I hear his song in my heart, the way the Psalmist did. The Lord is my shepherd. I shall not want."

"The twenty-third. While the only song I hear is the twenty-second."

She smiled wanly. " 'Why hast thou forsaken me?' " she quoted.

"And the part about the bulls of Bashan," said Ender. "I've always felt like I was surrounded by bulls."

She laughed. "Come to me when you can," she said. "I'll be here, when you're ready."

She almost left him then.

"Wait."

She waited.

"I brought you the viricide and the recolada."

"Ela's triumph," she said. "It was beyond me, you know. I cost you nothing, by abandoning my work. My time was past, and she had far surpassed me." Novinha took the sugar cube, let it melt for a moment, swallowed it.

Then she held the vial up against the last light of evening. "With the red sky, it looks like it's all afire inside." She drank it—sipped it, really, so that the flavor would linger. Even though, as Ender knew, the taste was bitter, and lingered unpleasantly in the mouth long afterward.

"Can I visit you?"

"Once a month," she said. Her answer was so quick that he knew she had already considered the question and reached a decision that she had no intention of altering.

"Then once a month I'll visit you," he said.

"Until you're ready to join me," she said.

"Until you're ready to return to *me*," he answered.

But he knew that she would never bend. Novinha was not a person who could easily change her mind. She had set the bounds of his future.

He should have been resentful, angry. He should have blustered about getting his freedom from a marriage to a woman who refused him. But he couldn't think what he might want his freedom *for*. Nothing is in my hands now, he realized. No part of the future depends on me. My work, such as it is, is done, and now my only influence on the future is what my children do—such as they are: the monster Peter, the impossibly perfect child Val.

And Miro, Grego, Quara, Ela, Olhado—aren't they my children, too? Can't I also claim to have helped create them, even if they came from Libo's love and Novinha's body, years before I even arrived in this place?

It was full dark when he found young Val, though he couldn't understand why he was even looking for her. She was in Olhado's house, with Plikt; but while Plikt leaned against a shadowed wall, her face inscrutable, young Val was among Olhado's children, playing with them.

Of course she's playing with them, thought Ender. She's still a child herself, however much experience she might have had thrust upon her out of my memories.

But as he stood in the doorway, watching, he realized that she wasn't playing equally with all the children. It was Nimbo who really had her attention. The boy who had been burned, in more ways than one, the night of the mob. The game the children played was simple enough, but it kept them from talking to each other. Still, there was eloquent conversation between Nimbo and young Val. Her smile toward him was warm, not in the manner of a woman encouraging a lover, but rather as a sister gives her brother the silent message of love, of confidence, of trust.

She's healing him, thought Ender. Just as Valentine, so many years ago, healed me. Not with words. Just with her company.

Could I have created her with even *that* ability intact? Was there that much truth and power in my dream of her? Then maybe Peter also has everything within him that my real brother had—all that was dangerous and terrible, but also that which created a new order.

Try as he might, Ender couldn't get himself to believe *that* story. Young Val might have healing in her eyes, but Peter had none of that in him. His was the face that, years before, Ender had seen looking back at him from a mirror in the Fantasy Game, in a terrible room where he died again and again before he could finally embrace the element of Peter within himself and go on.

I embraced Peter and destroyed a whole people. I took him into myself and committed xenocide. I thought, in all these years since then, that I had purged him. That he was gone. But he'll never leave me.

The idea of withdrawing from the world and entering into the order of the Children of the Mind of Christ—there was much to attract him in that. Perhaps there, Novinha and he together could purge themselves of the demons that had dwelt inside them all these years. Novinha has never been so much at peace, thought Ender, as she is tonight.

Young Val noticed him, came to him as he stood in the doorway.

"Why are you here?" she said.

"Looking for you," he said.

"Plikt and I are spending the night with Olhado's

family," she said. She glanced at Nimbo and smiled. The boy grinned foolishly.

"Jane says that you're going with the starship," Ender said softly.

"If Peter can hold Jane within himself, so can I," she answered. "Miro is going with me. To find habitable worlds."

"Only if you want to," said Ender.

"Don't be foolish," she said. "Since when have *you* done only what you *want* to do? I'll do what must be done, that only I can do."

He nodded.

"Is that all you came for?" she asked.

He nodded again. "I guess," he said.

"Or did you come because you wish that you could be the child you were when you last saw a girl with this face?"

The words stung—far worse than when Peter guessed what was in his heart. Her compassion was far more painful than his contempt.

She must have seen the expression of pain on his face, and misunderstood it. He was relieved that she was capable of misunderstanding. I do have some privacy left.

"Are you ashamed of me?" she asked.

"Embarrassed," he said. "To have my unconscious mind made so public. But not *ashamed*. Not of *you*." He glanced toward Nimbo, then back to her. "Stay here and finish what you started."

She smiled slightly. "He's a good boy who thought that he was doing something fine."

"Yes," he said. "But it got away from him."

"He didn't know what he was doing," she said. "When you don't understand the consequences of your acts, how can you be blamed for them?"

He knew that she was talking as much about him, Ender the Xenocide, as about Nimbo. "You don't take the blame," he answered. "But you still take responsibility. For healing the wounds you caused."

"Yes," she said. "The wounds you caused. But not all the wounds in the world."

"Oh?" he asked. "And why not? Because you plan to heal them all yourself?"

She laughed—a light, girlish laugh. "You haven't changed a bit, Andrew," she said. "Not in all these years."

He smiled at her, hugged her lightly, and sent her back into the light of the room. He himself, though, turned back out into the darkness and headed home. There was light enough for him to find his way, yet he stumbled and got lost several times.

"You're crying," said Jane in his ear.

"This is such a happy day," he said.

"It is, you know. You're just about the only person wasting any pity on *you* tonight."

"Fine, then," said Ender. "If I'm the only one, then at least there's one."

"You've got *me*," she said. "And *our* relationship has been chaste all along."

"I've really had enough of chastity in my life," he answered. "I wasn't hoping for more."

"Everyone is chaste in the end. Everyone ends up out of the reach of all the deadly sins."

"But *I'm* not *dead*," he said. "Not yet. Or am I?"

"Does this feel like heaven?" she asked.

He laughed, and not nicely.

"Well, then, you can't be dead."

"You forget," he said. "This could easily be hell."

"Is it?" she asked him.

He thought about all that had been accomplished. Ela's viruses. Miro's healing. Young Val's kindness to Nimbo. The smile of peace on Novinha's face. The pequeninos' rejoicing as their liberty began its passage through their world. Already, he knew, the viricide was cutting an ever-widening swath through the prairie of capim surrounding the colony; by now it must already have passed into other forests, the descolada, helpless now, giving way as the mute and passive recolada took its place. All these changes couldn't possibly take place in hell.

"I guess I'm still alive," he said.

"And so am I," she said. "That's something, too. Peter and Val, they're not the only people to spring from your mind."

"No, they're not," he said.

"We're both still alive, even if we have hard times coming."

He remembered what lay in store for her, the mental crippling that was only weeks away, and he was ashamed of himself for having mourned his own losses. "Better to have loved and lost," he murmured, "than never to have loved at all."

"It may be a cliché," said Jane, "but that doesn't mean it can't be true."

18

THE GOD OF PATH

<I couldn't taste the changes in the descolada virus until it was gone.>

<It was adapting to you?>

<It was beginning to taste like myself. It had included most of my genetic molecules into its own structure.>

<Perhaps it was preparing to change you, as it changed us.>

<But when it captured your ancestors, it paired them with the trees they lived in. Whom would we have been paired with?>

<What other forms of life are there on Lusitania, except the ones that are already paired?>

<Perhaps the descolada meant to combine us with an existing pair. Or replace one pair-member with us.>

<Or perhaps it meant to pair you with the humans.>

<It's dead now. It will never happen, whatever it planned.>

<What sort of life would you have led? Mating with human males?>

<This is disgusting.>

<Or giving live births, perhaps, in the human manner?>

<Stop this foulness.>

<I was merely speculating.>

<The descolada is gone. You're free of it.>

<But never free of what we *should* have been. I believe that we were sentient before the descolada came. I believe our history is older than the spacecraft that brought it here. I believe that somewhere in our genes is locked the secret of pequenino life when we were tree-dwellers, rather than the larval stage in the life of sentient trees.>

<If you had no third life, Human, you would be dead now.>

<Dead *now*, but while I lived I could have been, not a mere brother, but a father. While I lived I could have traveled anywhere, without worrying about returning to my forest if I ever hoped to mate. Never would I have stood day after day rooted to the same spot, living my life vicariously through the tales the brothers bring to me.>

<It's not enough for you to be free of the descolada, then? You must be free of all its consequences or you won't be content?>

<I'm always content. I am what I am, no matter how I got that way.>

<But still not free.>

<Males and females both, we still have to lose our lives in order to pass on our genes.>

<Poor fool. Do you think that I, the hive queen, am *free*? Do you think that human parents, once they bear young, are ever truly free again? If *life* to you means independence, a completely unfettered freedom to do as you like, then none of the sentient creatures is alive. None of us is ever fully free.>

<Put down roots, my friend, and then tell me how

unfree you were when you were yet unrooted.>

Wang-mu and Master Han waited together on the riverbank some hundred meters from their house, a pleasant walk through the garden. Jane had told them that someone would be coming to see them, someone from Lusitania. They both knew this meant that faster-than-light travel had been achieved, but beyond that they could only assume that their visitor must have come to an orbit around Path, shuttled down, and was now making his way stealthily toward them.

Instead, a ridiculously small metal structure appeared on the riverbank in front of them. The door opened. A man emerged. A young man—large-boned, Caucasian, but pleasant-looking anyway. He held a single glass tube in his hand.

He smiled.

Wang-mu had never seen such a smile. He looked right through her as if he owned her soul. As if he *knew* her, knew her better than she knew herself.

"Wang-mu," he said, gently. "Royal Mother of the West. And Fei-tzu, the great teacher of the Path."

He bowed. They bowed to him in return.

"My business here is brief," he said. He held the vial out to Master Han. "Here is the virus. As soon as I've gone—because I have no desire for genetic alteration myself, thank you—drink this down. I imagine it tastes like pus or something equally disgusting, but drink it anyway. Then make contact with as many people as possible, in your house and the town nearby. You'll have about six hours before you start feeling sick. With any luck, at the end of the second day you'll have not a single symptom left. Of *anything*." He grinned. "No more little air-dances for you, Master Han, eh?"

"No more servility for any of us," said Han Fei-tzu. "We're ready to release our messages at once."

"Don't spring this on anybody until you've already spread the infection for a few hours."

"Of course," said Master Han. "Your wisdom teaches me to be careful, though my heart tells me to hurry and proclaim the glorious revolution that this merciful plague will bring to us."

"Yes, very nice," said the man. Then he turned to Wang-mu. "But you don't need the virus, do you?"

"No, sir," said Wang-mu.

"Jane says you're as bright a human being as she's ever seen."

"Jane is too generous," said Wang-mu.

"No, she showed me the data." He looked her up and down. She didn't like the way his eyes took possession of her whole body in that single long glance. "You don't need to be here for the plague. In fact, you'd be better off leaving before it happens."

"Leaving?"

"What is there for you here?" asked the man. "I don't care how revolutionary it gets here, you'll still be a servant and the child of low-class parents. In a place like this, you could spend your whole life overcoming it and you'd still be nothing but a servant with a surprisingly good mind. Come with me and you'll be part of changing history. *Making* history."

"Come with you and do *what*?"

"Overthrow Congress, of course. Cut them off at the knees and send them all crawling back home. Make all the colony worlds equal members of the polity, clean out the corruption, expose all the vile secrets, and call home the Lusitania Fleet before it can commit an atrocity. Establish the rights of all ramen races. Peace and freedom."

"And you intend to do all this?"

"Not alone," he said.

She was relieved.

"I'll have *you*."

"To do what?"

"To write. To speak. To do whatever I need you to do."

"But I'm uneducated, sir. Master Han was only beginning to teach me."

"Who are you?" demanded Master Han. "How can you expect a modest girl like this to pick up and go with a stranger?"

"A modest girl? Who gives her body to the foreman in order to get a chance to be close to a godspoken girl who *might* just hire her to be a secret maid? No, Master Han, she may be putting on the attitudes of a modest girl, but that's because she's a chameleon. Changing hides whenever she thinks it'll get her something."

"I'm not a liar, sir," she said.

"No, I'm sure you sincerely become whatever it is you're pretending to be. So now I'm saying, Pretend to be a revolutionary with me. You hate the bastards who did all this to your world. To Qing-jao."

"How do you know so much about me?"

He tapped his ear. For the first time she noticed the jewel there. "Jane keeps me informed about the people I need to know."

"Jane will die soon," said Wang-mu.

"Oh, she may get semi-stupid for a while," said the man, "but die she will *not*. You helped save her. And in the meantime, I'll have you."

"I can't," she said. "I'm afraid."

"All right then," he said. "I offered."

He turned back to the door of his tiny craft.

"Wait," she said.

He faced her again.

"Can't you at least tell me who you are?"

"Peter Wiggin is my name," he said. "Though I imagine I'll use a false one for a while."

"Peter Wiggin," she whispered. "That's the name of the—"

"*My* name. I'll explain it to you later, if I feel like it. Let's just say that Andrew Wiggin sent me. Sent me off rather forcefully. I'm a man with a mission, and he figured I could only accomplish it on one of the worlds where Congress's power structures are most heavily concentrated. I was Hegemon once, Wang-mu, and I intend to have the job back, whatever the title might turn out to be when I get it. I'm going to break a lot of eggs and cause an amazing amount of trouble and turn this whole Hundred Worlds thing arse over teakettle, and I'm inviting you to help me. But I really don't give a damn whether you do or not, because even though it'd be nice to have your brains and your company, I'll do the job one way or another. So are you coming or what?"

She turned to Master Han in an agony of indecision.

"I had been hoping to teach you," said Master Han. "But if this man is going to work toward what he says he will, then with him you'll have a better chance to change the course of human history than you'd ever have here, where the virus will do our main work for us."

Wang-mu whispered to him. "Leaving you will be like losing a father."

"And if you go, I will have lost my second and last daughter."

"Don't break my heart, you two," said Peter. "I've got a faster-than-light starship here. Leaving Path with me isn't a lifetime thing, you know? If things don't work out I can always bring her back in a day or two. Fair enough?"

"You want to go, I know it," said Master Han.

"Don't you also know that I want to stay as well?"

"I know that, too," said Master Han. "But you *will* go."

"Yes," she said. "I will."

"May the gods watch over you, daughter Wang-mu," said Master Han.

"And may every direction be the east of sunrise to you, Father Han."

Then she stepped forward. The young man named Peter took her hand and led her into the starship. The door closed behind them. A moment later, the starship disappeared.

Master Han waited there ten minutes, meditating until he could compose his feelings. Then he opened the vial, drank its contents, and walked briskly back to the house. Old Mu-pao greeted him just inside the door. "Master Han," she said. "I didn't know where you had gone. And Wang-mu is missing, too."

"She'll be gone for a while," he said. Then he walked very close to the old servant, so that his breath would be in her face. "You have been more faithful to my house than we have ever deserved."

A look of fear came upon her face. "Master Han, you're not dismissing me, are you?"

"No," he said. "I thought that I was thanking you."

He left Mu-pao and ranged through the house. Qing-jao was not in her room. That was no surprise. She spent most of her time entertaining visitors. That would suit his purpose well. And indeed, that was where he found her, in the morning room, with three very distinguished old godspoken men from a town two hundred kilometers away.

Qing-jao introduced them graciously, and then adopted the role of submissive daughter in her father's presence. He bowed to each man, but then found occasion to reach out his hand and touch each one of them. Jane had explained that the virus was highly communicable. Mere physical closeness was usually enough; touching made it more sure.

And when they were greeted, he turned to his daughter. "Qing-jao," he said, "will you have a gift from me?"

She bowed and answered graciously, "Whatever my father has brought me, I will gratefully receive, though I know I am not worthy of his notice."

He reached out his arms and drew her in to him. She was stiff and awkward in his embrace—he had not done such an impulsive thing before dignitaries since she was a very little girl. But he held her all the same, tightly, for he knew that she would never forgive him for what came from this embrace, and therefore it would be the last time he held his Gloriously Bright within his arms.

———

Qing-jao knew what her father's embrace meant. She had watched her father walking in the garden with Wang-mu. She had seen the walnut-shaped starship appear on the riverbank. She had seen him take the vial from the round-eyed stranger. She saw him drink. Then she came here, to this room, to receive visitors on her father's behalf. I am dutiful, my honored father, even when you prepare to betray me.

And even now, knowing that his embrace was his cruelest effort to cut her off from the voice of the gods, knowing that he had so little respect for her that he thought he could deceive her, she nevertheless received whatever he determined to give her. Was he not her father? His virus from the world of Lusitania might or might not steal the voice of the gods from her; she could not guess what the gods would permit their enemies to do. But certainly if she rejected her father and disobeyed him, the gods would punish her. Better to remain worthy of the gods by showing proper respect and obedience to her father, than to disobey him in the name of the gods and thereby make herself unworthy of their gifts.

So she received his embrace, and breathed deeply of his breath.

When he had spoken briefly to his guests, he left. They took his visit with them as a signal honor; so faithfully had Qing-jao concealed her father's mad rebellion against the gods that Han Fei-tzu was still regarded as the greatest man of Path. She spoke to them softly, and smiled graciously, and saw them on their way. She gave them no hint that they would carry away with them a weapon. Why should she? Human weapons would be of no use against the power of the gods, unless the gods willed it. And if the gods wished to stop speaking to the people of Path, then this might well be the disguise they had chosen for their act. Let it seem to the unbeliever that Father's Lusitanian virus cut us off from the gods; *I* will know, as will all other faithful men and women, that the gods speak to whomever they wish, and nothing made by human hands could stop them if they so desired. All their acts were vanity. If Congress believed that they had caused the gods to speak on Path, let them believe it. If Father and the Lusitanians believe that they are causing the gods to fall silent, let them believe it. *I* know that if I am only worthy of it, the gods will speak to me.

A few hours later, Qing-jao fell deathly ill. The fever struck her like a blow from a strong man's hand; she collapsed, and barely noticed as servants carried her to her bed. The doctors came, though she could have told them there was nothing they could do, and that by coming they would only expose themselves to infection. But she said nothing, because her body was struggling too fiercely against the disease. Or rather, her body was struggling to reject her own tissues and organs, until at last the transformation of her genes was complete. Even then, it took time for her body to purge itself of the old antibodies. She slept and slept.

It was bright afternoon when she awoke. "Time," she croaked, and the computer in her room spoke the hour and day. The fever had taken two days from her life. She was on fire with thirst. She got to her feet and staggered to her bathroom, turned on the water, filled the cup and drank and drank until she was satisfied. It made her giddy, to stand upright. Her mouth tasted foul. Where were the servants who should have given her food and drink during her disease?

They must be sick as well. And Father—he would have fallen ill before me. Who will bring him water?

She found him sleeping, cold with last night's sweat, trembling. She woke him with a cup of water, which he drank eagerly, his eyes looking upward into hers. Questioning? Or, perhaps, pleading for forgiveness. Do your penance to the gods, Father; you owe no apologies to a mere daughter.

Qing-jao also found the servants, one by one, some of them so loyal that they had not taken to their beds with their sickness, but rather had fallen where their duties required them to be. All were alive. All were recovering, and soon would be up again. Only after all were accounted for and tended to did Qing-jao go to the kitchen and find something to eat. She could not hold down the first food she took. Only a thin soup, heated to lukewarm, stayed with her. She carried more of the soup to the others. They also ate.

Soon all were up again, and strong. Qing-jao took servants with her and carried water and soup to all the neighboring houses, rich and poor alike. All were grateful to receive what they brought, and many uttered prayers on their behalf. You would not be so grateful, thought Qing-jao, if you knew that the disease you suffered came from my father's house, by my father's will. But she said nothing.

In all this time, the gods did not demand any purification of her.

At last, she thought. At last I am pleasing them. At last I have done, perfectly, all that righteousness required.

When she came home, she wanted to sleep at once. But the servants who had remained in the house were gathered around the holo in the kitchen, watching news reports. Qing-jao almost never watched the holo news, getting all her information from the computer; but the servants looked so serious, so worried, that she entered the kitchen and stood in their circle around the holo-vision.

The news was of the plague sweeping the world of Path. Quarantine had been ineffective, or else always came too late. The woman reading the report had already recovered from the disease, and she was telling that the plague had killed almost no one, though it disrupted services for many. The virus had been isolated, but it died too quickly to be studied seriously. "It seems that a bacterium is following the virus, killing it almost as soon as each person recovers from the plague. The gods have truly favored us, to send us the cure along with the plague."

Fools, thought Qing-jao. If the gods wanted you cured, they wouldn't have sent the plague in the first place.

At once she realized that *she* was the fool. Of course the gods could send both the disease and the cure. If a disease came, and the cure followed, then the gods had sent them. How could she have called such a thing foolish? It was as if she had insulted the gods themselves.

She flinched inwardly, waiting for the onslaught of the gods' rage. She had gone so many hours without purification that she knew it would be a heavy burden when it came. Would she have to trace a whole room again?

But she felt nothing. No desire to trace woodgrain lines. No need to wash.

She looked at her hands. There was dirt on them, and yet she didn't care. She could wash them or not, as she desired.

For a moment she felt immense relief. Could it be that Father and Wang-mu and the Jane-thing were right all along? Had a genetic change, caused by this plague, freed her at last from a hideous crime committed by Congress centuries ago?

Almost as if the news reader had heard Qing-jao's thoughts, she began reading a report about a document that was turning up on computers all over the world. The document said that this plague was a gift from the gods, freeing the people of Path from a genetic alteration performed on them by Congress. Until now, genetic enhancements were almost always linked to an OCD-like condition whose victims were commonly referred to as *godspoken*. But as the plague ran its course, people would find that the genetic enhancements were now spread to all the people of Path, while the godspoken, who had previously borne the most terrible of burdens, had now been released by the gods from the necessity of constant purification.

"This document says that the whole world is now purified. The gods have accepted us." The news reader's voice trembled as she spoke. "It is not known where this document came from. Computer analysis has linked it with no known author's style. The fact that it turned up simultaneously on millions of computers suggests that it came from a source with unspeakable powers." She hesitated, and now her trembling was plainly visible. "If this unworthy reader of news may ask a question, hoping that the wise will hear it and answer her with wisdom, could it not be possible that the gods themselves have sent us this message, so that we will understand their great gift to the people of Path?"

Qing-jao listened for a while longer, as fury grew within her. It was Jane, obviously, who had written and spread this document. How dare she pretend to know what the gods were doing! She had gone too far. This document must be refuted. Jane must stand revealed, and also the whole conspiracy of the people of Lusitania.

The servants were looking at her. She met their gaze, looking for a moment at each of them around the circle.

"What do you want to ask me?" she said.

"O Mistress," said Mu-pao, "forgive our curiosity, but this news report has declared something that we can only believe if you tell us that it is true."

"What do *I* know?" answered Qing-jao. "I am only the foolish daughter of a great man."

"But you are one of the godspoken, Mistress," said Mu-pao.

You are very daring, thought Qing-jao, to speak of such things unbidden.

"In all this night, since you came among us with food and drink, and as you led so many of us out among the people, tending the sick, you have never once excused yourself for purification. We have never seen you go so long."

"Did it not occur to you," said Qing-jao, "that perhaps we were so well fulfilling the will of the gods that I had no need of purification during that time?"

Mu-pao looked abashed. "No, we did not think of that."

"Rest now," said Qing-jao. "None of us is strong yet. I must go and speak to my father."

She left them to gossip and speculate among themselves. Father was in his room, seated before the computer. Jane's face was in the display. Father turned to her as soon as she entered the room. His face was radiant. Triumphant.

"Did you see the message that Jane and I prepared?" he said.

"You!" cried Qing-jao. "My father, a teller of lies?"

To say such a thing to her father was unthinkable. But still she felt no need to purify herself. It frightened her, that she could speak with such disrespect and yet the gods did not rebuke her.

"Lies?" said Father. "Why do you think that they are lies, my daughter? How do you know that the gods did not cause this virus to come to us? How do you know that it is not their will to give these genetic enhancements to all of Path?"

His words maddened her; or perhaps she felt a new freedom; or perhaps she was testing the gods by speaking very disrespectfully so that they would *have* to rebuke her. "Do you think I am a fool?" shouted Qingjao. "Do you think that I don't know this is *your* strategy to keep the world of Path from erupting in revolution and slaughter? Do you think I don't know that all you care about is keeping people from dying?"

"And is there something wrong with that?" asked Father.

"It's a lie!" she answered.

"Or it's the disguise the gods have prepared to conceal their actions," said Father. "You had no trouble accepting Congress's stories as true. Why can't you accept mine?"

"Because I know about the virus, Father. I saw you take it from that stranger's hand. I saw Wang-mu step into his vehicle. I saw it disappear. I know that none of these things are of the gods. *She* did them—that devil that lives in the computers!"

"How do you know," said Father, "that she is not one of the gods?"

This was unbearable. "She was *made*," cried Qing-jao. "That's how I know! She's only a computer program, made by human beings, living in machines that human beings made. The gods are not made by any hand. The gods have always lived and will always live."

For the first time, Jane spoke. "Then *you* are a god, Qing-jao, and so am I, and so is every other person—human or raman—in the universe. No god made your soul, your inmost aiúa. You are as old as any god, and as young, and you will live as long."

Qing-jao screamed. She had never made such a sound before, that she remembered. It tore at her throat.

"My daughter," said Father, coming toward her, his arms outstretched to embrace her.

She could not bear his embrace. She could not endure it because it would mean his complete victory. It would mean that she had been defeated by the enemies of the gods; it would mean that Jane had overmastered her. It would mean that Wang-mu had been a truer daughter to Han Fei-tzu than Qing-jao had been. It would mean that all Qing-jao's worship for all these years had meant nothing. It would mean that it was evil of her to set in motion the destruction of Jane. It would mean that Jane was noble and good for having helped transform the people of Path. It would mean that Mother was *not* waiting for her when at last she came to the Infinite West.

Why don't you speak to me, O Gods! she cried out silently. Why don't you assure me that I have not served you in vain all these years? Why have you deserted me now, and given the triumph to your enemies?

And then the answer came to her, as simply and clearly as if her mother had whispered the words in her ear: This is a test, Qing-jao. The gods are watching what you do.

A test. Of course. The gods were testing all their servants on Path, to see which ones were deceived and which endured in perfect obedience.

If I am being tested, then there must be some correct thing for me to do.

I must do what I have always done, only this time I must not wait for the gods to instruct me. They have wearied of telling me every day and every hour when I needed to be purified. It is time for me to understand my own impurity without their instructions. I must purify myself, with utter perfection; then I will have passed the test, and the gods will receive me once again.

She dropped to her knees. She found a woodgrain line, and began to trace it.

There was no answering gift of release, no sense of

rightness; but that did not trouble her, because she understood that this was part of the test. If the gods answered her immediately, the way they used to, then how would it be a test of her dedication? Where before she had undergone her purification under their constant guidance, now she must purify herself alone. And how would she know if she had done it properly? The gods would come to her again.

The gods would speak to her again. Or perhaps they would carry her away, take her to the palace of the Royal Mother, where the noble Han Jiang-qing awaited her. There she would also meet Li Qing-jao, her ancestor-of-the-heart. There her ancestors would all greet her, and they would say, The gods determined to try all the godspoken of Path. Few indeed have passed this test; but you, Qing-jao, you have brought great honor to us all. Because your faithfulness never wavered. You performed your purifications as no other son or daughter has ever performed them. The ancestors of other men and women are all envious of us. For your sake the gods now favor us above them all.

"What are you doing?" asked Father. "Why are you tracing the woodgrain lines?"

She did not answer. She refused to be distracted.

"The need for that has been taken away. I know it has—*I* feel no need for purification."

Ah, Father! If only you could understand! But even though you will fail this test, I will pass it—and thus I will bring honor even to you, who have forsaken all honorable things.

"Qing-jao," he said. "I know what you're doing. Like those parents who force their mediocre children to wash and wash. You're calling the gods."

Give it that name if you wish, Father. Your words are nothing to me now. I will not listen to you again until we both are dead, and you say to me, My daughter, you were better and wiser than I; all my honor here in the house of the Royal Mother comes from your purity and selfless devotion to the service of the gods. You are truly a noble daughter. I have no joy except because of you.

———————

The world of Path accomplished its transformation peacefully. Here and there, a murder occurred; here and there, one of the godspoken who had been tyrannical was mobbed and cast out of his house. But by and large, the story given by the document was believed, and the former godspoken were treated with great honor because of their righteous sacrifice during the years when they were burdened with the rites of purification.

Still, the old order quickly passed away. The schools were opened equally to all children. Teachers soon reported that students were achieving remarkable things; the stupidest child now was surpassing all averages from former times. And despite Congress's outraged denials of any genetic alteration, scientists on Path at last turned their attention to the genes of their own people. Studying the records of what their genetic molecules had been, and how they were now, the women and men of Path confirmed all that the document had said.

What happened then, as the Hundred Worlds and all the colonies learned of Congress's crimes against Path—Qing-jao never knew of it. That was all a matter for a world that she had left behind. For she spent all her days now in the service of the gods, cleansing herself, purifying herself.

The story spread that Han Fei-tzu's mad daughter, alone of all the godspoken, persisted in her rituals. At first she was ridiculed for it—for many of the godspoken had, out of curiosity, attempted to perform their purifications again, and had discovered the rituals to be empty and meaningless now. But she heard little of the ridicule, and cared nothing for it. Her mind was devoted solely to the service of the gods—what did it matter if the people who had failed the test despised her for continuing to attempt to succeed?

As the years passed, many began to remember the old days as a graceful time, when the gods spoke to men and women, and many were bowed down in their service. Some of these began to think of Qing-jao, not as a madwoman, but as the only faithful woman left among those who had heard the voice of the gods. The word began to spread among the pious: "In the house of Han Fei-tzu there dwells the last of the godspoken."

They began to come then, at first a few, then more and more of them. Visitors, who wanted to speak with the only woman who still labored in her purification. At first she would speak to some of them; when she had finished tracing a board, she would go out into the garden and speak to them. But their words confused her. They spoke of her labor as being the purification of the whole planet. They said that she was calling the gods for the sake of all the people of Path. The more they talked, the harder it was for her to concentrate on what they said. She was soon eager to return to the house, to begin tracing another line. Didn't these people understand that they were wrong to praise her now? "I have accomplished nothing," she would tell them. "The gods are still silent. I have work to do." And then she would return to her tracing.

Her father died as a very old man, with much honor for his many deeds, though no one ever knew his role in the coming of the Plague of the Gods, as it was now called. Only Qing-jao understood. And as she burned a fortune in real money—no false funeral money would do for her father—she whispered to him so that no one else could hear, "Now you know, Father. Now you understand your errors, and how you angered the gods. But don't be afraid. I will continue the purification until all your mistakes are rectified. Then the gods will receive you with honor."

She herself became old, and the Journey to the House of Han Qing-jao was now the most famous pilgrimage of Path. Indeed, there were many who heard of her on other worlds, and came to Path just to see her. For it was well-known on many worlds that true holiness could be found in only one place, and in only one person, the old woman whose back was now permanently bent, whose eyes could now see nothing but the lines in the floors of her father's house.

Holy disciples, men and women, now tended the house where servants once had cared for her. They polished the floors. They prepared her simple food, and laid it where she could find it at the doors of the rooms; she would eat and drink only when a room was finished. When a man or woman somewhere in the world achieved some great honor, they would come to the House of Han Qing-jao, kneel down, and trace a wood-grain line; thus all honors were treated as if they were mere decorations on the honor of the Holy Han Qing-jao.

At last, only a few weeks after she completed her hundredth year, Han Qing-jao was found curled up on the floor of her father's room. Some said that it was the exact spot where her father always sat when he performed his labors; it was hard to be sure, since all the furniture of the house had been removed long before. The holy woman was not dead when they found her. She lay still for several days, murmuring, muttering, inching her hands across her own body as if she were tracing lines in her flesh. Her disciples took turns, ten at a time, listening to her, trying to understand her muttering, setting down the words as best they understood them. They were written in the book called *The God Whispers of Han Qing-jao*.

Most important of all her words were these, at the

very end. "Mother," she whispered. "Father. Did I do it right?" And then, said her disciples, she smiled and died.

She had not been dead for a month before the decision was made in every temple and shrine in every city and town and village of Path. At last there was a person of such surpassing holiness that Path could choose her as the protector and guardian of the world. No other world had such a god, and they admitted it freely.

Path is blessed above all other worlds, they said. For the God of Path is Gloriously Bright.